KILL THE QUEEN

Also by Jennifer Estep

THE ELEMENTAL ASSASSIN SERIES

THE MYTHOS ACADEMY SERIES

KILL THE QUEEN

A CROWN OF SHARDS NOVEL

JENNIFER ESTEP

HARPER Voyager
An Imprint of HarperCollins*Publishers*

KILL THE QUEEN. Copyright © 2018 by Jennifer Estep. Excerpt from PROTECT THE PRINCE copyright © 2019 by Jennifer Estep. All rights reserved. Printed in the United States of America. No part of this book may be used or reproduced in any manner whatsoever without written permission except in the case of brief quotations embodied in critical articles and reviews. For information, address HarperCollins Publishers, 195 Broadway, New York, NY 10007.

HarperCollins books may be purchased for educational, business, or sales promotional use. For information, please email the Special Markets Department at SPsales@harpercollins.com.

Harper Voyager and design are trademarks of HarperCollins Publishers LLC.

FIRST EDITION

Designed by Paula Russell Szafranski
Map designed by Virginia Norey
Title page and chapter opener art © mashakotcur/Shutterstock, Inc.

Library of Congress Cataloging-in-Publication Data has been applied for.

ISBN 978-0-06-279761-2

18 19 20 21 22   LSC   10 9 8 7 6 5 4 3 2 1

To my mom, my grandma, and Andre—for your love,
your patience, and everything else that you've given to me
over the years.

And to my teenage self, who devoured every single epic fantasy
book that she could get her hands on—for finally writing your
very own epic fantasy book.

Summer queens are fine and fair,
With pretty ribbons and flowers in their hair.

Winter queens are cold and hard,
With frosted crowns made of icy shards.

—BELLONAN FAIRY-TALE RHYME

ACKNOWLEDGMENTS

My heartfelt thanks go out to all the folks who helped turn my words into a book.

Thanks go to my agent, Annelise Robey, and my editor, Erika Tsang, for all their helpful advice, support, and encouragement. Thanks also to Nicole Fischer and everyone else at Harper Voyager and HarperCollins.

And finally, a big thanks to all the readers. Knowing that folks read and enjoy my books is truly humbling, and I hope that you all enjoy reading about Evie and her adventures.

I appreciate you all more than you will ever know.

Happy reading! ☺

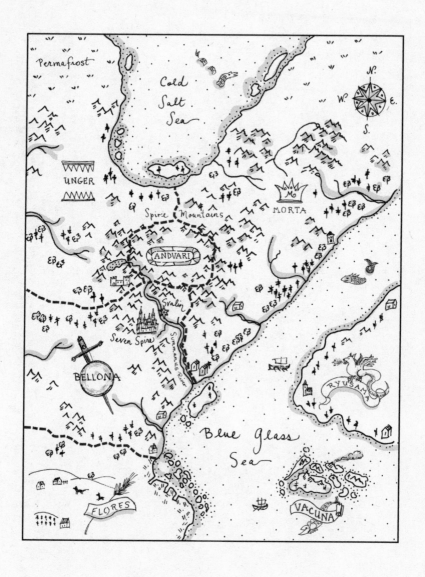

PART ONE

THE
ROYAL
MASSACRE

CHAPTER ONE

The day of the royal massacre started out like any other.

With me doing something completely, utterly useless.

"Why do *I* have to make the pie?" I grumbled.

I stared at the flour, sugar, and butter lined up on the table, along with measuring cups and spoons, a paring knife, a rolling pin, and bowls full of honey cranberries and bloodcrisp apples.

Isobel waved her hand over everything. "It's a sign of respect for a member of the royal family to make the traditional welcome pie for the Andvarian ambassador. Lord Hans requested cranberry-apple for today's luncheon."

"You're the cook master, not me," I grumbled again. "You should make the pie. Your magic will make it look and taste amazing."

Masters were those whose magic let them work with specific objects or elements, like metal, glass, and wood, to create astounding things. Isobel's power helped her craft amazing desserts out of ordinary flour, sugar, and butter, which was why she'd been the head baker at Seven Spire palace for more than twenty years.

She slapped her hands on her hips. "I might be a cook master, but the Andvarians have very finely tuned senses. They would know if I made the pie instead of you. They can sniff out the intentions of every single person who handles their food, even if it's only the servant who pours their wine. It's one of the reasons why they can't be poisoned."

I snorted. "That's just an old fairy tale started by the Andvarians themselves to keep people from trying to poison them. They don't have any better senses than anyone else. Only mutts like me have that sort of magic." I tapped my nose. "I might have an enhanced sense of smell, but even I can't always sniff out people's intentions."

Isobel frowned. "You know I don't like that word, especially when it's applied to you."

Unlike masters, who were sought after and lauded for their impressive skills, mutts were not, simply because our magic didn't let us create anything. Most mutts had only a small spark of power, a tiny flicker that enhanced something about themselves, like my supersensitive nose. Something that barely qualified as magic, especially when compared to the airy meringues, spun-sugar cakes, and other delicacies that Isobel whipped up. When it came to magic, mutts were considered far weaker and far, far inferior to masters, magiers, and morphs. Hence the term *mutts*.

I shrugged. "We both know that I am most definitely a mutt in every sense of the word."

Isobel winced, but she didn't disagree.

"Besides, Lord Hans has the constitution of a gargoyle. I've seen him eat pepper radishes like they were as sweet as those apples. Why, I could pour him a tall, frosty glass of wormroot poison, and it wouldn't give him much more than a stomachache. And a small one at that."

Isobel's lips twitched, but she summoned up a stern look, trying to keep me in line. Always a losing battle. I was rather incorrigible that way.

"Regardless, you need to make the pie, Lady Everleigh. You were the only one who was, ah, available."

"Oh, really?" I arched an eyebrow, and Isobel dropped her dark brown gaze from mine.

Available? Well, that was a nice way of saying that it was once again time for me to earn my keep as Lady Everleigh Saffira Winter Blair. A mouthful of fancy names that meant very little in the grand scheme of things, but they, and the lineage that went along with them, were good enough for my cousin Queen Cordelia Alexandra Summer Blair to have me trotted out like a trained monkey whenever a so-called royal presence was required. Like wasting a morning baking a pie for some foreign ambassador who probably wouldn't eat a single bite of it.

Isobel winced again, causing lines to groove into her bronze skin, then smoothed back her graying black hair, the way she always did whenever she had bad news. "I'm afraid that it's not just one pie. Lord Hans requested thirteen of them. It's his favorite dessert. The Andvarian king's granddaughter loves it too. She's also part of the ambassador's contingent. I believe her name is Gemma."

I glanced at the stacks of pie tins half hidden behind the bowls of apples. Anger pricked my heart that I was always the one singled out for such tasks, but the sharp sting was quickly replaced by cold, numbing acceptance.

Such was life at Seven Spire.

Such was *my* life at the palace anyway, ever since I'd first arrived here after my parents had been murdered fifteen years ago. I was expected to go where I was told, and do what I was ordered, all while wearing a sunny smile and spouting flowery platitudes about how grateful I was for everyone's meager, miserly generosity. Orphans didn't get to have choices, ambitions, or most especially opinions. I'd learned that long ago, but it was the one thing I could never quite accept, no matter how much meaningless protocol, empty niceties, and polite drudgery I was expected to reiterate, regurgitate, and perform on command.

"I forgot the orange flakes." Isobel's voice was soft and sympathetic. "Let me get those, and then we'll get started, Evie."

Besides my parents, Isobel was the only person who had ever called me *Evie*, although she did it only when no one else could hear. More silly protocol. She was also one of the few people who was kind to me not because she had to be, but because she simply wanted to be. When I was younger, I had spent countless hours in this kitchen, sitting in the corner, reading books, and watching her turn mounds of flour and pounds of sugar into dazzling displays of confectionary delights.

Isobel fondly referred to me as her taste tester, since my enhanced sense of smell always let me tell how well a cake had turned out before I'd had a single bite, but that was just an excuse for her to sneak me treats. She was the closest thing to a mother that I'd had since my own had died, but she still had to do her duty. And today, that duty included making me make pies.

Isobel placed a warm, comforting hand on my arm and gave it a gentle squeeze. Then she hurried over to one of the pantries full of syrups, spices, and other seasonings.

Our pie-making station was in the back corner, away from the other preparation stations, as well as the competing warmth of the ovens and the frost of the metal chillers, which lined opposite walls. It was just after eight o'clock, and a dizzying array of people moved through the kitchen. Young pages delivering breakfast orders. Teenage servers carrying trays. Cook masters cracking eggs and frying smoked sausages.

Everyone wore black boots and leggings, along with long-sleeve scarlet tunics trimmed with gold thread, in keeping with Queen Cordelia's colors. I wore the same thing, along with a black apron, and I blended in perfectly with the workers.

Then again, I *was* one of them—in every way that truly mattered.

Most of the kitchen staff ignored me. They had long ago realized that I was just another cog in the palace wheels, that I showed up, did my duty, and earned my keep, the same as them. Besides, they were much more interested in sharing the first gossip of the day, like who was sleeping in, who had asked for extra mochana to help their hangover, and who had been seen sneaking out of this or that married lord or lady's room.

Some of the newer workers eyed me, wondering if I might pitch a fit at being on pie patrol, but my expression remained blank. I never let my true emotions show, not so much as a flicker, not even here. You never knew who might be watching or what they might do with the information.

Life at the palace was cutthroat, with everyone always looking for an advantage over their friends and enemies alike. Business deals, political favors, arranged marriages, even something as small as who got to sit at the queen's table during today's luncheon. It was all a perpetual battlefield, with people rising and falling daily, as well as stabbing others in the back to further advance their own positions. From the kitchen to the throne room, the entire palace was one enormous arena, only everyone here fought with scathing words, poisonous rumors, and cold threats, instead of swords, shields, and daggers like real gladiators did.

My position, magic, and wealth might be insignificant— more like nonexistent—compared to others', but I was still a Blair, still a member of the royal family, and I had been the target of more than one scheme. At least, until people realized that I had no power to help them in any way. Still, I couldn't afford to show any weakness. Not trusting people, especially with my feelings, was a lesson I'd learned the hard way when I was twelve years old, during my first month at the palace. It was perhaps the one thing, the one useful skill, that I had completely mastered.

Still, the workers' curious glances made that sharp, stinging anger rise up in me again. It threatened to break through my calm facade, so I curled my hands around the edge of the table and focused on the feel of the cool stone under my palms. Sturdy, solid granite, worn smooth by the wear and tear of kitchen life.

Worn down, just like me.

Isobel returned with a jar filled with what looked like crystalized orange snowflakes. Even though it was tightly stoppered, I could still smell the sweet tang of citrus inside.

She placed the jar on the table with the other supplies. "Anytime you're ready, Lady Everleigh."

That was Isobel's soft, subtle way of letting me know that Evie was gone and that it was time for Everleigh to do her duty.

More anger pricked my heart that I couldn't have something as simple as a nickname from someone I loved. For a mad, mad moment, I thought about ripping off my apron and storming out of the kitchen. But Auster, the captain of the queen's guard, would track me down; give me a long, stern lecture about how my actions reflected poorly on Cordelia; and escort me back here. Which would be far more humiliating and time-consuming than making the bloody pies right now.

I served at the whim of the queen, just like everyone else did. And today, the queen wanted me to make thirteen pies.

"Dance, monkey, dance," I muttered.

Then I sighed and reached for a bowl to start mixing the ingredients together.

Two hours later, I poured the last of the cranberry-apple filling into the final pie crust, then reached for the orange flakes.

"Whether you're a cook master or not, the secret is not to overdo the orange," Isobel instructed, the same way she had on the previous pies. "Most people shake the flakes on like they're common salt. But too much orange, and that's all you'll taste. So go around the pie once, gently tapping on the jar three times with your index finger. That's the perfect amount."

I did as she said, watching the tiny, delicate granules melt into the fruit filling like perfumed snowflakes. Then I drew in a deep breath, letting the air roll in over my tongue and tasting all the scents in it. The buttery crust, the sugary fruit, the hint of orange that curled through it all. Delicious aromas that would bubble up and become even more pronounced, fragrant, and intense as this pie and the others baked.

Despite my own condescending view of my mutt magic, my enhanced sense of smell was one of the reasons why I had always gravitated toward Isobel and the kitchen. All the sweet scents here made the bitter reality of my life a little easier to bear.

"Perfect! That's my girl." Isobel beamed at me, and I smiled back at her.

She arranged a few strips of crust on top of the filling, creating a pretty lattice pattern, then slid the pie into the oven. Isobel had taken pity and had helped me make the pie crusts, although she had insisted on my preparing the cranberry-apple filling, orange flakes and all, claiming that it was the most important part.

I often helped Isobel, as I enjoyed spending time with her, and the kitchen was a welcome refuge from other, less-friendly sections of the palace. She had slowly turned me into a decent cook, despite my not being a master. But after making so many pies in a row, I had all the ingredients, measurements, and motions memorized, and I felt like I could craft them in my sleep now. Just as I could bow, curtsy, dance, and make polite, inane chitchat in several languages. And those were just some of the many trivial skills that I'd learned as the unofficial royal stand-in.

While Queen Cordelia and the rest of my Blair cousins were dealing with ambassadors and the like, I was attending all the functions they could not, due to their oh-so-important and exceedingly busy schedules.

Breakfast recitals, charity luncheons, afternoon teas. I went to all those and more every week, both here at the palace and out in the city. Most of the time, it wasn't so bad. Usually, all I had to do was smile, nod, and shake hands, along with thanking people for their time; admiring their music, artwork, or goods; and giving short and exceptionally vague speeches about how disappointed Queen Cordelia was that she herself couldn't attend. At the very least, I almost always got a free meal out of the proceedings.

But even that could be fraught with danger. A few months ago, when the third cousin of the king of Vacuna had visited from the southern islands, I had taken part in a traditional feast—one that involved eating the raw liver of a freshly killed wild boar.

Under the watchful eye and careful direction of the king's cousin, I had slit open the boar's side and rooted around through all sorts of slimy, squishy things better left to the imagination. The stench of blood and guts had almost knocked me over, but I'd found the liver, pulled it out, and eaten the smallest bite that was considered polite. Then, while the king's cousin and the rest of his contingent were enthusiastically butchering and grilling the rest of the boar, I'd slipped away and thrown up in the potted, golden persimmon tree they'd brought the queen as a sign of friendship. It had been the closest container, and I'd shifted the dirt around inside the bucket to hide what I'd done. The king's cousin had been very disappointed that the tree had died a few days later, though.

Given my magic, scents and memories were often tangled up together in my mind, and thinking about the liver made my nose twitch. Suddenly, the sweet, enticing smells of the baking pies turned sour and rotten. So I gathered up the dirty bowls, spoons, and measuring cups, dumped them in the closest sink, and stripped off my apron.

"Here." Isobel pushed a red paper bag into my hands. "Some plum tarts. For you and that old sourpuss down in the dungeon."

"Casting aspersions on Alvis's character again?"

She huffed. "They're not aspersions if they're true. And he is the grumpiest man I've ever met."

I grinned. "And Alvis would call you that old sunny-side up in the kitchen."

Isobel huffed again. "Better sunny than sour—"

Whispers surged through the room, cutting her off. In the distance, heels clacked on the floor, like thunder signaling an oncoming storm. Everyone quit gossiping and focused on their work, concentrating like they had never concentrated before. All conversation ceased, and the kitchen went deathly quiet, except for the *thwack-thwack-thwack*s of knives cutting through food and the *tick-tick-tick*s of the timers counting down the minutes left on the baking pies.

A forty-something woman appeared at the far end of the kitchen. She too wore a scarlet tunic, but hers featured Queen Cordelia's rising-sun crest stitched in gold thread over her heart. Her tunic had also been tailored to fit her strong, slender form, along with her black leggings, and short black heels adorned her feet, instead of more sensible boots. Everything about her was sleek and sharp at the same time, from her smooth blond bun to her angular cheekbones to the point of her nose. She would have been quite beautiful, if not for the faint pucker of her lips, as though she were perpetually displeased by everyone around her.

Maeven, the kitchen steward, surveyed the room, her gaze moving from one worker and cooking station to the next. After several seconds of silent scrutiny, she snapped her fingers at the three guards who were standing behind her, clutching wooden crates full of bottles. "Why are you just standing there? Put those down and go fetch the others from the wine cellar. I want the rest of the champagne for the luncheon brought up immediately."

The guards set the crates down and beat a hasty retreat.

Maeven snapped her fingers at some of the teenage servers. "You three. Go help them."

She didn't raise her smooth, silky voice, but the three servers still flinched and dashed away, almost tripping over their own feet in their hurry. Maeven had been running the kitchen for more than a year now, since the previous steward had retired, and the workers had quickly learned that hers was an iron fist on its best, gentlest day.

"The Andvarian ambassador is an important dignitary, and I want everything to be perfect for the luncheon," Maeven called out. "Understood?"

The workers ducked their heads, avoiding her gaze. Maeven nodded, satisfied that she had cowed everyone into continued obedience. She looked around the kitchen again, and she noticed me standing with Isobel. Her gaze cut back to the crates of champagne, but she plastered a smile on her face and walked over to us.

"Incoming." Isobel stepped back, grabbed a wet dishrag, and started wiping flour off the table, leaving me to face the kitchen steward alone.

"Coward," I whispered.

Isobel grinned and kept working.

Maeven stopped in front of me. Up close, she was even more beautiful, especially her deep, dark, amethyst eyes. "Lady Everleigh. I didn't realize that you were . . . visiting the kitchen."

Visiting? That was Maeven's way of stating that this was her territory, not mine, and that while my presence was tolerated, it would never truly be welcomed. As if I needed another reminder of my lowly position.

I pasted my usual bland, benign smile on my face, matching her supposed politeness. "Yes, I had to make the pies for the Andvarian ambassador. It's tradition."

"Oh, yes, the pies."

Maeven's gaze swept over me, and her lips puckered again. Not a speck of flour, sugar, or anything else marred her tunic, but the same could not be said for me. Sugar granules clung to my fingers like sticky sand, while flour stains streaked my clothes like stripes of chalky paint. Plus, several tendrils of my black hair had escaped from their braid and hung down the sides of my face. I blew one of the strands out of the way, but of course it dropped right back down again.

Maeven's face cleared, as though some other, far more pleasing thought had distracted her from my unkempt appearance. She waved her hand at the crates. "Can I interest you in some champagne? I would love to get a royal opinion on it. Besides, you're always . . . tasting things for Isobel."

It might have sounded like an innocent request, but suspicion filled me. Maeven never asked me to taste test anything. Besides, what kind of lush did she think I was? It was barely ten o'clock. Even Cousin Horatio, the Blair family drunk, wouldn't guzzle champagne at this hour. He'd wait until at least eleven.

"You're the expert. I'm sure that whatever champagne you've picked out will be fine. But thank you ever so much for the offer."

Disappointment flashed in her eyes, but she smiled at me again. Well, as much as she ever smiled at anyone. "I'll be sure to save you a glass."

"That sounds lovely."

The guards and the servers returned with more crates. Maeven tipped her head to me, then stalked over to them, her heels stabbing into the floor. She grabbed one of the bottles and examined the label. She nodded in satisfaction, then barked out more orders.

"What was that about?" I murmured to Isobel, who had finished wiping down the table.

She eyed the other woman. "I don't know, but I don't like it. You should leave now, while she's distracted."

"I can take care of myself, even against demanding kitchen stewards."

Instead of grinning at my joke, Isobel frowned. "There's something not quite right about that woman. Maybe because she's from Morta. I've never liked Mortans. Always invading, always trying to take more land that doesn't belong to them."

"Just because she's from another kingdom doesn't automatically make her evil."

"No," Isobel said. "But it doesn't make her a friend either."

"Be careful with that sourpuss tone," I teased. "You're starting to sound like Alvis."

She snorted. "I'd have to say a lot worse for a lot longer to sound like Alvis."

"Yes, you would. But you know how grumpy he gets when I'm late. I'll see you at the luncheon, okay? Save me a piece of pie."

"Of course. You earned it, Evie."

I winked at her, then headed out of the kitchen. My winding path through the pages, servers, and cook masters took me close to where Maeven was examining those bottles. Our gazes met, and she tipped her head to me again. I returned the gesture, then walked past her.

I reached the swinging doors that led out of the kitchen.

I started to push through them, but something made me stop and glance back over my shoulder. Maeven was still watching me, her fingers curled around a champagne bottle. Her dark, painted nails were the same color as her eyes, and they looked like amethyst talons trying to punch through the green glass.

Maeven smiled at me a final time, then turned and slid the bottle back into the crate with the others.

Three smiles in one morning, none of which had even come close to reaching or warming her cold eyes. Isobel was right. Definitely not a friend.

But that was nothing new at Seven Spire.

CHAPTER TWO

My duties, royal and otherwise, weren't finished for the day. So I left my unease about Maeven behind in the kitchen and wound through the spacious hallways that made up the first-floor common areas of Seven Spire.

The palace was the crown jewel of Svalin, the capital city of the kingdom of Bellona. Seven Spire had originally been a mine, where workers had chiseled tearstone, fluorestone, and more out of the mountain. But thanks to Ophelia Ruby Winter Blair, a stone master who had been one of my ancestors, the mine had been turned into a marvel of marble, granite, and tearstone. Over the years, the palace had been enlarged and expanded until now it was practically a mountain and a city unto itself.

Seven Spire reminded me of one of Isobel's elaborate, tiered cakes. A wide, sturdy base, with stone stairs and metal lifts climbing up both the inside and the outside, like strings of icing and ribbons of hardened sugar. The palace spiraled up and into the side of the mountain, with balconies and terraces adorning each level, before tapering to a series of seven tall tearstone spires that seemed to pierce the sky itself. Hence the name Seven Spire.

I stopped at one of the windows. Down below, the Summanus River glittered like a frothy carpet of sapphires and diamonds as it tumbled down from the surrounding Spire Mountains. Seven cobblestone bridges jutted out from the palace, spanned the river, and led into the city. Across the water, buildings of all shapes and sizes stretched out, most of them topped with smaller, metal versions of the palace's spires. I loved the view at night, when the city lights reflected off the spires, making them gleam like gold, silver, and bronze toppers on yule trees.

A white paddlewheel boat with the name *Delta Queen* painted on its side chugged along the river, slowly approaching an enormous, round, domed arena near the edge of the city. I squinted, but I couldn't make out the symbols on the white flags flying on top of the dome's spires that would tell me which gladiator troupe called that arena home.

Gladiator troupes were all the rage in Andvari, Unger, Morta, and the other kingdoms. Ask anyone, and they would proudly tell you who their favorite gladiator was, which troupes they rooted for in the various leagues and championships, and which gladiators and troupes they utterly despised.

But gladiator troupes had an especially frenzied popularity and special meaning here in Bellona. Once upon a time, Bryn Bellona Winter Blair had been a lowly gladiator who had risen through the ranks to unite the disparate regions into one kingdom, which had been named Bellona in her honor. Bryn had also driven back the Mortan invaders and had defeated the Mortan king in one-on-one combat in true gladiator style. She had been crowned the first queen of Bellona for her strength, bravery, and cunning, both in and out of the gladiator ring.

The stories about Bryn were some of my favorites. When I was younger, I had tried to be as strong, brave, and fierce as she had been, although life at the palace had quickly turned me cold, bitter, and jaded instead.

I had never been to one of the gladiator shows, but I had heard plenty about them. Part circus, part spectator sport, part combat. Most of the bouts were rather tame, with gladiators only drawing first blood or battling gargoyles, strixes, and other creatures. But every once in a while, a black-ring match would be announced, either between two rival troupes or sometimes even between two gladiators in the same troupe, much to the delight of the masses, who would pay through the nose to see the warriors battle to the death.

The paddlewheel boat churned on past the domed arena and disappeared from sight, so I walked on.

Sunlight streamed in through the windows and reflected off the gold, silver, and bronze threads that ran through the tapestries that covered the dark gray granite walls. The floor was made of the same stone, although it had been polished to a high, slick gloss. Wooden stands topped with glass cases lined the walls, each one boasting some historic statue, sword, or other treasure. The jewels on the artifacts burned as brightly as gargoyle eyes in the sunlight.

But the most impressive things inside the palace were the columns.

They used to be the supports for the old mining tunnels, although they had always seemed more like the bones of some great mythological creature to me. A few of the columns were slender enough for me to wrap my arms around, but most were massive monoliths that were larger than seven men standing shoulder to shoulder. Whether they were narrow or wide, short or tall, all the columns were covered with figures celebrating Bellona's history.

Gladiators clutching swords and shields. Spears that shot up from the floor or dropped down from the ceiling as though they were zooming toward targets. Stone gargoyles stretching their wings out wide and pointing the thick, curved horns on their heads at the strixes, enormous, hawklike birds with metallic feathers and razor-sharp beaks and talons. Caladriuses hovering above them all, their tiny, owlish bodies hiding their true power.

All the columns were made of tearstone, which was unusual in that it could shift color, from a light, bright starry gray to a dark, deep midnight-blue, depending on the sunlight and other factors. The tearstone's shifting color brought the gladiators and creatures to life, making it seem as though they were circling around the columns in a continuous battle for victory and supremacy. Similar columns also adorned the outside of the palace, supporting the structure.

I had been only twelve when I'd first arrived here from my parents' estate in the north, and I had been terrified of the flickering figures, despite the steady glow of the fluorestone lights embedded in the walls. I hadn't realized back then that the columns were just columns—and that it was the people inside the palace who could truly hurt me.

On a normal day, everyone would be out and about, conducting their business. Servants carrying food and drinks to meetings of palace stewards, guilders, and district senators tasked with running everything from Seven Spire to the city of Svalin to the rest of Bellona. Guards patrolling the hallways.

And nobles, of course, lords and ladies with money, power, privilege, and access, trying to worm their way into better favor and broker better deals with whatever steward, guilder, senator, or royal they were targeting.

But it was Saturday, which meant that the week's work was done, and the only scheduled event was the luncheon. So the hallways were empty, except for a few guards and servants making their rounds, although the area would fill up later.

I walked down several sets of stairs until I reached the bottom level of the palace, buried deep in the mountain's bedrock. The dungeon, as Isobel called it. This deep underground, I was closer to the river than I was to the sky, and the air felt cool and misty. The fluorestones clustered in the ceiling corners created more shadows than they banished, but I didn't mind the gloomy quiet, or the eerie echo of my boots on the flagstones. The chilly stillness was a welcome relief after the kitchen's heat, commotion, and tension.

I stopped in front of a door made of blue, black, and silver shards of stained glass that joined together like puzzle pieces to create a frosted forest. I admired the artistic scene, then banged my knuckles on the door, turned the knob, and stepped inside.

The door opened up into a workshop that was shaped like an eight-pointed star. A table covered with metal cutters, pliers, and stacks of soft polishing cloths took up the center of the circular room, while short, narrow hallways led to eight little nooks of additional space. Unlike the dim hallway outside, several rows of fluorestones were embedded in the low ceiling, all of them blazing with light, as though someone had set miniature suns into the dark granite.

The light flooded the entire workshop, including the eight

nooks with their glass cases full of precious gems and metals tucked into the corners. Each case was sorted by color, from the first holding only the clearest, whitest diamonds and silver sheets to the last boasting midnight onyx stones and the blackest bars of coldiron. Pinks, yellows, reds, greens, purples, blues. Gems and metals in all those colors glittered and gleamed in the other cases, making it seem as though I had stepped inside a jeweled rainbow.

An older man perched on a stool at the table, his head bowed, shining the fluorestone lamp clamped to his forehead onto his latest project. Wavy, salt-and-pepper hair puffed out all around the leather band that anchored the light to his head, and his skin was almost the same color as the slivers of polished onyx spread out on the white cloth by his elbow.

The man didn't raise his head or call out a greeting. Alvis wasn't big on politeness or protocol. Instead, he peered down through the large, freestanding magnifying glass sitting on the table and used the tweezers in his hand to pluck one of the onyx shards off the cloth. Then he hunched forward and dropped the shard into the appropriate slot on the piece in front of him.

Only when I heard the soft *tink* of the gem sliding into place did I move away from the door, walk over, and set the bag of plum tarts that Isobel had given me onto the table. Then I leaned over his shoulder and looked through the magnifying glass.

A rose-shaped brooch glittering with pink-diamond petals, emerald leaves, and onyx thorns was anchored to a padded work tray. The magnifying glass let me see every exquisite detail in super sharp focus, from the heart-shaped diamonds to the needle-thin slivers of onyx to the delicate filigree that had been etched into the gold setting.

"Nice design," I murmured. "Although all those pink diamonds are a bit much. I would have used plain old rubies."

"And how many times have I told you that we're not paid to think?" Alvis grumbled. "We're paid to design what the client wants, right down to the garishly colored stones."

He picked up another onyx sliver and dropped it into the next open slot. He waited for the gem to *tink* into place, then reached out and waved his hand over the piece. The scent of magic surged over the brooch, and tiny gold prongs curled in to hold the onyx shards in place.

Alvis was a metalstone master who'd been at Seven Spire for more than thirty years. Originally from Andvari, he'd decided long ago that he would much rather use his magic to shape the precious jewels and metal that his countrymen dug out of their mines than pry them out of the ground himself. So he'd left his homeland and had gotten an appointment at Seven Spire as the royal jeweler, making pieces for the nobles, senators, and anyone else who could afford them.

I had met Alvis about a month after I'd come to the palace, after rigorous testing had determined that I was a mutt with only an enhanced sense of smell and no other magic. Of course, that wasn't true, not at all, but my parents' murders had taught me to keep my other power to myself, lest someone try to use it—and me—for their own ill ends.

Since I was an orphan with no close family, money, or power, I had been required to learn a trade to help offset the cost of my royal education and upkeep. Hence my apprenticeship to Alvis. You didn't need magic to polish jewels or twist metal, and Alvis was notorious for going through apprentices like ladies went through ball gowns. A few hours of wear and tear was all that it took to send boys and girls sobbing from his workshop, vowing never to return.

Alvis hadn't liked having yet another apprentice foisted off on him, especially not a royal girl who kept having to leave to attend one silly function after another. He hadn't said a single word to me during the first three months that I'd worked here. He'd just grunted and pointed at whatever gem, metal, or tool he wanted me to fetch. I had been so heartbroken over my parents' deaths, and the cruel betrayal that had come next, that I hadn't minded his grumpy demeanor. His silent brooding had matched my own dark mood perfectly.

Still, being around all the glittering jewels and gleaming sheets of metal had helped pull me out of my heartbreak, and I'd grown curious enough to start playing around with the gems and settings, trying to shape them into something beautiful the way that Alvis always did. Of course, he had growled at me to stop, but I was as stubborn as he was, and I had worn him down, pestering him with questions and making a mess of things until he'd finally decided that he would be much better off to teach me everything he knew.

I would never be a true master like Alvis, and my finished pieces were pale imitations of his, but I enjoyed the work. Picking out the right jewels and metal and then bending, twisting, and shaping them into something new soothed me. I felt like I was bringing a little bit of beauty into someone's life, a small bauble that would remind them of a special time and bring them enjoyment for years to come. It gave me a sense of accomplishment and made me feel useful in a way that being the royal stand-in at all those boring recitals, luncheons, and teas did not.

Plus, I enjoyed the money.

I might have been the queen's cousin, but I still had to pay for my modest room and board, and being the royal jeweler's apprentice paid quite nicely. Plus, Alvis let me keep all the money I earned for any piece that I commissioned, made, and sold myself, minus supply costs. Thanks to Isobel's influence and my own hard work, I had a good business going with the kitchen staff. Even some of the poorer, er, minor nobles had started to request pieces from me.

Given my apprenticeship, I was well acquainted with frippery and frivolity, and I had seen more than one noble sent packing from the palace in disgrace after squandering his wealth. My finances were one of the few things that I could control, and I saved every penny I could, adding them to my accounts at the royal bank. My plan was to take all those pennies, return to my family's estate, and restore it to its former glory, along with opening up my own small jewelry shop. I'd been saving for that goal for years, and I was almost ready to make it a reality.

All I had to do was get the queen's permission to leave, something that I had been trying to secure for the last three months. Even though I would turn twenty-eight later this year, she was still my official guardian. But of course the queen was busy, and I had yet to snag a spot on her schedule. Perhaps I could speak with her at the luncheon.

I was hoping that Alvis and Isobel would come with me. Winterwind, my family's estate, was only a few miles from Andvari and not that far from Unger. I wanted to take care of them like they had taken care of me, and it would be a fine place for them to live out their golden years. Besides, their constant sniping would help keep them both young and vigorous. It certainly had during the years they'd been at the palace.

Alvis dropped the last few onyx slivers into place, then waved his hand over the brooch again. This time, the scent of his magic gusted through the workshop, much stronger than before, burning my nose with its sudden, sharp intensity.

Most people—or at least their emotions—smelled like food. Peppery anger, vinegar tension, garlic guilt. But not Alvis. He smelled like metal, mixed with crushed stone and a strong tang of magic, as if he had worked with so much gold and silver that their essences had seeped into his skin.

Alvis dropped his hand, and the scent of his magic vanished. I peered through the magnifying glass again. The final gold prongs curled into place, finishing the design, and the pink diamonds lit up one by one, each gem glowing much more brightly than it had before.

Not only was Alvis a master who could bend and shape metal, but he could also infuse his magic into the stones. Most jewels could absorb magic, but they reflected it back in different ways, adding to and augmenting their wearers' own power and abilities. Rubies radiated strength, emeralds increased speed, and the like.

Pink diamonds reflected back beauty. The rose brooch was lovely on its own, but thanks to the magic now pulsing through the diamonds, it would make its wearer seem more beautiful as well. A subtle magic and a small glamour, but one that Alvis's clients paid handsomely for.

"Very nice," I said when the diamonds had dimmed back to

their normal color. "They soaked up quite a bit of your power. That glamour should last for more than a year, even if the client wears the brooch every day."

"You should know," he replied. "You picked out those stones last week."

Most people scoffed at my mutt magic, but Alvis never had because it was quite helpful when picking out which gems to put in which pieces. Alvis might be a metalstone master, but all I had to do was sniff a tray of jewels, and my mutt magic told me which stones already had sparks of magic inside them, versus those that had little to no sparks. Jewels with more innate sparks had more potential and would absorb, store, and reflect back far more magic, letting Alvis craft more powerful pieces—and charge much higher prices for them.

"And I did an excellent job, as always."

Alvis waved away my smug self-compliment, but the corners of his mouth lifted up into a tiny smile. Then he looked at me, and his face creased into its usual frown. "What have you been doing? Rolling around in flour?"

I stared at the white stains that streaked my tunic. "Something like that."

"A page came down before you did. The queen wants an opal memory stone at today's luncheon." He shook his head. "I don't know why she would want to record that pit of vipers."

"Those vipers are my cousins."

He snorted. "And they would bite, poison, and kill you if they could, all to curry more favor with Cordelia."

He wasn't wrong. Life at the palace was always cutthroat, especially among the Blairs.

"Did the page say why Cordelia wanted the memory stone?"

"No." Alvis shrugged. "But it probably has something to do

with the rumors that she's planning to announce Vasilia's engagement to the Andvarian prince."

My stomach twisted at the mention of the crown princess, but Alvis's theory made sense. Rumors had been swirling for months that Queen Cordelia wanted to strengthen relations between Bellona and Andvari, and a royal marriage would be the best way to do that. Alvis wasn't the first to speculate that the main reason for the Andvarians' visit was to formally announce the engagement—something that Vasilia was vehemently opposed to. The crown princess thought that Bellona should negotiate with Morta, not help protect Andvari from the other larger kingdom. She'd proposed several new trade agreements with Morta, all of which the queen had vetoed, and relations between daughter and mother had been frosty for months.

Alvis pointed at the table in the corner that I used. "I prepared the stone. I have work to do, so you might as well take it with you to the luncheon."

"You're not coming? I thought Cordelia personally invited you."

He snorted again. "No, it was Vasilia, which means that she probably wants another jewel for her newest sword or dagger. Some little trinket to make her even more powerful than she already is. I'm staying here. If she wants her new bauble badly enough, she can come ask me for it herself."

My stomach twisted again, but I didn't respond. Words wouldn't change anything. Not when it came to my strained relationship with Vasilia—and how she had betrayed me.

Alvis handed the rose brooch to me. "Here. Take this over to your table, and get it out of my way while I clean up."

My fingers curled around the brooch. Not only could I

smell the magic clinging to the jewels, I could actually *feel* it, and the power burned like an ember in my palm. More importantly, I could feel my own cold, hard power rising up in response, wanting to snuff out all that hot, pulsing magic.

Alvis watched me, his hazel eyes narrowing with interest. This was another one of his tests. I didn't know why, but he was always searching for a sign, always looking for the smallest hint that I was more than what I appeared to be.

Then again, he was the only one who even suspected that I was immune to magic.

A magier's lightning, a morph's talons, a mutt's speed, a metalstone master's brooch. They could all hurt me, terribly so, but they didn't do nearly the damage they were supposed to. And I could overcome them all, if I really wanted to, if I was truly desperate enough to unleash my own magic in response. Depending on who was inherently more powerful, either a magier would roast me alive with her lightning or my immunity would smother her power, throttling it into nothingness. Although, thankfully, I hadn't had to use my immunity like that in years.

Back when I was younger, before I'd learned how to control my immunity, all I had to do was touch a ring or a necklace, and I would extinguish all the magic inside the jewels. At first, Alvis hadn't been able to figure out why it was happening, but he'd slowly grown suspicious, and he'd started giving me these little tests.

I loved and respected Alvis, but I'd never told him about my power. I'd never told *anyone* about it, not even Isobel. The only person I'd ever even been tempted to tell was Vasilia, and thank the gods that I had kept my mouth shut.

So as easy as it would have been for me to wrap my fingers around the brooch, unleash my power, and extinguish the magic in the pink diamonds, I pushed my immunity back down, walked over, and set the brooch on my table.

Disappointment flashed in Alvis's eyes, but he started getting things ready for his next design.

I looked at the memory stone on my table. It was a smooth, flat opal roughly the size of my palm, resting on top of a black velvet bag. The gem reeked of magic, and sparks of blue, red, green, and purple shimmered through the milky surface, like fireworks exploding over and over again.

Memory stones did exactly what their name implied—they captured and held memories. All I had to do was place the stone in a strategic position and tap on it three times, and it would record everything at the luncheon. People, conversations, even the decorations. Then, when the event was over, I would tap the stone three more times to stop its magic, and the queen would have a perfect recording of the day's festivities, which she could view by tapping on the stone herself at any time.

I dropped the opal into the black velvet bag and slid the whole thing into my pants pocket. Then I noticed a black velvet box tied with a blue ribbon sitting on the corner of my table. I picked up the box and shook it, but the velvet kept me from hearing what was inside.

"What's this? Another new piece for a client?"

"Sort of." Alvis fiddled with his tools. "It's for you. Consider it an early birthday present."

"My birthday isn't until the Winter Solstice. Besides, you don't believe in birthday presents."

Alvis always said that a person's birthday was just another day, although he always found an excuse to sneak me a treat on mine, whether it was a new set of metal cutters, some gems for my latest design, or a bag of chocolates that he claimed he didn't want.

"Well, I finished it early, so you're getting it now. Don't just look at it," he grumbled. "Go on, open it."

I undid the ribbon, set it aside, and slowly cracked open the box, enjoying the surprise for as long as possible.

A stunning bracelet lay inside the black velvet.

The wide band was made of curls of silver that had been twisted together to resemble thorns, which wrapped around and protected the elegant crown in the center of the design. Instead of being a single gem, the crown was made of seven tearstone shards that had been fitted together, making it glitter far more than one gem ever could. The bracelet was exquisite, but what was even more impressive was all the magic that pulsed through it.

Like other jewels, tearstone could absorb and reflect back magic, but it also had the unique property of offering protection from magic—deflecting it like a shield. Tearstone jewelry that reflected back magic was often light gray in color, while those pieces that deflected magic were often midnight-blue, like the ones in my bracelet.

Each shard in the crown was filled with a cold, hard power that was similar to my own immunity. I didn't know why Alvis had made the bracelet, since I didn't have anything to fear at the palace—at least, not when it came to physical danger—but I was touched by the gesture.

"It's beautiful," I whispered. "It must have taken you months to make this."

Alvis shrugged, but his lips twitched up again, as though he was holding back another smile. "Well, don't just look at it. Put it on."

I slid the bracelet onto my wrist and snapped the clasp. It fit perfectly, and the tearstone shards glittered a deep, vibrant blue.

"I know that shards are one of your signature designs, but why a crown made of them?" I asked, running my finger over the jewels. "I've never seen you make that before."

Alvis shrugged. "I've made a crown of shards before, although not for a long time. I only use it for special pieces."

I glanced at him, sensing there was something he wasn't telling me, but he fiddled with his tools again, and the stubborn set of his mouth told me that he wouldn't reveal anything else. Still, love and gratitude flowed through me, and I walked over and wrapped him up in a tight hug. If I'd had the strength, I would have lifted him off his feet and spun him around, but he was far too short and stocky for me to do that.

"Thank you!" I hugged him even tighter. "Thank you so much!"

Alvis awkwardly patted me on the back. "All right," he grumbled. "I have work to do, and you have a luncheon to attend, remember?"

I hugged him again, then drew back. Alvis stared at me, that small half smile still on his lips. I leaned forward and kissed him on the cheek.

"Bah!" He waved his hand. "That's quite enough of that."

"I know. You don't believe in affection either." I grinned. "I guess that it's lucky for both of us that I do."

I leaned forward and kissed his other cheek.

"Bah!" Alvis waved his hand at me again, but his lips were slowly creeping up. If he wasn't careful, he was going to break out into a bona fide smile.

I grinned even wider at him, and he actually did smile at

me. Then his hazel gaze dropped to the bracelet, and his smile vanished, as though something about the piece bothered him, even though he was the one who'd made it.

"Is something wrong? Did you not want me to wear the bracelet? It doesn't exactly go with my kitchen tunic," I joked.

He shook his head. "Don't be silly. Of course I want you to wear it."

"But?"

He hesitated. "Just . . . be careful."

"Of what?"

"I don't know, exactly. It just seems like there are a lot of new people around the palace lately. You know how I feel about new people."

"You don't like them."

Alvis nodded. "You can't trust new people."

I could have pointed out that he didn't like anyone, not even me most days, and that just because he didn't know someone didn't mean that they were up to something sinister, but I held my tongue. He'd given me such a lovely gift, and I didn't want to ruin the moment. Besides, he was right. I had a luncheon to attend and my freedom and future to secure.

"Go on," he said. "Before I change my mind and make you stay here and work."

I raised my hand and snapped off a salute. "Yes, sir."

Alvis gave me a chiding look, but his lips were twitching as though he was trying to hide another smile. Laughing, I gave him another salute, then left the workshop.

CHAPTER THREE

I trudged up to the first floor, which was much busier than before. Maeven must have lit a fire under the kitchen staff, because servants hustled to and fro, carrying everything from table linens to platters of cheeses to baskets of fresh fruit. The steady *thud-thud-thud-thud* of their footsteps was like a low, rolling drumbeat, accentuated by the clatter of dishes rattling together.

I eyed a couple of servants carrying crates full of bottles. How much champagne did Maeven think would be consumed at the luncheon? Perhaps she was just being cautious in having so much of it on hand. If Cordelia was going to announce Vasilia's engagement, then there would be several toasts wishing the couple well, congratulating each kingdom on a shrewd new alliance, and so on. Either way, I hugged the wall, steering clear of the scurrying servants.

But that put me in the path of other people—the palace guards.

Normally, a guard was stationed at either end of the common areas, with a few more roaming from one section of the palace to the next. Just to make sure that the political disagreements, drunken lords, and feuding ladies didn't get out of hand. But even those things were few and far between and almost always quickly resolved.

But today, guards were stationed every few feet. One, two, three . . . I counted more than a dozen in this hallway alone. Captain Auster must have brought in extra security for the luncheon. An ordinary enough occurrence, given the Andvarian dignitaries' importance, and one that wouldn't normally bother me. But I had been at the palace for a long time, and I knew every single one of the guards, along with their routes and duties.

I didn't recognize any of these people.

All the guards were wearing the standard uniform of a plain gold breastplate over a short-sleeve red tunic with black leggings and boots, and each one had a sword buckled to their black belt. Nothing unusual there. But the more I studied the guards, the more I noticed something very unusual about them.

They all reeked of magic.

A servant carrying a tray of champagne flutes hurried by, pushing me closer to two guards who were standing along the wall. I drew in a deep breath, tasting the scents in the air. Dozens of perfumes and colognes clashed together, their floral and spicy notes fighting for dominance, along with an undercurrent of sour, nervous sweat.

I expected the perfumes and colognes, given all the people who moved through Seven Spire on a daily basis, but the sweat was a surprise. Usually, that scent permeated the palace only when there were deals to be made, fortunes to be won and lost, and enemies to be struck down.

I drew in another breath, my nose twitching as I sorted through all the scents. The harsh, metallic tang of magic swirled through the hallway again, emanating from the two guards.

I stared at the men, but I didn't see any morph marks on their necks, and no lightning or fire sparked on their fingertips to indicate that they had any magier power. And they obviously weren't masters, since they weren't working with or wielding some specific element. They could be mutts like me, but mutts usually smelled of magic only when they were actively using their power, and all these two were doing was standing against the wall.

Sure, their posture was stiffer than normal, and sweat glistened on their foreheads, despite the cool air. But they were so tense and nervous that they were literally sweating magic out of their pores. What were they so concerned about?

The two guards realized that I was staring and tipped their heads to me. The polite nods increased my worry. I was still wearing a kitchen tunic, so I should have been invisible to them. Captain Auster didn't pay his men to be polite to servants. So why acknowledge my presence at all?

I opened my mouth to ask their names, but a group of servants rushing up behind me forced me to walk past the guards or risk getting trampled. It wasn't until I reached the far end of the hallway that I was able to step out of the servants' way, stop, and look back.

A third man had joined the other two—Nox, the personal guard to Princess Vasilia.

Unlike the other guards in their red tunics, Nox wore one that was a bright, vivid fuchsia and trimmed with gold thread, in keeping with Vasilia's colors, although he never bothered with a breastplate or any other armor. He was quite handsome, tall and muscled with broad shoulders, golden hair, purplish eyes, and tan skin, and more than one servant snuck an admiring glance at him.

Nox had come to Seven Spire about nine months ago with a group of visiting Mortan nobles. Vasilia had taken an immediate shine to him and had convinced him to stay on as her own personal guard, despite the fact that he was a minor royal in his own right. Ever since then, rumors had flown fast and furious that the two of them were sleeping together, despite Nox's flirting with every woman he encountered, even me, on occasion.

Sex was just as much a weapon at the palace as swords were in the gladiator ring. For some, it was their preferred weapon, wielded with cold cunning. More than one fresh-faced ingénue, male and female alike, had come to the palace only to leave a few weeks later in poverty, disgrace, tears, and heartbreak after being fucked over—literally and physically—by some more experienced lord or lady.

I didn't like Nox. Not because he was Mortan, as Isobel would have insisted, but because he knew exactly how handsome he was and used it to his advantage. He was always dazzling the servants with sly smiles and pretty words to get what he wanted, whether it was the best cuts of meat at dinner, a bottle of expensive wine from the cellar, or fine silk sheets for his bed. But his smile was always just a little too bright, and his laughter was always just a little too hearty to be genuine. He reminded me of a coral viper lying in the grass, waiting to strike the unsuspecting soul who was unlucky enough to step on him.

He was a perfect match for Vasilia that way.

Nox spoke to the guards, who nodded back to him, as well as to the servants who hurried by. Perhaps Captain Auster hadn't rounded these guards into shape yet, and they didn't realize that they should be watching people, instead of greeting them.

Either way, I couldn't do anything about Nox or the guards, so I pushed my unease aside, left the hallway, and headed up to my chambers on the seventh floor.

Contrary to popular belief, a person's living on a higher floor had absolutely nothing to do with their position, wealth, title, or magic. It just meant that I had to climb more than a dozen sets of bloody stairs every time I wanted to go to my room. Oh, I could have taken one of the metal lifts, but they were always far too slow and crowded.

Fifteen minutes later, I reached a door tucked into the back corner of that level. Much like Alvis's dungeon workshop, this area was deserted, and not a whisper of sound broke the silence. No one ever came up to this hidden nook unless they were looking for me, but even that was a rare occurrence. Usually Captain Auster was the one who came calling, to sternly remind me of my royal duty on the rare occasion when I skipped some tedious tea.

Since no one ever came up here, I never bothered to lock the door, so I opened it and stepped inside. Unlike the other members of the royal family with their spacious apartments on the lower levels, my quarters were shockingly small. An old, creaky table with a couple of mismatched chairs stood in the front of the room, with my bed pushed up against the back wall. In the corner, a wooden armoire loomed over the vanity table sitting next to it. A door set into the opposite wall opened up into a bathroom that was barely big enough for the white porcelain tub, toilet, and sink inside.

Since I didn't get any visitors, I didn't bother to keep my room clean. Childish, I know, but it was the only bit of rebellion that I could consistently get away with. Piles of books were stacked up on one of the chairs, the different colors, shapes, and sizes almost making it look like a person was sitting there. More books covered the table itself, along with gems, bits of metal, and tweezers. A magnifying glass like the one in Alvis's workshop stood on one side of the table, while a fluorestone headlamp was hooked over the back of one of the knobs on the empty chair.

Still more books were stacked up three and four dozen high on the floor, and I wound my way through the paper maze. Most of the volumes were research for one function or another, and colored ribbons stuck out of the pages, marking the passages that were the most pertinent. I might despise being the royal stand-in, but I prided myself on always being prepared and always doing a good job. That meant learning everything I could about the people, politics, and objects at every tea, recital, and art exhibit that I attended.

I sat down at the vanity table, sliding aside the newest stack of books that I'd borrowed from the palace library. A wooden music box shaped like an ogre's face perched on the top volume, although I could still read the book's title that glimmered in silver foil—*Step by Step: Traditional Dances of Unger.*

In addition to making pies for the Andvarian ambassador, I was also scheduled to perform the Tanzen Freund, a dance of friendship, for the Ungerian ambassador when she visited next week. The dance was far more complicated than the pies, and far more important, since relations between Bellona and Unger had been strained for years.

I had planned to spend a rare lazy morning in bed, listening to the music box, reading through the book, and reviewing the dance's intricate steps. At least, until Isobel had knocked on my door and told me about my new, last-minute, pie-making duties.

Once the music box and the books were out of the way, I studied my reflection in the mirror. Alvis was right. I looked like I'd been rolling around in flour. White stains covered my tunic and streaked across my cheeks like makeup that I'd forgotten to blend in. No wonder the strange guards had nodded at me. They'd probably felt sorry for me, the clueless servant wandering around with flour all over her face.

I sighed and dropped my gaze from the mirror to a silver framed portrait propped up on the corner of the table. The painting showed a beautiful woman with black hair sitting next to a handsome man with wavy dark brown hair. My mother, Leighton Larimar Winter Blair, and my father, Jarl Sancus.

The two of them had been sitting in front of the fireplace in our home. I had ducked behind the paint master and had made silly faces, trying to get them to laugh and break their poses. I could still see that silent laughter shining in their eyes and in the faint lift of their lips. The portrait had been painted a few weeks before their murders, and it was one of the few reminders I had of them.

My heart squeezed tight, but I stared at the portrait, studying my parents' faces, even though I'd long ago committed them to memory. Everyone told me that I looked just like my mother, since I had her black hair and gray-blue eyes.

All the Blairs had gray-blue eyes. Tearstone eyes, some people called them, named after all the tearstone that the Blairs had mined out of Seven Spire and the surrounding mountains. Some stories said that the royal family had dug so much tearstone out of the ground that it had turned our eyes the same shifting gray-blue color as the stone.

My eyes and features weren't nearly as pretty as my mother's had been. Still, I tried to look as much like her as possible, even braiding my long hair in the same elaborate style as in her portrait.

A series of bells rang out, warning everyone that there was only an hour left until the noon luncheon. I couldn't go to the event covered in flour. Queen Cordelia paid little attention to me, but even she would notice that.

My parents' portrait was a bit crooked, so I straightened the frame, lining it up with the edge of the table.

"There you go," I whispered.

It almost seemed as though their eyes brightened and their smiles widened, although it was just wishful thinking on my part. I wasn't a time magier, so I never got glimpses of the past or had visions of the future.

I stared at my parents' faces for a few seconds longer, then got to my feet to get ready for the luncheon. The ache in my heart lingered, though, the way it always did.

The way it always would.

I went into the bathroom and washed the flour off my face, then stripped off my dirty clothes and replaced them with black boots and leggings and a long-sleeve midnight-blue tunic trimmed with silver thread—the colors for the Winter line of the Blair family. I also grabbed the black velvet pouch with Alvis's memory stone and slid it into my pocket.

I checked my reflection in the bathroom mirror. More tendrils of my black hair had escaped their braid and curled up like tiny gargoyle horns all over my head, so I wet my hair and smoothed them down. I also dabbed some berry balm onto my lips, but I didn't bother with any more makeup. Most of my cousins were quite pretty, with servants and thread masters to help them make the most of their good looks. I could never compete with them, especially not with Vasilia and Madelena, the two princesses, so I didn't even try anymore.

I started to leave the bathroom when my gaze fell on the bracelet lying on the sink. I hesitated, wondering if I should wear it to the luncheon. It was a simple, elegant piece, compared to my cousins' ropes of pearls and cascades of diamonds, but I'd learned long ago that someone was always ready, willing, and eager to take away what little that I had. Not because they needed or wanted it, but just because they could, just because that sort of pettiness amused them.

But it had been such a lovely, thoughtful gift, and I didn't want to abandon it less than an hour after Alvis had given it to me. A compromise then. I slid the bracelet onto my wrist, but I pulled my sleeve down so that the fabric covered the band.

Once that was done, I left my room and walked back downstairs. By the time I reached the first floor, the hallways were empty, even of guards. Everyone must have already gone to the luncheon, which was being held on the royal lawn. I stepped into the hallway that would take me to the lawn when a snide voice called out behind me.

"Everleigh, a word, please."

I sighed. And the day had been going so well.

I plastered a smile on my face and turned around. A man strode toward me, his boots banging out a constant, annoying beat. Instead of the usual scarlet, his long-sleeve tunic was black, although it was adorned with several rows of gold thread, as were his black leggings. His black hair and mustache were brushed and curled just so, and his black boots were as polished and glossy as mirrors.

Felton, the queen's personal secretary, stopped in front of me and straightened up to his full height, which was little more than five feet, despite the ridiculously high heels on his boots. I'd never understood how he managed to walk in those things, but I'd never seen him wear anything else. A small red book dangled from his fingers like a sword he was about to snap up and bring down on top of someone's head—my head.

In addition to scheduling the queen's life, Felton also assigned me all my so-called royal duties, including baking those bloody pies this morning. Despite all my other royal relatives who lived at the palace, Felton always summoned me first. He knew that I didn't have the authority to say no to him, so he always singled me out for the most pointless, menial, and disgusting tasks, like eating that raw liver. Like everyone else at Seven Spire, Felton enjoyed wielding what power he had, and the bastard took great delight in humiliating me whenever possible.

Well, that was going to change. As soon as I had the queen's permission, I would leave Seven Spire, and I would never have to see the odious little toad again, much less swallow my pride and anger and obey his orders.

Felton didn't even deign to look at me as he snapped open his book, pulled out the gold pen inside, and made a little check mark on one of the pages. Even with his ridiculous boots, I was still a good six inches taller, and I leaned forward and discreetly scanned the page.

Felton had a list of names, probably of everyone attending the luncheon, and they all had check marks beside them, as my name did now. I was surprised that he'd given me a check mark, though, instead of a big, black *X*. Normally, he would have marked me as tardy just for the petty pleasure of getting me in trouble with the queen.

"Your meeting with the Ungerian ambassador next week has been canceled," Felton said in a distracted voice, still concentrating on the list of names.

"What?"

It had taken Cordelia and her advisors months of negotiations to get the Ungers to agree to travel to Bellona, and it was to be a historic goodwill trip, since no Ungerian ambassador had visited Seven Spire in the thirty years that Cordelia had been queen.

So why had the meeting been canceled? The whole point of the ambassador's trip was to shore up a treaty between Unger, Andvari, and Bellona, promising aid if the Mortans attacked any of the three kingdoms. The political ramifications of the trip not happening were enormous, like a pebble being dropped into a pond and making waves all the way over to the opposite shoreline.

Then another thought occurred to me. "But what about the dance?"

Felton flipped over to the next page in his book, which also contained a list of names, and ran his pen down the paper, double-checking his check marks. "What dance?"

Anger spiked through me, but I kept my voice level. "The Tanzen Freund. The traditional Ungerian dance of friendship. The one that I spent the last three months learning at your insistence."

Felton had been particularly gleeful when he'd informed me that I had to learn the dance, and even more so when he'd introduced me to my tutor, Lady Xenia, an Ungerian woman who had married a Bellonan lord and had moved to Svalin more than twenty years ago. Xenia's husband had died long ago, and she spent her days running a finishing school, teaching royal, noble, and other wealthy children things like etiquette, languages, and dances. Everything one needed to know in order to marry into money, snare a sponsor, and hobnob in Bellonan society and those in the other kingdoms.

I had enjoyed brushing up on the Ungerian language and customs, but Lady Xenia had quickly become the bane of my existence. She was a stern taskmaster who made Alvis seem as warm and cuddly as a baby gargoyle in comparison.

Then there was the dance itself. The Tanzen Freund was an intricate, complicated affair that was performed barefoot and had not one, not two, but thirteen separate sections. To make matters even worse, Xenia was overly fond of poking me with her cane whenever I got the smallest thing wrong, whether it was a step, a bow, or even a hand flourish. And I got them wrong quite frequently, given how bloody many of them there were. I still had the bruises on my arms, legs, and feet from our last session three days ago.

"It's just a dance," Felton said. "Nothing important."

My hands clenched into fists. Oh, no. Just my time, energy, and effort. Nothing important at all. But I forced myself to keep my voice level again. "Who canceled the meeting?"

"Vasilia, of course."

And just like that, all my anger, indignation, and resistance cracked away, like a brick bludgeoned to bits by a sledgehammer. I couldn't summon up another word of protest. There was no point. Nothing I could say would change things. Not with Felton, and especially not with Vasilia. The crown princess always got her way. Vasilia always *won*, especially when it came to hurting me, just as she had ever since we were children.

Still, once my surprise wore off, I frowned. The trip had been Cordelia's idea. If anyone should be canceling anything, it should be the queen.

"You can inform Xenia of the cancellation during the luncheon," Felton continued.

Not only had he casually dismissed all my months of hard work, but he was also going to make me break the bad news to Xenia, who would probably poke me with her cane for wasting her time as well. Terrific. Just bloody terrific.

Felton stuck his pen into his book and snapped it shut. He didn't even glance in my direction as he walked past me. "Well, come along then, Everleigh. We wouldn't want you to be any later than you already are. Then again, punctuality has never been one of your virtues. Not that you really have any virtues to start with." He delivered the insults without breaking stride, which was impressive, even for him.

A sick, empty feeling spread through my body. The same feeling that I had experienced countless times before. The same defeated, hollow feeling that I always had whenever Vasilia won and I lost.

Damned if I did, damned if I didn't. But that was duty for you, and I had as little choice in this matter as I did in all the others at the palace. So I sighed and trudged after Felton.

CHAPTER FOUR

elton opened one of the glass double doors at the end of the hallway. He didn't bother to hold it for me before he strode outside, and of course it slid shut before I could grab it. I sighed again, opened the door, and followed him.

The royal lawn was one of the largest common areas, a mixture of stone and grass that stretched out for thousands of feet before a wall cordoned it off from the cliffs on this side of the mountain and the two-hundred-foot drop to the Summanus River below. Towering trees dotted the lawn, although their branches were brown and bare for the winter. The flower beds were brown and bare as well, except for a few hardier blossoms, like the ice violets and snow pansies that bloomed year-round. Cobblestone paths wound across the grass, many of them lined with iron benches where people could sit and enjoy the view of the city. The lawn was one of my favorite places, and I tilted my face to the sun, soaking up the surprising heat of the late January day.

The royal lawn was used for all sorts of events, including

dance recitals, concerts, and even stargazing. If there was a large enough crowd, wooden bleachers would be erected on the grass, turning the lawn into a makeshift arena. Today's luncheon was on the small side, with fewer than two hundred guests, including the Andvarians, along with the Blair royal family and some notable nobles. A grand ball was planned for next week to properly celebrate the Andvarians' visit and let them mix and mingle with Bellonan society.

In keeping with the luncheon's small scale, the setup was simple. Round tables draped with scarlet linens covered the lawn, all of them arranged in front of a long, rectangular table where the core members of the royal family would sit—Queen Cordelia, Crown Princess Vasilia, the younger Princess Madelena, and Madelena's husband, Lord Durante.

Another long, rectangular table stood at an angle to that first one, indicating where the Andvarian ambassador and his contingent would sit. My pies, golden brown and perfect, were perched on one end of that table. Isobel was stationed there, handing out pieces of pie.

Felton scurried over to Queen Cordelia, who was standing in the center of the lawn. The queen was dressed in a scarlet gown trimmed with gold thread, and a gold crown studded with roses made of rubies circled her head. Despite the glints of gray in her golden hair, Cordelia was an impressive figure, with an imposing, authoritative air, as though she was somehow taller than everyone else, despite her petite size. I had thought her quite intimidating when I was a child. Now I just felt sorry for her.

For as much as I hated performing my so-called royal duties, Cordelia's were a thousand times worse. All I had to do was smile, nod, and learn dances. The queen made decisions that impacted people throughout Bellona and beyond. Her choices determined who succeeded and who failed, who flourished and who floundered, who lived and who died, a burden far, far heavier on the heart than the weight of that crown on her head.

A fifty-something man wearing a short-sleeve scarlet tunic topped with a gold breastplate with a rising-sun crest emblazoned over his heart stood three feet away from Cordelia. The crest and the feathered texture of the breastplate marked his importance and made him stand out from the other guards with their simpler armor. Captain Auster, the queen's personal guard.

With his short gray hair, dark bronze skin, and brown eyes, Auster looked as stern as Cordelia did, especially given his lumpy, crooked nose, which had obviously been broken multiple times, despite the efforts of various bone masters to put it back into place. Unlike everyone else, Auster wasn't laughing, talking, eating, or drinking. Instead, his sharp gaze scanned over everyone, and his hand rested on the sword hooked to his belt, ready to pull the blade free at a moment's notice.

Lord Hans, the Andvarian ambassador, stood next to the queen. He was a handsome older man, with short gray hair, dark brown eyes, and ebony skin, and his fine gray jacket was covered with medals and ribbons, denoting his former service as an army general. He was telling some story and kept waving his hand to punctuate his loud, boisterous words. In his other hand, he held an empty plate and a fork, as though he had already had a piece of one of my pies. He must have enjoyed it, since only a few crumbs littered the plate.

Princess Madelena laughed at Hans's story, as did her husband, Lord Durante, who had his arm draped protectively around her waist. Madelena wore a pink gown that highlighted her golden hair, her gray-blue eyes, and the round curve of her stomach. She was six months pregnant and seemed to grow larger and more beautiful each day, while Durante's green tunic accentuated his dark brown hair, eyes, and skin. Even though they had been married for more than two years, the couple was known for being thoroughly, disgustingly in love, and they spent more time sneaking adoring glances at each other than they did listening to the ambassador.

The final member of their group was Frederich, an Andvarian prince who was third in line for the throne. With his brown hair and blue eyes, he cut quite the dashing figure in his gray jacket, although it lacked the medals and ribbons that adorned Lord Hans's garment.

A servant wandered by with a tray of champagne, and I grabbed a glass so I could see why Maeven had been making such a fuss about it. I started to take a sip, but a foul, sulfuric stench wafted up out of the fizzing bubbles. My nose crinkled. I'd never heard of champagne going bad, but this certainly had, although you wouldn't know it from the way everyone else was guzzling it down. Perhaps it was just me. I tried again to take a sip, but I couldn't ignore the disgusting aroma. I placed the glass on the servant's tray and let him whisk it away. That's when I realized that someone was staring at me.

Maeven.

Her blond hair was swept up into its usual bun, but she'd traded in her kitchen garb for a midnight-purple gown, along with amethyst chandelier earrings and a matching ring. She looked far more like a noble lady than she did a kitchen steward.

Maeven's eyes locked with mine. Her face remained blank, and I couldn't tell what she was thinking. Then her gaze cut to the servant who had taken away my champagne. Perhaps she was wondering why I hadn't drunk it. Another servant came up and whispered something in her ear, and she turned to answer him.

Servants were coming and going through the doors behind me, streaming by with trays of champagne, along with fresh fruit, crackers, and cheeses, so I moved out of their way and surveyed the rest of the crowd, many of whom were my cousins.

Queen Cordelia's mother, Carnelia Blair, had been the oldest of nine siblings, including my grandmother Coralie, the third born and youngest sister. So all the children of those nine siblings were first cousins, including Queen Cordelia and Lady Leighton, my mother. That first generation of children had multiplied into many, many more, about fifty second cousins, including myself. That total crept up to about seventy-five cousins, if you counted all the bastard children. Currently, I was seventeenth in line for the throne. Soon to be eighteenth, after Madelena had her baby in a few months.

Genevieve, Owen, Bria, Finn . . .

Carmen, Sam, Fiona, Jasper . . .

My cousins were huddled in their usual cliques and keeping an eye on Cordelia, looking for the slightest opening to get some face time with her. Given the groups of people between us, I wouldn't be able to get anywhere near the queen, much less talk to her about leaving Seven Spire.

I still needed to find someplace to put Alvis's memory stone to record the luncheon, so I moved along the fringes of the crowd, searching for the spot with the best view where I could discreetly leave the stone.

Some of my younger cousins, including Gwendolyn, Logan, Lila, Devon, Rory, and Ian, waved and called out greetings as I passed them, which I returned. But for the most part, no one paid any attention to me as I roamed through the crowd. Which was fine, as it let me eavesdrop on all sorts of gossip, which I filed away for future use.

". . . juggling three mistresses at once must be exhausting . . ."

". . . can't believe she had the gall to wear the same dress as me . . ."

". . . Serilda Swanson's come back to the capital. Her gladiator troupe moved into that new arena along the river last week. Their first show is tonight."

My ears perked up at that last tidbit. A new gladiator troupe was always noteworthy, but this one was particularly interesting.

Serilda Swanson was a legend in Bellona. She used to be the queen's personal guard, under the command of Captain Auster, but she'd gotten embroiled in some scandal that had led to her dismissal about fifteen years ago. But instead of slinking away quietly into the night, Serilda had fully embraced and even added to her scandal by taking several of the queen's most trusted guards with her. She'd further thumbed her nose at Cordelia by using those same guards to start her own gladiator troupe. Now instead of protecting the queen, Serilda trained gladiators to entertain the masses and line her pockets with gold crowns. Everyone at the palace either applauded her ingenuity or hated her for it. Sometimes both.

Serilda had still been at Seven Spire when I'd first come here, so I had a few dim memories of her. What I mostly remembered was how many weapons she had always carried. She had once pulled them all out for me and laid them on the table in Alvis's workshop like the pieces of a jigsaw puzzle. I paused, hoping that I might hear more about her, but the conversation moved on to another topic, so I moved on as well.

Everyone kept glancing from Queen Cordelia to the doors, as though they were expecting someone else important to arrive. That's when I noticed who was missing—Vasilia.

Curious. I despised Vasilia, but she did her duty, the same as me, and it wasn't like her to be one minute late. Perhaps she was going to skip the luncheon in protest. She hadn't wanted Cordelia to meet with Lord Hans, and she certainly didn't want to be engaged to Prince Frederich. But Vasilia was the crown princess, and it was her duty to do what was best for Bellona. That meant a permanent alliance with the Andvarians—one that would be bound by blood.

A royal marriage between Vasilia and Frederich would ensure that the two kingdoms were united for years and generations to come, especially against the growing threat of the Mortans. Despite my hatred of her, I couldn't blame Vasilia for wanting to choose her own husband. True, Madelena had a love match, but Durante came from the Floresian royal family, and their marriage had been politically motivated as much as anything else.

But I still had to find a spot for the memory stone, so I pushed those thoughts away, finished my circuit of the lawn, and headed over to the Andvarian table, stopping a few feet away from where Isobel was still dishing up pieces of pie. This table had the best view of the proceedings, so I pulled the black velvet bag out of my pocket, opened the drawstrings, and fished out the memory stone.

I set the stone on the table in front of a crystal vase full of blue snow pansies, then tapped my finger on it three times. The bits of blue, red, green, and purple shimmered in the milky surface, and the opal began glowing with a faint light, although you had to squint to see it, given the bright sunshine.

I had just slid the black velvet bag back into my pocket when a cane poked into my upper arm, hard enough to shove me forward and make me bump up against the table. I winced and resisted the urge to massage away the pain. That would only make her poke me again, even harder than before. I plastered a smile on my face and turned around.

A woman stood in front of me. She was a few inches taller than me, with golden amber eyes and shoulder-length, coppery red hair that curled around her face in loose waves. Her tailored dark green tunic and black leggings highlighted her strong, lithe body. She leaned on a silver cane, although she didn't need it, despite the wrinkles that grooved into her sixty-something face. Her peony perfume washed over me, along with the faintest aroma of wet fur.

"Lady Xenia." I bowed my head, then executed the perfect Bellonan curtsy before straightening back up.

Xenia stared at me—as did the snarling ogre face on her neck.

Morph marks always reminded me of tattoos, if tattoos could ever be moving, thinking, living things. The ogre face on Xenia's neck was about the size of my palm. As I stared at it, the eyes on the face popped open, two bright slits of blinking liquid amber ink against Xenia's bronze skin. The ogre's eyes locked onto me, giving me a measuring look, as if it was thinking about how I might taste should it get hungry and want a snack before the luncheon started.

All morphs had some sort of tattoo—mark—on their bodies that showed what monster or creature they could shift into, but ogres were more powerful and far more frightening than most, with enough jagged teeth to give anyone nightmares. Xenia's morph mark even had a coppery strand of hair that curled around the ogre's face, just as the actual hair on her head did.

I didn't know if the mark was part of Xenia, or if Xenia was part of the mark, and I wasn't going to be stupid enough to ask. But I stared at the ogre, letting it know that I wasn't afraid of it. I had been wounded by far worse things than ogres, and I had the scars on my heart to prove it.

The ogre blinked, and its lips drew back into what seemed like a smile, despite the razor-sharp teeth the expression revealed. It was by far the friendliest look the ogre had ever shown me in all the months that I'd been working with Lady Xenia. For some reason, it approved of me today. Fantastic.

"What is this nonsense about the Ungerian ambassador's trip being canceled?" Xenia asked in a sharp tone.

Lady Xenia might instruct her students in the art of polite chitchat at her finishing school, but she didn't engage in it herself. Isobel heard her too, and she eyed Xenia as she cut into the final pie.

I focused on Xenia again. "I don't know why the trip has been canceled. Felton only told me about it a few minutes ago. How did you find out? He told me to tell you."

She tapped her index finger on her silver cane, which was topped with an ogre head that bore an eerie resemblance to the morph mark on her neck. "I don't need Felton to tell me what's going on. I have my own sources."

Of course she did. I had often wondered if Lady Xenia was a spy. People from every kingdom on this continent and the ones beyond were always coming and going from her school, and she always seemed to know about things the moment they happened, if not before.

"I'm sorry." I tried to be diplomatic, since that's what was expected. "I know you put a lot of time and effort into teaching me the Tanzen Freund—"

She snorted. "Perhaps it's better that the ambassador's trip was canceled. At least he won't have to watch you stumble through the dance and embarrass yourself, as well as me."

Xenia was never kind, but that was harsh, even for her. Anger surged through me, especially since her words weren't true. At least, not anymore. Yes, I had floundered through the dance for weeks, but over the past month, I had slowly mastered it, and I had performed it perfectly during our practice session earlier this week. She hadn't found a single reason to stab me with her cane. Not when it came to the dance, although she had still poked me a few times anyway, telling me not to get too confident.

"Well, perhaps if you had been a better teacher, and more interested in helping me learn the dance, rather than incessantly stabbing me with your bloody cane, I might not have stumbled so much."

The words popped out of my mouth before I could stop them, and Isobel sucked in a startled breath, shocked by them, along with my icy tone. The polite thing, the *proper* thing, would have been to bow my head and apologize. But I lifted my chin and crossed my arms over my chest. I didn't feel like bloody apologizing. Not when she had so casually dismissed all my hard work. Felton might be able to get away with that, but I didn't answer to Lady Xenia.

She blinked at my words. So did the ogre on her neck. I'd never spoken so harshly to either one of them, but she recovered quickly. "I am an *excellent* teacher."

"What is it you always say? Oh, yes. That a student is only as good as her teacher. So if there is any fault here, it lies with you, Lady Xenia." I arched an eyebrow. "You overestimate your excellence."

Her fingers clenched around the silver ogre head on her cane like she wanted to whip it up and brain me with it. But after a moment, her lips crept up into a begrudging smile, and the ogre on her neck grinned at me as well. "I underestimated you, Lady Everleigh. It seems like you actually have a bit of bite in you after all."

She tipped her head at me, then stalked back into the crowd, stabbing her cane into the grass every few steps.

Now I blinked in surprise. "What just happened? Did she give me a . . . compliment?"

"I think so," Isobel said. "Good for you, Evie, for standing up for yourself. You should do it more often."

She walked over and handed me the final piece of pie. Then she returned to the end of the table, gathered up the empty tins, and stacked them on a platter to take back to the kitchen.

I was proud of myself too, and the pie was my reward. I inhaled, enjoying the sweet aroma of the fruit filling wafting up out of the still-warm dessert. It smelled even better now than it had this morning, and my stomach rumbled in anticipation.

I picked up the fork, ready to enjoy the fruits of my labor, when I felt a tug on my sleeve. I looked down to find a girl with brown braids and blue eyes standing in front of me. I had never seen her before, although her gray dress matched the ambassador's tunic, telling me that she was part of the Andvarian contingent. Probably someone's granddaughter, since she looked about twelve.

"May I have a piece of pie?" she asked in a soft voice. "Please? It's my favorite."

This must be Gemma, the Andvarian king's granddaughter. I glanced at Isobel, but she had stacked up all the pie tins, and there wasn't a single crumb of crust left. My stomach grumbled in protest, and I sighed. I might have been bitchy to Xenia, but I would never be so rude to a visitor. Besides, the girl had said *please*. That made her more polite and far more worthy of my pie than anyone else here.

"Are you Gemma?"

She blinked, surprised that I knew her name, but she nodded.

"Of course you can have my pie, sweetheart."

I handed her my plate. A shy smile spread across her face, and she dropped into an awkward Bellonan curtsy. Polite, and she followed proper protocol. I liked her. I tilted my head in return, as was the custom, and winked at her.

Gemma giggled, then took the plate, sat down at a nearby table, and shoveled the dessert into her mouth.

If I couldn't have any pie, I'd try another glass of champagne. Hopefully, this one wouldn't smell as horrible as the first one had. I started to flag down one of the servants when the palace doors opened, and a woman strode outside. No trumpets blared, and no one announced her, but every eye still turned in her direction, and a hush fell over the lawn.

Vasilia had finally arrived.

CHAPTER FIVE

Princess Vasilia Victoria Summer Blair strode forward, then stopped in an open space on the lawn, so that everyone could properly admire her.

Vasilia was breathtakingly beautiful, even more so than Madelena. Her loose, wavy hair glimmered like gold as it cascaded past her shoulders, while her eyes were a light blue with the faintest tinge of gray, like the sky on a summer day. Understated makeup highlighted her delicate eyebrows, perfect cheekbones, and heart-shaped lips. Unlike Cordelia and Madelena in their gowns, Vasilia was dressed in her usual black boots and tight black leggings, along with a bright fuchsia tunic that featured her crest, a sword encircled by a wreath of laurel leaves, stitched in gold thread over her heart. A gold tiara studded with pink diamonds shaped like laurel flowers gleamed on her head.

Vasilia was far more than just a pretty face. She was also one of the best warriors in Bellona and could cut down opponents twice her size with the sword and the dagger hanging off her black leather belt. She was equally good with other weapons, everything from bows to staffs to spears. And then there was her magic. Vasilia was a powerful magier, able to summon up lightning with a mere thought, and she was as deadly with it as she was with everything else.

The crown princess smiled and nodded, acknowledging all the admiring and envious looks. She let everyone stare at her for a few seconds longer, then began moving from one group of people to another, all of whom stepped up, eager for her time and attention.

Perhaps it was our gladiator history, but there is a saying at Seven Spire, one that had spread throughout the kingdom and the rest of the continent—Bellonans are very good at playing the long game.

Sometimes in the arena, you killed your opponent in an instant. But other times, most times, you had to wait and plot and plan. You had to cut down your enemy one small, shallow slice at a time. Playing the long game meant being patient, inflicting the wounds you could along the way, and waiting for that perfect moment to strike and finally finish off your enemy.

All the royals and nobles excelled at the long game, as did the servants and guards. They knew that being nice to the crown princess now could go a long way toward getting certain favors granted to them when she was queen.

Nox trailed along behind Vasilia, hovering at her elbow and engaging in her conversations, as though he were her consort instead of just the guard she was currently fucking. Whispers surged across the lawn, and everyone glanced from Nox to Frederich and back again, wondering how the prince would react to the other man's presence.

Frederich must have heard the rumors about Nox and

Vasilia, because he frowned, as did Lord Hans. Queen Cordelia was standing next to them, and her lips were pinched into a tight, thin line that indicated she was quietly furious. Not only about Vasilia throwing Nox in Frederich's face, but also because Vasilia was flitting around, instead of greeting the Andvarians first.

The doors opened again. This time, instead of servants or some other late-arriving royal, more guards streamed onto the lawn. I started to ignore them, but then I realized that I didn't recognize any of the guards, just as I hadn't recognized the ones patrolling the hallways earlier.

It just seems like there are a lot of new people around the palace lately. Alvis's voice whispered in my mind. He was certainly right about that.

Vasilia's laughter rippled on the breeze, and the light, pealing sound made my heart squeeze tight with a mixture of anger, embarrassment, and resignation. I could almost feel myself shrinking, even though she wasn't anywhere near me.

It hadn't always been this way. Once upon a time, I had considered Vasilia to be my best friend, a warm, comforting light in the dark aftermath of my parents' murders. I hadn't realized back then that that warmth, comfort, and light came with a price—one that I could never pay.

Vasilia moved from one group to the next, smiling, laughing, and soaking up all the adoration. Eventually, she broke free of the crowd, and I thought she might finally deign to greet Cordelia, Hans, and Frederich, but Felton scurried up to her. He opened his red ledger, and she nodded at whatever he was showing her in the book.

Vasilia must have sensed my gaze, because she raised her head, and her eyes narrowed. I stared back at her, wondering if she would favor me with a smile too. A servant carrying a tray of champagne walked in front of me, and Vasilia tracked his movements as he handed out the glasses, and everyone started sipping the liquid.

She hadn't noticed me. Not for one second. Of course not. I hadn't been worthy of her time or attention in fifteen years now. My cheeks flamed, and I felt even smaller and more insignificant than before. I would have grabbed a glass of champagne and downed my sorrows, but the servants had already passed them all out, leaving me out of luck, just as I had been with the pie. Story of my life.

Queen Cordelia had had quite enough of being ignored, and she *tink-tink-tink*ed a fork against her glass, making the crystalline notes ring out across the lawn. She handed the fork to a servant, who slipped into the background with the others. Everyone on the lawn turned toward her.

Even Vasilia faced her mother, her hands clasped in front of her, since she hadn't bothered to get any champagne.

"I want to welcome our distinguished guests from Andvari, but especially Lord Hans and Prince Frederich," Cordelia called out. "They honor us with their presence and especially with their friendship."

She raised her glass in a toast to the two men, who returned the gesture, as did the rest of the Andvarians scattered throughout the crowd. Even Gemma, the girl who'd eaten my pie, lifted a glass, although hers contained sparkling apple cider.

"Today, we usher in a new era between our two kingdoms," Cordelia continued. "For centuries, Bellona and Andvari have been united in friendship and commerce. It is my intention that we will soon be united in marriage as well."

Prince Frederich smiled and dipped his head to the queen. Everyone looked at Vasilia, wondering how she would take the queen's pronouncement, but she nodded to her mother, then smiled at the prince, playing her role perfectly.

Cordelia raised her glass again. "To friendship!"

Everyone echoed her words, then tipped up their glasses and drank half their champagne, as was the Bellonan custom.

While everyone else was distracted, Cordelia glared at Vasilia and gave a sharp, pointed jerk of her head. The princess got the message loud and clear, and she moved through the crowd until she was standing beside Prince Frederich.

Lord Hans beamed at them. Cordelia eyed her daughter, but Vasilia's acquiescence must have satisfied her because she looked at the crowd again.

"In addition to our long-standing friendship, today we also celebrate several new trade agreements with Andvari . . ."

The queen launched into her speech, droning on about how happy she was that the ambassador was here, what an honor it was to host the prince, and all the other expected niceties. I tuned out her words, since I'd heard variations of them hundreds of times before at other events. By this point, I just wanted her speech to bloody *end* so that we could sit down and I could finally eat something. But a visit by an ambassador and a prince was no small thing, and the queen had prepared quite a lot of words in order to properly mark the occasion.

My stomach grumbled in protest, and I looked toward the doors, wondering if the kitchen staff might come back with another round of fruit, crackers, and cheeses to get us through the queen's speech. But the servants were clustered together near the edge of the lawn, clutching their empty trays, as if they had been told to stay put by the guards who flanked them.

For the first time, I noticed just how many guards were here. Dozens of them ringed the lawn, and each one had his hand on his sword. Strange that they would be on such high alert at such a routine event.

I wasn't the only one who noticed the extra guards. Captain Auster did as well, and he sidled closer to the queen, his fingers curling around the hilt of his sword. Worry flared up in my stomach, but I pushed it away. We were standing in the middle of the royal lawn. There was absolutely nothing to fear here, other than catty comments and backstabbing relatives.

"A toast!" Cordelia called out, wrapping up her speech. "To new beginnings!"

Everyone lifted their glasses again and downed the rest of their champagne, as was the custom.

Vasilia pointedly cleared her throat and stepped into the open space in front of the queen. Cordelia frowned, obviously wondering if she was going to stage some sort of protest, but Vasilia nodded at Hans and Frederich, then turned and nodded at the crowd as well, as though she was happy that so many people were here to witness her de facto engagement.

"As my mother said, we are quite pleased that you could all mark this special day with us," Vasilia said in her lovely, lilting voice. "It's not often that so many Blairs, so many members of my extended family, are gathered in one place, along with such distinguished guests, and I'm so honored that each and every one of you could be here . . ."

She was saying all the right things, expressing all the right sentiments, but her words made my stomach knot up with dread. I'd spent the last fifteen years watching Vasilia, analyzing her every word, gesture, and expression, and I recognized the cold, flat, distant note in her voice. It was the same one she'd used when she had betrayed our friendship.

I glanced around to see if anyone else had noticed the hollow ring to her speech, but everyone was nodding and smiling, hanging on her every word.

Except for Felton and Nox.

They were close to the palace wall, well behind the guards who ringed the lawn. Curious. Usually, the two of them were front and center, with Felton hovering around the queen and Nox doing the same to Vasilia. I frowned. Something was going on, something far more serious and worrisome than the usual cliques, politics, and infighting.

I looked at Captain Auster, who was standing by the queen's side, his hand still on his sword. He too was scanning the crowd, and the longer he looked around, the more his eyes narrowed, as if he had the same bad feeling that I did. His obvious concern increased my own worry.

"For far too long, our kingdoms have squabbled over small, petty things," Vasilia continued. "Well, I say no more. Soon, we will all be united, as my mother has said."

She glanced at Lord Hans, who winked back at her, apparently pleased by her words. Then she turned to Prince Frederich and gave him a small smile, the corners of her lips curving up, as though she was amused by some secret that only she knew.

Those knots of worry in my stomach doubled, tripled, in size, then crawled up into my chest, wrapped around my heart, and strangled it. I knew *that* smile. It was the same one that Vasilia always gave me right before she was particularly cruel. The smile that dazzled, tricked, and conned you into coming that much closer to her warmth, light, and beauty, so that she could finally, fully eviscerate you.

"Oh, yes." Vasilia's voice boomed like thunder. "Today is a new beginning for all of us. Starting with you, Prince Frederich."

Her eyes flashed with a dark, wicked light, and her lips curved up even more. Somehow, I knew exactly what was coming next, even though it was unthinkable.

Before I could shout a warning, Vasilia plucked the jeweled dagger off her belt, whipped it up, and buried it in Prince Frederich's heart.

CHAPTER SIX

The shock was like a cold, wet blanket dropping over the lawn and blotting out the heat, light, and normalcy of the day. Everyone blinked and blinked, but no one could quite believe what had happened. That the crown princess of Bellona had just attacked—*murdered*—the Andvarian prince.

Vasilia's smile widened, and she stared at Frederich as she ripped her dagger out of his chest. The prince's mouth opened, but only a small, strangled gasp escaped his lips. His eyes rolled up in the back of his head, and he dropped like a stone, dead before he even hit the grass.

Lord Hans yelled and lunged forward, but Vasilia coolly whirled around, executed the perfect spin move, and sliced her dagger across his stomach.

Hans screamed and stumbled into a table, sending the plates, glasses, and forks flying through the air. His face twisted with pain, but he growled, clamped his hand over the blood and guts spilling out of his stomach, and pushed away from the table. He staggered toward Vasilia, still determined to attack her.

The other Andvarians snapped out of their shock. They too yelled with rage, drew their swords, and shoved through the crowd, trying to reach Hans.

Vasilia watched them come, along with Hans, who was still stumbling toward her. She let out a small, pleased laugh, then snapped up her hand and reached for her magic.

White lightning streaked out of her fingertips and slammed into Lord Hans's chest.

For a moment, the ambassador resembled a fluorestone—this pillar of bright white light. Then the magic washed over his body, cooking his open guts, along with the rest of him. He screamed again and lurched back, but Vasilia had no mercy.

She never had *any* mercy.

She blasted Hans a second time with her power. Then a third, then a fourth. Or perhaps it was all one continuous stream of lightning. But her magic was just as deadly as her dagger had been, and seconds later, Lord Hans dropped to the ground, his dead body reduced to a burned husk.

The hot, caustic scent of Vasilia's magic filled my nose, along with the charred stench of Hans's fried flesh. My stomach roiled, but I was too shocked to vomit.

People yelled, screamed, and scrambled back, desperate to get away from Vasilia's lightning before she cooked them to death too. I wasn't close to Vasilia, but I still backed up until I hit the table behind me. Even the Andvarians stopped short, not sure what to do now that both of their leaders were dead.

Once again, that shocked silence descended over the lawn, and everyone was frozen in place—except for Queen Cordelia. She marched forward, moving past Captain Auster, who had drawn his sword and stepped in front of her the moment that Vasilia had attacked Frederich.

"Vasilia!" she barked. "Stop this madness at once!"

Cordelia raised her hand and reached for her own power, since she was a fire magier and one of the few who could go toe to toe with Vasilia's lightning. Her hand should have burst into flames, but only a few red-hot sparks flickered on her fingertips. Cordelia frowned and shook her hand, as though she didn't understand why her magic wasn't instantly igniting like usual.

"What's the matter, Mother?" Vasilia called out in a light, mocking voice. "It looks like you can't summon up a single spark of power. Luckily, I don't have that problem."

She waggled her hand, and more lightning sizzled on her fingertips. People sucked in ragged breaths and backed up a few more steps.

"What did you do?" Cordelia demanded.

"Nothing much. Just stood back and watched while you and everyone else guzzled down your champagne like usual." Vasilia tapped her finger on her lips. "Well, I suppose that it wasn't *just* like usual, since everyone's champagne has wormroot mixed in with all those golden bubbles."

Cordelia's eyes widened, and horrified gasps rang out. Everyone stared at the glasses in their hands, sick expressions twisting their faces.

Wormroot was a particularly sinister poison. First, it extinguished a person's magic, from the weakest mutt to the strongest magier. Then, when a person's magic was gone, the poison went to work on their internal organs, reducing them all to mush, until their eyes, nose, mouth, and even fingernails hemorrhaged blood. My father had been poisoned with wormroot, and it was a truly horrific way to die.

I would have drunk the champagne too, if not for the

foul stench. I just hadn't realized that I was smelling poison. I should have, though. I should have done something, should have warned people that something was wrong, but I hadn't, and now, everyone was going to die. My stomach roiled again, but I swallowed down the hot, bitter bile rising in my throat.

Most of my cousins were still clutching their glasses, fear filling their eyes, waiting for the poison to kick in. A few desperately snapped their fingers, trying to summon up their magier power, but all they could produce were weak sparks, like Cordelia.

Madelena looked particularly sick, and she dropped her glass and pressed both hands to her bulging belly, as if that would protect the baby growing inside. She had been drinking apple cider, along with the children. Madelena must have thought that Vasilia had poisoned their glasses too, because she let out a soft whimper and swayed on her feet. She would have fallen, if Durante hadn't steadied her.

Vasilia rolled her eyes. "Oh, don't worry, Maddie. I didn't poison you, and I didn't give our cousins all that much wormroot either. Just enough to keep everyone from using their magic. I wanted to do the final honors of finishing you all off myself."

Captain Auster stepped in front of the queen again and snapped up his sword. "You'll do no such thing," he growled. "Guards! To me! Now!"

Every single guard drew their weapon, but only about a dozen of them heeded Auster's command and flanked him and the queen. Auster's eyes narrowed as he studied the rest of the guards, who held their positions at the edge of the lawn, the sun glinting off the blades in their hands.

I recognized the men and women standing with Auster, but

none of the others. My heart sank. Alvis had been right about all the new people at the palace. And once again, I realized that the strange guards reeked of magic. Whatever power they had, they were getting ready to unleash it.

Nox moved away from his spot along the wall, stepped through the ring of guards, and strode over to stand beside Vasilia. "Sorry, old chap. But as you can see, I replaced your men with some of my own." He used his sword to snap off a mocking salute to Auster.

The captain's lips pressed together, but he tightened his grip on his weapon, ready to defend his queen to his last breath.

Cordelia placed a hand on his shoulder and shook her head. Then she sidestepped her guard and faced Vasilia again.

"Why are you doing this?" she asked.

Vasilia's eyes glittered with a cold light. "Because I'm tired of being the perfect little princess and taking orders from you. I'm tired of you ignoring my suggestions and undercutting my proposals at every turn."

"You mean imposing new taxes on Floresian goods? Annexing mines on Andvarian land? Sending troops to the Ungerian border?" Cordelia shook her head. "Your *proposals* would do nothing but plunge us into war."

"My proposals would make us *strong* again," Vasilia hissed. "A force to be reckoned with, just like Morta is. Something that you know nothing about, especially since you tried to betroth me to a weak, spineless man with no real power to his name." She stabbed the pointed toe of her boot into Frederich's body. "I can't believe that you expected *me* to marry *him*. Third in line for the Andvarian throne. What a bloody *insult*. Really, Mother. You could have done *so* much better."

The Andvarians growled and lifted their swords, and I

could almost see the wheels turning in their minds as they debated how they could avenge their fallen prince and ambassador. A few of them even crept forward, like they were thinking of charging at Vasilia.

She gave them a bored look, then flicked her fingers, shooting a few small streaks of lightning at them. The magic slammed into the ground, scorching the grass at their feet, and the Andvarians yelled and scrambled back.

Vasilia eyed the Andvarians a moment longer, making sure that they were properly cowed, along with everyone else. Then she turned back to her mother.

"What did you think was going to happen? That I was going to fall madly in love and start popping out babies like Madelena? That I would forget about becoming queen? Please. You should have known better. The only reason to even suggest such a ridiculous marriage was so you could ship me off to Andvari and get rid of me." Vasilia tilted her head, studying her mother the way that other people might examine a bug they were going to squash beneath their boot. "Or perhaps you were planning to have me assassinated in Andvari and eliminate me altogether."

"That was absolutely my plan." Cordelia's voice was as cold as Vasilia's was.

Shocked gasps rippled through the crowd, including one from my own mouth. She'd been planning to assassinate her own daughter? But my surprise lasted only an instant. Despite my dislike of her, Cordelia was a good queen in that she always did what was best for Bellona, and Vasilia's policies would do nothing but plunge us into war, just as Cordelia had said.

The queen looked at everyone on the lawn. The remaining Andvarians, her royal cousins, the nobles, the servants, the few loyal guards. For a moment, she focused on me, and something like remorse sparked in her eyes. Then she looked at her daughter again.

"You, my dear, are a power-hungry bitch who has no regard for anyone other than herself."

Vasilia laughed. "Do you think that's an insult? I consider it a fine compliment."

"Of course you would. But the truth is that killing you would be a mercy to all the people of Bellona and beyond." Cordelia smiled, but it was a grim, resigned expression. "My only regret is that I waited too long to do it. I kept hoping that you would change, even though I knew deep down that you never would. Silly sentiment, on my part, staying my hand."

How long had Cordelia been planning Vasilia's death? And who was going to help her kill her own daughter?

"I should have done it months ago," she continued. "As soon as your two new Mortan friends came to Seven Spire."

Cordelia looked at Nox, then Maeven. What did the kitchen steward have to do with this? The answer came to me a moment later. Maeven had poisoned the champagne. I had wondered why she'd wanted me to taste it earlier. A test, most likely, to make sure that the poison worked—and it probably would have. I might be immune to magic, but I didn't know if I could survive a bellyful of wormroot.

Cordelia glanced back and forth between Nox and Maeven, and for the first time, I noticed the resemblance between them. Same golden hair, same amethyst eyes, same sharp, angular cheekbones. The two of them were related. I was sure of it. I didn't get the sense that they were mother and son, though. Maybe aunt and nephew? Cousins?

Maeven had been at Seven Spire for more than a year, and Nox for about nine months. Other than Nox's scandalous relationship with Vasilia, both of them had gone about their jobs like everyone else. How long had they been plotting this? How many people were involved? Was the plot supported by the Mortan royal family?

My mind spun around with questions, but no answers were in sight. Only death for the queen and everyone else.

"I had hoped that you would come to your senses." Cordelia focused on Vasilia again. "That you would do your duty and put Bellona first, above your own ambitions. What a fool I was to think that you would ever do anything so selfless."

Vasilia rolled her eyes again. "I am so bloody tired of you harking to me about *duty* all the time. But mostly, I'm tired of waiting when *I* should be queen."

"Queen Vasilia has a lovely ring to it." Nox grabbed Vasilia's hand and gallantly pressed a kiss to her fingers, even though they were covered with Prince Frederich's and Lord Hans's blood. Then he shot Cordelia a saucy wink.

The queen's nostrils flared with anger. "I don't know what he's promised you, but you can't trust him."

Vasilia let out an amused laugh. "Of course I don't trust him. Just as he doesn't trust me. But who needs trust when you have a common goal?"

"And what would that be?" Cordelia snapped.

Vasilia smiled at her mother again, and for once, the expression was quite genuine. "Why be queen of a single kingdom, when I can rule an entire empire?"

Murmurs rippled through the crowd. Cordelia looked from her daughter to the two dead Andvarians to Nox and then finally over to Maeven, who was still standing quietly in the background. Understanding flashed in her eyes, and she shook her head.

"You will never be queen of any *empire*." Cordelia spat out the words. "The Mortans will use you to get our land, our resources, our magic. And then, when they are ready, they will take Bellona from you. They will slit your throat, burn your body, and grind your bones to dust, like they do to everyone. And the sad part is that you won't even realize what's happening until it's too late."

The princess waved her hand, dismissing her mother's concerns. "You should know by now that no one takes anything from me—ever."

Vasilia slid her dagger back into the scabbard on her belt and drew her sword. Nox raised his weapon as well, as did all the turncoat guards. Captain Auster stepped up beside the queen, as did the few remaining guards who were still loyal to him.

An eerie silence descended over the lawn. Then, with one thought, one breath, one roar of sound and motion, everyone sprang into action.

CHAPTER SEVEN

asilia and Nox charged forward, attacking the people closest to them.

"Guards!" Captain Auster roared. "To me! To me! Protect the queen!"

Despite the fact that they were terribly outnumbered, the guards formed a tight, protective circle around Cordelia.

"Back!" Auster roared again. "Retreat!"

He was trying to get the queen away from the center of the lawn and back inside the palace, where he could better protect her, or perhaps even get her to safety altogether. But there was nowhere for them to go. The turncoat guards had formed a ring around the lawn, penning everyone inside their ranks like animals in a slaughterhouse. The turncoats surged forward, their swords flashing like lightning bolts in the sunlight. Only instead of striking the earth, these bolts had far more sinister targets—all the people gathered here.

Screams and shouts ripped through the air, along with blood—so much blood. In an instant, the coppery scent of it filled the air. The sickening stench slithered down my throat and made me want to vomit again. Blood spattered everywhere, like a sideways rain soaking everything in its path. Tables, chairs, dishes, people. A couple of drops hit my cheek, and I hissed at their sudden, stinging warmth and slapped my hand to my face, like they were bees that I could shoo away.

Several magiers, including my Blair cousins and the Andvarians, tried to summon up their power so that they could fight back, but the wormroot had done its job, and they got the same pitiful results as Cordelia—all sparks and no sizzle. Their magic was so weak that I couldn't even smell it over the thick, heavy scent of all the blood.

Some of the morphs tried to shift into their larger, stronger shapes, but the wormroot had dampened their magic too, and they were stuck in their weaker, human forms.

The only one who successfully shifted was Lady Xenia, given the loud roars that spewed out of her throat. She must not have drunk any of the champagne. I couldn't see her face through the crowd, although I did catch a glimpse of the long, pointed black talons on her fingertips as she laid open the throat of a turncoat who attacked her.

With their magic out of reach, people were forced to rely on their own physical strength, speed, and fighting skills, and they tried to force their way through the ring of guards. But that's when the second, sinister phase of the wormroot kicked in, and several people pulled up short, including the Andvarians, clutching their stomachs, doubling over, and vomiting up the champagne they'd drunk, along with mouthfuls of blood. Their sudden sickness made it easy for the turncoats to step up and finish them off.

The guards cut down every single person with merciless efficiency. Servants, nobles, royals. Men, women, even the children. No one was spared as the traitors hacked and slashed their way through the crowd. The guards were particularly vicious when it came to my Blair cousins, stabbing them over and over again and then slitting their throats for good measure. And the guards had plenty of magic to help them with their murderous rampage. Most of them were mutts, with extra strength or speed, along with a few magiers and morphs.

They were all equally brutal and ruthless.

Through the mass of moving, screaming, fighting bodies, I spotted Maeven still standing close to the palace wall, a small, satisfied smile on her lips. Felton was beside her, staring at the chaos with a calm expression, holding his red ledger. I thought of that list I'd seen in Felton's book, the pages with all those check marks. He'd been keeping track of the Blairs and other guests and making sure that they were all here before Vasilia had sprung her trap.

Vasilia had planned this very carefully. Not only were she, Nox, Maeven, and Felton going to kill the queen, but they were also going to assassinate every single person here with even a drop of Blair blood. They were going to eliminate anyone who might miraculously survive the massacre, rise up, and potentially challenge Vasilia for the Bellonan throne later on.

Including me.

A guard ran his sword through the man in front of him, then pulled his weapon free and charged at me, the next person in his path. Panic filled me, and I stepped back, bumping up against the table again. My hand hit something slick and hard—the crystal vase of snow pansies that I'd admired earlier. Cold determination surged through me, freezing out my panic, and I snatched up the vase, my fingers curling tight around the top of it.

The guard charged at me, and I found myself thinking of the strangest thing—all those recent dance lessons with Lady Xenia. I didn't know why, but I could almost *hear* the music playing in my mind, and I listened to the strange phantom beat. The guard raised his sword, even as the music in my head swelled to a roaring crescendo.

Move, Everleigh! Now!

Xenia's voice snapped in my head, the way that she had snapped at me during those lessons, and I pivoted to the side, out of the way of the guard's slashing sword, like it was a sharp blow from Xenia's cane that I was avoiding.

The guard rushed past me, slamming his weapon into the table instead of my chest. The blade stuck in the wood, and he cursed, trying to yank it out.

Before he could free the weapon, I stepped up and slammed the vase into the back of his head.

The crystal shattered, and the guard screamed. Somehow, I wound up with a long, dagger-like shard in my hand, which I rammed into the guard's back. He screamed again, but I didn't stop. I yanked the shard out and then stabbed it into his back over and over again until he finally quit screaming and slumped down onto the table.

I dropped the bloody shard and staggered away, breathing hard. The guard's head lay on the table, his mouth open in a silent scream. I'd killed him. I had actually killed him.

It had been a long, long time since I had killed someone.

"Evie! Evie!"

I whirled around. Isobel was running toward me, doing

her best to avoid the swarming guards. Our gazes locked, and I saw the fear and panic in her eyes.

More determination surged through me. I had to protect her. I wasn't going to lose her to an assassination plot the same way that I had my parents.

I shoved the dead guard out of the way, stepped up, and took hold of his sword, which was still stuck in the table. I had to brace my foot against the wood, but I wrenched the weapon free. I staggered back, holding the sword, and something slid off the table and landed in the grass at my feet.

The memory stone.

The opal was glowing with a soft white light, telling me that it was still recording. Vasilia murdering Prince Frederich and Lord Hans, her confrontation with Cordelia, the guards attacking everyone. The stone had recorded everything. I had to take it with me.

I dropped the sword, yanked the black velvet bag out of my pocket, and fell to my knees. I tapped on the opal three times to stop the recording, then shoved it into the bag and yanked the drawstrings tight. My hands were shaking, but I looped the strings around my wrist and tied them together so that I wouldn't lose the bag. Then I grabbed the sword again and surged back up onto my feet.

"Evie!" Isobel screamed. "Evie, look out!"

Two guards had realized that I'd killed their friend, and they both charged at me. I wasn't a great warrior like Vasilia was, but Captain Auster had spent a fair amount of time training me over the years—or at least attempting to train me. I desperately tried to remember just one of those lessons, but I heard that phantom music in my mind again, and I let it carry me away.

Whatever it was, it worked.

I sidestepped the first guard, whipped around, and sliced my sword across his back. He screamed and tumbled to the ground. I stepped up and kicked him in the face, making his head snap back. Then, while he was still dazed, I rammed my sword into his chest. The guard gurgled once, then was still.

"Evie! Evie, look out!" Isobel screamed a third time.

The second guard whirled around and lunged at me. Even as I turned toward him, I knew that I wasn't going to be fast enough to avoid the blow. I grimaced and braced myself to die—

At the last instant, Isobel raced up and latched on to the guard's arm, stopping him from killing me.

"Get out of the way!" the guard growled.

He shook her off, then stepped forward and shoved his sword into her chest. The guard must have had some mutt magic that gave him extra strength, because he thrust his sword so deep into her body that it punched out her back. Isobel hung there on his blade, eyes wide, gasping for breath, like a butterfly pinned in place.

"Isobel!" I screamed. "Isobel!"

I moved around her and lashed out with my own sword. The blade stuck in the guard's neck, and blood erupted like a fountain from the wound. He shrieked and tumbled to the ground, losing his grip on his sword and taking mine with him as well. Isobel staggered back, the guard's sword still buried in her body, and crumpled to the grass.

My legs buckled, and I dropped to my knees beside her. It took me only a second to grab her hand, although it seemed much, much longer. I was no bone master, but even I could tell that there was nothing I could do. Not given the sword still stuck in her chest and all the blood that had already soaked into the grass underneath her body.

Isobel gasped for air, even as tears of pain streamed down her face. Her head lolled to the side, and her gaze fixed on mine. "There's . . . my . . . girl . . ." she rasped. "There's . . . my . . . Evie . . ."

Her eyes warmed, her face softened, and her lips curved up into a small smile. Then she shuddered out a breath, her chest sagged, and her hand slipped out of mine.

"Isobel!" I screamed. "Isobel!"

But she was gone—dead.

Even though it was no use, I shook Isobel's shoulders and screamed her name over and over again, although the continued chaos of the fight drowned out my hoarse, heartbroken cries.

A guard ran past me, chasing one of the servants, and his leg clipped my shoulder and sent me toppling over onto Isobel. For a moment, I got a whiff of her scent—powdered sugar mixed with cinnamon—the one that had always made me feel so warm, welcome, and safe. Then her blood gushed over my hands, hot and sticky, drowning out that sweet scent and replacing it with the coppery, rotting stench of fresh death. My heart squeezed tight, tears streamed down my cheeks, and bile rose in my throat again—

A sharp whimper sounded, and my head snapped to the right. Gemma, the Andvarian girl, had taken refuge under a nearby table, one of the few that was still standing upright. She was huddled on her knees, trying to make herself as small as possible, although her blue eyes were wide with fear and shock.

The turncoat guards hadn't noticed the girl yet, but they would soon enough, and then they would kill her too—unless I saved her.

I hadn't managed to protect Isobel, and I had no illusions

that I could do any better with Gemma, but I had to *try*. That was what Isobel would have wanted. She would have wanted me to do my best to save this lost little girl, just as she'd taken me in when I had come to Seven Spire.

And I realized that I just might be able to do it, thanks to Lady Xenia.

Xenia let out another loud bellow, picked up a guard, spun him around, and slung him into a pack of men coming at her, knocking them all down to the ground. That created an opening in the ring of guards, and Xenia charged forward, raking her talons across the stomach of another guard, and widening the gap between the turncoats. A few people took advantage and darted past her, sprinting for the palace doors.

But they didn't count on Maeven.

She snapped up her hand, and bright purple lightning flashed to life on her fingertips. I could smell the stench of her magic all the way across the lawn. A magier. She was a fucking magier, and a very strong one at that. Of course she was. Because this couldn't get any worse.

"Watch out!" I screamed, but it was no use.

Maeven threw her lightning at the doors, driving people away from them. Everyone dove for cover behind the overturned tables and chairs, and she kept tossing bolt after bolt of lightning at them, smiling all the while, like a cat playing with an entire den of mice.

She was so busy trying to kill people that she didn't notice that her lightning had shattered the glass doors, creating a jagged opening. All I had to do was distract Maeven long enough for Gemma to escape. That bitch might be a magier, but this mutt knew more than one trick, and I could handle a little lightning.

But first, I had to get Gemma over to the doors. I was still sprawled on top of Isobel, and I scrambled to my feet. "Forgive me," I whispered, although she was far beyond any sort of hearing now.

Then I reached down, grabbed hold of the sword still stuck in her chest, and yanked it free. Isobel thumped back down to the ground, and I had to remind myself that I wasn't hurting her, that she was gone, *dead,* and that I would be too if I didn't move. More tears streamed down my face, but I gritted my teeth and turned away from her.

Keeping low, I darted over to Gemma, grabbed her arm, and yanked her out from under the table. She yelped and started to pull away, but I gave her a small shake, trying to snap her out of her panic. After a moment, she realized that I wasn't one of the guards and that I wasn't trying to hurt her.

"Do you know Alvis?" I yelled over the chaos. "The Andvarian master? Do you know where his workshop is?"

The Andvarians always visited with Alvis whenever they came to Seven Spire, and I was hoping that Gemma had been to his dungeon workshop. Her eyes were so wide that I thought they might pop off her face and roll away like marbles, but she finally nodded.

I pointed out the opening in the glass to her. "Then you go through those doors and run to his workshop as fast as you can. Don't you dare stop for anything. You tell him what's going on and that Evie said to get out of the palace. Do you understand?"

I hadn't been able to save Isobel, but maybe I could help Alvis. It was a long shot at best, but it was the girl's only hope of escape, and Alvis's too.

More tears rolled down Gemma's cheeks, but she nodded again.

"That's a brave girl. Here we go. One, two, three, go!"

I grabbed her hand, and we sprinted toward the shattered doors. But as soon as we started running, I realized that we weren't going to make it. One of the guards, a mutt with some speed magic, was closing in on us. Together, Gemma and I were too slow and too much of a target to reach the doors. But she might be able to make it—if I cut him off.

So I shoved her forward, put my shoulder down, and veered to my right, barreling into the guard and knocking him as far away from her as I could. Gemma stopped and looked over her shoulder, but I waved at her.

"Don't stop! Keep going!" I yelled.

Her lips flattened out into a grim, determined line, and she stepped in my direction, as if she was going to come to my rescue. But she never got the chance. Xenia grabbed the girl around the waist and scooped her up.

My eyes widened. I had studied the ogre face on her neck dozens of times, but I had never seen Xenia's actual morph form before, and it was truly terrifying.

Lady Xenia had grown to more than six feet tall, and the muscles in her arms and legs bulged against her clothes, straining the fabric. Long black talons tipped her fingers, each one dripping blood. More blood covered her face, including each and every one of the sharp, jagged teeth that now filled her mouth. Her amber eyes burned like torches, and her coppery hair glimmered with a dark red light, even as the strands whipped around her face, almost like they were coral vipers that were writhing around her head.

Our gazes locked, and I shook off my surprise and waved at her.

"Go! Save the girl!"

I didn't know if she heard me, but Xenia loped away, sprinting for the shattered doors.

I started to follow her, but the guard I'd knocked down got up, surged forward, and slammed his fist into my face. Pain exploded in my jaw, and white stars winked on and off in my eyes, but I blinked them away and focused on Xenia, who was still racing toward the doors.

Maeven tossed a bolt of lightning at the morph. The magic clipped Xenia's shoulder, spinning her around and making her yelp like a wounded animal. She staggered, almost dropping the girl, but she tightened her grip and kept going, and she crashed through what little glass was left in the doors and into the palace. Xenia and Gemma disappeared from sight.

Maeven snapped her fingers at the closest guards. "No one escapes!" she hissed. "After them! Now!"

A couple of guards peeled off from the main part of the battle and headed in that direction, darting through the opening after Xenia and Gemma.

I hoped that the two of them made it to safety. I hoped that they were able to reach Alvis and warn him. But I'd done all that I could for them, and now it was time to try to save myself.

I blinked away the last of the stars and faced the guard. He surged toward me again, but his boot slipped on a bloody patch of grass. Before he could recover his balance, I lunged forward and buried my sword in his stomach. His eyes bulged, and he screamed with pain. I shoved the sword in a little deeper, then yanked it free.

He toppled to the ground, and I turned toward the doors again. Maybe if I was lucky I could sneak up behind the guards who had gone after Xenia and Gemma and kill them—

"No!" a deep, familiar voice shouted. "No! Stay away from her!"

I whirled around. Vasilia was clutching her sword and advancing on Durante, who was standing in front of Madelena, shielding his pregnant wife with his own body, and holding out the stem of a broken champagne flute like it was some sort of weapon. I hesitated, torn between running toward the doors and whatever safety might lie beyond and trying to save them. Madelena had never been particularly kind to me, but she had never been cruel either. And her baby was innocent of everything.

I cursed and ran in that direction, darting around the panicked people who were still alive, ducking the turncoat guards who tried to attack me, and hopscotching over the bloody bodies, broken glasses, and cracked tables that littered the lawn. But I was too far away, and I wasn't going to reach them in time. Even if I had, Vasilia could easily cut me down with her sword. Still, I had to try. Vasilia might not have a conscience, but I did, and I wouldn't be able to live with myself if I didn't at least try.

Durante lashed out with his broken glass, but Vasilia avoided the clumsy blow, snapped up her hand, and unleashed her lightning. Durante screamed, his body convulsed, and the stench of fried flesh filled the air again. A few seconds later, Durante crumpled to the ground, smoke rising off his charred skin. His chest convulsed a few more times, and then he was still, his gaze locked onto his wife, as if he was still trying to protect her, even in death.

Madelena put her hands over her stomach and backed up. "Please, Vasilia," she begged, tears streaming down her face.

"You don't have to do this. I'm not a threat to you. I never have been."

"I know," Vasilia said. "But I don't care."

She snapped up her sword, lunged forward, and stabbed her sister in the heart. Madelena didn't even have time to scream before Vasilia twisted her sword in even deeper, then yanked it free. Madelena crumpled to the ground, one hand stretched out toward her husband and the other curled over her stomach, still trying to protect her unborn baby, even though it was as dead as she was.

Vasilia smiled with satisfaction, whirled around, and waded back into the fight, using her sword and her lightning to kill everyone in her path.

My steps slowed, and I stopped in the middle of the lawn, staring at Madelena and swaying from side to side, as the chaos raged all around me. Something wet stung my cheeks, and I realized that more tears were streaming down my face. I had always known that Vasilia was cruel, but I had never thought that she would be so *heartless* as to murder her own pregnant sister.

What kind of nightmare was this? And how could I escape from it? I wanted to rewind time and go back to this morning, when the worst thing in my world was making pies.

But the screams, shrieks, and vicious attacks continued, and I knew that I could never escape this. Even if I somehow survived the massacre, I would never, ever forget *this*—

"To me! To me!" Captain Auster's voice rang out. "Protect the queen!"

My head snapped in that direction. Auster had managed to get Cordelia out of the kill zone in the center of the lawn, and he'd maneuvered what few men he had left so that their backs were to the stone wall that overlooked the cliffs and the river below. Auster headed to his left, toward the shattered doors that Lady Xenia had gone through, but Nox and several turncoats charged forward to block his path.

Auster and his men were closer to the doors than I was now, and I darted through the melee, trying to reach them and swinging my sword at every single turncoat who came near me. Not because I thought the remaining guards would protect me—the queen was and should be their top priority—but because they were the only ones left standing.

Everyone else was dead or dying.

I was probably going to wind up that way too, but I couldn't reach the doors by myself, and Auster and his men at least gave me a fighting chance. And if I was going to die, then I wanted to die protecting the queen, the same as them. I wanted to do my royal duty one last time, maybe the only time that it would ever matter, that it would ever truly help someone.

But once again, I was too late.

Auster was busy fighting Nox and two turncoats, so he didn't see Vasilia sprint up and slice her sword across the stomach of the guard who was the closest to the queen. That man screamed and toppled to the ground, giving Vasilia a clear path to her mother.

Cordelia leaned down and fumbled for the dead man's sword, but Vasilia kicked the blade out of her hand. Cordelia scrambled up and backed away from her daughter, but there was nowhere for her to go, and she hit the wall a second later.

Vasilia knew that she had her mother trapped, and she stopped, another smile filling her face as she twirled her sword around in her hand. The bitch was savoring the moment.

Cordelia lifted her chin and squared her shoulders. Then

she bowed her head, congratulating her daughter on her treacherous victory, and raised her arms out to her sides, accepting her fate.

"Trying to die with a little bit of dignity?" Vasilia sneered. "You should know by now that there's no such thing."

"You'll discover that for yourself soon enough when your Mortan friends betray you," Cordelia said. "My only regret is that I won't be alive to see it."

She stared at her daughter, her face as cold as ice, and widened her arms, embracing the death in front of her.

Rage sparked in Vasilia's eyes, and she drew her sword back and then swung it forward, determined to kill her mother.

"No!" I screamed. "No! Stop!"

My shouts surprised Vasilia, and she didn't put the full force of her body behind the blow, but she still did plenty of damage. Her sword bit into the queen's side, and Cordelia screamed and staggered back. She hit the wall behind her again and bounced off, her legs buckling and her body crumpling to the ground.

Vasilia turned toward me, but I rammed my shoulder into hers, knocking her down to the ground and away from the queen. Then I hurried over and dropped to my knees beside Cordelia. Her back was up against the wall, with her legs tucked under her body. She had her hand clamped on her side, but blood still gushed out from between her fingers.

"Get up!" I yelled. "You have to get up! You have to move!"

I reached out to grab her arm and haul her to her feet, but Cordelia caught my hand in hers. She blinked several times, as if she was having trouble focusing on me through the pain of her gruesome wound, but she finally managed it.

"Everleigh," she murmured, surprise flashing in her gray-blue eyes. "Of course it's you. The little orphan girl nobody wanted. First your parents, and now me. You're surprisingly good at surviving assassinations."

My mouth dropped open, but I didn't know what to say. Why was she talking about my parents? Why now? Was her mind already gone?

Cordelia's lips curved up into a smile, and she actually laughed, as if she found something about this whole situation highly amusing. But her laughter soon turned into a racking cough, and blood bubbled up out of her mouth and trickled down her chin. Her gaze moved past me, and she stared at the bodies that littered the lawn like dead, brittle leaves. Sorrow sparked in her gaze, and a single tear escaped from the corner of her eye, but she focused on me again.

"Summer queens are fine and fair, with pretty ribbons and flowers in their hair. Winter queens are cold and hard, with frosted crowns made of icy shards," she rasped in a low, urgent voice.

It took me a moment to recognize the phrase as an old fairy-tale rhyme, one that my mother used to sing to get me to sleep. "Why would you say that? What are you talking about?"

"Because you're the last one left. The last Winter queen. You have to live," Cordelia rasped. "You have to survive, no matter what you have to do, no matter who you have to cheat and hurt and kill, no matter what the cost is to your heart and soul. Do you hear me, Everleigh? You have to *live*. You have to protect Bellona. Promise me you'll do that."

Vasilia shook off her daze and got back up onto her feet. Behind her, more and more turncoats advanced on our position. I wasn't getting off the lawn alive, but there was no need to make the queen's death any more painful than it already was.

"I promise," I said. "I promise to protect Bellona until my dying breath."

A smile flitted across Cordelia's face, and she nodded. Then she reached up, dug her fingers into my loose, tangled hair, and pulled my face down to hers, so close that her gray-blue eyes filled my vision. Tearstone eyes, Blair eyes, just like mine.

"Find Serilda Swanson," she whispered in a low voice that only I could hear. "She'll . . . protect you, help you, train you. Tell her . . . that you're the last Winter queen. She'll understand. And tell her . . . tell her . . . that I was . . . wrong . . . and that . . . I'm sorry . . . for *everything* . . ."

Cordelia sucked in another breath, like she was going to say something else, but her breath escaped in a soft puff of air that kissed my cheek. Her fingers slid free from my hair, and her head lolled to the side, her gaze fixed on something far, far beyond me.

My heart ached, and more tears streamed down my face, but I didn't bother saying her name or shaking her shoulders like I had with Isobel. There was no use.

The queen was dead.

CHAPTER EIGHT

didn't know how long I stared at Cordelia. It seemed like forever, although it probably wasn't more than a few seconds. I reached out and gently closed her eyes. I studied her face, committing it to memory, along with her cryptic last words. I wasn't sure why. It wasn't like I was going to have time to puzzle out her meaning.

I would be joining her in death soon enough.

Footsteps scuffed through the grass behind me. I'd dropped my sword when I'd been trying to help Cordelia, but I didn't bother to pick it up, since I was now trapped up against the wall. Instead, I drew in a breath, got to my feet, and turned around, determined to meet my death with the same dignity that the queen had.

Vasilia stood in front of me, her sword dangling from her hand. Her gray-blue gaze, the one that was so much like mine, swept over me, taking in my wild, disheveled hair, the cuts and bruises on my face and hands, the grass stains on my clothes, and the blood that covered me from head to toe, like I'd been dipped in rusty paint.

"Well, well, well, if it isn't Everleigh," Vasilia said, a mocking note in her voice. "You surprised me, cousin. I wouldn't have thought that you would have survived this long."

"And I wouldn't have thought that you would have slaughtered everyone. But I should have known better. You always were a treacherous bitch, even when we were kids."

She smiled, as though my hateful words amused her. She had always been able to smile, no matter how I tried to best her, no matter how hard I tried to hurt her the same way that she had hurt me. My hands clenched into fists, and I longed to slam them into her over and over again until she was as bloody, broken, and dead as everyone else. But she would kill me with her sword before I landed a single punch, so I forced myself to stand still.

Felton was hovering behind her, along with the turncoat guards. More turncoats surrounded Auster, who was still on his feet, although he had been disarmed, and Nox had his sword pressed up against the captain's throat. Maeven stood off to the side, all by herself, her arms crossed over her chest, staring at me with a thoughtful expression.

I peered past them, my gaze sweeping over the lawn. It looked like a waterspout had surged up from the river, arced over the stone wall, and crashed down onto the area. Broken tables and splintered chairs stuck up out of the grass at crazy angles, many of them marking the spots where the dead lay.

My gaze rested on Madelena's crumpled form, then flicked to Isobel's body. I wanted to fall to my knees and scream and scream, but I couldn't do that. I *wouldn't* do that. Vasilia and the others were going to kill me, but I wasn't going to beg, and they weren't going to see me cry—

Thwack-thwack-thwack.

That strange sound, along with a few soft moans and groans, startled me out of my grim thoughts. Some people were still alive, and the turncoats were moving from one person to the next, stabbing them until they were dead.

The weak, whimpering pleas of the injured, and the resounding, unrelenting *thwack*s of the turncoats' swords biting into flesh and bone, were almost more than I could bear. But I watched while what was left of the Blair royal family—*my* family—was slaughtered.

It didn't take long.

Vasilia stared at me the whole damn time, smiling at the horror, disgust, and rage that pinched my face. I had never felt so weak and helpless and utterly useless.

In that moment, I made a silent vow to myself. If I somehow survived this, I would *never* be weak and helpless and useless again. I would *never* let anyone ever make me feel this way again. And I especially would *never* let anyone hurt the people I cared about ever again.

An easy, empty promise to make, since everyone that I cared about had already been slaughtered, and I would be too soon enough.

When it was finished, and everyone else was dead, Vasilia stabbed her sword at Cordelia's body, still slumped up against the wall. "I saw your little scene with my mother. How touching. I didn't realize that the two of you were so close."

I barked out a harsh laugh. "Your mother had as little use and regard for me as you do."

"But you still tried to save her. Why?"

"I don't know," I growled. "Maybe it had something to do with all those history lessons about being a Blair and always doing my duty to queen and country."

Vasilia shook her head. "Poor, silly, stupid Everleigh. Still trying to be a good little girl. Still trying to win everyone's approval. Still trying to beat me. You should know by now that I always win—*always*."

My fists clenched tighter, but she was right. She had won, and everyone else had lost.

Vasilia glanced at my hands, and amusement sparked in her gaze, along with a bit of curiosity. "What's that on your wrist?"

I looked down. Sometime during the massacre, the bottom half of my tunic sleeve had been ripped away, revealing my right arm from my elbow down to my wrist. My silver bracelet still circled my wrist, although blood coated the crown in the center of the design, blackening the blue tearstone shards. It was a good thing that Alvis had given me the bracelet today.

I wasn't going to be alive to appreciate it tomorrow.

But the bracelet wasn't the only thing on my wrist. The black velvet bag was hanging right alongside it. The bag's drawstrings had tangled themselves around the bracelet's thorns, and together, the two of them felt as tight as a noose digging into my skin.

"What's in the bag?" Vasilia asked.

I didn't answer. She would kill me soon enough, open the bag, and see the memory stone. Making her go to that small trouble was the last bit of petty satisfaction I would ever have.

Vasilia waited, but when I didn't answer, she shrugged, as if it didn't matter. And it didn't, not really, not at all. Because she had won, and I was going to die.

She turned her attention to Auster, who was being guarded, with Nox's sword still at his throat. "And you, captain," she said. "I can't imagine how horribly *you* must feel, knowing that you had one job, to protect your queen, and seeing how spectacularly you failed at it."

Anger stained Auster's cheeks a bright scarlet, and his eyes glittered with grief and rage, but he couldn't deny the truth of her words any more than I'd been able to.

"You see, Captain Auster helped the Andvarian assassins kill the queen he was sworn to protect. What a betrayal." Vasilia clucked her tongue in mock sympathy.

Auster sucked in a surprised breath, and horror filled his face. Shock jolted through me as well, followed by sick understanding.

Vasilia might be heartless, but she was also smart, and she was going to make Auster her scapegoat. It was plausible enough, given Auster's access to the queen, the guards, and the palace, and it would garner Vasilia sympathy from all corners of Bellona. And, since she'd killed the rest of our cousins, there was no one left to challenge her for the throne. Oh, a few Blairs were always scattered at their estates throughout the countryside, but no one with enough magic to take on Vasilia and win.

"Why *did* you betray your queen, Auster? Was that Andvarian gold really worth it? Was that why you helped the assassins?" Vasilia continued spinning her lies. "Felton discovered your secret bank accounts too late to save my mother, although he did warn me in time."

Felton smirked and waggled his red ledger at the captain. Rage replaced Auster's shock, and he glared at the queen's secretary.

Vasilia shook her head. "I managed to save myself from

your assassins, and then, with my loyal guards, I cut down the Andvarian traitors and captured you, but not before you had murdered everyone else. But traitors always pay for their sins, Auster. And a nice, public execution will be the perfect reward for your crimes."

Auster turned his hot stare back to Vasilia. "Your mother was right," he growled. "All you want to do is plunge us into war."

My mind spun at their words. Blaming Auster for the queen's murder was bad enough. But claiming that he was working with the Andvarians, and that the ambassador and the prince had orchestrated the massacre, had potentially catastrophic ramifications for both Bellona and Andvari.

It meant war.

I looked at Maeven, who had remained quiet through Vasilia's preening. Somehow, I knew that she was the ultimate architect of this. But who was she working for? Morta? Relations with Morta, especially with the royal family, had always been strained, ever since Bryn Blair had defeated their king and driven the Mortan invaders out of Bellona centuries ago.

But this was about far, far more than just putting Vasilia on the throne. Morta was going to use the queen's death to get Bellona to invade Andvari. And that was just the beginning. The ramifications stretched on and on, like a web weaving itself together, each strand darker and more ominous than the last, a black, poisonous web that could potentially destroy Bellona and Andvari and let Morta conquer the entire continent.

Maeven stared back at me, then her gaze dropped to the bracelet on my wrist. She frowned, as though something about the silver band annoyed her. "She's a Winter, isn't she?"

"So what?" Vasilia said.

"So kill her and be done with it," Maeven snapped. "That was our agreement. We help you murder the queen, and you eliminate the Winter line of the Blair family—forever."

Two types of magic ran through the Blair family—Summer and Winter, named after Bryn Blair, who'd had the powers of both a magier and a master. Those with Summer magic were often powerful magiers, like Cordelia with her fire and Vasilia with her lightning. Those with Winter magic could be magiers too, like my mother with her control over ice and snow, but they were more often masters, like those who had built Seven Spire. Thanks to my mother, I was considered a Winter, despite my seeming lack of magic.

I could understand why Maeven wanted to eliminate the Blairs, so that no one could challenge Vasilia for the throne. But the Summer line was widely considered to be the more powerful. So why target the Winter line specifically?

I thought back to Cordelia's words, about how I was a Winter queen. I had thought that she'd just been babbling, that she'd been in too much pain to be thinking clearly. But what if there was more to it than that? Although I couldn't imagine what that *more* might be.

"Kill her now, or I'll do it myself." Maeven held up her hand, and a ball of purple lightning crackled to life in her palm.

Vasilia huffed. "Fine. I was going to do it anyway."

My cousin stepped up so that she was standing about five feet away. Everyone tensed. Felton, Nox, the turncoat guards, and especially Maeven.

"Everleigh," Auster rasped, breaking the silence. "I'm sorry. So sorry. For all of this. I failed in my duty to protect you and the queen and everyone else."

I forced myself to smile at him. "It's all right, Auster. You did your best. No one could have fought harder. You did your duty, and you honored your queen today."

A stricken expression filled his face, and tears gleamed in his eyes. Auster nodded at me, and I nodded back. Then I looked at Vasilia again.

She raised her hand, white lightning sparking on her fingertips. The cold, hard power of my own immunity rose up in response, the way it always did whenever I was around any magic.

For the first time since my parents had died, I didn't flinch at my immunity or ignore it or push it down. Instead, I reached for my power, grasping and clawing and holding on to it in a way that I never had before. I pulled it up and up and up until I could almost *feel* the invisible strength of it crackling along my skin, the same way that Vasilia's lightning was on her fingertips. I didn't know what good it would do, since I doubted that my immunity was stronger than her lightning, but I was going to fight until the bitter, bitter end.

Vasilia smiled at me, savoring the moment. The smug, sneering triumph on her face made icy rage spread through my body, and my resolve hardened, along with my magic.

"The queen is dead," Vasilia sneered. "Long live the queen."

Then she reared back and threw her lightning at me.

The bolt hit me square in the chest, lifting me up and off my feet, and throwing me over the side of the wall.

CHAPTER NINE

For a moment, I was suspended high in midair, and I could see the entire lawn.

The debris. The blood. The bodies. They all seemed small and far away, as though I was peering through the window of a child's dollhouse at the tiny people and furnishings inside.

Then another bolt of lightning streaked out of Vasilia's fingertips, shot through the air, and slammed into my chest.

And I started to fall.

My bird's-eye view of the lawn vanished, and the last thing I saw was Vasilia's sneering face before the lightning filled my vision, turning everything a bright, eerie white. The lightning danced over my body, trying to fry me alive. I screamed and batted my hands at my chest, even though it wouldn't do any good. I sucked in another breath to scream, and the hot, caustic stench of Vasilia's magic filled my nose. For some reason, the stench cut through my panic, and I quit screaming, gritted my teeth, and pushed back against the lightning with my own power.

I imagined my immunity like a cold fist, wrapping around my body and squeezing, squeezing tight, throttling every single spark of Vasilia's lightning. For the last fifteen years, I had hidden my power the same way that I did my feelings, but I didn't have to do that anymore. No one was watching, and I wanted to keep my promise to Cordelia. I wanted to *live*. So for the first time since my parents had died, I fully embraced my power, this strange little quirk that let me destroy other people's magic.

And it *worked*.

My immunity smothered Vasilia's lightning like a bucket of water dousing a candle flame. The sharp, stinging jolts of power vanished, although smoke wafted up from my body where her magic had singed my clothes. My vision cleared. I blinked the world back into focus and then immediately wished that I hadn't.

Because I was still going to die.

Vasilia's lightning had knocked me clear of the sharp, jagged cliffs on this side of the palace, so I wasn't going to tumble end over end down the rocks and break every single bone in my body. Instead, I was going to hit the river far, far below, which would probably still break every single bone in my body.

The world spun around and around in a crazy, disjointed blur of white clouds, gray rocks, and blue water. If I had any hope of surviving, I couldn't hit the water headfirst, and I managed to flip myself over in midair so that my feet were pointing downward, even as the rippling surface rushed up to meet me—

WHOOSH!

I hit the water, and everything went cold, wet, and black.

Everything was cold, wet, and black.

I stood in front of a window, watching the rain spatter down onto the palace. A bit of snow mixed in, but the rain washed it away before it could stick to anything. Back home at Winterwind, my family's estate in the northern mountains, it would have been all snow, and the fat, fluffy flakes would have turned the evergreen woods into an icy wonderland. Here, the rain reigned, turning everything a cold, wet, miserable black.

I missed the snow. The mountains. My home. My parents. Everything I had lost.

It had been more than a month since my parents had been murdered. Ever since then, I had been passed from one cousin and estate to the next. No one had kept me for more than a few days. This cousin already had two children. That one never wanted kids. This one was far too busy with her social engagements to bother with her own children, much less a distant orphan cousin.

I had moved from relative to relative, traveling south all the while, until I had ended up in the capital city of Svalin. Now I was at Seven Spire, waiting for someone to tell me where to go next. I hadn't seen Queen Cordelia yet, and I had no idea when or even if that might happen. After all, she had far more pressing things to worry about than one little girl. I wondered if she would take me in and make me part of her family. Probably not. No one else had. But maybe she would at least order someone else to do it for her.

"Hmm-hmm-hmm . . . hmm-hmm-hmm . . ."

The sound of light, happy humming caught my ear, breaking the steady slap of the rain against the glass, and a girl skipped down the hallway toward me. She was quite pretty, with long, golden curls and a pink silk dress that bounced and swished with every step. She looked like a ray of sunshine on this gloomy day.

I expected the girl to skip past me, but to my surprise, she stopped, as if she'd been looking for me.

"Hello!" she chirped. "My name is Vasilia. I'm the crown princess."

Of course she was the crown princess, with a dress like that, not to mention the pink-diamond tiara that sparkled like a ring of stars on her head. I was suddenly aware of how plain and shabby my own blue dress was, as well as the fact that it was three inches too short. It had been a castoff from one of my younger cousins. All my clothes had been at my home—a home that had been destroyed when my parents had been murdered.

I gritted my teeth and dropped into a curtsy. "Forgive me, Your Highness. I'm new here, and I didn't know—"

Vasilia stepped forward, grabbed my arm, and lifted me to my feet. "There's no need for any of that nonsense. You can call me Vasilia. After all, our grandmothers were sisters, so that makes us second cousins. That makes us family."

She had a far different idea of family than our other cousins did. They couldn't wait to pass me along to someone else. But I didn't trust anyone, not after what had happened to my parents, so I drew in a breath, tasting her scent. Cinnamon curiosity. Well, that was better than the sour-milk reluctance I'd sensed from everyone else.

"You're Everleigh, right?"

I nodded.

"Excellent. Come with me."

Before I could protest, Vasilia grabbed my hand and tugged me along the hallway with her. A few minutes later, she pushed open a large door and led me inside an enormous room.

She let go of my hand and skipped around. "This is my playroom."

Playroom? It was more like a treasure vault. Every toy imaginable lined the floor-to-ceiling shelves that took up two of the walls. Dolls, balls, hoops, games, puzzles, wooden swords and shields. And still more toys peeked up out of the chests that were scattered here and there. And they weren't just mere toys. They were works of art, gilded with gold and studded with jewels.

As if the toys weren't wonderful enough, a padded seat with books scattered on the cushions ran the length of the picture window that took up the back wall. My heart ached. I'd had a seat like that in my own room back home.

Vasilia grabbed my hand and led me over to a glass-topped table with four chairs. Dolls had been propped up in two of the seats. One of them was your typical princess in a frilly purple dress, while the other was an ogre morph with a scary face and teeth jutting out of its mouth. A diorama of a miniature arena perched on that end of the table, complete with two tiny figures with swords, as if the dolls were watching a gladiator bout.

Vasilia dropped into one of the empty chairs and tugged me down, so that I was sitting next to her. A fine tea set had been laid out, along with plates of real food—crustless sandwiches with slivers of cucumber, honey cranberries dipped in powdered sugar, and dark chocolates shaped like Vasilia's tiara.

I stared at the food. My stomach rumbled, an embarrassingly loud sound that reminded me how long it had been since I had eaten.

"Poor thing," Vasilia crooned. "Are you hungry? Here, have some hot chocolate."

She picked up a teapot and poured the chocolate into my cup. I was so hungry that I gulped it all down. The hot, steaming liquid burned my tongue, but the rich, dark chocolate slowly warmed me from the inside out, and I felt calmer, stronger, and more like myself than I had in weeks.

Vasilia smiled. "There. Isn't that better?"

"Yes. Thank you."

She patted my hand, her gray-blue eyes bright in her pretty face. "You know what, Everleigh? You and I are going to be fabulous friends."

For the first time since my parents had died, someone was treating me like an actual person, instead of an unwanted piece of furniture to be hauled off to a new location. Someone wanted to be around me. Someone wanted to take care of me. Someone wanted to be my friend.

For the first time in weeks, my heart ached with gratitude instead of sorrow. Tears stung my eyes, but I blinked them back. I wasn't going to start bawling like a baby.

Vasilia didn't seem to notice my turbulent emotions as she poured herself some hot chocolate, then refilled my cup. She picked up her cup and gestured for me to do the same.

"So . . . friends?" she said, smiling at me again.

Despite everything that had happened, I found myself smiling back at her. "Friends."

Her smile sharpened, and we clinked our cups together . . .

For a moment, I could still smell the warm, rich steam rising off that hot chocolate. But it was just a dream, just a memory, one that splintered into shards as something cold and wet slapped me in the face, jolting me awake.

My eyes snapped open, and I sucked down a breath, not knowing where I was or what was going on. Then another wave washed over me, dousing me from head to toe, and I realized that I was in the Summanus River.

My right arm was splayed over a dead tree that had fallen from the riverbank over into the water. A tangle of thorns ringed the tree, and they'd embedded themselves into what was left of my tunic sleeve and my skin underneath, hooking me like a fish. The thorns had also caught on my silver bracelet and the black velvet bag, both of which were still wrapped around my wrist, so tightly that my fingers had gone numb.

I didn't remember anything after hitting the water, but the current must have swept me downriver and into this tree. The thorns stabbing into my clothes and skin were probably the only reason that the river hadn't sucked me under and finished drowning me.

I lay there, getting my breath back, and feeling the water pushing against my back, trying to drag me even farther downriver. Then, when I felt strong enough, I raised my head and straightened up. To my surprise, my feet touched the bottom, and I was able to stand up, since the water only came up to my chest.

It took me several minutes to dig the thorns out of my shirt and skin, but I managed it, although I got long, stinging scrapes in return. I also managed to untangle the bracelet and the bag from the thorns.

The water ebbed to shallows, before giving way to mud and rocks, and I slogged through it all until I reached the grassy shore.

Sweat slid down my face, mixing with the water, and my breath came in ragged gasps. For a long time, all I could do was sit there, sucking down gulp after gulp of air, not quite believing that I was still alive. That Vasilia's lightning, the fall off the cliffs, and the wild ride through the river hadn't killed me. But eventually, my fear and panic faded, and I looked around, trying to figure out where I was.

Woods surrounded both sides of the river, the trees and branches blocking out everything else. No boats or people appeared, no voices sounded, and nothing moved except the river as it rushed by. All I could smell was water and mud, telling me that I was completely alone.

But I could still see Seven Spire in the distance.

The palace jutted out of the side of the mountain like always, although the longer I stared at it, the more the balconies, the steps, and especially the gladiators and creatures on the massive columns seemed to move, writhe, and twist themselves into grotesque shapes. I felt like I was staring at the dark, gaping maw of some horrible monster that was about to break free of the mountain and gobble me up, along with everything else.

Memories of the massacre rose up in my mind. The screams tearing through the air. The solid *thunk*s of swords hitting bones. The disgusting stench of blood covering everything. Isobel, Madelena, Cordelia, and all the others lying broken, battered, beaten, and dead on the lawn.

I shuddered and dropped my gaze from the palace. I couldn't stand to look at it right now, much less think about what had happened.

I didn't know how long I sat there, my arms wrapped around my knees, hugging myself into a little ball, and rocking back and forth, as if that would protect me from my memories or anything else. But my shock slowly receded, and I realized how cold and wet I was, not to mention the way my stomach kept rumbling, demanding food. Like it or not, I had survived, and I couldn't sit here and pretend that the rest of the world didn't exist, no matter how much I wanted to.

But where could I go? My cousins were dead, and I didn't have any friends. I felt like I was twelve years old again. For the second time in my life, everything that I loved had been ripped away. Isobel, Alvis, all my hopes, dreams, and plans for the future. They were all gone, and this time, no one was going to help me.

Even if I did know someone who might take me in, I couldn't trust them not to betray me to Vasilia. After all, what better way to gain the new queen's favor than by handing me over to her? As far as Vasilia knew, her cousin Everleigh was dead, and it needed to stay that way if I had any hope of surviving for any length of time.

I couldn't tell anyone who I was, which meant that I couldn't access my bank accounts. No accounts meant no savings and no money. My clothes were ruined, and the only things that I had of value were my silver bracelet and the black velvet bag on my wrist—

My eyes widened, and I fumbled for the bag, untangling the drawstrings and sliding it off my wrist. I opened the strings, then tipped the bag upside down.

The memory stone dropped into my hand with a whisper.

I held the stone up, examining it, but the opal was smooth, whole, and unbroken, and I could feel the magic pulsing inside it. The stone had recorded every single second of the massacre, right up until I'd grabbed it from the grass.

It was proof of Vasilia's crimes, which made it powerful, valuable, and extremely dangerous. Favors, blackmail, another coup. The memory stone could be used for all that and more. If anyone—*anyone*—knew about the stone, they would kill me for it.

I was tempted to hurl the opal into the river and let the water drown it forever. I even went so far as to rear back my hand. But I let out a breath, lowered my hand, and dropped the memory stone back into its black velvet bag. I didn't know what I was going to do with it, but I couldn't get rid of it either.

I set the bag on the ground, then undid the clasp on my bracelet. I examined it the same way I had the memory stone, but the bracelet had also survived unscathed. Not so much as a scratch marred the silver, and the tearstone shards were all intact and as blue as ever, since the river had washed all the blood off them.

Staring at it made my heart ache again, so I dropped the bracelet into the bag as well, then pulled the drawstrings together, hiding it and the memory stone. I started to hook the strings back around my wrist, but I thought better of it, lifted up my tunic, and slid the strings through one of my belt loops before tying them together. Then I pulled my tunic back down into place, hiding the bag.

But that still didn't solve the problem of where I should go, and I stared up at Seven Spire again, as though all those gladiators battling each other in the columns would give me some brilliant inspiration—

Serilda Swanson's come back to the capital. Her gladiator troupe moved into that new arena along the river last week.

That bit of gossip that I'd overheard during the luncheon popped into my mind, along with Cordelia's voice.

Find Serilda Swanson. She'll . . . protect you, help you, train you. Tell her . . . that you're the last Winter queen. She'll understand.

I still had no idea what Cordelia had meant about my being a Winter queen or why she thought that was so important, and I couldn't trust Serilda Swanson any more than I could trust anyone else. But I couldn't come up with a better idea. At least I knew where Serilda was and what she did for a living.

Everyone else I knew was dead.

My heart squeezed tight again, but I forced myself to keep thinking, and I came to two sad, inescapable conclusions—I couldn't sit here forever, and I didn't have anywhere else to go. Besides, a gladiator troupe would be large, crowded, and the last place that anyone would look for me, on the slim chance that anyone realized that I was still alive.

So I sighed, pushed myself to my feet, and started walking, heading back toward the city.

PART TWO

THE
BLACK
SWAN

CHAPTER TEN

I hadn't gone as far down the river as I'd thought, and I reached the city just as the sun was setting behind the palace. The towering spires looked like swords stabbing into the sun, with red rays of blood oozing everywhere. My lips curled with disgust, but I kept walking, finally reaching the slums on the outskirts of the city.

I stepped out of the trees and onto a hard-packed dirt road that split off in a dozen different directions. I picked the path that stayed the closest to the river and trudged on.

Bellona was a prosperous kingdom with its mining, timber, and other industries, but not everyone shared in the wealth. Shacks made of rotten wood lashed together with equally rotten ropes jutted up like crooked teeth, topped with flimsy tin roofs that glinted like dull fillings in this mouth of squalor.

Through the open doors, I spotted women feeding fires and stirring pots of bubbling stews inside the tiny, cramped quarters. Children with bare feet and dirty faces chased each other through the maze of shacks, hopscotching over broken boards, shattered glass, and other odds and ends. A few thin, mangy dogs barked and nipped at their heels, joining in the fun, while equally thin, scruffy cats perched on the roofs, blinking sleepily and soaking up the evening sun.

This wasn't the first time I had been to the slums. Vasilia and the rest of my Blair cousins wouldn't have been caught dead here, so I had been the royal stand-in at more than one soup kitchen and other charity. Coming here always made my own problems seem so insignificant. Sorrow filled my heart that people lived like this, that *my* people lived like this, but I couldn't help them. I was so tired, battered, and bruised that I could barely help myself right now.

I rounded a shack and passed a group of men huddled around a fire, passing a brown bottle back and forth. They stared at me, their gazes sharpening with predatory interest, and I hurried on. Sorrow or not, I had to be careful. I might have only my torn clothes and muddy boots, but that was still enough to make me a target.

The closer I got to the city proper, the nicer the shacks became, with straighter walls and fewer spaces in between the boards. Some were whitewashed, and a few boasted small metal spires at the corners, as though they were trying to emulate the larger homes in the distance.

Wire lines stretched from one shack to another, and the clothes on them snapped like flags in the breeze. Women chatted with each other as they hung out their wet laundry and checked to see if their other clothes had dried yet. I walked past them and slipped behind one of the shacks. Then I crept up and peered around the corner, watching the women. It seemed to take forever, although it couldn't have been more than a few minutes, but the women said their goodbyes, gathered up their laundry baskets, and disappeared back inside their homes.

When I was sure that they were all inside, I darted over and snatched a blue tunic and a pair of black leggings off one of the wires. I ducked my head, balled the clothes up under my arm, and hurried on. My heart pounded, and I expected someone to yell at me to stop, but no cries sounded.

I hated stealing, especially from people who had so little, but I didn't have a choice. My own clothes were ruined, and I didn't dare ask anyone for anything. I didn't want anyone remembering me, the waterlogged woman who had come from downriver the day of the royal massacre. Oh, I doubted that anyone would connect me with what had happened and realize that I had survived, but it wasn't a risk that I was willing to take.

When I was a safe distance away, I stopped behind one of the shacks, stripped off my clothes, and shimmied into my stolen ones. They were still damp, and they didn't fit well, but beggars couldn't be choosers, and I was lower than the lowest beggar right now. I tied the bag with the memory stone and my bracelet to one of the belt loops on my new leggings, made sure that my new tunic covered the bulge, and pulled my muddy boots back on. Then I shoved my ruined clothes under a pile of wood and scurried away.

Eventually, the hard-packed dirt gave way to cobblestone streets, and the shacks were replaced by small homes made of wood that actually fit together. The streets opened up into large plazas with fountains bubbling in the center and wooden carts selling everything from fruits and vegetables to loaves of fresh-baked bread. Wisps of steam curled up, bringing the delicious scent of the bread with it. My stomach grumbled again, but I didn't dare swipe so much as an apple from the carts. The last thing I needed was for the city guards to arrest me for stealing.

I wasn't familiar with this part of Svalin, and all I knew was that Serilda Swanson's gladiator troupe was located in the arena by the river, but it was easier to find than I'd expected.

I just followed the crowd.

"Free show! Free show tonight!" a boy bellowed at one of the street corners, waving a stack of flyers. "Straight ahead at the new Black Swan arena!"

Black Swan? That must be Serilda's name for her troupe. They all had colorful names and crests like that, all the better to help them sell tunics, flags, jewelry, replica weapons, and more to their adoring fans. I'd never been to a gladiator show, but I had still heard the names—the Scarlet Knights, the Blue Thorns, the Coral Vipers, and dozens more.

The boy shoved a flyer into my hand. The paper said the same things that he already had, but my gaze focused on the crest at the top—several shards fitted together to form an elegant black swan with a bright blue eye and a matching beak.

The longer I stared at the crest, the more familiar it seemed. I traced my finger over the symbol, and I remembered something else about Serilda. When she had been the queen's personal guard, she had been called the Black Swan because she had been so graceful in battle and had brought death to so many of Cordelia's enemies.

"See gladiators battle for the glory of your applause!" the boy yelled. "Free show! Free food! Over at the Black Swan arena!"

Free food? My stomach grumbled again. That alone was enough reason to keep going.

I folded up the flyer, slid it into my pocket, and headed toward the arena. People of all shapes, sizes, and stations walked along the streets, everyone from poor, bedraggled bums to miners in blue coveralls coated with gray fluorestone dust to lords and ladies in expensive, flashy, fashionable garb. Everyone loved a free show.

Several folks glanced curiously at me. At first, I wondered why, but then I caught a glimpse of my reflection in one of the store windows. A fist-shaped bruise darkened my right cheek from where the turncoat guard had punched me, and several other cuts and bruises dotted my face as well. I grimaced, ducked my head, and hurried on.

Eventually, the street opened up into another plaza. More vendors and carts lined the area, selling everything from clothes to flags to silver medallion necklaces, all of which were embroidered, embellished, or stamped with the black-swan crest. Even the stone fountain in the center of the plaza was shaped like a large black swan with jets of water rising and falling all around it. The swan's blue beak looked as sharp as an arrow, while its two fluorestone eyes burned a bright, steady blue, giving it a fierce, combative look, like it was about to rise up out of the water and attack anyone who came near it.

A twelve-foot stone wall cordoned off the plaza from the domed arena, and I got in line, heading toward the open iron gate. A girl on the far side was passing out free bags of cornucopia from a wooden cart. My stomach grumbled again, and I snatched the last two bags off her cart.

"Hey!" she called out. "You're only supposed to take one!"

I ignored her and kept going, already shoving my hand into one of the paper bags and then the cornucopia into my mouth. The rich flavor of the buttery popped corn, covered with sticky salted caramel, exploded on my tongue, along with toasted almonds, crunchy sunflower seeds, and bits of sweet dried bloodcrisp apples.

Cornucopia had never been my favorite treat, but this was fantastic. I was so hungry that I could have upended the entire bag into my mouth, then the second one, but I forced myself to chew only a few clusters at a time, trying to make it last as long as possible.

The line of people in front of me slowed, giving me plenty of time to nibble on my food and look around. The enormous arena with its round dome took up much of the space behind the wall, but gladiator troupes didn't just have arenas. Oh, no. They had entire *compounds* devoted to their training, feeding, housing, and everything else that went into putting on their shows.

Several buildings squatted around the arena. A dining hall, barracks for the gladiators and other workers, stables for the gargoyles, strixes, and other creatures used in the shows. The Black Swan compound was a city unto itself, like Seven Spire was.

I glanced up at the palace in the distance. The sun had set more than an hour ago, and blackness cloaked the mountain. Lights burned in the palace windows, but they did little to drive back the darkness, although the tearstone spires gleamed with a soft, silvery light, thanks to the moon and stars high above.

I wondered what Vasilia was doing right now. Probably still enjoying her bloody triumph over her mother and the rest of the Blairs. I wondered what she had done with Cordelia's body, and Madelena's, and Isobel's, and all the others. My stomach churned, and I almost vomited up the cornucopia. I forced the bile down, dropped my gaze from the palace, and shuffled forward.

There was no going back.

By the time I got inside the arena, all the good seats down front had been taken, and I had to climb up to the top of the stone bleachers. I didn't mind too much, though, as it gave me a bird's-eye view of the entire arena.

A stone wall cordoned off the bleachers from the arena floor. Down below, three enormous wooden rings, each one only about a foot high, stood on the hard-packed dirt. The two outer rings were white, but the center one was painted a bright, glossy red, indicating that tonight's bout would be only to first blood. Of course. You had to pay big money to see gladiators battle to the death. Serilda Swanson was no fool. Tonight's free show was just a taste, just a tease of bloodier, deadlier things to come.

But the action wasn't just going to be on the ground. Thick cables crisscrossed the open air above the rings and connected to stone platforms that jutted out from the arena walls. Some of the cables and platforms were fairly low, only about ten feet off the ground, but others were much higher, twenty, fifty, and even a hundred feet up.

I scanned the crowd, and I realized that a large box had been built into the middle of the bleachers. Us common folk were sitting on hard slabs of stone, but cushioned chairs lined the box, along with carts filled with food and drinks. That must be where Serilda Swanson would sit and entertain wealthy and important guests. I stared at the box, but no one approached it. Perhaps Serilda took part in the show instead of watching it from on high.

I was among the last people to snag a seat, and a few minutes later, the white fluorestones embedded in the ceiling slowly dimmed, and a hush fell over the crowd.

Showtime.

A lone spotlight snapped on and focused on the red ring in the center of the arena, and a man wearing a short, tight bloodred tailcoat trimmed with silver buttons stepped into the light. His leggings were black, and his black boots had been polished to a high gloss. His black hair gleamed under the spotlight, as did his black eyes and golden skin. A morph mark peeked up above the collar on his white ruffled shirt, although from this distance, I couldn't tell what creature he could shift into.

"Lords and ladies, high and low," he called out in a deep, booming voice. "Welcome to the Black Swan arena. My name is Cho Yamato, and we are here to entertain you."

The crowd roared, and Cho made an elaborate flourish with his hand and bowed low. The spotlight snapped off, plunging everything into darkness. Then, a moment later, all the fluorestones blazed to life, and an explosion of sound, color, and magic erupted in the arena.

Acrobats tumbled from one ring to another, while wire walkers raced across the cables above. Magiers summoned up fire and ice in their hands, juggling them like balls and knives, as well as tossing them back and forth to each other. Morphs shifted into their other forms, using their sharp talons to scale the walls and do other amazing tricks. The performers were dressed in bright, sequined costumes, and many of their faces were adorned with sparkling crystals and shimmering paint, adding to the dazzling atmosphere. Despite everything that had happened, I oohed and aahed along with everyone else.

The first part of the show went on for about thirty minutes, with each feat, trick, and tumble more dazzling and death-defying than the last. Then the acrobats, wire walkers, magiers, and morphs waved their goodbyes, and the lights dimmed. A minute later, the fluorestones blazed to life again.

And the gladiators appeared.

They entered at one end of the arena and walked forward, going slowly so that everyone could get a good, long look at them. They were dressed in tight, sleeveless shirts, knee-length kilts, and flat sandals with straps that wound up past their ankles. A black swan with a blue eye and beak stretched across everyone's chest, but the rest of their shirts, along with their kilts and sandals, were made of pale gray leather. The light color must have made it easier to see the gladiators bleed, which was what the crowd was really here for. The harsh reality made me quit cheering.

Young, old, men, women, short, tall, heavy, thin. All ages, sexes, and sizes were represented in the troupe's ranks, along with magiers, morphs, mutts, and even a few mortals without magic. Some of the gladiators were carrying swords, while others clutched spears, but each one had a silver shield with that black-swan crest strapped to their forearm.

The gladiators started beating their swords and spears against their shields, creating a low, rolling drumbeat. The farther they walked out into the arena, the harder and faster they beat their weapons against the shields, and the quicker and louder the drumbeat became. The crowd surged to their feet, cheering wildly.

The gladiators reached the red ring and spread out, forming ranks. Everyone fell into line except for a single woman who stood in front of the others. She looked to be about my age—twenty-seven or so—but she was a couple of inches taller and carried a spiked mace that was as big as my head. Her long blond hair was done up in elaborate braids, showing off the morph mark on her neck, although she was too far away for me to make out exactly what kind of mark it was. An ogre, if I had to guess, like Xenia.

The lights snapped off for a third time, and when they blazed back on, another woman was standing in the center of the red ring. Unlike the gladiators in their gray fighting leathers, this woman was wearing a white, long-sleeve tunic and matching leggings, although her knee-high boots were a shiny, glossy black. Thin lines of black thread crawled up her arms before thickening and spreading out across her chest to create the image of a black swan swimming in a pool framed by flowers and vines.

Serilda Swanson had finally appeared.

Serilda smiled and waved to the crowd, who applauded even louder. Then, slowly, everyone quieted and took their seats again. I leaned forward, studying everything about her, from her blond hair to her confident stance to the way that her hand unconsciously flexed over the sword that hung off her black leather belt.

"As you've all probably guessed, I am Serilda Swanson," she said. "Welcome to my not-so-humble arena."

Laughter rippled through the crowd.

"Since this is our first show, I wanted to greet you all," Serilda continued. "It's been many years since I've been in Bellona, but now that I'm home, I plan to stay. And to bring you the best, bloodiest gladiator matches that your black hearts desire!"

She punched her fist into the air to punctuate her words,

and the crowd cheered again. Serilda smiled and nodded, accepting their praise, although she held her hand up, asking for quiet.

She turned to the tall blond woman with the spiked mace. "Tonight, for your entertainment, the one, the only, Paloma the Powerful!"

Serilda left the ring, and Paloma stepped forward and raised her mace over her head. She must have been quite popular, since the crowd roared for her even louder than they had for Serilda. Once the applause died down, Paloma turned to the other gladiators and lowered her mace.

The gladiators spread out, swinging their swords, stabbing out with their spears, and blocking blows with their shields. Not fighting, but getting warmed up for the battles to come. The crowd loved it, and I did too. It was all just an elaborate dance, like the one that Xenia had taught me.

Eventually, the warm-ups ended, and the gladiators fell back into their previous ranks, except for Paloma, who held her position in the center of the ring. Paloma gestured, and one of the gladiators stepped forward, lifted his sword, and charged at her.

And the fight was on.

Paloma waited until the man was almost in range, then smoothly spun to the side, out of the way of his charge. Sometime during the warm-ups, she had traded her mace for a sword, and she sliced the weapon across the man's back.

I could smell the coppery stench of his blood all the way up here at the top of the bleachers.

The man yelled, stumbled forward, and fell to the ground. The crowd sucked in a collective breath, wondering if she might have killed him, but the man slowly pushed himself to his knees and then back up onto his feet. She didn't seem to have hurt him too badly.

Paloma nodded to the man, and he nodded back before limping out of the ring, probably to get healed by a bone master. Paloma gestured at the other gladiators standing in front of her.

"Next!" she barked out.

Another gladiator left the ranks to attack her, although she dealt with the second man as easily as she had the first.

For the next fifteen minutes, Paloma dispatched one gladiator after another, drawing first blood every time, and asserting herself as the troupe's champion. She could have easily killed her opponents, especially if she had shifted into her larger, stronger morph form like some of the other gladiators did, but I got the impression that she was holding back so as to not accidentally kill anyone. Powerful, indeed.

Finally, Paloma stepped aside, and the remaining gladiators began to battle each other, two at a time, until first blood was drawn.

Magiers' fire and lightning. Morphs' teeth and talons. Mutts' strength and speed. Mortals' mastery of weapons and tactics.

The gladiators battled each other with a captivating, gruesome mix of magic, weapons, and skills. Vicious slices, punishing punches, and brutal blocks rang out in a violent symphony, and blood spattered everywhere until the dirt glistened like a carpet of dusty rubies.

The crowd loved every single moment, cheering with the victors, groaning with the losers, and eagerly betting on the outcomes of the matches. Money changed hands all around me, the gold, silver, and bronze crowns *clink-clink-clink*ing together like a softer, more profitable version of the gladiators' swords, spears, and shields crashing together.

An hour later, all the gladiators had battled at least once and had emerged either happy and victorious or bloody and defeated. Then Cho, the ringmaster, reappeared.

"Remember to come back to our next show," he called out. "Good night!"

He bowed low, and the lights snapped off. When they came back on again, everyone who had participated in the show, from the acrobats to the wire walkers to the gladiators, was standing on the arena floor, and they all bowed low. Everyone got to their feet to cheer and give all the performers one last hearty round of applause.

And then people started leaving.

Some folks hurried down to the wall that separated the bleachers from the arena floor, stretching their flyers, flags, tunics, and more through the gaps in the iron gates, and begging the gladiators to come over and sign their items. But most people headed for the exit, and I found myself asking one troubling question.

What was I going to do now?

Since I was at the top of the bleachers, I had to wait for the people below to clear out of the way. That gave me a few minutes to figure out what to do.

I had been so focused on getting to the arena that I hadn't thought about what would happen after the show ended. Panic sparked in my stomach, but I ignored it. I had come this far. I would figure out something . . . even if I didn't know what that something was right now.

I glanced down at the arena floor, but I didn't see Serilda Swanson with the performers. She had left after she had introduced the gladiators, which meant that she could be anywhere in the compound by now. I needed to find her and tell her . . . what, exactly? That Vasilia had killed the queen and most of the royal family? That I was the only Blair who had survived the massacre? That I was a Winter queen, whatever that meant?

Cordelia had said that I could trust Serilda, but how could I trust the queen when she had been so wrong about her own daughter? My head ached. I didn't know what to do, and I was running out of time to figure it out.

The people below me walked down the bleacher steps, and I had no choice but to follow them and step outside with everyone else.

Thanks to all the people packed inside, the arena had been warm, but the winter wind was bitterly cold. I shivered. I would freeze to death if I didn't find shelter for the night.

The crowd streamed toward the open gate and the plaza beyond, but I didn't follow them. Going out into the plaza wouldn't help me. If I left the Black Swan compound, there was no telling when I might be able to get back inside, and I would be far safer in here than I would be on the city streets. That left me with only one option.

I had to find someplace to hide.

I slipped away from the crowd and stepped into the shadows next to a concessions cart that had already closed for the night. Then I examined what I could see of the compound.

The crowd was sticking to the wide street that ran from the

arena over to the main gate, but the performers were peeling off and heading toward the dining hall, which was on the opposite side of the street from me. Several gladiators were limping into another building, probably to get the bone masters to heal their injuries. Lights burned in the windows of a third building, the barracks that I had noticed earlier, and I could see the female gladiators through the glass, laying down their swords and shields.

I couldn't go into any of those buildings, but other structures farther back in the compound were still dark. I would have to take a chance on one of them. So I left the shadows and crossed over to the opposite side of the street where the dining hall and other buildings were. I walked at a steady clip, with my head held high, as though I had every right to be here and knew exactly where I was going. The confident charade had helped me navigate through more than one treacherous palace party.

No one called out to me, and I quickly moved deeper into the compound. The buildings back here were smaller and looked more like homes, rather than communal areas. Probably private residences for the senior workers and their families.

I avoided the homes with clotheslines, toys in the yard, and clay pots of herbs by the front door. People left things outside only if they knew that they were coming back to get them.

Finally, I found a house near the back of the compound. No personal objects were scattered around outside, and no lights were on inside. Perhaps no one lived here yet, since the troupe had recently come to the city. By this point, I had run out of places to look, along with the energy to keep searching. This would have to do.

Still keeping my confident stride, I walked over and grabbed the front door knob—

And almost shrieked at the intense shock that I received.

Blue lightning crackled around the knob the second I touched it, and the smell of magic filled the air. Not the hot, caustic stench of Vasilia's or Maeven's magic, but a colder, cleaner aroma. Truth be told, it was a pleasant scent, although I wasn't in a charitable mood right now. I glared at the knob and shook the sharp, stinging shock out of my hand. Bloody magier booby-trapping his door with lightning.

Well, I could fix that.

I hadn't come all this way to be defeated by a mere door and a little bit of magic, so I gritted my teeth and wrapped my hand around the knob again. And just like I had at the palace, I reached for my immunity and imagined my power throttling the lightning.

It was far more painful than I expected. Oh, it wasn't as intense as Vasilia's lightning had been, but getting shocked over and over again wasn't fun either. The magier had coated the knob with a healthy amount of his power, creating a very effective lock.

Maybe I should have gone somewhere else. Breaking into a magier's house wasn't the smartest idea, but I could hear people talking on the street behind me, their voices growing louder and closer. The other performers were coming home, and I could be discovered at any moment. I just had to hope that the magier was sleeping somewhere else tonight.

It was now or never, so I wrapped my hand even tighter around the knob and reached for even more of my immunity. Sweat slid down my face, and my hand shook from the strain, but I held on . . . and on . . . and on . . .

The lightning dissolved in a shower of blue sparks.

I let out a breath and rested my forehead on the door. It

took me a few seconds to get my hand to actually move again, but I turned the knob, and the door opened. Before I could change my mind, I slipped inside and shut and locked the door behind me.

Fluorestones clicked on in the ceiling, burning with soft white light, and almost making me shriek again. I froze, wondering if the magier might be home after all, but no one appeared to blast me with lightning, so I felt safe enough to keep going.

An open door to my left led into a bathroom, but the rest of the home was one large area. Half of it was the magier's living quarters. A kitchen table with two chairs, a bed, a nightstand bristling with books, an armoire filled with clothes, a writing desk covered with papers, pens, and maps.

The dark mahogany furniture was surprisingly expensive, and I noted with some jealousy that he had nicer sheets on his bed than I had had on mine at the palace. I even spotted what looked like a freestanding Cardea mirror in the corner, which would let him see and communicate with people in other cities and kingdoms. The magier must be fairly powerful and important to the troupe to enjoy this level of luxury. Or perhaps he came from a wealthy family.

Weapons filled the other half of the room. Swords, shields, and spears were stacked in wooden racks like wine bottles, while sharpening stones, polishing cloths, and other supplies perched on floor-to-ceiling shelves. The magier must be involved in the gladiators' training.

I was so exhausted that I was about to pass out, so I shuffled forward, searching for a place to sleep. I eyed the bed with longing, but I resisted the urge to crawl underneath those fine sheets. Despite my desperation, that would have been rude.

But I did steal a hip-length royal-blue jacket and an extra pillow from the armoire.

I took both items over to the very back corner of the room, got down on the floor, and wedged myself in between a rack of swords and a supply shelf. Back here, I was out of sight of the front door and much of the rest of the home, so maybe the magier wouldn't notice me if he did come back tonight. Either way, I was about to drop, so I would have to take my chances.

Besides, if he did find and kill me, then at least this would all be over.

I shrugged into the jacket, which was as fine as everything else the magier owned. It was too big for me, but the fabric felt as soft and light as silk against my skin, even though it was as warm as a much heavier fleece. And the pillow? A cloud of comfort behind my head. I sighed and wormed even deeper into my hidey-hole. He even had better pillows than I did.

Or rather, than I had had.

Walking back to the city, getting to the arena, and seeing the gladiator show had been enough of a distraction to push the massacre to the bottom of my mind. But now that I was alone and relatively safe, the memories bubbled back up to the surface. The shock of Vasilia's betrayal. Isobel's death. Cordelia's final words. All of it soaked in blood and screams and death.

So much death.

A sob rose in my throat, but I choked it down, although I couldn't stop the tears from leaking out of my eyes. And I sat there, silently crying, for a long, long time.

CHAPTER ELEVEN

I hadn't cried myself to sleep since my parents had been murdered and Vasilia had betrayed me as a child, but that's what happened. I thought I might dream about the massacre, but I fell down into the blackness, and I didn't see or hear anything for the rest of the night.

The sharp point of a sword kissing my throat woke me the next morning.

At first, I thought some spider was crawling on me and tickling my skin with its tiny legs. I tried to flick it away, but it kept coming back. Slowly, I realized that spiders weren't that hard and sharp, and that someone else was in here. Someone who smelled cold, crisp, and clean, just like the magic that had coated the front door, along with a strong undercurrent of hot, peppery anger.

I opened my eyes and looked up to find the magier of the house looming over me.

He wore a tailored black tunic that stretched across his firm, muscled chest, along with black leggings and boots. A long dark gray coat with silver buttons hung off his broad shoulders. It reminded me of the uniform that Lord Hans had worn to the luncheon.

The magier looked to be in his early thirties, with sharp cheekbones, a straight nose, and a strong jaw. His short dark brown hair gleamed under the fluorestones, and his eyes were a light, bright, piercing blue—the same blue as the magic that had shocked me last night. He was quite handsome, with a powerful, authoritative air that made him even more attractive. A natural-born leader, and not just because of his magier power. I drew in another breath, tasting his scent again. He even smelled good, like crushed ice mixed with vanilla and a hint of spice.

"And a good morning to you too," I drawled. "Do you greet all your guests this way?"

"You are not a guest," he growled. "In case you missed it, this is the part where you start begging for your life."

I laughed.

After everything that had happened yesterday, the threat of this man running me through with his sword didn't bother me at all.

"Well, go ahead then," I said. "Although it would be a shame to ruin this jacket with my blood. Is this Andvarian silkfleece? It's exquisite. Not to mention the pillow. Floresian down, right?"

I wasn't sure why I said that. Maybe yesterday's horrors had addled my brain. Or maybe I was simply tired of biting my tongue. Of always having to do and say the polite thing, the nice thing, instead of what I really thought and felt. And what had all that politeness and nicety gotten me? *Nothing*—absolutely nothing but memories of death in my mind, screams echoing in my ears, and the stench of blood in my nose.

So, no, I wasn't going to cower, and I certainly wasn't going to beg for anything, not even my own miserable life. No, from now on, I was going to do and say exactly what I wanted, when I wanted, and damn the consequences. It was the first step in keeping that promise I had made to myself to never be weak and helpless again.

"Who are you?" he growled again. "How did you get in here?"

"The door was open."

It wasn't a total lie. The door had been open . . . after I had snuffed out all his lightning.

The magier's eyes narrowed, and he dug the point of his sword a little deeper into my throat. Not enough to break the skin, but almost. I resisted the urge to retreat and sink deeper into the pillow propped up behind my head.

"That door is never, ever open," he said in a soft, deadly voice. "So how did you get in here? What do you want?"

"Well, I, for one, would like to have a civilized conversation instead of all these vague threats that you keep spewing."

He turned the sword point the tiniest bit, like it was a nail he was about to hammer into my throat. "My threats are anything but vague."

"Perhaps *vague* was the wrong word. How about *nonexistent*?"

He blinked in surprise. "Nonexistent?"

I shrugged. Well, as much as I could with his sword still at my throat. "If you really wanted to kill me, you would have done it while I was sleeping. Not woken me up in such dramatic fashion."

He didn't say anything. He couldn't argue with my logic.

"So, why don't you let me up, and we can have a normal conversation like two adults."

My gaze locked with his, and I carefully reached out and touched my finger to his sword. He tensed, but he let me slowly push the blade away from my throat. After a moment, he stepped back, although he kept his weapon raised, ready to stab me if I did anything he didn't like.

I scooted out of the tight space and into the middle of the floor, but then I realized how cold, heavy, and numb my legs were.

"Well?" the magier demanded. "What are you waiting for? You're the one who wanted to talk, so get up."

"Um, this is a bit embarrassing, but my legs are asleep."

A cold, evil light flared in his eyes. "Really? Well, let me help with that."

He snapped up his hand, and blue lightning crackled on his fingertips. Before I could move or react, he stepped forward.

And then the bastard shocked me.

I shrieked as his magic slammed into my legs. In an instant, my limbs went from cold, heavy, and numb to hot, twitching, and burning. I started to smother his power with my immunity, but I thought better of it and gritted my teeth instead. I might not be at Seven Spire anymore, but I couldn't let anyone know about my immunity, especially not some magier.

I expected him to keep shocking me, but after about fifteen seconds, he released his hold on his magic, and the lightning on his hand vanished.

"How is that, highness?" he mocked. "Are your legs feeling a bit livelier now?"

It took me a moment to unclench my jaw. "Oh, yes. Thank you ever so much."

A razor-thin smile creased his face. It made him look even more handsome. Bastard. "You're quite welcome. Now get up."

My legs felt like they were on fire, but I reached out, grabbed hold of one of the weapons racks, and pulled myself to my feet. Then the magier and I faced each other.

In addition to the sword still clenched in his hand, a dagger gleamed in a slot on his black leather belt, and I got the impression that he could wield both weapons as easily as he did his magic. But perhaps the most curious thing was the fact that he wasn't wearing the black-swan emblem. No crest of any sort adorned his clothes. Odd. You would think that the magier would wear his troupe's symbol.

His icy gaze swept over me. Once he determined that I didn't have any weapons, he focused on my face again. I raised my hand to my cheek, wondering what he was staring at, and winced as my fingers touched the puffy bruise. Oh, that.

"I'll ask you again," he said. "What do you want?"

"I want to speak to Serilda Swanson. She's the one who runs things around here, right?"

A speculative look filled his eyes, and another razor-thin smile creased his face. Handsome and smug. A dangerous combination.

"You want to talk to Serilda?" he drawled. "I'm happy to arrange that, highness."

The magier grabbed my arm. A firm grip, but not tight enough to bruise. Seemed he had a bit of manners after all, despite shocking the shit out of me. I was still wearing his jacket, and before he could drag me away, I leaned down, snatched the pillow off the floor, and stuffed it under my other arm.

"What are you doing?" he snapped.

I shrugged. "I should get something out of sleeping on the floor. Besides, do you really want it back after I've drooled on it all night?"

He opened his mouth to argue, but once again, no words came out. He sighed and shook his head, admitting defeat.

The magier strong-armed me out of the house and onto the street. The sun was up, but it was still early, and only a few folks were moving through the compound. Two men were sitting on a bench outside the dining hall, drinking mochana. The rich, steaming fumes tickled my nose.

"Who do you have there, Sullivan?" one of the men asked. "Another runaway?"

They both snickered. Must be some kind of inside joke. Although I supposed that I *was* a runaway, despite the fact that I was too old for that sort of thing.

"Something like that," he muttered, and muscled me on past them.

"Sullivan?" I said. "So the mysterious magier has a name."

"Yes," he growled. "My name is Lucas Sullivan. Not that it's any of your business."

"Sullivan is a bit formal, don't you think? Especially after I've spent the night drooling on your pillow. I'll call you Sully. I think that it's appropriate in this stage of our relationship." I was rather enjoying this whole speaking-my-mind thing, especially when it came to needling him. Besides, words were the only way that I could wound him.

His nostrils flared, and his jaw clenched. Not a fan of nicknames. "I wouldn't worry about it, highness. You're not going to be here long enough to call me anything."

"We'll see."

We kept walking. Eventually, we turned off the street and

stepped onto a path that led around the side of the dining hall and into a series of connected gardens with towering trees, winter flowers, black wrought-iron benches, and fluorestone streetlamps. Sullivan marched me through the gardens and across a stone bridge that arched over a stream that disappeared into the trees.

The path led to a three-story manor house surrounded by more trees and flowers, along with an iron gate. Stone turrets topped with silver spires stood at all four corners of the house. Serilda Swanson had to live here, since it was much nicer and larger than the other homes.

The arena, the other buildings, the gardens, and now this manor house. Running a gladiator troupe paid far better than I'd realized. How else could Serilda have gotten her hands on such a large piece of property in the city? Much less built all of this?

Sullivan knocked on the front door, but he didn't wait for a response before opening it and dragging me inside. Stained-glass lamps, gilded silver mirrors, and dark mahogany furniture filled the rooms. Oh, yes. Serilda had done very well for herself since leaving the queen's guard.

Sullivan strong-armed me into a library that took up the back half of the manor. The furnishings in here were as fine as everything else, with a crystal chandelier dangling from the ceiling, bookcases covering two of the walls, and a large mahogany desk perched in the center. But the most prominent thing was the white pennant that featured a black swan with a blue eye and beak that adorned the back wall.

An impressive collection of weapons adorned the rest of that wall. Swords, maces, daggers, axes, spears, and shields glinted in the early-morning sunlight streaming in through the windows. Each object featured a variety of jewels and was polished to a high gloss.

I started to look past the weapons when I noticed a separate set tucked away in the corner—a sword, a dagger, and a shield. Unlike the other weapons, with their fist-size rubies, emeralds, and more, this set boasted only a few small jewels, although I was too far away to tell exactly what the gems were.

Several delicious scents tickled my nose, and I glanced to my right. Silver platters piled with scrambled eggs, black-pepper-crusted bacon, and fried fruit pies perched on a table, along with carafes of mochana, hot chocolate, iced teas, and juices. My stomach growled, reminding me that I hadn't eaten anything since those two bags of cornucopia last night. But my gnawing hunger was the least of my worries, so I focused on the people in the library.

Cho Yamato, the ringmaster, was standing next to the table, surveying the breakfast spread with a critical gaze. Paloma, the gladiator, was sitting in a chair in front of the desk, next to another female gladiator with auburn hair and light brown eyes. Emilie, a mutt with speed magic. I remembered her from the show. She had been one of the few who had actually challenged Paloma and made the other woman work for her victory.

And finally, there was Serilda Swanson, who was sitting in a white plush chair behind the desk.

She was wearing a fresh white tunic with the same black-thread swan design that she had had on last night. She was tallying numbers in a ledger, and several bags of gold, silver, and bronze crowns lined the desk. I drew in a breath, tasting her scent. Sharp, hard, and metallic, like coldiron mixed with blood. A warrior's scent.

Sullivan shoved me forward, and I staggered to a stop on top of a white rug that I had already ruined with my muddy boots.

Serilda didn't look up from her ledger. "Yes?"

"I found her sleeping in my house," Sullivan growled.

"I didn't realize that having a woman in your bed was such an unusual occurrence, Lucas."

I hid a grin. Seemed like I wasn't the only one who enjoyed needling the magier.

Sullivan stabbed his finger at me. "It is when I come home this morning and find her snoring in the corner."

"I don't usually snore," I said. "It must have been your fine Floresian pillow."

Sullivan's right eye twitched. So did the fingers on his right hand, as though he wanted to shock me with his lightning again.

My quip finally made Serilda look up at me. Her short blond hair was slicked back from her face, smoky shadow brought out her dark blue eyes, and red gloss covered her lips. She was quite beautiful—except for the sunburst-shaped scar near the corner of her right eye.

I had seen more than one fight between noble ladies, so I recognized the mark for what it was. Someone had backhanded Serilda, and her ring had left behind a lasting impression. Still, any bone master could have fixed it, so why have a scar like that? Especially on your face, where everyone could see it.

Of course I didn't know the answer, so I studied the rest of her. The top few buttons of her tunic were undone, revealing a small black-swan pendant that rested in the hollow of her throat. The jet shards that made up the swan's body glittered with every breath she took, as did its blue tearstone eye and beak, making it seem as though the swan was floating on top of the steady pulse beating in her throat. Jet was another jewel that deflected magic, although not nearly as well as tearstone. Interesting. I would have thought that a famed warrior like Serilda would have worn rubies to increase her strength, or emeralds to increase her speed.

But the most striking thing about her pendant was the fact that Alvis had made it.

The jeweled shards. The simple, elegant design. The delicate silver chain. I recognized his work immediately. My heart lifted, but I doused my hope with cold reason. Serilda had been Cordelia's personal guard for years. She could have gotten that pendant—and her matching swan crest—from Alvis at any time. It didn't mean anything, not really, and it certainly didn't indicate whether I could trust her.

Cho also stared at me, and Paloma and Emilie turned in their seats so they could see me too. I shifted on my feet and tried not to grimace at how dirty and disheveled I was.

"And how exactly did she get into your house?" Serilda murmured. "I thought you kept all the doors and windows locked with your magic."

"I do," Sullivan growled. "I don't know how she got in. I thought you might want to question her before I throw her out."

Not exactly a warm welcome. I chewed on my lip, debating what to do. Cordelia had told me that I could trust Serilda, but right now, I didn't trust anyone. Not after watching Vasilia, Nox, Felton, and Maeven slaughter the rest of the royals. For all I knew, Vasilia could have Serilda in her pocket too.

"Why would I want to question her? She didn't break into *my* house." Serilda waved her hand. "Take her to the front gate and throw her out if you're so inclined. Just make sure that she doesn't come back."

I should have realized that something like this would happen, but I didn't know how to stop it. Panic rose up in me. If Sullivan threw me out of the compound, I didn't know what I would do or where I would go.

I moved toward the desk. "No, you can't do that—"

Before I could take another step, Paloma surged up out of her chair, grabbed my arm, spun her body into mine, and flipped me over her shoulder. I landed hard on my back on the floor, and a fresh wave of pain shot through my battered body. I also lost my grip on the pillow that had been stuffed under my arm, and it rolled end over end across the floor before silently plopping to a stop.

Sullivan grinned again, while Emilie snickered, both of them enjoying my suffering. Serilda made another note in her ledger, while Cho grabbed a fried pie from one of the platters. The sudden bit of drama bored them.

Paloma bent down over me. Not only was she a skilled gladiator, but she was also quite pretty with her braided blond hair and beautiful bronze skin. I focused on the morph mark on her neck—a snarling ogre face with the same golden amber eyes that Paloma herself had. The ogre reminded me of the one on Lady Xenia's neck, right down to the lock of blond hair that curled around its face. Both Paloma and the ogre regarded me with a flat expression.

As much as I would have liked to lie still until the pain subsided, it would be a sign of weakness, so I forced myself to roll over onto my knees and push myself up and onto my feet. I might have wobbled a bit—I might have wobbled quite a bit—but I lifted my chin and faced them all again.

"You can't throw me out," I said.

Serilda arched an eyebrow. "Paloma just proved that she can throw you out quite easily."

"You don't understand."

She rolled her eyes, set down her pen, and leaned back in her chair. "Let me guess. You came to the show last night, hid out in the compound, and now you want to join the troupe."

"Yes! Exactly! I want to join the troupe."

They laughed at me.

Sullivan, Emilie, Cho, Paloma, even the ogre on Paloma's neck opened its lips and silently chuckled. The longer they laughed, the angrier I got. It was just like being back at the palace and listening to Vasilia and her friends snicker about how small, shabby, and insignificant everything about me was in comparison to them.

The only one who didn't laugh was Serilda, who watched me closely, her blue gaze taking in my clenched fists and stiff posture. But even more than that, I felt like she was looking past my bruised face and false bravado and actually seeing *into* me, and I had to stop myself from shivering at her intense scrutiny. She waved her hand, and the others quit laughing. She stared at me another moment, then waved her hand again.

"All right then. Tell me your life story, girl, such as it is."

I bristled. I hadn't been a *girl* since my parents had died, but I swallowed my anger. This was my one chance to convince her to let me stay. My mind spun, trying to figure out how to tell her what had happened with Isobel, Cordelia, and Vasilia without revealing my true identity.

"I don't have all day," Serilda said. "Now or never."

"My . . . foster mother recently passed away, as did our . . .

mistress, the woman we both served. The new mistress wasn't as . . . kind as the old one had been." It wasn't exactly a lie. I had just left out some pertinent details. Names, dates, places, murders.

"So this new mistress is the one who gave you that nasty shiner?" Serilda asked.

"No, not exactly. She told her . . . men to give it to me."

"So you ran away from home, came here, and now you want to join the troupe so you can get your revenge on her," Serilda finished in a bored voice.

Revenge? Of course I wanted revenge on Vasilia, but I also knew that I could never, ever get it. She was the fucking queen now, with practically unlimited money, magic, and resources. I couldn't have gotten close to her, much less actually hurt her, not even if I'd had an army at my disposal.

Serilda shook her head, and a little bubble of laughter escaped her lips. Somehow, that small, soft sound was far more mocking than all the others' guffaws put together.

"What's so funny?" I growled.

"Do you know how many people have told me this same sob story? Someone did them wrong, and they want to learn how to fight, become a great gladiator, and win countless riches, along with the adoration of the public, all so they can take their revenge on their enemy." Serilda laughed again. "It's all so ridiculous that it might as well be a fairy tale, or a story in the penny papers that the children sell on the street corners every morning. The only thing that would make it even more cliché is if you claimed that you were some long-lost princess, desperate to become a warrior so you can reclaim your kingdom from evildoers."

Vasilia's smug, triumphant face flashed before my eyes. That was exactly what I wanted, and it was utterly ridiculous, like Serilda had said.

"I'm no bloody *princess*." I spat out the word. "But, yes, I want to become a gladiator. Not for revenge, but for myself. So that no one can ever do what my . . . mistress did to me again. So that no one can ever hurt me like she did again."

Serilda's eyes narrowed, although her gaze was as sharp and blue as the eye of the swan on the pennant on the wall behind her. Once again, I got the feeling that she could see much more than I wanted her to. "And why should I give you a chance instead of someone else?"

A small opening, but I latched onto it. "Because I'll do anything you want."

She arched her eyebrow again. "Anything?"

I lifted my chin. "Anything."

"I almost think you mean that."

I gave her a thin smile. "If there's one thing that you should never question, it's my resolve. My new mistress . . . humiliated me. Nothing you could ever do would be worse than what she put me through. *Nothing.*"

"That sounds like a challenge."

I shrugged. "Call it what you will."

She kept staring at me, and I met her gaze with a steady one of my own. Sullivan, Emilie, Paloma, and Cho glanced back and forth between us.

Serilda leaned forward and steepled her hands together on her desk. "Well, you obviously have no fighting skills, given how easily Paloma tossed you around. So what can you do?" She examined my face, neck, and hands. "Are you a morph? Magier? Master? Mutt?"

"Mutt."

"With what skills?"

I sighed, knowing that they were going to laugh at me again. "I have an enhanced sense of smell."

And laugh they did, long, hard, and loud.

"So you can't fight, and you don't have any real magic," Serilda said when everyone's laughter finally died down. "That makes you officially useless."

Maybe it was the faint, sneering note in her voice, or the fact that everyone at the palace had treated me that way for so long, or the hard truth that I had thought of myself that way more than once, but my hands clenched into tight fists. "I am *not* useless."

"Then what *can* you do?" she asked. "What can you do better than anyone else already here?"

I opened my mouth, but nothing came out. I didn't have an answer. Oh, there were lots of things that I could do better than anyone else here. Dancing, curtsying, engaging in polite, inane chitchat about art, music, and books. But I couldn't tell Serilda that, much less where I had learned all those skills. Besides, she was right. They were completely useless here.

Sullivan, Emilie, and Paloma were still watching me, waiting to see what I would say. So was the morph mark on Paloma's neck. The ogre was frowning as if it felt sorry for me, telling me how much trouble I was in and how I needed to come up with an answer—any answer.

"Well?" Serilda snapped. "What can you do?"

Desperate, I glanced over at Cho just in time to see him sink his teeth into a fruit pie. He made a face, as though it tasted bad, and set it down on the platter with the others.

"I can make pies."

The words popped out of my mouth before I could stop them, but they weren't a lie. I *could* make pies, thanks to all the hours that I'd spent with Isobel in the kitchen.

"Pies? Really? That's your big skill?" Serilda said. "Anyone can make a mere pie."

I stepped forward. Paloma started toward me, but I held up my hand, and she stopped. I made sure that she wasn't going to flip me over her shoulder again, then looked at Serilda.

"Not just *mere* pies. The most delicious pies you've ever tasted. Buttery crusts. Sweet fruit fillings. Decadent mousses. Spiced nuts that will make your tongue tingle with delight." I had heard more than one overwrought, flowery speech at the palace, and I made my descriptions as rich and inviting as, well, pudding in a pie crust.

Silence descended over the library, and I wondered if I had exaggerated too much.

"Those sound like my kind of pies." To my surprise, Cho was the one who spoke.

Serilda snorted. "Don't encourage her."

Cho strolled over and sat down on the corner of her desk. He looked to be in his midforties, the same as Serilda, and was a few inches taller than me, with a lean, wiry body. He reached up and scratched his neck, drawing my attention to the morph mark there—a dragon's face made of ruby-red scales. Cho might not be as big and strong as Sullivan, but in his own way, he was just as dangerous.

"Tell me more about these pies. What flavor is your specialty?"

"Cranberry-apple." It was the first flavor I thought of, since I had made so many of them yesterday.

His black eyes gleamed, as did those of the dragon on his neck. "That's my favorite."

Serilda sighed. "Forget it, Cho. We already have a baker who can make pies."

"No, we don't. Kiko stayed behind in Andvari with her lover, remember?" He stabbed his finger at the breakfast platters. "I don't know who made those, but they are definitely *not* pies. I wouldn't feed those sour, soggy things to the gargoyles."

"Well, I don't feel like taking in any more strays, especially not to appease your sweet tooth," Serilda grumbled back.

I opened my mouth to protest that I wasn't a stray, but Paloma shook her head, warning me to keep quiet.

Serilda glared at Cho, who smiled back at her, as did the dragon on his neck. After several moments, Serilda rolled her eyes again and gave a sharp nod.

"A test?" Cho asked, an eager note in his voice.

She sighed. "A test."

He clapped his hands together and hopped off the desk. "Excellent! Let's do it now."

Serilda nodded at Sullivan, who stepped toward me. I leaned down and snatched my stolen pillow off the floor before he latched onto my arm again.

"What's going on?" I asked, thinking that they were going to throw me out after all.

Serilda got to her feet and gave me a thin smile. "We're going to see how good your pies really are."

CHAPTER TWELVE

Serilda walked out of the library, followed by Cho, Paloma, and Emilie.

"I hope your pies are as good as you think they are, highness," Sullivan said. "Cho doesn't like to be disappointed. And neither does his dragon."

I got the message loud and clear. If Cho didn't like the pie, his inner dragon would come out and snack on my bones.

Sullivan marched me out of the manor, and we followed the others through the gardens and to the dining hall. Sullivan opened one of the doors and shoved me inside.

The building was split into two sections. The front was a large, open dining space, with long, rectangular wooden tables and chairs in the center. Other, smaller tables ran along either wall, all of them covered with platters of eggs, bacon, hotcakes, and more. A wooden partition that was about three feet high separated the dining area from the kitchen in the back.

Dozens of people were sitting at the tables, chowing down on their breakfasts before going about their day's work. They were dressed in regular tunics, leggings, and boots, instead of the glitzy costumes and glamorous makeup they had sported during the show. Everyone glanced curiously at our group, but they went back to their food and conversations.

We walked through the dining space, pushed through a swinging gate in the wooden partition, and stepped into the kitchen. Preparation stations in the center, ovens lining one wall, metal chillers against another, sinks full of dirty dishes in the back, workers scurrying everywhere. My heart ached. It was so much like the palace kitchen that I half expected Isobel to appear with a smile on her face and a plate of cookies in her hand.

But Isobel was dead, and I would be too if I didn't focus.

A man standing at one of the prep stations spotted Serilda. He was tall, with a broad, thick body; short, curly black hair; dark brown eyes; and ebony skin. He was wearing a long-sleeve white tunic like the other workers, but the swan crest stitched in black thread over his heart marked him as the kitchen steward. Given the exceptionally large knife in his hand, and the garlicky tang of magic that wafted off him, he was a cook master as well.

He finished chopping an onion, then wiped his hands on a cloth and came over to us. "Serilda. What's going on?"

"Theroux, this woman says that she can make pies," Cho said in an eager voice. "Cranberry-apple pies."

Theroux's lips pressed together. He seemed to be as well acquainted with and unhappy about Cho's love of pie as Serilda was. Theroux's gaze raked over me the way that everyone else's had. At this point, I was used to the constant scrutiny and silent judgments.

"You could use a new baker now that Kiko is gone," Cho

said in a wheedling tone. "Especially since pies and pastries aren't your specialties."

Theroux gave him a flat look, but it didn't faze the other man.

"Let's see what she can do," Serilda said. "Then we'll talk about whether she can stay."

Theroux didn't like that much either, but she was the boss, so he nodded to her and crooked his finger at me. Sullivan let go of my arm. I shoved my pillow into his chest, and he instinctively grabbed it.

"Be a dear, and hold this for me, Sully."

His eyes narrowed, but I gave him a sunny smile, then followed Theroux into the back of the kitchen. Theroux gestured at one of the sinks, and I rolled up my sleeves and washed my hands. My hair was a mess, half in and half out of its original braid, but I didn't have time to fix it, so I wet it and smoothed it back away from my face.

While I cleaned myself up, Theroux moved around the kitchen, pulling out butter, flour, and more, along with bowls, a rolling pin, and measuring cups and spoons. He lined everything up in a neat row on an empty countertop. The other kitchen workers eyed us, but they soon returned to their chores.

Theroux snapped his fingers at me. I bristled at the summons, but I walked over and stared at the ingredients and the utensils. Yesterday, I had been doing this exact same thing with Isobel. If only I could go back and change what had happened to her and everyone else. Hot tears pricked my eyes, but I squeezed them shut before the treacherous drops could escape.

I couldn't afford to let anyone see my tears.

"Any time you're ready, highness," Sullivan said in a snide voice.

My hands curled around the counter. The stone was smooth and worn, just like the one at the palace. But I wasn't at the palace anymore, and I had to make the best damn pie that I'd ever made, or I would be kicked out of the compound, at the very least, and possibly become dragon food, at the very worst. So I pushed my pain, sadness, and heartbreak away and thought about Isobel and everything that she had taught me. Then I let out a breath, opened my eyes, and reached for the butter to start making the crust.

Paloma and Emilie left the kitchen, but Cho, Serilda, and Sullivan stayed and watched me work. Cho with obvious excitement, and Serilda and Sullivan with open suspicion. It reminded me of the time a few weeks ago when I had built gingerbread houses for the children of several Bellonan senators who had traveled to the palace to celebrate the yuletide season. I supposed that I should be grateful that my audience today wasn't trying to run off with all the spearmint sticks, black-forest gumdrops, and cherry candy canes like the kids had.

I ignored my watchers and mixed the ingredients together for the crust. Once it was ready, I rolled out the crust, cut it into a large circle, and draped it over a metal pie tin. Theroux, in particular, studied every move I made, assessing my technique.

I held up one of the scraps of dough. "Would you like to taste it?"

He crossed his arms over his chest and gave me another flat stare. I shrugged and popped the piece into my mouth. I was so hungry that I didn't care that the dough was raw. I would have eaten the rest of the pieces if I didn't need them for the lattice pattern on the top.

When I finished with the dough, I grabbed a paring knife,

sliced the bloodcrisp apples, and placed them in a bowl with the honey cranberries, along with cinnamon, sugar, and more. I combined everything, then poured the filling into the crust. Then I looked at the bottles of flavored sugars, spices, and salts on the counter, ready to give the pie its finishing touch. Finally, I turned to Theroux.

"Where are the orange flakes?"

Cho looked at me. "What are you talking about?"

"You can't make a proper cranberry-apple pie without orange flakes." I turned to Theroux again. "Don't tell me that you don't have any. Why, I would think that a fine kitchen steward such as yourself would have all the appropriate seasonings on hand."

Theroux's dark eyes narrowed, and Cho, Sullivan, and Serilda looked back and forth between the two of us. Everyone recognized my words as the insult they were. Tongues had always been sharper than razors at Seven Spire, and I wielded mine as well as anyone. Besides, I had learned a long time ago that just because someone saw me as a useless decoration didn't mean that I had to act like one, and that people respected their enemies far more than those that they thought they could walk all over.

Cho laughed and clapped Theroux on the back. "She's got you there, my friend."

Theroux gave the other man a sour look, but he went over to one of the cabinets and returned with a bottle of orange flakes, which he shoved into my hand.

I pulled the stopper out of the bottle. The sweet citrus tang punched me in the nose and made me think of Isobel again, but I forced the memories away. I leaned forward and went around the pie, carefully sprinkling on the orange flakes. One, two, three light taps on the bottle, like Isobel had taught me. The orange crystals landed on top of the luscious fruit filling and slowly melted into the mixture.

"That's it?" Theroux asked, a challenging note in his voice. "That's all you're going to use?"

I capped the bottle and shoved it back at him. "Yes."

I arranged the final strips of crust onto the top of the pie, creating a pretty lattice pattern, then slid it into one of the hot ovens and set a timer that was sitting on the counter.

I expected the others to drift away to their chores, work, or whatever they did during the day, but Cho, Sullivan, and Serilda stayed in the kitchen, alternating between watching me and the pie baking in the oven. I didn't want to stand around and be stared at, so I grabbed the dirty bowls and utensils and moved away from the counter.

Sullivan stepped in front of me. "Where do you think you're going?"

I held up the bowls. "Where does it look like I'm going? Over to the sinks to wash the dishes. Unless, of course, *you* want to wash them for me, Sully."

He glared at me, but he moved out of my way. I dumped the dishes in one of the sinks and turned on the hot water.

Theroux watched me for a few moments before barking out orders to the rest of the staff and going back to his own prep station. Cho started talking to Sullivan about the merits of cranberry-apple versus plain apple pie, although the magier just grunted in response. Serilda leaned a shoulder against the wall and stared at me, a speculative look on her face, as if I had surprised her. I stared back at her a moment, letting her know that her silent scrutiny didn't bother me, then washed the dishes.

I had just finished drying off the last spoon when the timer dinged. I slid a pair of mitts onto my hands, took the pie out of the oven, and set the hot tin on the counter.

The crust was a perfect golden brown, and the fruit filling bubbled up like ruby lava in between the gaps in the lattice strips. I drew in a breath, tasting the scents in the air. The buttery crust, the sugary fruit, the hint of orange that curled through it all. The aromas were the same as they had been in the palace kitchen, and this pie would be just as good as those had been. I smiled, even as more sadness surged through me. Isobel would have been so proud of me.

"That looks amazing!" Cho reached for the pie, but I smacked his hand away.

"You have to let it cool first, or the fruit filling will run everywhere. And you don't want to burn your tongue."

He frowned, as did the morph mark on his neck. I wondered if I might end up being dragon food after all, but his frown melted into a sheepish grin. Even his dragon grinned at me, and I found myself grinning back at both of them.

When the pie had cooled, I cut the first piece and handed it to Cho, who dug his fork into it. He chewed, tasting the flavors, then swallowed. Everyone looked at him, but Cho ignored them and shoved another bite of pie into his mouth.

"Mmm . . ." he mumbled. "So good. She stays, Serilda. She definitely stays!"

I sighed with relief. They could still throw me out of the compound, but at least I wouldn't wind up getting eaten.

Serilda rolled her eyes. "Let's see what the rest of us think of it first."

I dished up pieces to her, Theroux, and Sullivan. The two men dug in right away.

"It's good." Theroux's voice was far less hostile than before. "Not as good as a cook master's, but it's close." He looked at me. "What else can you make?"

I shrugged. "Cakes, cookies, candies."

"Cakes *and* cookies *and* candies?" Cho sighed and clutched his empty plate to his chest. "Be still my heart."

Serilda ignored his theatrics. "Lucas?"

Sullivan had almost polished off his piece of pie, and he popped the last bite into his mouth with a guilty look. He shrugged. "It will do."

Anger spurted through me. He had loved the bloody pie, given how quickly he had inhaled it. He was just being difficult because I had annoyed him before, and he was still clutching my pillow under his arm.

"What do you think, Serilda?" Theroux asked.

She finally took a bite. For a moment, her eyes brightened, but then she swallowed, set her plate on the counter, and pushed it away. My heart sank. She hadn't liked it.

"I think that it's the best pie I've had in a long, long time."

Her words surprised me, especially since they didn't match her expression. Her eyes dimmed, her lips twisted, and her shoulders slumped. She almost seemed . . . sad.

But the moment passed, and she was her usual cool, detached self again. Serilda looked at Cho, Theroux, and Sullivan. Cho smiled, Theroux shrugged, and Sullivan shook his head. One vote for, one neutral, and one against. Up to Serilda then.

Finally, she turned to me. "What's your name?"

I opened my mouth to say *Everleigh,* but then I remembered that I couldn't use that name ever again. Lady Everleigh Saffira Winter Blair was dead, along with the rest of the royals.

"Well?" Serilda said. "You do have a name, don't you?"

A name. I needed a name right bloody *now* before she became any more suspicious than she already was. My gaze darted around the kitchen, looking for inspiration. I focused on Cho, who was cutting himself a second piece of pie. And I realized that I did have a name—the one I had always wanted.

"Evie." I looked at Serilda again. "My name is Evie."

Her eyes narrowed. She had noticed my hesitation and knew that I was lying, but I lifted my chin and stared back at her.

"Well, then, *Evie,* let me warmly welcome you to the Black Swan." She gave me a thin smile that was neither warm nor welcoming. "I suggest that you get busy making another pie, since Cho is going to eat the rest of this one right now."

CHAPTER THIRTEEN

Serilda was right. Cho had polished off the first pie by the time that I slid a second one into the oven.

Cho smiled as he gobbled up the last few bites of the pie, and the dragon on his neck winked at me. Well, at least someone around here liked me. Everyone else? Not so much, judging from the suspicious stares that Theroux, Sullivan, and Serilda kept giving me.

But I had done enough to earn a spot in the kitchen, because Theroux stabbed his knife at me. "Come back at four this afternoon to help with dinner. And don't be late."

That was hours from now. What was I supposed to do until then? Judging from Sullivan's smug smile, it wasn't going to be pleasant.

"Yes, sir."

Theroux glowered at me, thinking that I was being sarcastic, but I kept my gaze steady on his, letting him know that I wouldn't be intimidated. The kitchen steward might be my new boss, but I wasn't going to bow and scrape to him like I had to Felton. I wasn't going to do that ever again, no matter how tenuous it made my position here. At this point, my pride was the only thing that I had left.

After a few seconds, Theroux went back to slicing vegetables.

Serilda glanced at Cho. "If you've finished stuffing your face, perhaps we can finally get on with the day's business?"

He scraped up a few final crumbs and popped them into his mouth. Cho glanced longingly at the pie in the oven, but it wasn't close to being done, so he sighed and set his empty plate on the counter. "If I must."

"You must." Serilda looked at Sullivan. "You know what to do with her."

He nodded, and Serilda strode out of the kitchen. Cho smiled at me again, then followed her.

Sullivan shoved my stolen pillow into my chest. "Here you go. You're going to need this."

"For what?"

He gave me another one of his sharp, devastating smiles. "To cry into after I get done with you."

A bit of magic flashed in his eyes, making them burn bright and blue. He was trying to intimidate me. A week ago, it probably would have worked. But not now.

"Oh, Sully," I drawled. "Are you threatening me? How adorable."

I had already antagonized him plenty, and the wise thing to do would have been to keep my mouth shut. But I was still pissed at his dismissive comment about my pie, so I stepped forward, close enough that the pillow in my hand brushed up against his solid, muscled chest, and stared him down, just like I had Theroux.

Not the response Sullivan expected or wanted, judging from how quickly the magic vanished from his gaze.

A bark of laughter rang out, and we both looked over at Theroux. The kitchen steward cleared his throat, dropped his gaze, and started chopping his vegetables again.

Sullivan glared at him another second before turning back to me. "Follow me, highness, and we'll see how tough you really are."

"That sounds like a challenge." I waved my pillow out to the side. "Lead the way, Sully."

His right eye twitched, along with his hand, as if he was thinking about shocking the shit out of me with his lightning again, but Sullivan restrained himself, whirled around, and stormed out of the kitchen.

We walked through the dining hall, which was empty now, since breakfast had come and gone while I'd been making the pies, and stepped outside.

Sullivan set off at a quick pace, and I had to hurry to keep up with him. Long-legged bastard. I expected him to keep stewing in his silent anger, but he started talking.

"You've already seen the dining hall. Breakfast is at eight, dinner is at six. You'll report to the kitchen every morning and afternoon to help Theroux and the staff prepare meals for everyone, as well as cornucopia and other treats to sell to the arena crowds. We host a matinee on Saturday afternoon, then the two main shows on Saturday and Sunday nights. You get two meals a day, clothing, and a bed in the barracks. Every-one gets a cut of the ticket and food sales. The gladiators can earn more, depending on how well they fight in the arena. The compound is our home base, but if you stay long enough, you'll come with us when we go on tour to Andvari later this year."

I doubted that anyone in Bellona would want to go to Andvari after word of Queen Cordelia's assassination got out, but of course I couldn't say that.

"Whether they are a cook master, an acrobat, or a gladiator, everyone around here pulls their own weight without complaint. In case you haven't guessed by now, I'm the troupe enforcer."

"What does that mean?" I asked.

"It means that I enforce the rules. And that if you make any trouble, if you lie, cheat, steal, or anything else, I will personally fry you to a crisp before throwing your rotting carcass out onto the street. Understand?"

I opened my mouth, but he walked on before I could answer. Definitely a rhetorical question.

He pointed out the structures on this side of the street. "The gargoyles, strixes, and other creatures are housed in those stables, the bone masters are over there, and don't step into that building without knocking or an acrobat will likely tumble into you. Or worse, one of the wire walkers will lose his balance and land right on top of you."

We kept going until we reached a three-foot-high stone wall close to Sullivan's house. Several iron gates were set into the wall, which formed a large circle around a flat clearing of hard-packed dirt that was the same shape and size as the center ring inside the arena.

"After you finish your morning work in the kitchen, you will change into your fighting leathers and train with the rest of the gladiators," Sullivan said.

"Serilda said that I wasn't a fighter," I said in a snide voice. "So why bother training me?"

"Everyone trains until Serilda says otherwise. She'll decide whether we can make a fighter out of you or not." He eyed me. "My money is on not, though."

My money was on not too. Captain Auster hadn't had any luck training me. Why would this be any different?

"There's only one rule here—what happens in the ring, stays in the ring," Sullivan said. "Someone knocks you down or hurts you, too bad. That's what happens to gladiators. You fight, you bleed, and sometimes, you die. Don't come crying to me about any of it, and don't take it outside the ring. You have a problem with someone, then you solve it with your sword, shield, and fists in there. Got it?"

Another rhetorical question.

The gladiators were already here, dressed in their pale gray fighting leathers and sandals. Some were talking and relaxing on benches that were pushed up against the wall, while others were clustered around the racks of swords, shields, and other weapons at one end of the ring. A blackboard covered with names and numbers stood a few feet away from the weapons racks. It must have denoted the gladiators' rankings, since *Paloma* was scrawled across the top in white chalk, with *Emilie* right below it.

Both women were already inside the ring. Paloma was sitting on a bench, talking with several other gladiators, while Emilie stood in front of a weapons rack, pulling out first one sword, then another, as if trying to figure out which one would give her an edge.

"Why aren't they fighting yet? What are they waiting for?" I asked.

"Me."

Sullivan pushed through the nearest gate, walked over to one of the benches, and shrugged out of his long gray coat. Apparently, being the troupe enforcer also involved training the gladiators, as well as disciplining them. The warriors all snapped to attention and faced him.

I had no choice but to follow Sullivan into the ring. Someone snickered, and I realized that I was still carrying that pillow around like an unruly child. I grimaced. I was getting tired of people laughing at me, but I tightened my grip on the pillow. I had stolen it fair and square, and I wasn't giving it up.

Sullivan rolled up his tunic sleeves, revealing brown, muscled forearms. The whole time he had been wearing his coat, he had seemed stiff, formal, and, well, buttoned-up. But now, without the garment, he seemed more relaxed, more natural, more like a warrior. Both versions were attractive in their own way, far more than I should have noticed.

Sullivan drew the sword from the scabbard belted to his waist and pointed the weapon at me. "Sit here and be quiet until I call for you."

I opened my mouth to snipe back at him, but he had already stalked away.

Sullivan strode out into the middle of the ring. He raised his sword high overhead, and the gladiators moved into two squads, forming the same ranks that they had in the arena last night. I had been right about the blackboard denoting the rankings, since Paloma stood at the head of one squad, while Emilie was at the front of the other one.

"Weapons drills!" Sullivan barked out. "Now!"

The gladiators raised their own swords high, saluting him, and then started the drills. I sat on the bench and watched as the gladiators split into teams of two and went through a series of attacks, defenses, and counterattacks.

Sullivan moved from one team to the next, barking out orders or congratulating someone on a particularly good strike. Occasionally, he would stop and show one of the gladiators how to position his sword or shield, or how to block an attack and then lash out with a quick counterstrike. Most magiers thought that their power was enough to protect them, so they didn't bother learning how to use weapons, but Sullivan seemed to be an exception. Sword, spear, dagger, shield. He was comfortable with all of them.

The winter sun warmed the arena, and the smells of sweat and leather filled the air. The familiar aromas reminded me of standing on one of the balconies at Seven Spire, watching Captain Auster and his men train. My stomach twisted. All those men were dead, and Auster was probably rotting in the palace dungeon, if Vasilia hadn't already executed him.

Sullivan made three laps around the ring before coming back to the center. "Now with magic!"

The gladiators kept doing their drills, but this time, they added magic. The magiers conjured up balls of fire, shards of ice, and bolts of lightning and hurled them at their opponents, many of whom were mutts who used their strength and speed to either absorb the blows or duck out of the way.

The remaining gladiators shifted into their morph forms, revealing the teeth, talons, fur, and scales that lurked beneath their human skin—except for Paloma.

Instead of shifting, she fought as her regular mortal self, even though she would have had much greater strength and speed, not to mention razor-sharp teeth and talons, if she had shifted into her ogre form. Perhaps she was holding back since this was training time. Or perhaps Paloma simply didn't need to shift, given how badly she was beating her opponent.

Paloma was sparring with Emilie, who had incredible speed and some enhanced strength, and was smashing her sword into Paloma's shield over and over again.

But she was still losing.

Paloma dug her feet into the ground and absorbed the blows. Emilie might as well have been whacking at a tree with a butter knife. It would have been more effective than what she was doing to Paloma. Emilie knew it too, and she darted this way and that, trying to use her speed to get past the other woman's defenses, but Paloma pivoted back and forth, blocking every attack with her shield.

Exertion stained Emilie's cheeks tomato-red, and I could hear her huffing and puffing even over the repeated clashes and clangs of the swords and shields, but Paloma wasn't winded at all. Emilie let out a loud, frustrated scream and made a reckless lunge, and that's when Paloma finally went on the offensive. She spun to the side and used her longer reach to slap Emilie's sword out of her hand. In an instant, Paloma had her blade up against the other woman's throat.

"Good match," Paloma said.

She lowered her sword, smiled, and clapped Emilie on the shoulder before turning to see who Sullivan was instructing.

Emilie's face twisted with rage the second that Paloma turned away, and she snatched her sword off the ground and twirled it around in her hand, staring at Paloma's back. I knew that cold, calculating look. I had seen it before many, many times at the palace, whenever someone got an expensive necklace, or a fine new hunting dog, or a lucrative business deal.

Jealousy truly was an ugly, ugly thing.

Paloma apparently thought that they were friends, but it was obvious that Emilie did not. Paloma was her competition, and Emilie seemed fed up with being the second-best gladiator in the Black Swan troupe. But she didn't get the chance to do anything about it, since Sullivan halted the drills.

"That's enough for now," he said. "I'm sure you've noticed that we have a new recruit."

He looked at me, and I realized that this was my summons. So I got to my feet, shrugged out of his blue jacket, set it down on the bench next to my stolen pillow, and walked out to the center of the ring.

Sullivan arched an eyebrow. He wanted me to introduce myself.

I waved at the gladiators. "Hi. My name is Evie."

No one responded. No one smiled, nodded, or gave me any sort of welcoming look or gesture. Tough crowd.

Sullivan gestured at Paloma, who handed me her sword and shield. I almost dropped them on the ground. It was all that I could do to lift the sword, and I had to hold on to one of the straps on the back of the shield instead of sliding my arm through it.

"How do you even carry these things?" I muttered. "Much less fight with them?"

Paloma shook her head, as though she already felt sorry for me. So did the ogre on her neck. This was not going to be pleasant.

"Let's see what you've got," Sullivan said.

I looked at the gladiators, expecting one of them to step forward, but Sullivan pointedly cleared his throat. I tensed, finally realizing what was going on, then slowly faced him. Sure enough, he was holding a sword. He smiled at me, his eyes gleaming with anticipation.

Not going to be pleasant at all.

I barely had time to lift my shield before he whipped up his sword and charged.

Clang!

That first sharp blow almost knocked the shield from my hand, but I gritted my teeth and tightened my grip on it.

Clang!

Clang! Clang!

Clang!

Sullivan smashed his sword into my shield over and over again. He wasn't using his lightning, but he didn't have to, given how much faster, stronger, and more skilled he was than me. Every blow made my entire body ache and vibrate, like I was a drum that he was beating.

"Come on," he said. "You can do better than that. Here. I'll even give you a free shot."

He backed away and held his arms out to his sides. His smile was even wider than it had been before, his eyes brighter. The bastard was enjoying this.

I blinked, and suddenly, I wasn't seeing Sullivan anymore. Instead, I was back at Seven Spire, in one of the training yards, watching Vasilia give me that same sort of smug smirk as she lazily twirled one of her jeweled swords around in her hand, getting ready to cut me with it again. She had always beaten me when it came to weapons. She had always beaten me at *everything,* just as she had taunted before she had blasted me off that cliff.

"Well, come on," Sullivan said again. "Take your shot."

A cold fist of rage wrapped around my heart, squeezing tight. I wasn't going to best Sullivan, but I had to try. I couldn't afford for him or any of the other gladiators to think that I was weak. More importantly, *I* didn't want to be weak. I didn't want to keep my mouth shut and plaster a smile on my face and stay in the background like I had all those years at the palace. I just wanted to be *myself*, for the first time in a long time.

The shield was far too heavy for me to wield properly, so I tossed it aside. Surprise flashed across Sullivan's face, but he kept his arms out to his sides. Then, before I could think too much about how badly this was going to end, I wrapped both hands around my borrowed sword, screamed, and charged forward.

I raised my sword as though I was going to slash it across his chest, but at the last second, I went low, swiping out at his legs instead. But of course Sullivan still easily avoided the blow.

For a moment, I thought I heard faint music playing in the distance, and I found myself moving in time to the beat. I whirled around, brought my sword up, and—

Clang!

I actually managed to block his counterstrike. We stood there, seesawing back and forth, our swords scraping together. More surprise filled his face, along with the tiniest bit of grudging respect. Then he smiled again, and I knew how much trouble I was in.

Sullivan leaned forward, using his strength and weight to make me fall to one knee. I managed to keep my sword up in between us, although my arms shook from the effort.

"Trying to fight dirty?" he mocked, looming over me. "That's a bit desperate, don't you think?"

"Tell me something I don't know," I muttered.

He smiled again. I tensed, realizing that he was about to attack, but he was still too fast and strong. Sullivan whirled around, knocked my sword out of my hand, and kicked my leg out from under me.

An instant later, I was flat on my back in the dirt, and Sullivan had the point of his sword pressed up against my throat, just as he had when I had woken up in his house this morning.

"You lose, highness."

I sighed. I always did.

I thought he might slice my neck with his sword, to make sure that I really got the point, but Sullivan lowered his weapon, leaned down, and offered me his forearm. I hesitated, then reached out and grabbed it. He easily pulled me to my feet.

We stood in the middle of the ring, our arms locked together like our swords had been a moment ago. Sullivan's breath kissed my cheek, and the heat from his body mixed with my own, warming me far more than our sparring had. An answering warmth sparked in Sullivan's eyes, which weren't nearly as cold as they had been before.

He cleared his throat, let go of my arm, and stepped back. "You dropped your shield and used your sword to attack me. Interesting."

My eyes narrowed. "Wait a second. Was this some sort of test?"

"Of course it was a test. Everything here is a test."

"And what did it tell you?"

He studied me with a sharp, penetrating gaze. "That there might actually be some hope for you yet." He jerked his head at the sword and shield lying on the ground. "Give those back to Paloma, then pick out a lighter sword from the weapons racks."

Sullivan turned back to the rest of the gladiators and barked out more orders. I started to grab the fallen weapons, but Paloma beat me to them. The ogre morph easily picked up the shield and secured it to her forearm before grabbing the sword.

She looked at me. "Not bad. Most newbs don't last that long against Sullivan their first time out."

Her voice and expression were both neutral, and the ogre on her neck blinked its amber eyes, as if trying to figure me out. Paloma seemed a bit friendlier than she had in Serilda's library, so I decided to take a chance.

"What kind of test was that? What did Sullivan mean that there might be hope for me?"

Paloma lifted her sword and shield. "You realized that my weapons were too heavy for you, and you decided to use the sword instead of the shield."

"So?"

"So it means that you would rather attack then defend yourself."

"And why is that important?"

She shrugged. "Because that's the sign of a true gladiator."

Paloma jogged off to join the rest of the gladiators as they resumed their drills. Sullivan pointed at me, then over at the weapons racks. I sighed and limped in that direction. I reached the racks and picked out a lighter sword, although it still felt as heavy as a gargoyle.

I started to limp back to the center of the ring when a glimmer of glass caught my eye. I looked up.

Serilda Swanson was watching me.

The back of the training ring butted up against the gardens, along with the manor house. Serilda was lounging in a chair on one of the second-story balconies, sipping a drink, and watching her gladiators.

She stared at me, her index finger tapping against her

glass. Her face was as blank as a canvas, and I couldn't tell what she might be thinking about Sullivan's test, or me—

"Let's go, highness!" Sullivan yelled.

Whatever Serilda thought, it wasn't going to save me from the training session. So I sighed, turned around, and shuffled back to the center of the ring, bracing myself for several more hours of hurt and humiliation.

A couple of other gladiators had recently joined the troupe, and I trained with them through the rest of the morning and into the afternoon, although they were all far more skilled than I was.

After that, I washed off the dust and dirt and returned to the dining hall. Theroux put me to work chopping carrots, onions, potatoes, and celery for some beef stew. By the time the stew was finished, I was so ravenous that I stood in a corner of the kitchen and ate three bowls of it, along with half a loaf of sourdough bread slathered with honey butter. Theroux didn't comment on my appetite, but he did give me a piece of the second cranberry-apple pie that I'd made earlier.

It was one of the best meals I'd ever had.

Once dinner was finished and the dishes had been washed, Theroux pointed me over to the barracks for the female gladiators. I opened the door and stepped inside.

The front of the barracks was a common area, with tables, chairs, and writing desks covered with paper, pens, and pots of ink. Flames crackled in a fireplace in the front wall, and a shelf in the corner held books, along with a few board games.

Several gladiators were gathered in that area, writing letters, reading, or dozing in front of the warm fire. I shuffled past them into the back half of the barracks, which featured two rows of cots running down either wall. A wooden trunk sat at the end of each cot, with nightstands, lamps, and other pieces of furniture scattered here and there.

The sleeping spaces might all be the same, but each one had a personal touch, like ribbons wrapped around the bedframe, or a pretty embroidered tunic lying over the trunk, or a framed portrait propped up on the nightstand.

The only empty cot was in the back corner, far away from the heat of the fireplace but right next to the bathrooms that lined the back wall. So not only would I be cold, but I would also get to listen to the other women use the toilets all night. Terrific. Just terrific. But I supposed that it was better than sleeping in Sullivan's house again.

I still had the blue jacket and the pillow that I had stolen from Sullivan, and I laid the jacket across the foot of the bed. The pillow was a bit dirty and grimy from where I had carried it around all day, but the cot didn't have a pillow, so I set it at the head of the bed. Then I leaned down and tested the mattress with my hand. Hard as a rock, but the sheets were clean. Good enough for me.

The trunk at the foot of the bed was open, and I bent down and rifled through the items inside. A couple of white kitchen tunics, black leggings and work boots, gray sandals, and some gray fighting leathers, all of which looked to be about my size. Someone had already stocked the trunk with clothes, along with some soap, a hairbrush, and other toiletry items.

I grabbed a black nightgown, a toothbrush, and some other things and shuffled toward the only bathroom that wasn't occupied. Right before I was going to step inside, an arm shot out and grabbed the doorframe, blocking me.

"Newbs go last." Emilie gave me an evil grin, then stepped into the bathroom and slammed the door shut in my face.

I sighed, but all I could do was stand there and wait. The other gladiators gave me curious looks, but no one talked to me, and I was too tired to make the effort to speak to them.

Finally, another bathroom opened up, and I stepped inside and shut and locked the door behind me. It had been a long, long day, and I was bruised, sore, and utterly exhausted, but I forced myself to unwind what was left of my braid, shake out my hair, and strip off my dirty clothes.

I untied the black velvet bag with my bracelet and the memory stone from the belt loop on my leggings. Even though I was bone-tired, I still hid the bag under my pile of dirty clothes before I got into the shower.

Since everyone else had gone before me, the water was luke-warm, at best, although it quickly turned ice-cold. I ground my teeth to keep them from chattering and washed myself from head to toe three times, including my hair.

Thirty minutes later, I had finished my bedtime routine and was standing in front of the mirror over the sink, star-ing at my reflection. Long black hair, gray-blue eyes, cheek-bones, nose, lips. My features looked the same as always, and yet strangely foreign at the same time. Perhaps that was due to my injuries. Tiny cuts crisscrossed my chin like stitches on a rag doll's face, while my right cheek was one massive mix of black-and-blue bruises from where the turncoat guard had punched me. My hair was just about the only part of me that had survived unscathed, but even it felt like a chilly, heavy weight dragging me down.

I touched my hair and shivered. Given how far away I was from the fireplace, it would take hours for it to dry. If I had still been at the palace, I would have used a brush with heated bristles or crawled into bed and read until my long locks dried enough for me to go to sleep. But Lady Everleigh was gone, and so were all her books and other creature comforts. Evie the gladiator needed to do something different with her hair. Besides, the cuts and bruises on my face would soon fade, and the less that I looked like my old self, the safer I would be.

Someone had left a pair of scissors sitting on the back of the toilet, and I picked them up. I turned the scissors over in my hands. Then, before I could think too much about what I was doing, I grabbed a piece of my hair, held it out, and cut it off.

Snip.

Just like that, it was gone. Just like my former life. Just like Isobel, Alvis, Xenia, Cordelia, and everyone else that I had ever known.

Sorrow filled me, but I grabbed another piece of hair and cut it off as well, pretending that I was cutting the emotion out of my body at the same time.

Snip.

The sorrow vanished, but heartache rose up to take its place.

Snip.

Then fear, worry, dread, and helplessness.

Snip-snip-snip-snip.

I kept cutting, going as fast as I could. Piece by piece, I hacked off my hair until it just brushed the tops of my shoulders. By the time I put the scissors down, my hands were shaking, but I actually felt lighter, better, *freer,* as if I really had cut away the horrors of everything that had happened.

Oh, I knew that it wasn't true. That I had just cut my hair and nothing else. That the memories were still there, that they would *always* be there, right along with the sorrow, heartache, and rage.

Especially the rage.

That was the one thing that I hadn't imagined cutting out of myself. That was the one thing that I didn't want to get rid of. That was the only thing that had helped me survive, and it was the only thing that would keep me going through all the long days ahead.

But I had made my choice, and this was my life—and hair—now, for better or worse.

So I gathered up the wet locks and dumped them in the trash can, then grabbed my meager possessions and left the bathroom to go to bed.

CHAPTER FOURTEEN

The sounds of cots squeaking woke me the next morning.

Even though I desperately wanted to stay in bed and rest my tired, aching body, I got up and put on one of the white tunics from my trunk. I also tied the black velvet bag with my bracelet and the memory stone to one of the belt loops on my leggings, then pulled my tunic down to hide it. I didn't dare leave it in the barracks. Not until I found a good hiding spot for it.

Three other female gladiators also worked in the kitchen, and I followed them to the dining hall. They chatted with each other, but I didn't join in the conversation. Instead, I listened, putting names with faces and seeing who were friends, who weren't, and how they all got along.

"We have a good shot to win the Svalin city title this year. Maybe even the Bellonan national one too."

"With Paloma as our champion? Absolutely."

"Don't forget about Emilie. She's only a few points behind Paloma for the top spot."

I didn't understand the talk about the gladiator rankings, but the women soon switched to a far more relatable topic.

"Maybe I should ask Sullivan for a little one-on-one training. To improve my . . . technique."

"I wouldn't mind getting a little extra instruction from Sullivan."

"Me neither."

The gladiators' giggles reminded me of the noble ladies tittering about how they would enjoy certain attributes of various lords.

Getting *instruction* from Sullivan? He was so smug and arrogant that he'd probably expect his partner to climb on top and do all the work of pleasing him. Still, I couldn't help but picture Sullivan lying in bed, white sheets draped low on his hips, his tan, muscled chest laid bare, his brown hair rumpled, his blue eyes glittering with desire. A sexy, devilish grin would spread across his face, and he would reach out, thread his fingers through mine, and pull me down on top of him, even as his lips rose up to meet mine . . .

I shook my head to banish the unwanted thoughts.

One of the women turned to me. "What do you think . . . um . . ."

"Evie," I said, when it became apparent that she had forgotten my name.

She snapped her fingers. "Evie! That's right. Well, what do you think about Sullivan?"

All three women looked at me. I thought about their conversation so far.

"Well, I had some *instruction* from Sullivan in the ring yesterday, remember? I got tossed onto my back for nothing," I drawled. "He might have had fun, but it certainly wasn't satisfying for me. Then again, isn't that the way it always is with men?"

The women howled with laughter, like I had hoped. It was always better to make fun of yourself first, rather than wait for other people to do it. Another survival skill that I had learned at Seven Spire.

The trick worked, and the women included me in their conversation the rest of the way, although I still kept listening more than I talked.

I followed the gladiators into the dining hall and back to the kitchen. I walked over to Theroux, who was sprinkling dillweed and other dried herbs into a cast-iron skillet filled with yellow, red, and purple potatoes.

"Good morning," I said.

He grunted at me, then pointed over to another prep station that was covered with butter, flour, sugar, and more. "Can you make cherry-almond scones?"

My heart ached. Those were one of my favorite treats, and I had made them with Isobel many, many times.

"Well?" he snapped.

"Yes," I croaked. "I can make them."

"Good. Then get to work." Theroux turned his back to me and focused on his pan again.

I went over to that prep station. First, I mixed the butter, flour, sugar, and more together for the base of the scones, before submerging fresh tart cherries into a sweet almond liqueur. Forty-five minutes later, I took several trays out of the ovens. The three gladiators I had walked over here with gathered around me.

"Those smell delicious."

"Can I try one?"

"Oh, it's so good!"

The scones helped to further break the ice, and soon, all the workers were gathered around and chatting at me. I smiled and nodded at everyone, still doing far more listening than talking, but I seemed to have earned my place. Even Theroux snatched a scone from one of the trays when he thought I wasn't looking.

Eventually, the rest of the troupe came into the dining hall to eat breakfast, and Theroux told me to start serving food. So I left the kitchen and moved from one table to the next, using a set of tongs to dish out the scones.

Cho and Sullivan were sitting at a table by themselves. The dragon morph spotted me and waved his hand, an eager smile stretching across his face. Sullivan was far less enthused.

I counted the scones on my tray and the people in between us. Then I headed in their direction, stopping every few feet to dish out another scone. Eventually, I made it to their table.

Cho held out his plate, his black eyes locked onto the tray.

"Here you go, sir. I saved two scones just for you."

I had never liked kissing ass, but I was new here, and I had to be smart, quick, and ruthless about carving out and securing my position within the group. Getting Cho, the troupe's second-in-command, on my side was an excellent place to start. Besides, I had another ulterior motive in mind.

I dished out the treats to him. Sullivan lifted his plate as well.

"Oh, sorry. I'm all out."

His eyes narrowed. He knew that I had run out on purpose. I smiled at him.

Cho took a big bite. "Mmm-mmm-mmm! This is just as good as that pie yesterday." He shoved the rest of the scone into his mouth, then reached out and grabbed my hand. "Ah, if only I were twenty years younger, I would marry you in a heartbeat, Evie, and let you ply me with pastries until I was old, fat, and gray."

The dragon on his neck winked at me. Apparently, the creature agreed with Cho.

I wasn't quite sure what to say, but I didn't have to answer. Serilda opened one of the doors and stepped into the dining hall. Her face was its usual blank mask, although her eyes were a bit red, her lips were pinched tight, and she was moving slowly, as though she was in tremendous physical pain, although I didn't see any injuries on her body.

She strode to the center of the room. Everyone stopped talking and eating and faced her. Serilda looked at the acrobats, gladiators, and other workers. Then she drew in a breath and slowly let it out.

My stomach clenched. I knew what she was going to say. The horrible news would come out sooner or later. I was surprised that Vasilia had managed to keep it quiet this long.

"Queen Cordelia is dead," Serilda said.

An eerie silence descended over the dining hall. Then everyone started shouting at once.

"The queen? Dead? It can't be!"

"How did it happen?"

"Was there an accident?"

And on and on it went.

I stood beside Cho and Sullivan, the empty tray and tongs still clutched in my hands. My stomach roiled, and I wanted to vomit up the scone that I had eaten earlier, but I swallowed down the bile rising in my throat. This was perhaps the most dangerous moment, when someone might connect me with the massacre, and I couldn't afford to attract any attention to myself.

Serilda held her hands up, asking for silence. Slowly, everyone quieted down.

"I'm just as shocked and saddened as you all are. I don't know what happened, although believe me when I tell you that I will find out." Her voice was as cold as ice. She meant what she said, although I had no idea how she would get any more information. "The rumor is that assassins snuck into the palace and murdered the queen, along with the royal family and several nobles."

Everyone sucked in a collective breath as though they were going to start shouting again, but Serilda held her hands up again, and everyone remained quiet, except for a few muttered curses.

"There is some other news." Serilda's mouth twisted. "Vasilia survived the massacre. She is now queen of Bellona."

"Princess Vasilia? That is good news!"

"She's a great warrior!"

"She'll put things right!"

Disgust filled me. The people had always adored and lauded Vasilia for her beauty and fighting skills. Now they would love her even more for supposedly surviving the massacre. Once again, the bitch had gotten exactly what she wanted.

Serilda waited until everyone had fallen silent before she spoke again. "Vasilia and her guards killed most of the assassins, although she has one of them in the palace dungeon. Auster, the captain of the queen's guard. Supposedly, he helped plan the massacre."

She looked at Cho, who rocked back in his seat, his remaining scone forgotten. Like Serilda, his face remained blank, although his nostrils flared, and several soft *scrape-scrape-scrape*s sounded. Black talons had sprouted on Cho's fingertips, and he was digging them into the tabletop. I looked at the morph mark on his neck. The dragon's black eyes were narrowed to slits, and black smoke boiled out of its mouth, telling me how furious Cho and his inner self were.

Why would Cho care about Captain Auster? The answer came to me a moment later. Cho must have been one of the queen's guards who had gone with Serilda when she had left Seven Spire all those years ago. If that was the case, then he would know Auster well.

"What about the assassins?" Cho growled. "Do you know anything about them?"

"Supposedly, the assassins were from Andvari." This time, Serilda stared at Sullivan. "The rumor is that they were working for the royal family."

Sullivan jerked back as though someone had slapped him. Lightning flashed on his fingertips, although he quickly curled his hand into a fist, snuffing out the magic. His lips pressed together, and he ducked his head, as though he was trying to shrink down into his gray coat.

I stared at his coat, which had reminded me of Lord Hans's jacket. The style, cut, color, and fabric were definitely Andvarian, as were his black shirt, leggings, and boots. So Sullivan was from Andvari. Interesting. Perhaps he was worried that the rest of the troupe would take their anger out on him.

"Training, practice, show prep. Everything is canceled," Serilda said. "Take the rest of the day to mourn your fallen queen. Dinner will be served as usual, and a candlelight vigil will be held on the plaza tonight for those of you who wish to pay your respects. That is all."

She nodded to everyone, then turned and strode out of the dining hall.

As soon as the door shut behind her, everyone started talking at once.

"I can't believe the queen is dead!"

"Assassins in the palace? That captain should be drawn and quartered!"

"Andvarian scum! They'll pay for this . . ."

And on and on it went, each comment more violent and vicious than the last.

Cho left the dining hall, heading after Serilda, but Sullivan stayed in his seat, staring off into space, a sick look on his face. I wasn't the only one who noticed him. People at the surrounding tables turned their angry glares to him, and more than one comment cursing Andvarians rang out, although no one was stupid enough to confront him.

Still, in that moment, I felt sorry for him. I knew what it was like to be the subject of other people's scorn and derision, especially when it wasn't deserved.

And I decided to do something about it.

I went into the kitchen, grabbed another tray of scones, and stepped back into the dining area. I marched over to where Sullivan was still sitting, leaned down, and dropped two scones onto his empty plate. I wasn't sure why I did it. He hadn't exactly been kind to me during my brief time at the Black Swan. Perhaps I had simply seen enough cruelty during the massacre and didn't want to take part in any myself.

Sullivan reared back in surprise, then looked up at me. I pointedly glanced at his coat, letting him know that I realized that he was from Andvari and that I didn't blame him for what had happened.

More surprise filled his face, along with a tiny flicker of gratitude. "Thank you," he murmured.

"You're welcome."

I stared at him a moment longer, then walked away to hand out the remaining scones.

After breakfast, I spent the rest of the day in the barracks. Several of the gladiators, including Paloma and Emilie, huddled around the fireplace, speculating what the queen's murder would mean for the troupe, the city, and the kingdom.

I perched on the edges of the crowd, nodding when appropriate and speaking when spoken to, but otherwise, I kept quiet. Now that Cordelia's murder had been made public, my situation was even more precarious, and I didn't want anyone to connect my arrival here with the queen's assassination. Then again, why would they? As far as they knew, I was a runaway servant who had escaped from a mean mistress. Still, dread, worry, and paranoia simmered in my stomach, and I tensed every time the door opened, expecting Serilda to storm inside and confront me about who I really was.

But the day passed, and nothing happened.

Dinner that evening was a quiet, somber affair. After the meal, black candles shaped like slender spires were passed out to everyone in the dining hall, and we all headed toward the main gate. A lone torch was burning inside the gate, and everyone stopped to light their candle before streaming out into the plaza.

People clutching lit black candles had crammed into this plaza, just as they would in plazas throughout the city. More candles burned in the windows of the surrounding buildings, and torches blazed on the rooftops, as was the Bellonan custom whenever the queen died. The torches made the spires on the buildings gleam like gold, silver, and bronze stars.

It was beautiful and eerie and heartbreaking.

Everyone was quiet, except for a few sniffles as people held back their sobs. The collective scents of salty grief and ashy heartache hung in the air like thick clouds, the aromas as sharp as swords stabbing into my heart with every breath I took.

I kept to the fringes of the crowd, staying close to the compound gate and cupping my hand in front of my candle to keep the flame from going out. Like everyone else, I stared up at the palace high, high above.

Seven Spire was completely dark.

All the candles, torches, fluorestones, and other lights had been snuffed out or turned off, and the palace was as black as the night itself. I didn't know how long we stood there, staring up at the palace, but eventually, a series of bells chimed, starting at the palace and booming throughout the entire city as other bells joined in. The bells rang thirty times, one for each year of Queen Cordelia's rule.

I didn't think of her rule, though. No, each time the bells rang, I thought of Cordelia herself, and Madelena, and Isobel, and my cousins, and everyone else who had been slaughtered. And then I thought of Alvis, and Lady Xenia, and Gemma, the Andvarian girl. I hoped they had escaped, but I would probably never know what had happened to them.

Finally, the echoes of the bells faded away, and everyone looked up at the palace again. Waiting, just waiting, for what they knew was coming next.

A single candle flared to life in the throne-room windows.

Everyone sucked in a breath, and the cheers began, with the crowd chanting *Long live the queen! Long live the queen!* over and over again.

I found myself roaring with the rest of the crowd. Not because I wished Vasilia any kind of long, happy life. No, I cheered because despite Vasilia and her evil plot, despite the blood, betrayal, pain, and death, despite everything, I had survived the massacre, and I knew that Bellona would too.

The people around me were proof enough of that.

From the crowd's gossip, I learned that Cordelia's and Madelena's bodies would be displayed in gold caskets in the main plaza that fronted Seven Spire tomorrow morning, as was the custom. People would be able to file by and pay their respects all day before the queen and the princess were laid to rest in the royal Blair crypt deep within the palace at midnight. Well, at least Vasilia was giving her mother and sister and everyone else a proper burial. Then again, I supposed that she had to, in order to keep up appearances.

Many people would stay in the plaza through the night, mourning the old queen and celebrating the new, but ten minutes after the first palace light appeared, I blew out my candle and went back inside the compound. I couldn't stand to listen to them cheer for Vasilia any longer.

I was almost back to the dining hall when a loud *crack* sounded, like someone had kicked a stone up against something.

"That bitch," a voice growled. "That smug, arrogant *bitch*."

I froze, wondering where the sound and the voice had come from. I looked around, and I spotted Serilda and Cho standing at the edge of the gardens behind the dining hall. Perhaps it was my paranoia, or perhaps my curiosity got the best of me, but instead of walking on, I darted forward and slipped in between the metal trash bins that stood next to the dining hall. Then I sidled forward and peered through a gap in the bins, watching them.

Serilda was pacing back and forth. Every once in a while, she would stop, lash out with her boot, and kick a stone into a nearby tree or bench. Cho leaned against one of the streetlamps, his arms crossed over his chest, watching her.

"I told Cordelia that this would happen," Serilda snarled. "I *told* her. Over and over again. For *years*. But she didn't listen to me. And now she's dead, and Vasilia is queen."

I frowned. From the rumors I had always heard, Serilda had left Seven Spire in scandal and disgrace. So why would she care that Cordelia was dead? And who was the bitch that she was referring to? Cordelia? Vasilia? Both?

"We should leave," Cho said. "Pack up the troupe and leave Bellona while we still can. Before Vasilia closes the borders—or worse."

Serilda whirled around and stabbed her finger at him. "*No.* I am not leaving. Not again. Not until I find out what happened."

Cho snorted. "We know what happened. Cordelia is dead, and Vasilia is queen. Nothing else matters."

A stricken look filled Serilda's face, but she whipped around and started pacing again. "It matters if someone survived. If a *Blair* survived. Any one of them would be a better ruler than Vasilia, that smug, treacherous bitch."

Well, that answered my bitch question, although more rose up to take its place. Why would Serilda care if any of the other royals had survived? Unless . . . she somehow knew that Vasilia was responsible for the massacre. But how could she know that?

"And what about Auster?" Cho asked. "Have you forgotten about him? Because he's the one who is going to suffer the most at Vasilia's hands."

Serilda closed her eyes and rubbed her forehead, as though it were aching. Then she dropped her hand, opened her eyes, and looked at Cho again. "No, I haven't forgotten about Auster. But we can't get to him. The tunnels are blocked."

Tunnels? What tunnels? Everything she said only made me more confused.

Sadness filled Cho's face, but he nodded in agreement. Serilda started pacing again.

"We need to put out feelers and see if any of the Blairs survived," she said. "Someone, anyone. I don't care who. I would even take that old drunk Horatio right now."

Cho nodded. "I've already got my contacts in the palace working on it."

"Good. I want every scrap of information about the massacre that you can get. Every rumor, every innuendo, every damn whisper. I want it all. Some royal had to have survived, and we're going to find them."

This was my chance. My big moment. I could get to my feet, step out from behind the trash bins, and tell them who I really was. That I was a Blair, that the queen had sent me here, and that everyone else was dead, except for the few of my royal cousins who had had the good fortune not to be at the palace. I could have done that. I probably *should* have done that.

But I didn't.

Cordelia had told me that I could trust Serilda, and based on Serilda's own words, it seemed as though she despised Vasilia as much as I did. That was definitely a point in her favor. But she had also said that she wanted to find a survivor—a Blair survivor.

Serilda wanted a royal to use for something, although I wasn't quite sure what. I had already been used as a figurehead, as the royal stand-in, and I had no desire to become someone else's puppet, especially since I didn't know what game Serilda wanted to play. So I held my tongue and stayed hidden.

More voices filled the air, along with footsteps. The other workers were returning to the compound.

Serilda and Cho heard them too, and they both stared in my direction. I froze, scarcely daring to breathe for fear that they would spot me and realize that I'd been eavesdropping.

"Let's go," Serilda said. "We can discuss this more at the manor."

Cho nodded, and the two of them moved deeper into the gardens. I let out a soft, relieved breath. When I was sure that they were gone, I got to my feet and slipped away into the night, my secrets still intact.

For now.

CHAPTER FIFTEEN

Despite Cordelia's death, the next morning was business as usual at the Black Swan.

The troupe, the city, the kingdom, the continent didn't stop turning just because the queen had been assassinated. There were always meals to cook and eat, chores to be done, sleep to be had. Bellonans were a rather practical people that way.

My days quickly fell into a routine. Up early in the morning to help Theroux and the kitchen staff make breakfast, then off to the ring to train with the other gladiators until late in the afternoon. After that, it was back to the kitchen to make dinner. And finally, off to the barracks for a cold shower before going to bed.

On the weekends, I spent most of my time in the kitchen, helping Theroux and the others make batches of sweet and savory cornucopia, candied fruits, flavored ices, and more for the concession carts outside and inside the arena. On Saturday and Sunday nights, I walked up and down the bleachers, selling the treats before, during, and after the shows.

I wasn't a skilled enough gladiator to participate in the arena fights yet, although I was making progress. I had all the simple sword and shield drills memorized and could execute them in unison with everyone else.

It was when I actually tried to fight someone that I ran into problems.

On rare occasions, I was able to win a sparring round or two against the weaker gladiators. But most of the time, I fumbled through the bouts until the other warriors finally put me out of my misery. I lost my way somewhere between the drills and the sparring, and I couldn't put all the moves together with any consistency.

Sullivan didn't help matters, since he made it his mission to point out my flaws. He singled me out for one-on-one combat during every training session, and every one of our fights ended with me on my back on the ground, and his sword resting against my throat.

Not satisfying at all, just like I had told the female gladiators.

Afterward, Sullivan would help me up. Then he would shake his head, as if his kicking my ass yet again was somehow a disappointment. "You're better than this, highness."

He said that over and over again, until it became like a hated song running through my mind whenever I stepped into the training ring, but I gritted my teeth, picked up my sword, and tried again.

As the days passed, I discovered that my new life at the Black Swan wasn't all that different from my old one at the palace. I did my job and went where I was told, the same as always. Despite the hard work of the kitchen and the even harder blows in the gladiator ring, I enjoyed life here far more than I ever had at Seven Spire.

For the first time since my parents had died, I felt *free*.

I didn't always have to smile and pretend that everything was fine, although I still mostly kept my thoughts and feelings to myself, too schooled in the lifelong habit to break it so easily. But no one was watching me, no one was waiting for me to screw up so that they could spread nasty gossip, and Vasilia wasn't around to dish out meanness whenever the mood struck her.

And best of all, I didn't have to take shit from anyone.

If someone made a joke at my expense, I made one at theirs. If someone snapped at me, I snapped right back at them. I didn't back down from anyone, not even Sullivan. Strength equaled respect here, just like it had at the palace. I didn't have the physical strength of Paloma and some of the other gladiators, but I quickly made it clear that I would not be cowed, bullied, or intimidated in any way.

At Seven Spire, I had kept my head down and stayed in the background so that I wouldn't draw attention to myself, so that I wouldn't be targeted, so that I wouldn't be hurt. But a gladiator's life was all about hurting others, and sparring with people, whether it was with swords in the training ring, or sharp words outside it, drew me out of my shell. Even when I lost a fight or someone cracked a better joke than me, I still knew that I had tried my best, and that made me feel stronger and more powerful than I ever had at the palace.

Oh, it wasn't all pies, scones, and sunshine at the Black Swan. An undercurrent of tension ran between the Bellonans and the Andvarians in the troupe, especially Sullivan, since he was the most visible. But the Bellonans limited themselves to dirty looks and snide whispers, so no real damage was done. For now.

The acrobats, wire walkers, gargoyle and strix trainers, and other workers were split into various cliques, just like the royals, nobles, senators, guilders, and guards had been at Seven Spire. Most people were nice enough to me, but I didn't go out of my way to make friends with anyone. Vasilia had taught me a long time ago that your so-called friends were the people who could wound you the worst. Besides, I didn't dare get close to anyone, lest a slip of the tongue make the whole flimsy house of cards that I had concocted about who I was come tumbling down and reveal my true identity.

The cliques were the most noticeable and the most difficult to navigate when it came to the gladiators, especially since they spent almost as much time fucking as they did fighting. Sex wasn't a weapon here, not like it had been at Seven Spire, but it was still best to know who was currently sleeping with whom, and who was in it for casual fun, versus those with more serious feelings.

As for the fighting, many of the gladiators were newbs like me, trying to learn how to better their skills in hopes of making a few more crowns to support themselves and their families. Others simply loved fighting, and the more pain and injuries they could inflict on their opponents, the better they felt themselves. And then there were the divas, men and women alike, with insufferable, overinflated egos that filled them with supreme confidence about their fighting skills and popularity. Adding to those egos were the flyers of the gladiators that were strung up all over the compound, as well as the fans who lurked on the plaza outside, waiting for the gladiators to appear and sign autographs after the daily training sessions.

If anyone had the right to be a diva, it was Paloma, the troupe star and the highest-ranked gladiator in the city. But she never signed autographs on the plaza, and she was one of the few fighters who treated everyone equally, whether they were a gladiator or not.

But the strangest thing about Paloma was that she never shifted into her ogre form.

All the other morphs shifted when we trained, but not Paloma, not even once. She was strong and skilled enough with her shield and her spiked mace that she didn't need the extra boost of magic, but I still found it odd. Most morphs *loved* being in their other, stronger, faster forms. By not shifting, Paloma seemed determined to stay in the background as much as possible, despite her wild success in the arena.

I wouldn't have paid nearly as much attention to Paloma if not for Emilie.

For as humble as Paloma was, Emilie was three times as arrogant. She was always the first one to go to the plaza to sign autographs and the last one to leave, and she ordered everyone around like they were her own personal servants. Emilie's mutt speed made her a formidable opponent, and she was one of the highest-ranked gladiators in the city. But she had one fatal flaw—she couldn't beat Paloma, no matter how hard she tried.

And she certainly tried.

After signing autographs, Emilie would return to the ring and train for another hour or two, or sometimes longer. On the weekends, she was always the first gladiator in the arena and the last one to leave. But no matter how long she trained or how hard she tried, Paloma was just naturally that much better, and it drove Emilie crazy.

Emilie's frustration had long ago boiled up to jealousy and

then condensed down to anger, although no one seemed to notice but me. Then again, I had seen her type many, many times before at the palace. Perhaps the saddest thing was that Paloma actually thought that Emilie was her friend. Paloma was always deferring to her, always stepping back and keeping quiet so that Emilie could be the center of attention. All Paloma's niceness did was further infuriate the other gladiator, so much so that Emilie started cheating.

At first, it was small things. Paloma's favorite sword not being in the weapons racks. The soles on her sandals splitting apart during drills. The leather straps on her shield snapping and leaving her defenseless during sparring. Things that were overlooked or explained away as accidents, but Emilie was behind them all. She left the stench of her rose perfume on everything she ruined.

I casually asked around, wondering how long Emilie had been sabotaging the other gladiator. The supposed accidents and bouts of bad luck had been going on for several months, although no one else seemed to suspect what was really happening. Of course I thought about speaking up, but no one would believe me, the awkward newb, against one of the troupe's most skilled and popular gladiators, so I kept my mouth shut.

A month after the massacre, I was standing in the training ring, watching Paloma and Emilie battle two other gladiators and wondering what petty thing Emilie was going to do today. It had become my own personal guessing game. I was betting on snapped shield straps again.

For this match, Paloma and Emilie were teammates, and their goal was to disarm the other two gladiators. Paloma whirled around to attack one of the other fighters. Emilie was supposed to protect Paloma's blind side, but instead, she pretended to trip over her own feet, and she sliced her sword across her friend's back.

Paloma screamed and fell to the ground. Everyone sucked in a surprised breath, then rushed forward. I grabbed some towels from a nearby bench and hurried over as well.

Sullivan was already crouching beside Paloma, a concerned look on his face. He saw me holding the towels and waved me forward.

"I'm going to roll you over so we can see how bad the wound is," he said in a gentle voice. "It's going to hurt, but just try to get through it the best you can. Okay?"

Paloma gritted her teeth and nodded.

"On three. One, two, three!"

Sullivan took hold of her shoulder and rolled the gladiator onto her side, causing Paloma to snarl. Her leather shirt had been sliced open, and blood poured from the nasty wound that cut across her back. I drew in a breath, tasting the scent of her blood. A clean coppery tang, with no hint of punctured organs. A deep wound, but not a mortal one.

"Help me get her up!" Sullivan said. "Quickly!"

Two gladiators stepped up, grabbed Paloma's arms, and set her on her feet. Sweat beaded on her forehead, pain glazed her amber eyes, and the ogre face on her neck scrunched up with misery, but she stayed upright. Sullivan gestured at me, and I stepped forward and pressed the towels up against her wound.

"Paloma!" Emilie said, her voice dripping with fake concern. "I'm so sorry!"

Paloma smiled at her supposed friend. "Don't worry. Accidents happen."

Emilie touched her fingers to the corners of her eyes, as if fighting back tears. Duplicitous, treacherous bitch. She wasn't sorry. She had done that on purpose. Her only regret was that she hadn't killed Paloma outright.

"Get her to the bone masters," Sullivan barked out. "I'll be there in a few minutes."

The two gladiators nodded and helped Paloma limp out of the ring. I followed along behind them, still keeping the towels pressed up against her back.

We made it to the building that housed the bone masters, and a bell over the front door chimed as we stepped inside, announcing our presence. Just like the dining hall, this area featured rows of tables marching down the middle of the room, while shelves full of herbs, medicines, bandages, and more hugged the walls. But these tables weren't for eating, and the strong scent of lemony soap couldn't overpower the sharp tang of blood that lingered in the air.

The two gladiators helped Paloma lie down on her stomach on one of the tables. She snarled again, and her breath came in ragged gasps. The shock had worn off, and she could fully feel the pain of her injury now.

"I'll stay with her," I said. "You two go back to the ring and see if Sullivan needs anything."

They nodded and left the building.

A door in the back opened, and a woman with short black hair, hazel eyes, and lovely ebony skin hurried over to us. Aisha, one of the bone masters. She had healed my cuts and bruises more than once over the past few weeks.

Aisha stared at Paloma with a critical gaze. "Training accident?"

"Something like that," I muttered.

"You're going to be fine," Aisha said. "It's a nasty wound, but nothing that I can't fix."

Paloma nodded with understanding.

Aisha turned to me. "Evie, get me some clean cloths, and fill a bowl with warm water from the pot on the stove."

I did as she asked and set the items on another table. Aisha grabbed a pair of shears and cut away Paloma's bloody shirt so that she could see the entire wound. Then she pushed up the sleeves of her red tunic and laid her hands on either side of the deep, ugly slice. Power flared to life in Aisha's eyes, making them glow like citrines, and the scent of her magic filled the room. Fresh, clean, and lemony, like the soap.

Aisha stared at the wound, and her hands began to glow with the same bright golden power that filled her eyes. The glow spread out and sank into Paloma's skin, like magic was running through her veins, instead of blood. That was exactly what was happening. Bone masters had complete control over their element, which was the human body. A bone master's magic let her mend broken bones, stitch skin together, and fade out bruises— or cause them. Bone masters were dangerous in that they could heal you or crack your neck with a snap of their fingers.

Getting healed was usually just as painful as getting wounded, and Paloma latched onto my hand, trying to focus on something other than the fact that Aisha was pulling her skin, muscles, and tendons back together. Paloma's grip was so tight that it felt like she was crushing my bones, but I grimaced and kept quiet.

Aisha was strong in her magic, and it didn't take her long to heal the gladiator. She released her power, stepped back, and looked at me. "Help her get cleaned up. I'll find a fresh shirt for her."

I nodded, and she went through the door in the back of the room and shut it behind her.

I helped Paloma sit up, then turned my back while she took off what was left of her shirt and covered herself with a towel. When she was ready, I dipped a soft cloth into the bowl of warm water and washed the blood off her back. Neither one of us said anything. I couldn't have spoken even if I wanted to. The smell of her blood reminded me of the massacre, and it was all that I could do to keep from vomiting.

I cleaned her back, then dried it off and set the bloody cloth and bowl of water aside.

Paloma turned so that she could see me. "Thank you for helping me." She nodded at me, as did the ogre mark on her neck.

"You know this wasn't an accident, right?"

The words popped out before I could stop them. I didn't want to get involved. I *shouldn't* get involved. Not if I wanted to stay here with my secrets intact. Maybe it was the sight of all that blood, or how Emilie's cruelty reminded me of Vasilia's, or even how Paloma had crushed my hand trying to hold back the pain, but I couldn't keep quiet any longer.

I didn't *want* to keep quiet any longer. That's what the old Everleigh would have done back at the palace, and I didn't want to be that person anymore. I didn't want to stand by while other people got hurt. Not if I could do something to stop it. In some ways, being quiet was even worse than being helpless.

"Emilie cut you on purpose," I said. "She was deliberately trying to hurt you. Maybe even kill you."

Paloma laughed. "What? That's ridiculous. Emilie is my best friend. I've known her for years. She would never hurt me."

I shook my head. "Emilie is *not* your friend. She just acts like it. Deep down inside, she hates you. She's jealous of your success in the arena and how easily it comes to you."

Paloma frowned at the conviction in my voice, and I thought she was listening to me. But then, she shook her head. "No. You're wrong."

"No, I'm not. Trust me. I've known people like her before. My own personal nemesis, as a matter of fact." My stomach twisted, but I kept talking. "Think about everything that's happened lately. Your practice sword going missing. Your sandals coming apart. Your shield straps snapping. Those weren't accidents. Emilie was behind them and everything else that's gone wrong for you. That rose perfume she wears is better than a bloody confession. At least, it is to this mutt."

Paloma's frown deepened, and her gaze grew distant, as if she was thinking back over all those incidents, so I kept talking, hoping to convince her.

"And I imagine that Emilie especially hates you since you don't even have to morph to beat her over and over again." My gaze dropped to the ogre on her neck, who was staring at me with the same disbelief that Paloma was. "Why don't you shift? All the other morphs do. It would make you an even better, stronger, faster gladiator than you already are."

Anger sparked in Paloma's eyes, and she leaped off the table. She was still holding that towel to her chest, but her other hand clenched into a fist, and I thought she was going to punch me. She settled for glaring at me instead, and the ogre on her neck silently snarled, showing me its many sharp teeth.

"My morphing is nobody's business," she hissed. "Get out."

"But I just want to help you—"

"Get out!" she roared.

Her amber eyes glinted with rage, as did the eyes of the ogre on her neck. Once again, I thought she might punch me, and I gritted my teeth, bracing myself for the brutal blow.

Aisha opened the door and stuck her head into the room. "Is everything okay?"

"Everything's fine," Paloma snarled. "The newb was just leaving."

She said that to insult me, and it totally worked.

"Fine," I muttered. "It's your funeral."

I marched across the room, opened the door, and stepped outside. Then I slammed the door shut behind me as hard as I could.

"Problems?" a dry voice called out.

I whirled around to find Sullivan standing there. On an impulse, I stalked forward and grabbed his arm. Paloma hadn't listened to me, but maybe he would.

"You know that Emilie did this on purpose, right? She didn't trip. She knew *exactly* what she was doing."

His eyes narrowed, but unlike Paloma, he didn't automatically discount my words. "And why would she do that?"

"Because she hates Paloma and her success. Emilie is a seething mass of jealousy."

"Are you sure that you aren't talking about yourself, highness?"

I let out a bitter laugh. "Oh, I am well acquainted with jealousy and all the crazy things it makes you do."

"You, crazy with jealousy? Now that's something I would like to see."

The cold speculation in his eyes vanished, replaced by something hotter, more intense, and far more dangerous. The hard, corded muscles in his forearm bunched and flexed under my fingers, and the warmth of his body mingled with my own. His clean vanilla scent washed over me, and I suddenly felt dizzy for another reason besides my anger. In that moment, I realized exactly how easily fighting could turn into something much more pleasurable, although still extremely dangerous to my heart.

I shoved those thoughts away, dropped his arm, and stepped back. Sullivan's gaze dimmed, but he kept staring at me.

I shook my head and forced myself to focus on something besides how blue his eyes were. "You need to watch Emilie."

"Why?"

"Because next time, she'll do something worse."

I stared at him again, letting him see how serious I was, then brushed past him and headed back to the training ring.

Despite my dire prediction, everything was quiet for the next few days, and I went about my usual routine of cooking and training. I didn't speak to Paloma, and she didn't say anything to me, but every time she came into the dining hall or walked by me in the training ring, she stared at me, and I looked back at her. I had warned her about Emilie. The rest was up to her.

Aisha had fully healed Paloma, so everything returned to normal, including how easily Paloma beat Emilie in the ring. Emilie smiled, laughed, and joked with Paloma like always, but I didn't like the sly glint in her eyes whenever she looked at her so-called friend. Even more telling, she smelled . . . *eager*. Like she already had something else planned and was just waiting for the right moment to strike.

A week after the supposed accident, I was in the dining hall dishing out lemon-blackberry cookies. I glanced at Paloma, who was sitting at her usual table, with Emilie across from her. Paloma was talking and gesturing, reenacting some move from last night's bout, which she had won. Emilie smiled and nodded, although her gaze remained cold.

I turned to finish passing out the cookies when a foul, sulfuric stench wafted across the room. My nose twitched, and I drew in a breath, tasting the air. The stench came again, stronger and more caustic. My stomach lurched. I knew that horrible, horrible odor. Thanks to Maeven and her poisonous champagne, I would never, ever forget it.

Wormroot.

I whirled around. Paloma was talking to the woman next to her, so she didn't see Emilie casually stretch her arm out and reach across the table. A small vial gleamed in Emilie's fingers, and she quickly tilted it up and dropped the contents into Paloma's glass. Then, just as casually, Emilie leaned back in her seat, picked up her fork, and started eating again.

Paloma finished her conversation with the other gladiator and picked up her glass.

"Stop!" I yelled, dropping my tray of cookies and sprinting in that direction. "Paloma! Stop! Don't drink that!"

But the dining hall was packed, and the other conversations drowned out my voice. Sullivan was the only one who paid any attention to my shouts, and he frowned as I ran past. I ignored him and kept going, darting around people and tables, but I was too late.

Paloma tilted up her glass, drained the wine inside, and set it down on the table.

She said something to Emilie, who smiled back at her.

It was the same smug look that Vasilia had always given me whenever she had triumphed, whether it was with a simple meanness, like eating all the chocolate mousse that Isobel had made for my birthday, or a crueler calculation, like blaming me for making a visiting noble girl cry when Vasilia was the one who'd ripped the girl to pieces with her insults. The look that had always made me feel so small and insignificant, knowing that I had lost to her yet again.

Paloma started coughing—and she didn't stop. She reached for her glass to take a drink and clear her throat, but of course it was empty. She stared at her glass, then looked at Emilie, whose smile twisted into a satisfied sneer.

Paloma's eyes widened with horrific understanding. She pushed back her chair and surged to her feet, but the wormroot was already working its way through her body. She took a step and toppled to the floor, gasping for breath.

People yelled in surprise and jumped to their feet, not realizing what was going on, but I shoved them out of my way and dropped to my knees beside Paloma. She stared up at me, still gasping for breath, her features twisting with pain.

"Help . . . me . . ." she rasped, tears leaking out of her eyes.

The troupe members surged forward and formed a semicircle around Paloma and me, jockeying back and forth for position and trying to figure out what was happening.

"What's wrong?"

"Paloma's sick! She needs help!"

"Aisha! Aisha, are you in here?" Sullivan's voice boomed out, asking for the bone master.

But wormroot was one of the deadliest poisons, and Aisha couldn't help Paloma. No one could help her now. Sadness shot through me, and I grabbed Paloma's hand, hoping to at least comfort her as she died.

A strange thing happened. As soon as my skin touched

hers, I realized that I could actually *feel* the poison running through her body, like ribbons of fire unspooling in her veins, burning and liquefying everything they touched. Even more importantly, I could feel my own power rising up in response. Even though I wasn't the one who had been poisoned, my immunity was still responding to the magic in the wormroot and trying to snuff it out.

Maybe I could save Paloma after all.

I drew in a breath, and the foul, sulfuric stench of the wormroot burned my nose. Paloma was sweating the poison out of her pores, and it wouldn't be long before she started bleeding from her eyes, nose, and mouth. I didn't know if this would work, but I had to try. So I leaned down, wrapped my other hand around Paloma's, and reached out with my immunity.

The poison hit me a second later.

A red-hot spark flared to life in the pit of my stomach, as though I had swallowed a burning ember. That one spark exploded into a dozen more, all of them spreading through my body like wildfire. In an instant, I was sweating just like Paloma was, and I had to grind my teeth together to keep from screaming at the intense, searing pain. I tightened my grip on her hand, digging my nails into her skin so that I wouldn't be tempted to let go to stop my own pain.

Somehow, I managed to push past the poison and focus on my immunity, on that cold, hard, unyielding power deep inside me. I grabbed hold of that power, pulling it up, up, up, and sent it surging out through my entire body, like it was a protective, malleable shield that I could bend and twist into any shape that I wanted.

Everything else fell away. The troupe members clustered

around us, their surprised murmurs, Sullivan's continued shouts for Aisha and the other bone masters. It all faded to a dull roar in the back of my mind, and all I was aware of was the poison, the magic, raging through my own body, trying to kill me along with Paloma. Sweat slid down my neck, my breath came in thin, ragged gasps, and my heart was pounding so hard that I thought it was going to beat out of my chest and skitter away across the floor.

But finally—*finally*—the burning sparks of pain flickered and started to fade away. I reached for even more of my immunity, using that malleable shield to snuff out the sparks. My heart slowed down to its normal rhythm, and my breath came much easier than before. I was going to be okay.

And so was Paloma.

I leaned forward, stared at our interlocked hands, and focused on sharing my immunity with her. On taking the power inside my body and wrapping it around her like a fist, and then using that fist to crush the poison to nothingness.

And it worked.

Her heart slowed, and her breathing became easier. Paloma stared up at me with shocked eyes, as did the ogre on her neck, both of them wondering what had happened, and how I had managed to save all three of us. I was wondering how I was going to explain that myself.

Paloma let out a long, tired sigh, and I felt the last of the poison fizzle out of her body, like champagne that had suddenly gone flat. It took me a moment, but I pried my fingernails out of her skin, let go of her hand, and slumped down on the floor next to her.

The whole thing had taken fifteen seconds, maybe less, but

it seemed much, much longer than that. The troupe members were still gathered around us, wondering what had just happened, although I didn't hear Sullivan shouting anymore.

I wiped the sweat off my forehead and looked at Paloma. "Are you okay?"

She nodded, still too busy sucking down air to speak.

"Paloma!" Emilie fell to her knees beside us. "Are you okay? What happened?"

Icy rage surged through me, even colder than my magic. I lunged over, tackled Emilie, and knocked her down to the floor.

"You know exactly what happened!" I yelled, punching her in the face. "You poisoned her!"

For once, I landed the perfect punch, and Emilie's nose broke with a loud, satisfying *crunch*. Blood sprayed everywhere, but the gladiator wasn't stunned for long.

"You bitch!" she hissed. "I'll kill you for this!"

She slapped me, but I shook off the hard, stinging blow and shoved my hand down in between us. Emilie slapped me again, but I managed to reach into the pocket on the front of her tunic. My hand closed around something small and thin, and I yanked it out and held it up where everyone could see it.

A glass vial glinted in my fingers.

Emilie froze, her hand reared back to slap me again. Everyone stared at the empty vial in my fingers, then at her. Silence dropped over the dining hall.

Emilie snarled and shoved me away. I hit the floor, and the vial tumbled from my fingers and rolled away. I didn't see where it went, but I didn't care. I scrambled back up onto my feet. So did Emilie, who lunged forward, grabbed a butter knife off the table, and brandished it at me.

I pulled up just short of tackling her again. She was a skilled gladiator, and she could kill me with that dull little blade if she stabbed me in the right place. Emilie screamed with rage and lunged at me—

Blue lightning zipped through the air, slamming into her body and knocking her away from me. Emilie hit the floor and slid back into one of the tables. Several plates slipped off and landed right on top of her head. *Splat-splat-splat.* In an instant, she was dripping with salad, gravy, and mashed potatoes.

I snarled and headed toward her, but Sullivan grabbed my arm and yanked me back. Blue lightning crackled on his fingertips, shocking me, and I reached for my immunity to throttle his magic like I had the wormroot—

"Enough!" he snapped. "Restrain them!"

Sullivan let go, but strong hands grabbed me from behind, keeping me from lunging at Emilie again. Two other gladiators grabbed Emilie's arms and hauled her to her feet.

Silence dropped over the dining hall again. Sullivan made sure that we were both restrained, then walked over, knelt down, and picked up the empty vial. He stared at it, then at Emilie, and finally at me. He jerked his head at the gladiators holding both of us.

"Bring them," he said. "We'll get to the bottom of this—one way or another."

CHAPTER SIXTEEN

I wound up sitting in a chair in front of Serilda's desk in the manor library. Cho and Sullivan were standing behind the desk on either side of Serilda, who was seated in her own chair, studying the empty vial.

For the last fifteen minutes, I had stood in the hallway outside the library with my two guards and listened to Emilie's muffled shouts about how I was the one who'd poisoned Paloma, how she'd just been trying to help her friend, how I'd attacked her for no reason, and all the other lies that had dripped off her venomous tongue.

When she had finished, her guards had escorted her out of the library, and my guards had brought me in to plead my case. It reminded me of all the times that Felton had me marched into Cordelia's library to face the queen's cold displeasure whenever I had shirked one of my so-called royal duties.

Serilda passed the vial to Cho, who examined it for a few moments before setting it down. Sullivan had already seen it.

Serilda leaned forward and steepled her hands together on top of her desk. "Tell me what happened."

Well, that was a far more neutral opening than I had expected, but I didn't like the way that she was studying me, so I decided to keep my answers short and simple.

"I saw Emilie pour poison into Paloma's glass."

"And how did you know that it was poison?" she asked. "Much less wormroot?"

I tapped my nose. "I could smell it. Seems my mutt magic is good for something after all."

She arched an eyebrow at my sarcasm, but she tilted her head, ceding my point and telling me to continue.

"I yelled at Paloma to put her wine down, but she didn't hear me, and she drank it. Paloma collapsed, and I rushed over to see if she was okay. Everyone saw what happened next."

"Actually, there is some confusion about what happened next. Everyone was surprised when Paloma collapsed, and they agree that you were on the floor next to her. But some of them said that you held her hand for several seconds. Why would you do that? What were you trying to accomplish?"

"I wasn't trying to accomplish anything," I snapped. "I thought she was dying. I just wanted to comfort her."

Serilda studied me, almost as if she could hear the lie in my words. But after a moment, she tilted her head, ceding my point again. "Well, everyone definitely remembers you attacking Emilie and yelling that she poisoned Paloma. Only Emilie claims that *you* poisoned Paloma instead."

"Of course she would say that," I snapped again. "She just poisoned someone. Do you really think that lying would be a challenge for her?"

"I think that you should keep your attitude to yourself," Serilda snapped back. "You don't seem to understand how much trouble you're in."

Her annoyed tone made me even angrier. "Oh, I know *exactly* how much trouble I'm in. I'm just a lowly newb, and Emilie is one of your top gladiators. It's easy to see who you're going to believe, and the answer is not me because I don't make any money for you. Not like she does."

Serilda's lips pressed into a tight, thin line. Cho winced, and even Sullivan looked uncomfortable. Disgust filled me. I had thought—*hoped*—that things would be different here, but in many ways, life at the Black Swan was exactly the same as it had been at Seven Spire, right down to how money could make people overlook a multitude of sins.

Yes, that might be the same, but *I* was different now, and I wasn't going to acquiesce to Serilda like I had to Cordelia so many times before. Not when I knew that I was right.

"We all know that Paloma was poisoned, and Sullivan has studied the vial and agrees that it contained wormroot," Serilda said. "What I want to know is how you, a mutt with very little magic, managed to heal her?"

I had been expecting the question, but I still had to work to keep my face blank and my body from tensing. "I have no idea what you're talking about. I'm not a bone master or a magier. Like you said, I'm just a mutt."

"No one, not even a gladiator as strong as Paloma, survives being poisoned with wormroot," Serilda said in a harsh tone. "Everyone saw you leaning over her after she collapsed. Then, less than a minute later, she's better."

"I was checking to see if she was okay. That's all."

"Then how do you explain the fact that she's not dead?"

I shrugged. "I don't know. Maybe Emilie was as sloppy with the poison as she is in the arena. Maybe she didn't use enough."

Serilda's eyes narrowed. I kept my gaze steady on hers, desperately hoping that she wouldn't see through all my lies. Cho and Sullivan remained still and silent.

After several long, tense seconds, Serilda leaned back in her chair. "Luckily for you, Paloma supports your story. She says that Emilie is the one who poisoned her and that you were just trying to help."

So she had already questioned the gladiator. I wondered what else Paloma had told her, but I wasn't going to be stupid enough to ask. That would only make Serilda even more suspicious. Maybe Paloma hadn't realized that I'd used my immunity to neutralize the poison.

"But I wasn't there, and no one seems to know for sure who poisoned Paloma, only that it was either you or Emilie."

"So?" I asked, not liking where this was going.

"So I can't let this doubt and drama fester, lest it divide the gladiators, along with the rest of the troupe. You and Emilie are both gladiators, both bound by the same rules, so the two of you will settle this in the arena."

A finger of cold dread crept down my spine. "What do you mean?"

She smiled, but there was no warmth in her expression. "You and Emilie will fight in a black-ring match."

A black-ring match? But that meant . . .

Serilda nodded, confirming my fear. "The two of you will fight to the death."

All the air drained out of my lungs, taking my anger along with it, and I slumped back in my chair, too stunned to speak. I glanced at Cho, but his face was hard and remote. He would support Serilda in this. I looked at Sullivan. He grimaced, dropped his gaze from mine, and shifted on his feet, as though the silent plea in my eyes made him feel guilty. Of course it did. I had warned him about Emilie, and he hadn't listened. Now I was going to pay the price for his mistake.

Panic surged through me, and I thought about telling them who I really was. That I was a member of the royal family, that I was a Blair, not a gladiator, and that I had come here for protection, not to be executed for others' amusement. I sucked in a breath and opened my mouth to launch into my confession, but then I looked at Serilda again.

She was drumming her fingers on the desk, a resigned expression on her face, as if she was waiting for me to spit out my tearful plea so she could tell me no and get on with more important business. It was the same bored look that Cordelia had always given me whenever I had complained about Vasilia or tried to ask her for something.

Just like that, my confession died on my lips, and icy rage blasted through me, freezing out my panic. The old Everleigh would have given in to her fear. The old Everleigh would have bowed and scraped and done everything possible to avoid any sort of conflict, much less something as deadly as a black-ring match. The old Everleigh would have begged, pleaded, and even groveled to stay in her safe little bubble, no matter what the cost was to her own pride and sense of self-worth.

But the old Everleigh had died on the royal lawn, and this new, stronger, fiercer Evie had risen to take her place. I might not be a bona fide gladiator, but I wasn't someone to be dismissed and brushed aside, not by Serilda Swanson or anyone else. Not anymore. Never again.

"Fine," I snarled. "I'll play your little game. I'll fight Emilie."

Surprise flickered in Serilda's eyes, along with what looked like a tiny bit of respect, although cold calculation quickly replaced both emotions. "Very well. Emilie has already agreed to the match."

Of course she had. She wouldn't even have to break a sweat to kill me.

"The black-ring match will be the finale of the Saturday night show," she continued.

Saturday night was always the most lucrative, and Serilda would make even more money once the black-ring match was announced. Not only from the ticket sales and concessions, but also from the betting that would go on inside the arena. She could potentially make hundreds of thousands of crowns, if not more. Well, she wasn't going to be the only one who profited.

"I want triple the prize money."

More surprise flickered in her eyes. "You really think that you can beat Emilie?"

"Why not? Stranger things have happened."

"And you expect me to give you triple the prize money if you do?" She laughed. "Well, you're certainly not lacking for confidence."

"Do we have a deal or not?"

Serilda smiled. "I do like a woman who knows her own worth. Very well. If you kill Emilie, I will give you triple the prize money."

She got to her feet and held out her hand. I stood as well, and we shook on it. I started to drop her hand, but Serilda tightened her grip.

"I wouldn't go spending your prize money just yet. You have to earn it first."

I gave her a thin smile. "Don't worry. I will."

My two gladiator guards were waiting outside the library, but Sullivan stepped into the hallway and waved them off.

"I'll take her back to the barracks. Serilda wants you to help her with something else."

The two men nodded, went into the library, and shut the door behind them. Sullivan gestured with his hand, and we walked down the hallway and left the manor house.

Night had fallen while I'd been pleading my case, and the moon had already risen over the arena, bathing the round dome in soft, silvery light. Tonight was Monday, which meant that I had less than a week to prepare for the black-ring match. Less than a week to live, despite my earlier bravado in the library. I shivered and crossed my arms over my chest.

Sullivan and I left the manor house and walked through the gardens. The streetlamps that lined the path bathed everything in a dreamy, golden haze, from the trees, to the evergreen bushes, to the stream that ran under the stone bridge. It would have been a lovely, romantic stroll, if not for the fact that I could still see the arena dome looming over the trees. We reached the center of the bridge and stopped, right in the middle of all that golden light.

Sullivan cleared his throat. "I'm sorry that I didn't believe you. Emilie did cut Paloma on purpose, and now she's done something worse, like you said."

I shrugged, not really accepting his apology but not entirely rejecting it either.

"But don't worry. I'm going to make this right."

"How are you going to do that?" I arched an eyebrow. "Unless, of course, you plan to concoct some sort of elaborate disguise and fight in the arena for me. You wouldn't look so good with a ponytail, though." I tugged on my own short black ponytail at the nape of my neck.

For the first time since I had known him, a genuine smile lifted Sullivan's lips, and he actually laughed, just a bit. I liked his smile and the sound far more than I should have.

"Nothing like that," he said. "But I'm going to help you. All you have to do is trust me. Can you do that, highness?"

Highness. I had always despised the mocking nickname, but this time, it came out as a low rasp that made me shiver even more than the chilly night air did. The golden haze highlighted his strong, handsome features, and for once, his blue eyes blazed with warmth instead of cold disdain. An answering bit of warmth curled through my stomach, but I forced myself to look away.

"Sure, why not? It's not like I have a choice."

He grabbed my arm, making me face him again. "I am going to *fix* this. I promise."

His voice rang with so much determination that I almost believed him—until I caught sight of the arena dome again. Sullivan was wrong. Even a magier couldn't fix this.

Still, he was trying to make me feel better, so I forced myself to smile at him. "I'll hold you to that."

⚜

Sullivan escorted me back to the barracks. He nodded at me, then turned and strode away, probably heading back to his home. I waited until he had disappeared from sight, then opened the door and went into the barracks.

The female gladiators were gathered in the common area in front of the fireplace, talking, writing letters, and playing games. The second that I stepped inside, all conversation cut off, and everyone stared at me. I grimaced and moved forward, trying to ignore the curious stares and sharp whispers that sprang up. This was definitely one of those times when the troupe was far too much like the palace for my liking.

I headed for my cot. Given what had happened, I expected the bed to be pushed even farther back into the corner, but to my surprise, my cot was in its usual spot, and someone had crammed her bed and belongings in next to mine.

Paloma.

She was sitting on her cot and using a cloth to polish the spikes on her enormous mace. Several other weapons, ranging in size from a large ax to a not-so-small pair of daggers, covered the rest of the mattress. All the weapons had been freshly polished, as well as sharpened. Besides the weapons, the only personal item that I could see was a soft green blanket with tattered satin edges and a faded ogre face in the middle that was draped across the foot of her bed. It was far too small for Paloma to use, so it must have had some sentimental value. Maybe her baby blanket?

I looked at Paloma, then glanced over my shoulder at the other gladiators, wondering if this was some kind of joke. The other women watched us for a few seconds, then went back to their previous conversations and activities. I turned to face the gladiator again.

"Um, Paloma?"

She put down her mace. "Yes, Evie?"

"What are you doing?"

"Trying to figure out what you can use to kill Emilie. But all my weapons are too big and heavy for you." Paloma studied the assortment on her bed. She picked up a sword and gave it an experimental swing before shaking her head and setting it down. "Why? What does it look like I'm doing?"

I gestured at her cot, which was inches away from mine now. "It looks like you've moved in next to me."

"Of course I moved in next to you. I certainly wasn't going to sleep next to Emilie anymore. Not after she tried to kill me."

I couldn't argue with that. I wouldn't have wanted to sleep next to her either.

I glanced toward the front of the room again. I hadn't noticed it before, but Emilie's cot was missing, along with the rest of her things. "Where is she?"

"Under guard in another building," Paloma said in a matter-of-fact voice. "I told Serilda that if I saw that bitch again, I would kill her with my bare hands. I wanted to kill her anyway, but you know the rules. Gladiators settle their disputes in the arena. I only wish that I was the one who was going to face her."

She stared at me, as did the ogre on her neck, telling me how serious they both were. Paloma had every right to be angry, but I hadn't expected her to get Emilie kicked out of the barracks, much less drag her cot back here next to mine. I had assumed that everyone would shun me until the match, since I was a newb and had so little hope of winning it. But Paloma was acting like we were . . . friends.

She sensed my confusion. "What's wrong? Don't you want me to help you? I thought that after what happened in the dining hall . . ." Her face hardened, and she surged to her feet. "Don't worry. I know when I'm not wanted. I'll leave."

I held out my hands and stepped in front of her. "No! That's not what I meant. I do want you to help me. You just . . . surprised me. I didn't think that you liked me very much."

She shrugged. "You weren't a threat to me as a fighter, so I didn't think very much of you at all."

Of course she didn't. No one else here had taken me seriously as a gladiator, including myself. I had just been going through the motions, treading water until I could figure out what to do next.

You have to live. *You have to protect Bellona. Promise me you'll do that.* Cordelia's voice whispered in my mind, but I forced the memory away. I could barely protect myself right now, much less an entire kingdom.

"You saved my life," Paloma continued. "I owe you a debt, Evie."

I sighed. She sounded exactly like some noble at the palace. Sometimes, I thought everyone should have walked around like Felton, carrying little ledger books, and keeping a list of all the favors we owed and all the ones that we wanted to collect on in return.

"I didn't save your life. I didn't do anything."

Her eyes narrowed. "Yes, you did. I don't know how, but you got rid of the poison. You saved me, Evie, and nothing that you say will convince me otherwise."

I sighed again, too tired to deny it. "So why didn't you tell Serilda and the others that?"

She shrugged again. "If you want to keep your magic, or whatever it is, a secret, then that's your business, not mine."

I wasn't about to try to explain my immunity, so I eased past her and flopped down onto my own cot. "You don't owe me anything. I would have saved your life anyway. I don't expect anything in return. You don't have to pretend to be my friend just because I helped you."

I'd had a lifetime of that at the palace. And every time—*every single time*—people had only pretended to like me because they wanted something. Even a royal with no money and no magic could be useful on occasion. But the worst people had been the ones who had genuinely wanted to be my friend . . . until Vasilia had offered them something better. The regret on their faces had been sharper than a sword in my heart. They had liked me well enough, but they had their families, businesses, and fortunes to consider, and I had never been as important as any of that. I couldn't even blame those people for their choices, but they had still hurt me all the same.

"And I can't think of a better reason to be your friend than the fact that you helped me," Paloma said with absolute conviction. "You saved my life, Evie. I'll never forget that."

"So what you're saying is that we're friends now, whether I like it or not?" I couldn't keep the amusement out of my voice.

She thought about it for a moment, then smiled. "Yes. We are friends now, whether you like it or not." Her smile slowly faded away. "Is that okay?"

Uncertainty filled her face, and even the ogre on her neck seemed small and hesitant. In that moment, she reminded me of, well, myself, and all the times that I had opened myself up to someone. Almost all those times had ended in heartache, but I wasn't going to do that to her.

"It's more than okay. Just promise me one thing."

"What's that?"

I threw my pillow at her, which she easily caught. "Don't you dare snore. Or I might have to kill you myself."

Paloma smiled at my black humor and tossed the pillow back at me. I, of course, did not catch it, and the soft lump hit me square in the chest. "I can make no such promises."

I smiled back at her. "I can live with that."

CHAPTER SEVENTEEN

The next morning, Paloma roused me out of bed well before dawn, while everyone else was still asleep. Despite my grumbles, she made me get dressed, grab some of her many weapons, and head out to the training ring for a practice session before I had to report for kitchen duty.

Winter was slowly giving way to spring, but the early-morning air was still quite chilly, since the sun hadn't risen yet. But Paloma was not to be denied. She made me strip off my blue jacket, pick up a sword, and face her. I didn't want to be out here, but I was glad that no one else was out here either. I didn't want anyone to witness my humiliation—or realize how easily Emilie was going to kill me.

While we went through the drills and warmed up, I asked Paloma something that I had been wondering about for weeks. "How are you always able to beat Emilie? What's your secret?"

"Emilie is fast. That's her mutt magic, and that's her main advantage. She always tries to end a fight as quickly as possible. But she's no match for my strength or my endurance, so I just wait for her to wear herself out. When she gets tired, she gets slow, and that's when I move in and knock her out of the fight." Paloma shrugged. "But you aren't as strong as me, and you're certainly not as quick as Emilie. She's going to kill you unless you find some way to counter her speed."

I flexed my hand. My immunity rippled through my fingers, waiting to be used. "I might be able to do that."

"Well, you'd better, or you're going to die."

I grimaced. My new friend definitely wasn't one to sugarcoat things. She also wasn't one to take it easy on me, as I found out when we started sparring.

"Pitiful," Paloma said as she slapped my sword out of my hand for the tenth time in as many minutes. "Absolutely pitiful. You're not nearly as far along in your training as you should be, given the weeks you've been here. And I thought you said that you'd had some instruction before you came to the Black Swan. Who did it come from? A blind man?"

I winced, thinking of Captain Auster. He would have demanded that I drop and start doing push-ups as punishment for being disarmed so many times.

My gaze moved past Paloma and up to the palace in the distance. Only a few lights burned in the windows at Seven Spire, and the gladiators and gargoyles carved into the massive tearstone columns were the same pale gray as the approaching dawn.

From the gossip I'd heard, Captain Auster hadn't been executed yet, but it was only a matter of time before Vasilia grew tired of torturing him. My heart ached, not just for Auster, but for everyone who had died during the massacre—and all the other people who would still die.

According to the rumors, the Andvarian royal family had

vehemently denied having anything to do with Queen Cordelia's assassination, and relations between Bellona and Andvari had broken down completely. Now whispers curled through the air like smoke, all saying the same thing—that war between the two kingdoms was coming soon. Just like Maeven, Nox, and their Mortan masters wanted.

"Well?" Paloma asked, cutting into my dark thoughts. "Did you have other training?"

I sighed. "I did, but it never went very well. I could never get the hang of fighting. Not like I could other things."

"What other things? What's more important than fighting?"

I snorted. Spoken like a true gladiator. "Well, dancing, for one thing. My mistress was very . . . concerned with dancing, parties, and protocol."

Paloma frowned, and the ogre on her neck gave me an incredulous look as if it couldn't even fathom such a thing.

It wasn't a lie. Queen Cordelia had been quite fond of royal balls, and she had demanded that everyone at the palace learn the steps to all the traditional Bellonan waltzes, reels, and more. Dancing was one of the few things that I had always excelled at. The music, the hand movements, the quick turns, the low bows, the ebb and flow of steps as the dancers moved together, apart, and back together again. I loved it all. Plus, there were always so many people dancing during the balls that it was one of the few times when I could truly enjoy myself without fear of attracting Vasilia's attention. Even when Lady Xenia had been poking me with her cane, I had still enjoyed learning the Tanzen Freund, and it had given me a sense of pride and accomplishment to master something so intricate and graceful.

Paloma kept staring at me like I was some exotic creature that she had never seen before, so I tugged the sword out of her hand and laid it on a nearby bench. Then I took her hand again, curtsied low, and moved this way and that, twirling around her in the traditional Bellonan courting waltz.

Paloma looked at me like I was crazy, but I smiled and hummed the music that was in my mind, timing my movements to the soft, steady beat—

"You move quite well," a voice called out. "Too bad dancing is not fighting. Then you would win for sure."

Startled, I dropped Paloma's hand and whirled around. Sullivan was leaning against the wall, amusement creasing his face. A hot blush scalded my cheeks. I wondered how long he had been standing there, watching me twirl around Paloma like an idiot.

I crossed my arms over my chest. "Well, dancing is a form of fighting. At least where I come from."

Again, it wasn't a lie. Who danced with whom and how many times had been a spectator sport at Seven Spire, and the competition for certain lords' and ladies' time and attention had been equally as fierce, especially among those hoping to snare a wealthy, powerful spouse.

Sullivan's gaze sharpened. "And where is that?"

Too late I realized my mistake, but I shrugged off his pointed question. "Nowhere important."

He stared at me, but when he realized that I wasn't going to answer, he shook his head. "Well, you need to forget about dancing and focus on fighting because Emilie is going to do her best to kill you. Have you ever been in a fight before, highness?"

I thought of the turncoat guards, trying to hack me to

pieces with their swords, and Vasilia, gleefully blasting me with her lightning. Not to mention all the terrible things that had happened when my parents had been murdered. "Yes, I have been in a fight before."

He snorted in disbelief. "Really? What kind? Some slap-fight with another woman? Some petty squabble with another kitchen worker? This won't be like that."

My hands clenched into fists. He had no idea what I had been through—*no fucking idea*.

"I've seen the gladiator bouts," I snapped. "I know what they're like."

He shook his head again, moved away from the wall, and stalked toward me. He pushed back his coat, revealing the sword belted to his waist. "You might have seen the bouts, but you've never been in one, especially not a black-ring match."

Sullivan drew his sword, charged forward, and swung his weapon at me. Paloma and I both lurched out of the way. She managed to get clear of him, but I tripped over the sword that she had knocked out of my hand earlier. In an instant, I was flat on my back on the ground, with Sullivan looming over me and the point of his sword resting against my throat, just like always.

Not satisfying at all and particularly humiliating right now.

"You're dead," he said in a cold voice. "Five seconds into the fight, and you're already dead. You're going to have to do better than this if you want to stay alive. Much less actually win."

He leaned down and offered me his hand, but I slapped it away and scrambled to my feet on my own. Paloma looked back and forth between the two of us and backed up another step.

"You've made your point," I snapped again. "I'm a terrible fighter. Do you think that I don't know that? Emilie might not be able to beat Paloma, but she can certainly beat *me*. I'm not an idiot."

"I never said you were."

"You didn't have to. You think that I'm not taking this seriously? Well, I assure you that I am taking it very, very seriously. After all, it's *my* life that's on the line." I let out a low, angry, bitter laugh. "You have no idea what I've been through. The fights that I've been in. The blood that I've seen. The death that I've witnessed. So don't pretend like you're better than me, and don't you dare judge me, princeling."

Sullivan stiffened, and a muscle ticked in his jaw. "What did you call me?"

"Princeling," I sneered. "You walk around like you're something special with your fine coat and your fancy sword and your lightning magic. You act like you're some handsome prince that we should all bow down to because you know what's best for everyone. Well, I have news for you, Sully. You are *not* a prince. You're just another cog in the wheel, like the rest of us."

My insults were rather tame, compared to others that I had heard at the palace, but something about my words must have hit home. For the first time since I had joined the troupe, I had completely smashed through Sullivan's smug facade. He flinched as though I had stabbed him in the heart, and hurt flashed in his eyes. But the emotion vanished, replaced by anger that stained his cheeks a dark red. He glared at me, and I smirked back at him.

Sullivan stepped back and sheathed his sword. "I was trying to help you, but I see now that it's a lost cause, just like you are. Good luck in the ring, highness. You're going to need it."

He whipped around and stalked away. The long tails of his gray coat nipped at his bootheels, as if they were bristling with the same anger that he felt. Sullivan shoved through one of the gates and vanished from view.

"What was that about?" Paloma asked.

"I have no idea," I muttered.

She shook her head, then went over to grab her sword. I started to do the same when I spotted a gleam of glass out of the corner of my eye. I turned in that direction.

Serilda was watching me.

She was sitting on the second-floor balcony of her manor house, wrapped in a white silk robe and sipping a mug of mochana. Judging from her amused smile, she had seen my little spat with Sullivan. Of course she had. I sighed, then turned away from her and picked up my sword.

"Come on." I lifted the weapon and faced Paloma again. "Let's get back to work, and see if we can figure out some way to save my miserable life."

For the rest of the week, Paloma did her best to train me. Getting me up early, working with me during regular training, even dragging me back to the ring after dinner. I didn't know that I made any real progress, but it was nice to have someone who cared whether I lived or died.

But the days passed by all too quickly, and before I knew it, Saturday night had rolled around.

Instead of trudging up and down the bleachers, selling cornucopia and other treats, like I had during the other shows, I was in a dressing room deep in the bowels of the arena, getting ready for the black-ring match, which was the final event of the night.

Vanity tables with lighted mirrors ran down one side of the dressing room. Scissors, needles, spools of thread, and bottles of makeup and perfume littered the tabletops, while leotards, masks, and feather boas stuck up out of the overstuffed drawers. Metal racks full of costumes lined the walls like guards, each brightly colored sequin winking at me like an evil eye.

Paloma had helped me get ready, and now I was sitting at one of the vanity tables, staring at my reflection and trying to make sense of the person looking back at me in the mirror.

Oh, I was wearing the same sort of fighting leathers that I always wore—a tight, fitted, sleeveless shirt, a knee-length kilt, and sandals with straps that wound up past my ankles. The only difference was that they were made of black leather tonight. Still, the clothes were familiar enough.

But my face was entirely unfamiliar.

Normally, the gladiators fought in the arena just as they were. But for a black-ring match, each gladiator's face was heavily painted. I wasn't quite sure why. Perhaps to make us look more like characters, creatures, these abstract *things,* instead of real people fighting, bleeding, and dying for others' amusement.

My face had been painted to look like a black swan.

Midnight-black makeup ringed my eyes in thick, heavy circles before fanning out into thin, delicate streaks that resembled shard-like feathers. Bright slashes of silver had been painted over the unrelenting black, adding to the feathery look, and several small blue crystals had been glued at the corners of my eyes. Bloodred gloss covered my lips, while silver glitter shimmered on my arms, hands, and legs. For a final touch, my black hair had been pulled into three separate knots that ran down the back of my head. Black feathers bristled up out of each knot. They had been glued in place, along with more blue crystals.

The paint master had finished working on my face five minutes ago, and I had been sitting here staring at myself ever since, wondering why Serilda had wanted me to look like the embodiment of her crest. Why me instead of Emilie, who was far more likely to win? It was probably just a cruel joke on Serilda's part.

"Are you okay?" Paloma asked. "You've been fiddling with that bag for a while now."

My gaze dropped to the black velvet bag sitting on the table. I'd had to remove it from its usual hiding place on my belt loop when I had put on the fighting leathers. I couldn't leave it here, but I couldn't take it into the ring with me either. That left me with only one option.

"Here." I handed it to Paloma. "Keep this safe, will you?"

She hefted the bag. "What's in here?"

"Nothing much. Just a bracelet, along with a memory stone. But if I don't make it through this, keep the bracelet for yourself and give the stone to Serilda." My mouth twisted. "She might find it interesting."

She would probably find it much more than that. I still didn't know if I could trust Serilda, but at least if I died, the memory stone would be her problem, instead of mine.

Paloma slipped the bag into her pocket. "I'll hold on to this for you, but I'm not keeping anything, because you're going to win, Evie."

I gave her a flat look.

"You are going to *win*." She poked her finger into my shoulder for emphasis, and the ogre on her neck glowered at me as well.

Before I could respond, a soft knock sounded, and the door opened. Sullivan stepped inside the dressing room.

He glanced at me, then Paloma. "Can you give us a moment, please?"

She nodded, then smiled at me, left the room, and shut the door behind her.

I got to my feet and faced the magier. We hadn't spoken since our argument, and he hadn't singled me out during any of the regular training sessions this week. He had watched me spar with Paloma, though, just as I had watched him work with the other gladiators. Despite how angry he had made me, I couldn't take my eyes off him whenever he was around, and he didn't seem to be able to look away from me either.

Sullivan studied me, his gaze tracing over the makeup and crystals on my face and the feathers in my hair. "You look lovely," he said, an odd rasp in his voice. "Strong and fierce. Like a true gladiator."

I snorted. "Don't you mean like a gladiator who's about to die in a few minutes?"

His face hardened. "Not if I can help it."

He glanced around the room, making sure that we were truly alone, then pulled something out of his pocket, stepped forward, and held it out to me.

A single white feather.

"Here," he said. "Take this."

My nose twitched, and I drew in a breath, tasting all the scents in the air. The soft, powdery makeup on my face. The faint tang of sweat that permeated the costumes.

The stench of poison on the white feather.

I squinted. A small needle had been attached to the tip

of the feather, one that reeked of poison. It didn't smell like wormroot, but I could still sense the death in the harsh aroma.

"What am I supposed to do with that?"

"Tuck it into your hair with all the others," Sullivan said. "Take it into the arena with you, and use it, when the time is right."

My eyes narrowed. "I can smell the poison on it. You want me to kill Emilie with it."

He winced, but he didn't deny it.

"You don't think that I have even the smallest chance of winning. That's why you want me to use your pretty little poisoned feather. That's why you want me to *cheat*."

His wince deepened. "It's my fault that you're in this position. If I had listened when you told me about Emilie, none of this would be happening. I told you that I would fix things, and this is how I'm doing it."

"By cheating?" I gave him a disgusted look. "That's exactly what Emilie did when she poisoned Paloma. She couldn't win on her own, so she took the easy way out. And now you're telling me to do the same thing. Well, guess what? I won't do it."

Anger sparked in his eyes. "Emilie is a trained gladiator. *She will kill you.* Is your stubborn pride worth more than your life?"

I looked at the feather. I could pretend to be injured, wait for Emilie to lean over me, and then pluck it out of my hair. Given how strong the poison smelled, all I would have to do was scratch her with the needle, and the fight would be over. Sullivan was right. I could kill Emilie, I could survive, if I used the feather.

But I didn't want to win—not like that.

Because it was just like something that Vasilia would have done. It was just like a dozen things that she *had* done to me. And it was exactly what she had done during the massacre. Vasilia knew that she couldn't defeat Cordelia face-to-face, magier-to-magier, so she had poisoned her mother with wormroot to take away the queen's magic.

The shock, the screams, the blood, the death. Memories of the massacre flashed through my mind, hardening my resolve. I might not be a gladiator, and I might die in the arena tonight, but I would *not* be like Vasilia—not even if it cost me my life.

I crossed my arms over my chest, stepped back, and shook my head. "No. I won't use it."

Surprise filled his face, and he opened his mouth, probably to argue, but I shook my head again. He stared at me, emotions crackling like lightning in his blue, blue eyes.

"I'm trying to save your life," he growled, a desperate edge to his voice. "Why won't you let me save you, Evie?"

Evie. That was the first time that he had ever said my name, ever called me anything other than the mocking *highness,* and it resonated through the air between us like the last note of a sweet, sweet song. My heart did a funny little lurch, and suddenly, I wasn't thinking about the match, the poisoned feather, or my own principles.

I was thinking about how much I wanted him.

About how much I wanted to crush my lips to his. To run my hands through his silky brown hair, along his broad shoulders, and all the way down his chest. To draw his rich, vanilla scent deep down into my lungs. To feel his warm, bare skin next to mine. To touch him, and have him touch me in return. To move with him. To lose myself in him and finally satisfy this electricity that continuously hummed, sparked, and crackled between us.

For a mad, mad moment, I seriously considered it. Why shouldn't I fuck Sullivan? Why shouldn't I wring every single drop of pleasure I could out of this moment? It wasn't like I was ever going to get another chance.

The other gladiators did it all the time. They were always sneaking off after training bouts and before and after the arena matches. Fighting and fucking made them feel alive, and I knew that it would do the same for me. I *wanted* to feel alive tonight; I *needed* to feel alive tonight. Even more importantly, I could sense how good it would be between Sullivan and me.

I drew in a breath to tell him exactly what I wanted, and the scent of poison on the feather filled my nose again. The harsh stench made me hesitate.

"Please, Evie," Sullivan growled again. "Let me help you. Let me save you."

Save me? No one had ever fucking *saved* me. Not from my parents being murdered, not from Vasilia's cruelty, not from the massacre. And Sullivan couldn't save me now, either. Not really. Not from going into the arena.

And I didn't want him to.

The old Everleigh would have taken that poisoned feather without a second thought. She would have been so grateful that someone was trying to help her that she would have done whatever they wanted without question. But I was the new Evie, and I did things on my own terms. The new Evie didn't want to cheat. Even more importantly, the new Evie believed that she was strong enough to win all by herself.

My resolve hardened again, along with my heart. I squared

my shoulders and lifted my chin. "I am perfectly capable of saving myself."

His anger and all the other emotions in his gaze snuffed out, replaced by sad, weary resignation. "Then you're a fool."

"Probably. But at least I'll die an honest fool."

Sullivan's lips pressed into a thin, unhappy line, but he stepped forward, his body inches away from mine. He loomed over me, and I stared up at him. Neither one of us said anything, but tension crackled in the air between us, along with other, deeper things that I didn't want to think about. That I couldn't *let* myself think about.

Sullivan leaned forward and laid the white feather on the vanity table. Then he moved away from me. "In case you change your mind."

"I won't."

His lips lifted a bit. "I know. That's one of the things I like about you, highness."

Before I could respond, he turned around, stalked across the dressing room, and opened the door. I thought he might slam it shut behind him, but he closed it softly instead.

I stood there, frozen in place, listening until the sound of his footsteps faded away.

CHAPTER EIGHTEEN

A minute later, a knock sounded on the door, and Paloma stepped inside the dressing room. She didn't say anything, but the look on her face—and the one of the ogre on her neck—told me that she had heard everything.

I sighed, picked up the white feather, and handed it to her. "Here. Put this in the bag too. And be careful. It's poisoned."

Paloma twirled the feather back and forth in her fingers. "He's just trying to help."

I snorted. "By telling me to cheat? Some help. Besides, even if I managed to kill Emilie with the poison, isn't the penalty for cheating in a black-ring match automatic death?"

"Yes, but Serilda would probably overlook it. She knows that Emilie is guilty. She just can't take your side. Not without definitive proof." Paloma held the feather out to me, like Sullivan had. "Are you sure that you don't want this?"

I shook my head. "No. I might kill Emilie with it, and Serilda might even let me get away with it, but *I* would know that I cheated. I won't fight like that. Not in the ring."

Paloma nodded, accepting my decision, and dropped the feather into the bag.

A trumpet blared, so loud that it seemed to shake the walls, signaling the end of the regular show. I grabbed my sword, and Paloma held up the matching shield so that I could slip my forearm through the straps. They were the only things that I was allowed to take into the ring. They were the lightest weapons Paloma had, but both objects still weighed me down in more ways than one.

The trumpet blared again, signaling that I had five minutes to get to the arena or forfeit the match. If I forfeited, the other gladiators would hunt me down and drag me out to the ring, where Emilie would have free rein to execute me on the spot. At least if I went of my own volition, I had a fighting chance.

Before I could think too much about the fact that I was most likely heading toward my own death, I marched over, opened the door, and left the dressing room. Paloma walked with me through the tunnels until we reached one of the entrances to the arena floor.

I had been to the gladiator shows before, but I had never seen them from this angle. The stone bleachers rose up all around the floor, seeming much larger and higher than I remembered, and they were absolutely packed with people. Still more people were standing on the bleacher steps or along the wall. I suddenly felt very, very small, like an ant surrounded by gargoyles, just waiting for one of the creatures to step on and crush me to death.

Normally, three low rings would have been sitting on the arena floor, but the outer two rings had been removed, leaving only the center one behind, and the wood had been painted a slick, glossy black, indicating the blood, pain, and death to come.

Cho stood outside the black ring, wearing his red ring-master's jacket. He glanced up and made a signal with his hand. The lights slowly dimmed, then abruptly cut off, plunging the arena into darkness. The audience went still and silent, knowing what was coming next.

"And now . . ." Cho's voice rang out. "Introducing the White Swan!"

A spotlight popped on, illuminating the opposite end of the arena, and Emilie strode forward. She was wearing white fighting leathers and sandals, and she too had a sword in her hand and a shield on her forearm. Her face had also been painted, only with a different creature and color scheme than mine. White paint ringed her eyes before thinning out into the shard-like feather pattern. Gold streaks shimmered on top of the white paint, while gold crystals winked at the corners of her eyes. Gold glitter gleamed on her skin, although her lips were bloodred, like mine. White feathers bristled from the three knots of her auburn hair, completing her ethereal look.

A sick feeling filled my stomach. We were mirror opposites. A white swan and a black swan, a seasoned gladiator and a newb, battling to the death. The only thing we had in common was the blood we were going to spill.

Cho waited until Emilie had entered the black ring before he spoke again. "And now . . . introducing the Black Swan!"

A spotlight fell on me, and I had no choice but to squint against the harsh glare and plod forward into the center of the arena.

The crowd had stayed quiet this whole time, but once I appeared, everyone surged to their feet, screaming, clapping, and whistling at the top of their lungs. Emilie loved the attention, and she stabbed her sword into the air over and over again, encouraging the crowd to cheer even louder for her.

"White Swan! White Swan! White Swan!" The chants reverberated through the arena.

I had always loved all those old stories about my ancestor Bryn Bellona Winter Blair and her gladiator history. I had always thought that it must have been so wonderful to be a gladiator, to be a hero like she had been.

There was nothing wonderful about this.

The chants, cheers, and screams that twisted people's faces; the sharp, shrieking whistles that spewed from their lips; and especially the sour, sweaty eagerness that soaked the air. They all made me sick, and I wanted to vomit, even though I hadn't eaten anything today. Somehow, I managed to push down the thin, watery bile rising in my throat, along with my disgust. I had brought this upon myself, and all I could do now was see it through to the end.

Even if that end was most likely going to be my death.

I stepped into the black ring. Emilie kept firing up the crowd, but I looked at the troupe box. Serilda was relaxing in her plush chair, a glass of sangria in her hand. Sullivan was sitting on the edge of his seat, his body tight with tension.

Our gazes met and held. For some reason that I didn't want to think too much about, the sight of him loosened some of the tight knots of disgust, worry, fear, and dread in my stomach. I snapped my sword up, silently saluting him. After a moment, he nodded and forced himself to smile back at me. He didn't relax his tense posture, though.

My gaze cut to Serilda. A smile curved her lips, and she

lifted her glass in a silent toast. I reached around and deliberately, mockingly flicked the black feathers in my hair, telling her exactly what I thought of her blood sport. Her smile widened. My insult hadn't bothered her at all. Smug bitch.

I let out a breath and faced Emilie. The gladiator had been sequestered from the rest of the troupe this whole week, so I had seen her only in passing, whenever she was in the training ring, sparring by herself. But I could clearly see the hate in her brown eyes now, and I could definitely smell the hot, peppery anger wafting off her body.

Cho lifted his hands, calling for silence, although it took a while before the crowd finally quieted down.

"This is a black-ring match," he said in a loud, somber voice. "The winner lives. The loser dies."

Instead of cheers, another small but distinctive sound rang out all around the arena—the *clink-clink-clink* of gold, silver, and bronze crowns being passed from one hand to another. The thought of strangers betting on my life filled me with disgust again. This time, I grabbed on to the emotion, along with the accompanying anger.

Cho gestured for Emilie and me to step forward so that we were both standing in the middle of the ring. He bowed to Emilie first. She returned the gesture; then he turned and did the same thing to me. I bowed back to him. Cho straightened up and gave me a sly wink. So did the dragon on his neck. The gesture touched me. I winked back at them both, then tightened my grip on my sword and focused on Emilie.

The ringmaster raised his hand and looked back and forth between the two of us, drawing out the moment and amping up the tension and suspense.

"Begin!" Cho yelled, and scurried back out of the way.

Emilie snapped up her sword. With a loud, angry roar, she charged at me.

Even though I had seen her fight in the training ring, as well as in the arena bouts, I had never faced Emilie myself, and I hadn't realized how fast she was. She closed the distance between us in the blink of an eye, and I barely had time to snap up my shield before she was swinging her sword at me.

Her sword slammed into my shield with a harsh *clang* that seemed even louder than the crowd's screams. That one *clang* kept ringing in my ears, like someone playing the same note on a piano over and over again, even as I whirled around, barely dodging Emilie's next blow. Her sword bit into the dirt instead of my leg, but she didn't seem to mind. She smiled, and her eyes glowed with an eerie, almost fanatical light as she twirled her weapon around in her hand, getting ready for another strike.

I expected her to use her speed to move in for another quick blow, but Emilie circled around me, moving slower now and slashing her sword through the air in wide arcs. Not trying to hit me, not at all, but playing to the crowd. Emilie thought there was no way that I could beat her, and she was going to enjoy every single second in the spotlight.

The crowd loved her theatrics, and everyone surged to their feet, clapping, yelling, and cheering. The crowd's encouragement made Emilie further exaggerate her movements. Soon, the yells and cheers turned to snickering laughter, all of it aimed at me, since I kept lurching away from her.

So many things about the Black Swan had reminded me of the palace. But none as much as this moment, with Emilie and the crowd openly mocking me the way that Vasilia and everyone else at the palace had so many times. Seven Spire had been its own arena, and I had survived there for fifteen years.

I could survive this arena too.

I ignored the bright glare of the spotlights burning against my face. The yells, screams, and snickers of the crowd. The soft thud of Emilie's footsteps on the hard-packed dirt. The sneer on her painted face. I tuned it all out and focused on myself.

I let go of my emotions—all my disgust, anger, fear, panic, worry, and heartache. Everything that had weighed me down since the massacre, everything that had made me timid and cautious, everything that had ever made me feel small and weak and helpless. I let go of them all until the only thing left was cold calculation.

Then I focused on Emilie, analyzing everything I knew about her and searching for a weakness, like I had done so many times before at the palace, whenever I had listened to the tone of someone's voice, instead of their words, or noticed the faint cracks of emotion around the edges of someone's mouth, instead of their pleasant smile.

Emilie kept prancing around the ring, taunting me. Her arrogance was clearly her weakness. Now, how to best use that to my advantage?

My gaze flicked past Emilie, and I looked at Paloma, who was standing in the tunnel entrance along with Cho, both of them with worried looks on their faces—

Emilie must have sensed my distraction because she lunged forward and lashed out with her sword, moving almost too fast for me to follow. I barely managed to lurch to the side, but this time, I couldn't completely avoid the blow, and her sword sliced into my right arm.

I hissed with pain, staggered back, and glanced down. Emilie had opened up a deep gash above my elbow, and blood was already sliding down my skin and plopping to the dirt. Not a practice swing, but she hadn't been trying to kill me either. She could have easily taken my entire arm off with that blow, but she wanted to hurt and humiliate me first.

Emilie held up her bloody sword, and the crowd cheered even louder.

She's going to kill you unless you find some way to counter her speed. Paloma's voice whispered in my mind. She had told me that the first morning we'd started training for the black-ring match.

I flexed my fingers, feeling the icy power of my immunity running through my body. It would let me neutralize Emilie's speed, at least temporarily, just as it had let me overcome the poison in Paloma's body. The only problem was that I actually had to *touch* Emilie to make it work. So how could I do that without getting her sword in my gut in return?

A hasty plan formed in my mind. I didn't know if it would work, but it was my only chance. So I drew in a breath to steady myself and slowly let it out.

And then I threw down my sword.

The cheers cut off, replaced by mocking jeers and sharp guffaws of laughter.

"What is she doing?"

"Doesn't she know how to fight?"

"Idiot! You're supposed to actually *use* the sword!"

I ignored the insults. They were nothing compared to all the horrible things that Vasilia had done to me. Besides, the sword was no big loss. Given how badly my arm was throbbing, I wouldn't have been able to hold on to it much longer anyway. Instead, I stared at my sword, marking the spot where it had landed carefully in my mind, like the way that Lady Xenia had covered the floor of her dance hall with large paper *X*s when she had first started teaching me the Tanzen Freund.

When I had that spot firmly fixed in my mind, I pulled the shield off my other arm, gripped it by the edges, and held it out in front of me.

Emilie smirked. "Killing you is going to be even easier than I imagined."

"Then shut up and do it already, you arrogant, preening bitch," I hissed back.

She let out a loud, angry scream, charged at me, and swung her sword at my head, trying to lop it off with one brutal blow. Playtime was definitely over.

I sidestepped the strike, but instead of lurching away like before, I whirled around, lunged forward, and rammed my shield into her chest, along with the rest of my body.

I put as much force into the move as I could, and we both fell to the ground, with me on top of Emilie. She slammed into the dirt, and she lost her grip on her own sword and shield, both of which skittered away.

"Get off me, you bitch!" she snarled.

She kept shouting curses, even as she squirmed and squirmed, trying to wriggle out from under me, but I didn't let her get away. She wouldn't fall for the same trick twice, and this was the only chance I had to throttle her speed with my immunity. So I wormed along the ground with her, keeping the shield in between us and my body on top of it to keep her pinned down.

My dead weight was putting pressure on Emilie's lungs, and she slowed her struggles to suck down some much-needed air. Before she could start squirming again, I snapped up my fist and drove it into her face.

Crunch.

For the second time this week, I landed the perfect punch and broke her nose. Emilie screamed, but the sound quickly turned into a cough, as she tried not to choke on her own blood.

"Did you see that?"

"She punched her right in the face!"

"Now we've got a fight!"

Those jeers from the crowd turned into shouts of approval, but I tuned them out. I didn't need any encouragement to punch her again.

I drew my fist back for another strike, but Emilie snarled, put her hands on my shield, and shoved it and me off her. I lost my grip on the shield, which rolled away, and landed hard on my left hip. She lashed out and kicked me in the ribs. This time, I was the one who screamed with pain.

Emilie scrambled to her feet, her head snapping left and right, searching for her sword. I was still on the ground, and I didn't have time to get back up onto my own feet before she darted away, so I lunged forward and wrapped my hand around her leg, right above her sandal straps. I sensed her magic the second that my skin touched hers, and I reached for my own power and sent my immunity racing out into her body, trying to snuff out all her speed.

Emilie screeched again and tried to wrench away, but I dug my nails into her skin, deep enough to draw blood, and forced her to drag me along the ground behind her.

"What are you doing?" she yelled. "Get on your feet and die with some damn dignity!"

I could have told her that dignity was overrated, and that I had lost all of mine long ago, but I couldn't afford to waste a single breath. My right arm felt like it was on fire from where she had cut it, and more and more blood was oozing from the wound and dripping down my skin. Sweat also dripped down the sides of my face, not just from the exertion of the fight, but also from trying to throttle her speed. I could feel her magic rising up and fighting back against my own power. I gritted my teeth and reached for even more of my immunity. I imagined it flowing out of me and into her, as though I was dunking her in an icy river.

And it worked.

All at once, her magic fizzled out, like a soufflé caving in on itself. The second that I felt her magic, her speed, vanish, I let go of her leg and rolled away. Emilie wasn't expecting me to release her, and she stumbled forward, since I wasn't holding her back anymore.

I had no idea how long it would take for Emilie's speed to return, but I couldn't afford to waste a single second. I scrambled to my feet, whipped around, and darted forward, heading toward the center of the ring where I had thrown down my sword earlier.

X marks the spot. The weapon was right where I had left it.

My hand had just closed over the hilt when gasps rang out. Emilie must have picked up her weapon again too. Out of the corner of my eye, I saw her shadow zooming toward me on the arena floor. It looked like she had regained some of her speed as well.

There was no time to think. I picked up my sword, whirled around, and thrust it up and out—right into her stomach.

Emilie screamed, and her sword slipped from her fingers and clattered to the ground. She tried to wrench away, but I gritted my teeth, wrapped both hands around the hilt of my sword, and shoved the blade deeper into her body. She looked at me, surprise flashing in her eyes, along with pain—so much pain.

Emilie opened her mouth as if she were going to scream again, but she coughed instead, spewing blood all over my face, neck, arms, and chest. The drops stung my skin like wet, warm bees, making me hiss, although they didn't do any damage. Emilie stared at me a second longer, then her legs buckled, and she dropped to the ground, with my sword still stuck in her stomach.

Dead—she was dead, which meant that tonight's victor was the newb gladiator.

The Black Swan.

CHAPTER NINETEEN

I loomed over Emilie, watching her blood seep into the dirt. Then I looked down at my own body.

Her blood had spattered all over my fighting leathers, turning them even blacker than they already were. My own blood was also still trickling down my arm from where she had cut me. A few drops slid off my fingertips and landed on a white feather that was still stuck in Emilie's hair. I shuddered with revulsion.

Serilda had given me the wrong costume, the wrong name. I wasn't the Black Swan—more like the Bloody Swan.

A dull roar filled my ears, slowly sharpening into a cacophony of sound. I glanced up. Everyone was on their feet, cheering, clapping, yelling, and whistling louder than ever before, all because I had killed Emilie.

Cho must have sensed my anger and disgust because he stepped into the ring, rushed over, grabbed my hand, and raised it high into the air. "And our champion is the Black Swan!" he called out in a booming voice, much to the delight of the crowd, who roared again.

I ground my teeth, letting the cheers wash over me, even though each loud shout, piercing whistle, and appreciative clap made my stomach twist into tighter knots. I had never enjoyed being the center of attention, and I longed to run out of the arena, but I couldn't do that. Not with the crowd still yelling, cheering, and screaming in delight.

"How much longer is this going to last?" I muttered to Cho.

He started to answer, but a sharp trill of music cut him off. The loud notes sounded over and over again, each trumpet blast louder than the one before, and the music quickly drowned out the cheers. But even stranger was the fact that I recognized the tune—the Blair family royal march.

Why would they be playing that? Was it some Bellonan tradition to mark the end of a black-ring match?

The crowd stopped cheering, and everyone turned toward the main entrance. Beside me, Cho let out a soft, muttered curse and looked up at Serilda, who was still in her box, along with Sullivan, although both of them were standing now. What was going on?

Serilda made a sharp motion with her hand. One by one, the arena lights snapped off, but the royal march kept playing and playing. Sickening dread punched me in the gut, and my heart hammered in time to the beat.

The music roared to a climatic finish, then abruptly cut off. For a moment, everything was still, dark, and quiet. Then a single spotlight snapped on, highlighting a woman standing at the main entrance to the bleachers.

She was dressed in black boots and leggings, along with a tunic made of fuchsia silk. The bold color perfectly accentuated her gray-blue eyes, along with her blond hair, which hung in thick, loose waves. A sword with a large pink diamond set into the hilt was sheathed in a gold scabbard that dangled from her gold belt. A matching dagger was also hooked to her belt. All put together, she looked like a fairy-tale princess come to life.

I focused on the gold crown studded with pink diamonds that were shaped like laurel flowers that rested on her head. No, not a princess anymore. A queen now—one who was drenched in even more blood than I was.

Vasilia was here.

The new queen smiled into the bright glare, and everyone started cheering again. Of course they did. They thought that she had survived a brutal assassination attempt—not that she'd been the one behind it.

The louder the crowd cheered, the wider Vasilia smiled. She lifted her hand and waved at everyone. Then her smile slipped away, her face sombered, and she lowered her hand, as if she were suddenly overcome with emotion thinking about everything that she—and the rest of Bellona—had lost.

Vasilia bowed her head, her gold crown glowing under the spotlight. Silence swept over the crowd, and more than a few people sniffled and wiped away tears.

The moment passed. Vasilia lifted her head and waved at the crowd again, who cheered for her even more wildly than before. She waved to them again, then headed into the arena.

And the bitch wasn't alone.

Nox strode in behind her, the spotlight making his blond

hair gleam almost as brightly as Vasilia's crown, and Felton trotted in as well, clutching a red ledger. A dozen guards, all wearing fuchsia tunics and gold breastplates, also entered. There was no sign of Maeven.

Vasilia moved over to the bottom row of bleachers and started shaking hands with her well-wishers. Nox, Felton, and the guards trailed along behind her, eyeing the crowd. Please. As if she was in any real danger. Even if someone was stupid enough to attack, Vasilia could easily cut them down with her weapons or fry them with her lightning.

Up in her box, Serilda stabbed her finger at Cho, then at me, and made a sharp, waving motion with her hand.

"Come on," Cho muttered. "Our presence has been requested by her royal highness."

For a moment, I didn't understand what he meant, but then I realized that Vasilia was slowly but surely making her way up the bleachers to where Serilda and Sullivan were in the troupe box. Vasilia must have seen the match, and now, she wanted to meet the winner.

She wanted to meet *me*.

Shock spiked through my body, but it was quickly replaced by panic. I opened my mouth to tell him that I couldn't go up there, but Cho clamped his hand on my arm and marched me forward. It would look far more suspicious if I tried to wrench free and run away, so I had no choice but to follow him.

Cho pushed through one of the gates in the wall, and we climbed up to the troupe box. In addition to Serilda and Sullivan, Theroux was now standing along one side of the box, along with several kitchen workers clutching trays of food and drinks. Everyone looked tense, and one man's hands were shaking so badly that the glasses on his tray rattled together.

Serilda gestured for us to form a receiving line, with her first, followed by Sullivan, then Cho, and finally me at the end.

And then we waited.

Vasilia took her sweet time reaching the box, and my worry grew with each passing moment. The second she looked at me, she would realize that her cousin Everleigh wasn't nearly as dead as she wanted me to be.

I glanced around, searching for an escape route, but there wasn't one. Even if I hopped over the stone wall that cordoned off the box, I wouldn't make it down the bleachers, much less out of the arena, before the guards caught me.

I was well and truly stuck—and about to be well and truly dead.

Finally, Vasilia reached the box, along with her entourage. She, Nox, and Felton stepped inside the box, while the guards ringed it on all sides. My heart sank lower. No escape now.

Serilda executed the perfect Bellonan curtsy. "I am Serilda Swanson. Welcome to my humble arena."

Vasilia let out a light, trilling laugh. "Oh, Serilda. There's no need for such formality. I recognize you from your many years of service to my mother."

Serilda held her curtsy a moment longer, as protocol dictated, before rising to her feet. "It was my great honor to serve Queen Cordelia."

"Of course it was," Vasilia murmured.

"This is my resident magier, enforcer, and gladiator trainer, Lucas Sullivan."

She gestured at Sullivan, who stepped forward. Unlike Serilda, he didn't curtsy but instead pressed his fist to his heart and gave a traditional Andvarian bow. Given the poor relations between the two kingdoms, everyone tensed at the gesture, even Serilda, and the guards dropped their hands to their weapons, ready to defend their treacherous queen.

Sullivan straightened, the faintest hint of a sneer curving his lips, and I realized that he was actually mocking Vasilia. I didn't know why he was doing it, but in that moment, I fell a little bit in love with him for simply having the courage and audacity to stand up to her, even if it was in this one small way.

Vasilia recognized the gesture as the insult that it truly was, but she waved her hand, telling the guards to stand down. Everyone relaxed except for me. They thought the danger was over, but Vasilia's sharp smile told me that she was getting ready to gut Sullivan with her words.

"Oh, yes. I've heard quite a bit about you and your Andvarian family in recent weeks, Lucas." Vasilia stepped forward, reached out, and toyed with one of the silver buttons on his coat. "You actually remind me quite a bit of your younger brother Frederich. Although I hadn't imagined that you would be so handsome. Or so very polite. Then again, I suppose bastard princes have to mind their manners more than most, don't they?"

Shock blasted through me, drowning out my worry. *Bastard prince? Of Andvari?*

I thought about that Cardea mirror that I'd seen in his house. He must have talked to the Andvarians, to his family. That's how he knew that they had nothing to do with the massacre, and that's why he was mocking Vasilia now.

Sullivan's eyes glittered like two chips of ice, and a muscle ticked in his jaw, as though he was grinding his teeth to keep from snapping back at her. Vasilia's smile widened. She knew that she had scored a direct hit with that insult.

I eyed the magier. No wonder he had been so angry when I had mockingly called him *princeling*. A bastard royal was one of the worst things to be in any kingdom. At Seven Spire, his position would have been even lower than mine.

Vasilia stared at Sullivan, basking in her verbal triumph, then looked at Cho, who also bowed to her, but in the Ryusaman style, tilting his body forward with his hands by his sides.

"Cho Yamato, another one of my mother's former guards," Vasilia murmured. "Still stuck to Serilda's side, eh? I would have thought that you would have grown tired of servicing her by now."

Servicing her? Did she mean . . . were Cho and Serilda . . . *lovers*?

I had never seen them so much as touch, let alone do anything more, but Cho's nostrils flared at Vasilia's words. So did the ones of the dragon face on his neck, and a bit of ashy smoke wafted out of the creature's mouth and floated across his skin before fading away.

Vasilia noticed the smoke too, and she pressed her lips together, biting back her next insult. Even she wouldn't want to fight a dragon morph.

Serilda cleared her throat, breaking the awkward silence. "And finally, tonight's champion."

I tensed, getting ready for the battle to come. As soon as Vasilia realized who I was, she would blast me with her lightning. I would have to reach for my immunity and hope that it would save me from her magic the same way it had before—

Vasilia stepped in front of me and looked directly into my face.

If this had happened before the massacre, I would have

ducked my head and slumped down, trying to make myself as small and invisible as possible in hopes of avoiding her wrath, just as I had done hundreds of times before.

Not tonight.

For the first time in years, I squared my shoulders, lifted my chin, and stared right back at the bitch. I would not be cowed by her, and I would not hide from her. Never again. Not even if it meant my death here.

My cousin kept staring at me. The longer she looked, the more confusion and apprehension trickled through my body. Why wasn't she yelling, screaming, and cursing my name? Why wasn't she ordering the guards to cut me down?

What was she waiting for?

Her gaze lifted, locking onto the stupid black feathers that were still sticking up out of my hair, then swept down, focusing on the blood that coated my hands, arms, and black fighting leathers. Understanding filled me.

She didn't recognize me.

I wondered how she could have forgotten me so quickly, but then I remembered the black and silver paint on my face. Combine that with the ridiculous feathers, the fighting leathers, and all the blood, and I didn't look anything like her cousin Everleigh. Not even close. No, I was just a gladiator who had survived a fight to the death. Nothing more, nothing less, and not worth more than a few seconds of her time and attention.

Vasilia stared at the blood on my hands a moment longer, then turned back to Serilda. "I see that you're still using the black swan as your crest. Isn't that what the other guards used to call you? Because of all the death that you brought to my mother's enemies?"

"Something like that," Serilda murmured.

"Mmm." Vasilia smiled, but her expression had that sharp edge again. "I was most disappointed not to get an invitation to tonight's event. The black-ring matches are my favorites. They have been ever since I was a child. Luckily, my men were able to sneak me inside."

Serilda bowed her head. "Forgive my oversight. I assumed that you would be far too busy dealing with the recent tensions between Bellona and Andvari to attend our humble little show."

Vasilia's gaze flicked to Sullivan. "Tensions. Yes." She focused on Serilda again. "That's actually what I wanted to speak to you about. And to see the rest of the show. We arrived late, so I didn't get to watch the acrobats and wire walkers perform."

Her lips turned down into a pretty pout that I had seen a hundred times before. The one that signaled that you should give Vasilia exactly what she wanted—or else.

Serilda also heard the underlying order in Vasilia's words loud and clear. "Of course. Please make yourself comfortable, and enjoy our hospitality."

She hadn't even finished speaking before Vasilia swept forward and settled herself in Serilda's chair, the largest and most comfortable one in the box. Nox smirked at Lucas, then moved forward and sat down in the magier's chair next to Vasilia. Felton took a seat beside Nox, his red ledger still clutched in his hand.

Serilda squeezed into a small seat in the corner close to Vasilia, then jerked her head at Cho, who left the box. He didn't gesture for me to follow him, so I didn't know what to do. Vasilia noticed me hovering over her, and she looked at me again.

Sullivan saved me. He moved in between us, cutting off her view of me, then put his hand on my arm and steered me around the chairs to the far side of the box.

"Just stand still and stay quiet until this is over," he whispered.

Once we were out of the way, Theroux stepped forward and bowed low. "My queen, may I offer you some refreshments?"

Vasilia waved her hand, and Theroux and the other workers served the food and drinks. Vasilia daintily nibbled on a few small kiwi cakes, while Felton sipped a glass of sangria. Nox was much more gluttonous. He downed a whole tray of kiwi cakes and other desserts, along with a bottle of champagne.

The three of them were eating and drinking as though they had done nothing wrong, as though they hadn't orchestrated the brutal murders of Isobel, Cordelia, Madelena, and so many other innocent people. My hands tightened into fists, but there was nothing that I could do. Even if I gave in to my murderous rage and attacked them, Vasilia would incinerate me with her lightning, or Nox would cut me down with his sword. Not to mention the guards still lurking around the box.

As much as I longed to surge forward, wrap my hands around Vasilia's neck, and choke her to death for all the pain, misery, and heartache she'd caused, all I could do was stand still and stay quiet, as Sullivan had said.

A few minutes later, the lights dimmed, and Cho strode out into the arena and restarted the show. The music began, the acrobats tumbled into view, and the wire walkers resumed their positions on the platforms. The crowd took their seats again and started clapping and cheering, excited that they were getting another show. Nox ignored the performance in favor of guzzling down more champagne, while Felton set his glass aside and started writing in his ledger.

Vasilia smiled and clapped along with the crowd. To the

casual observer, she would seem as interested in the performance as everyone else, but getting Serilda to restart the show was simply a way for Vasilia to assert her influence and control. And she didn't care that she hadn't been invited to the black-ring match. The event had just been an excuse for her to show up. No, my cousin had some other purpose in mind with this little visit.

Sure enough, less than five minutes into the show, Vasilia quit clapping, dropped her hands to her lap, and turned to Serilda, who was still scrunched up in that chair in the corner.

"Thank you for your hospitality. It's most welcome, especially during this stressful time, dealing with the aftermath of my mother's and sister's assassinations."

Vasilia's lips turned down, and her face darkened, as though she was truly saddened by her family's deaths. Despite all the times that she had stabbed me in the back with her sly words and actions, even I would have thought that she was being genuine if I hadn't been there that awful day. She should have joined the troupe. The bitch was a terrific actress.

Vasilia cleared her throat, then cleared it again, as though she was having trouble getting her words out through her supposed sadness. Serilda gestured at Theroux, who poured a glass of iced cucumber water and handed it to Vasilia.

But it was just another power play on Vasilia's part, and she took only one tiny sip of the water before setting it aside. "Tonight has been wonderful. It's been good for me to get out of the palace. And to show the people that their queen is not afraid of Andvarian assassins."

Her gaze cut to Sullivan, who was still standing next to me. His lips pressed together, and a bit of magic crackled in his eyes, but he didn't take the bait and snap back at her. I could smell his anger, though. The strong, peppery scent matched my own silent rage.

"Of course," Serilda murmured. "I'm so glad to see you out and about, especially given the terrible tragedy at the palace just a few weeks ago."

Vasilia brought her hand up to the corner of her eye, as though she was dabbing away a tear. My fists tightened even more.

"Although I'm afraid to say that I have been hearing some rather nasty rumors," Serilda said.

Vasilia raised her head, her fake tear forgotten. "What rumors?"

Serilda shrugged, as though they weren't important. Vasilia's lips pressed together, and I could almost see the wheels turning in her mind as she debated whether to pursue the matter. She had come here with her own agenda, but Serilda was forcing her away from that. It was a skillful piece of manipulation. My estimation of the troupe leader went up several notches. She had learned the long game well during her time at Seven Spire.

"What rumors?" Vasilia asked again, falling neatly into Serilda's trap.

"The rumors that some members of the royal family escaped the massacre," Serilda said. "That some of the Blairs fled from the palace and are in hiding."

Vasilia blinked in surprise. Nox lowered his champagne flute, and even Felton stopped scribbling in his ledger.

The night of the candlelight vigil, Serilda had told Cho to reach out to his contacts to learn everything he could about the massacre and whether there had been any survivors. Serilda clearly wanted to get her hands on a Blair—any Blair, given her own words—but I still didn't understand why.

Nox snorted and took another slug of champagne, while Felton started writing again. Vasilia's worry melted into a smug smile that she didn't bother to hide. Serilda saw it too, and her fingers clenched around her glass.

"Unfortunately, I'm sad to say that every royal who was at the palace was slaughtered," Vasilia said. "Believe me, we have searched high and low for survivors, but the plot was much larger than we originally thought."

"What do you mean?" Serilda asked.

Now it was Vasilia's turn to shrug. "Some of my cousins were at their estates out in the countryside. I sent guards to check on them as soon as possible, but it was too late. They had all been murdered. I'm the only Blair left."

My heart sank. I had hoped that at least a few of my cousins had survived, but it sounded as though Vasilia had arranged for them to be killed as well. Of course she had.

Serilda lowered her glass and slumped back in her chair, as though all the strength had left her body. Not what she had wanted to hear. Vasilia's lips twitched, although this time, she managed to hold back her smug smile.

For a moment, Serilda looked sad, weary, and defeated, but then her gaze lifted, and she stared at the pink diamonds shaped like laurel flowers that adorned the gold crown on Vasilia's head.

"Summer queens are fine and fair, with pretty ribbons and flowers in their hair," Serilda murmured. "Winter queens are cold and hard, with frosted crowns made of icy shards."

Her words were soft, especially compared to the raucous calliope music that drifted up from the arena floor, but they still made me tense. And I wasn't the only one they affected. Nox jerked in his seat and sloshed champagne down the front of his tunic, turning the fabric more bloodred than bright pink. Felton eyed him a moment, then returned to his writing.

Vasilia frowned at Nox before focusing on Serilda again. "What did you say?"

She didn't repeat the phrase. "It's an old Bellonan fairy-tale rhyme. I'm sure you've heard it before."

"Of course I have," Vasilia snapped.

She clearly had no idea why Serilda had quoted those words. Me neither. Like Serilda herself had said, it was just an old rhyme. So why had she said the phrase now? And why had Cordelia said the exact same thing to me before she had died?

Vasilia and Serilda eyed each other, both of them smiling, but neither expression was genuine or particularly friendly, and it was more a pause to give them both time to regroup.

"Is that the only rumor you've heard?" Vasilia asked, getting back down to business.

"Oh, no," Serilda replied. "Some people are saying that the Andvarians weren't responsible for the attack. That they were framed. That it's all an elaborate Mortan plot to pit Bellona and Andvari against each other so that Morta can swoop in and conquer both kingdoms."

Nox and Felton both froze, while Vasilia blinked in surprise again.

It sounded as if Serilda knew *exactly* what had happened during the massacre. But how could she know that Nox, Felton, and Vasilia had orchestrated it? Who had told her so much of what had been going on inside the palace?

Serilda took a sip of her sangria before speaking again.

"Despite all the nasty rumors going around, you need to think about your future. And Bellona's as well."

"How so?"

"If you truly are the last Blair, then you need to produce an heir. Immediately. We wouldn't want you to meet the same unfortunate fate as Cordelia and for some usurper to grab the throne and plunge Bellona into civil war."

Vasilia's face hardened. "I will produce an heir when *I* am ready, and not one second before. In the meantime, you can rest assured that no one will be assassinating *me*." She must have realized how harsh her voice was, because she cleared her throat again and reined in her anger. "If any good has come out of this horrible situation, it's that I've learned from my mother's mistakes. My security is excellent, and there are no traitors in my ranks."

Serilda glanced at Nox and Felton, then at the guards ringing the box. "Of course. You've already proven what a fine, strong queen you are by leading us through this terrible tragedy."

Vasilia nodded, seemingly placated by the compliment. Then she leaned forward, her eyes brightening, and her smile widening. I tensed again. That was the same look that she had given Prince Frederich right before she had stabbed him to death.

"Actually, my security is one of the reasons why I came here. You were the finest guard my mother ever had, and I would like you to work for me, to help me prepare for war."

Serilda blinked, clearly not expecting the offer, although she recovered quickly. "What are you planning?"

"I cannot—will not—let my mother's and sister's deaths go unavenged. Bellona will mourn for them and everyone else until the Summer Solstice. On that day, a coronation ceremony will be held at Seven Spire, and I will be formally crowned queen, as is the custom."

"And then?" Serilda asked, her voice thick with worry.

Vasilia shrugged. "And then I will march on Andvari. I will go to war."

Everyone in the box tensed again. Serilda, Sullivan, Theroux, the workers, me. Everyone except for Nox and Felton, who already knew about Vasilia's evil plan. Sullivan let out a soft curse, although no one heard it except for me.

My mind spun around, trying to make sense of Vasilia's poisonous plot. She had become queen the moment she had killed Cordelia, but Bellonan custom dictated that an official coronation ceremony must be held on the next closest solstice, the Summer Solstice, in this case. A grand party would be thrown at Seven Spire to formally mark the start of Vasilia's reign. Then, as soon as the party was over, and the queen's crown was on her head, off to war she would go, forcing thousands of Bellonans to invade a kingdom and fight a people who had done nothing wrong.

No doubt Vasilia would spend these next few months leading up to the Summer Solstice drumming up support for her war effort and spreading even more lies about the Andvarians. By the time the solstice rolled around, the entire kingdom would be screaming for Andvarian blood.

"Well?" Vasilia demanded.

Serilda leaned back in her chair. My heart sank again. Now came the moment when Serilda would show her true colors. She would be seduced by Vasilia's pretty words and the promise of power, like everyone always was.

"I'm honored. Truly, I am."

"But?" Vasilia said in a sharp voice.

Serilda gestured out at the arena. "But this is my business, my responsibility. I have commitments that I cannot abandon."

"Not even for your queen in her hour of need?" Vasilia asked.

She had boxed Serilda into a corner, but the other woman bowed her head again. "Perhaps there is another way—a better way—that I may serve you."

"How so?"

Serilda gestured out at the arena again. "My troupe is going on tour—to Andvari."

Sullivan had mentioned a tour when I had first come to the compound, but I hadn't heard anything else about it, so I had assumed that it was off. But Serilda was making it sound like it was happening soon.

"Our tour will take us to several cities throughout Andvari, including the capital," Serilda continued. "Perhaps I can use our wanderings as a way to gather intelligence on border security, troop movements, and the like. To make your march into Andvari that much smoother and assure you a quick, decisive victory."

Vasilia drummed her fingers, pretending to think about it, but I noticed the faint flicker of satisfaction on her face. She didn't want Serilda to work for her. No, for some reason, she wanted Serilda out of the way, out of Bellona, although I couldn't imagine why. Maybe because Serilda had dared to suggest that another royal might have survived the massacre.

"Yes, I see your point." Vasilia nodded. "That sort of information would be quite useful, especially since I intend to burn Andvari to the ground. When do you plan to leave?"

"In three weeks," Serilda said, although I could smell the smoky lie in her words.

Vasilia nodded again. "Good. Then let's talk about exactly where you are going and how you can best keep me updated."

Serilda bowed her head.

And just like that, the deal was struck, and the two of them started talking about the logistics of communicating across such a long distance.

Vasilia leaned forward again, listening to everything that Serilda said and asking questions in return. She did everything one would expect of a queen in this situation, including telling Felton to take notes and ordering Nox to make sure that Serilda had everything that she would need for her new spy mission.

But the longer the two of them talked, the colder Vasilia's eyes became, and the more I got a sinking feeling that she had just sentenced Serilda and everyone else in the Black Swan troupe to death.

CHAPTER TWENTY

The acrobats finished their tumbles, the wire walkers climbed down from their platforms, and the second show finally ended.

Vasilia and Serilda finished their negotiations. The spotlight focused on Vasilia again, and she gave a brief speech about how much she had enjoyed the show. Then she walked down to the bottom of the bleachers and mingled with the crowd, shaking hands again, with Nox, Felton, and her guards trailing along behind her. A few minutes later, she exited the arena, and everyone else left as well.

Two hours later, I stepped out of one of the bathrooms in the barracks, my hair loose and wet, my clothes sticking to my damp skin, and several black feathers clenched in my hand. As soon as the crowd had cleared out of the compound, and the front gate had been shut and locked, the troupe members had gone to the dining hall to eat and celebrate another successful show. I had skipped the festivities, gotten Aisha to heal my arm, and come to the barracks instead.

I didn't want Emilie's blood on me a second longer than necessary.

I had taken a long, hot shower to wash away all the blood, sweat, and grime of the arena, as well as the ridiculous black-swan makeup. It had taken me a bit longer to peel the blue crystals off my face and pull the black feathers out of my hair. I had thrown the crystals into the trash, but I had saved the feathers. I wasn't quite sure why.

I had expected the barracks to be deserted, but Paloma had come inside while I'd been in the shower. She was sitting on her cot staring at the three objects that were laid out on her green ogre blanket—the poisoned white feather that Sullivan had given me, the silver bracelet that Alvis had made for me, and the opal memory stone that I had picked up from the royal lawn.

I hadn't told Paloma *not* to look in the bag, and of course she would be curious enough to open it. My stomach clenched with worry, but I walked over, sat down on my cot next to hers, and laid the black feathers on the nightstand.

Paloma picked up the bracelet and studied the design. "Pretty." She handed it to me. "Where did you get it?"

"A . . . friend gave it to me, right before I . . . left my new mistress. I never even got the chance to wear it. Not really."

I hadn't opened the bag in all the weeks that I had been here, and it was almost like I was seeing the bracelet for the first time. The curls of silver were much brighter than I remembered, and the band of thorns that they formed seemed sharper and more pronounced, like the tips would draw blood if you so much as touched them. And then there was the crown in the center. The seven tearstone shards fitted together perfectly, although they seemed a much darker midnight-blue, despite their constant glittering.

Summer queens are fine and fair, with pretty ribbons and flowers in their hair. Winter queens are cold and hard, with frosted crowns made of icy shards. Cordelia's and Serilda's voices whispered in my mind.

Shock rippled through me, and I traced my finger over the jewels. That certainly looked like a frosted crown made of icy shards, although I still had no idea what the fairy-tale rhyme meant, why both women had quoted it, or even why Alvis had made this bracelet for me. What did they all know that I didn't?

I dropped the bracelet into the black velvet bag, along with the poisoned feather and the memory stone. I hesitated, then slid one of the black feathers into the bag as well, before pulling the drawstrings tight and tying the bag to my belt loop like usual.

Paloma leaned back against the bedframe. "Are you going to tell me what kind of magic you have now?"

My head snapped up. "What do you mean?"

"First, you get rid of the poison in my body. Then, tonight, you took away Emilie's speed just like you said you would."

I opened my mouth to protest, but Paloma shook her head.

"I've fought Emilie more than anyone else in the troupe. I know *exactly* how fast she is. But after you hit her with your shield, she was much slower. It's like all her magic vanished. Just like that." Paloma snapped her fingers. The harsh sound made me wince. "Emilie lost her magic. Only for a few seconds, but it was long enough for you to kill her. So how did you do it, Evie?"

My gaze fell to the ogre mark on her neck. "I'll tell you what kind of magic I have if you'll tell me why you never morph."

Paloma's face scrunched up. I thought she wasn't going to answer, but then she started talking in a low voice. "My mother was an ogre morph. She disappeared when I was a kid. I don't know what happened to her. If she got sick and died, if she was killed, or if she just ran off. But my father never got over it. As I got older, I looked more and more like her, especially when it came to my morph mark."

She touched the blond lock of hair that wrapped around the ogre face on her neck. She grimaced, and so did the ogre. Then she dropped her hand and started speaking again, the words pouring out faster, as if they left a bad taste in her mouth, and she wanted to spit them out as quickly as possible. "My father hated that I looked so much like my mother, but he especially hated it when I morphed. I never really understood why. I guess it reminded him of her that much more. I tried to stop changing, but morphs have to, well, *morph* every so often, especially when we're younger. It's just part of who we are. When I was sixteen, my father said that he couldn't live with a monster in his house any longer, and he kicked me out. Eventually, I joined the Black Swan troupe, and I've been here ever since."

I could tell that there was more to her story—much more—but I also knew that she had told me everything that she was going to tonight. My heart ached for Paloma. My parents might have been murdered, but they had loved me, and my mother had died trying to protect me. Even at Seven Spire, Isobel and Alvis had cared for me in their own ways, and no one had ever made me feel like a monster, like I was some freak of nature who shouldn't exist. Well, no one except for Vasilia, but that was just because she was a heartless bitch.

I grabbed Paloma's hand and gave it a gentle squeeze. "I'm so sorry. Your father shouldn't have treated you like that. You are *not* a monster."

She shrugged, trying to pretend like it didn't matter, but hurt flickered in her amber eyes, as well as in the ogre's matching ones. "Your turn."

All those old whispers and warnings from my mother rose up in my mind, about how I could never tell anyone—*ever*—about my power. About how they would hurt and use me if they knew about my immunity. But Paloma had shared her secret, and now it was my turn. Besides, I liked her, and I really did want us to be friends, and not just because I had saved her life. So I drew in a breath, let it out, and said the words that I had never said to anyone except my parents.

"I'm immune to magic."

She frowned. "What?"

"I'm immune to magic. That's how I got rid of the poison in your body, and that's how I took away Emilie's speed. All I have to do is touch something, or someone, with magic, and I can snuff out their power. At least, for a little while."

Paloma looked at my hand on top of hers. "So you could take away my morph magic right now? Just by touching me?"

I could feel the magic crackling through Paloma, and I could feel how strong she was. As a gladiator, she was a fierce warrior, but as an ogre morph, she would truly be a force to be reckoned with, maybe even stronger than Lady Xenia. But I could also feel my own immunity pulsing through my body, wanting to lash out and destroy Paloma's power.

"Yes, I could take your magic away just by touching you."

To her credit, Paloma didn't pull away, even though worry

pinched her face. No one ever wanted to lose their magic, their power, the thing that made them who and what they were. I carefully removed my hand from hers.

"I would appreciate it if you didn't tell Serilda, Cho, Sullivan, or anyone else about my immunity."

"Why wouldn't you want them to know?"

"I don't want anyone to know."

"But you told me."

"Yes."

Her eyes narrowed. "Why?"

I let out an exasperated breath. "Because we're friends. Isn't that why you told me about your father?"

She stared at me, a thoughtful look on her face. "We *are* friends, aren't we? True friends."

"You sound surprised," I drawled.

"It's hard to be friends with someone with secrets. It makes it hard to trust them." Paloma was blunt as always. "Maybe one day you'll trust me enough to tell me the rest of your secrets."

"Fair enough. And maybe one day you'll trust me enough to let me see you morph."

She shrugged again, but her features weren't as tense, and the ogre on her neck gave me a small, brief smile. Paloma swung her feet off the cot and onto the floor. "But right now, we need to go. Serilda wants to see you."

"Why?"

"I don't know. She just told me to bring you over to the manor after you got cleaned up."

Paloma headed toward the barracks door. I grabbed one of the black feathers off the nightstand and followed her.

❦

Paloma walked me over to the manor house, then headed back to the dining hall to get us some food before the kitchen closed for the night. I promised to meet her back in the barracks.

The front door was open, so I stepped inside. I expected to run into Sullivan or some of the other performers, but the manor was empty, and I walked to the library in the back.

"It's over," a voice muttered. "It's well and truly over, and we are well and truly fucked."

The voice had come from inside the library. Keeping to the shadows, I sidled forward until I could peer in through the doors, which were cracked open.

Serilda was slumped in a chair in front of her desk with a glass of sangria in her hand. Cho was sitting across from her, also holding a glass of sangria. An open bottle was sitting on the desk in between them.

"It's over," Serilda repeated in a grim voice.

"You don't know that," Cho said in a far more reasonable tone. "Of course Vasilia would claim that there were no survivors. You know what a viper she is. My sources are still searching. She couldn't have killed all the Blairs. Someone must have slipped through the cracks and escaped. All we have to do is find them."

It was more or less the same thing he had said the night that I had eavesdropped on them behind the dining hall. Once again, I wondered how they seemed to know so much about the massacre. They must have their own spies inside Seven Spire. Some of the older guards who had served with Serilda and Cho might still be friendly with them. At least friendly enough to tell them what had really happened.

Vasilia might have murdered the Blairs and everyone else at the luncheon, but hundreds of people worked at the palace, and she hadn't killed them all. That would have been far too suspicious. And not even Vasilia was powerful or intimidating enough to keep all the turncoat guards from bragging about what they had done. Rumors, whispers, and gossip had always been a form of currency at Seven Spire.

Serilda shook her head and let out a bitter laugh. "No, it's over. I can *see* that it's over. That's all that I can bloody see right now."

I frowned. What did she mean? What could she see that Cho couldn't?

"Vasilia has won," she continued. "Even if there was another Blair, even if we found them, I doubt that person would have the fighting skills or the magic to challenge her according to the old laws."

Old laws? My heart clenched, my stomach twisted, and I finally realized what game she wanted to play. Of course. I should have known all along. Serilda wanted to find a royal, a Blair, and put that person on the throne instead of Vasilia, and now I knew exactly how she wanted to do it.

Through a royal challenge.

In many ways, a royal challenge was exactly like a black-ring match. Two royals battled to the death for the right to rule. It was how Bryn Blair had held on to her power and been queen for so long, despite all those who had wanted to take away her fledgling kingdom. Bryn had killed anyone who dared to fight her in a challenge—royal and otherwise—until Bellona had been stabilized and the people had accepted her rule. Some historians claimed that the gladiators' black-ring matches had been born from the royal challenges, while other historians said that it was the other way around.

Whichever had come first, Serilda's plan was a foolish

dream, at best. Vasilia had plotted to murder her mother for far too long to give up the throne without a fight, and she was simply too good a warrior and too strong in her magic to battle. Even if Vasilia was killed in a royal challenge, even if someone assassinated her the way that she had Cordelia, Maeven was still waiting in the wings. She wouldn't let her scheme to start a war between Bellona and Andvari unravel so easily.

But most of all, I couldn't help but wonder *why* Serilda wanted to do this. Cordelia had kicked her out of Seven Spire in scandal and disgrace. So why would Serilda care so much about who was queen? She seemed to know that Vasilia was behind the massacre. Perhaps Serilda wanted to do what was right, and see Vasilia brought to justice, and war averted. I had my doubts, though. In my cynical experience, people did what was easy, convenient, or profitable. They rarely, if ever, did what was *right*.

The far more likely scenario was that Serilda saw this as a chance to finally get her revenge on Cordelia, even though the queen was dead, and to assert her own influence over Bellona. After all, if Serilda put someone else on the throne, then that person would be beholden to her. It would be as good as being queen herself. No, it would be even *better*, because the queen would be the target of everyone's plots and schemes, instead of Serilda.

"Besides, we have no proof of Vasilia's treachery," Serilda muttered. "For all intents and purposes, she is the lawful, rightful queen of Bellona, and there is nothing we can do to change that."

I shifted on my feet. The memory stone tied to my belt loop suddenly felt as heavy as a gargoyle. It was proof of what Vasilia had done, along with the Andvarians' innocence.

Cho shrugged, not quite agreeing with her, but not dismissing her words either. "Well, if the Mortans have their way, Vasilia won't be queen for long. As soon as she takes Andvari for them, they'll turn their sights to Bellona. Once it falls, the Mortans will kill her and put one of their own royals on the throne. And they won't stop there. Andvari, Bellona, Unger, Ryusama, Vacuna. They'll conquer all the kingdoms."

He fell silent, and the two of them sipped their sangria, contemplating that horrible possibility.

Finally, Serilda shook her head again, as if clearing away the troubling thoughts. "Well, it's not our problem anymore." Her mouth twisted. "We're going on tour, remember?"

"You know that Vasilia will come after us, come after *you*," Cho said.

"Which is why we're leaving Bellona as soon as possible. Lucas says that the Andvarians will take us in. If we can't save Bellona from Vasilia, we might as well try to save Andvari from her and the Mortans."

Why would Vasilia come after Serilda? Why would she care about her mother's old guard? Especially if Serilda was leaving? Something else was going on here, something that I wasn't seeing.

"Well, then it looks like it's you and me against the world again." Cho held out his glass. "To the end?"

Serilda smiled, as though it were an old joke between them. She clinked her glass against his, completing the somber toast. "To the end."

They each took another sip of sangria, staring at each other. Cho hesitated, then reached out and gently touched Serilda's cheek. He stroked his thumb over the sunburst scar at the corner of her eye, his emotions clear on his face. Vasilia had been right. I didn't know what this thing was between them, or if they had ever acted on it, but it was obvious that Cho loved Serilda. And she loved him too, given the way that her face softened and the longing in her eyes.

But she didn't reach out to him, and she didn't encourage him to lean forward and kiss her. After several more seconds, Cho dropped his hand from her face, looked away, and set his glass on the desk.

"I should go make sure that the gate guards are on high alert. Just in case Vasilia sends someone to kill us in our sleep tonight." His tone was light, but he wasn't really joking.

"Good idea," Serilda murmured.

Cho stood up and turned toward the doors. I stepped forward and knocked on the wood, as though I had just arrived.

"Ah, there you are." Serilda got to her feet and went around behind her desk.

Cho smiled at me. "Congratulations, Evie."

It felt wrong to thank him when I had killed someone, so I nodded back. Cho winked at me, then left the library, shutting the doors behind him.

Serilda waved me over to her desk. She unlocked the center drawer, pulled out a small black ledger, and handed it to me. "Your earnings from tonight's match, as promised. Already deposited in a Bellonan bank. You can access the funds any time you like."

I opened the ledger and read the amount recorded on the first page. My eyes widened as I counted the zeroes. "Thirty thousand gold crowns? You're giving me *thirty thousand gold crowns* for winning?"

It was a not-so-small fortune. Despite all my scrimping, saving, and working for Alvis, I hadn't had this much money in all my accounts at the palace bank, not even close. Thirty thousand gold crowns . . . With this kind of money, I could go anywhere and do almost anything. I could even return to Winterwind, my family's estate in the northern mountains, and buy the property. Under an alias, of course.

If this had happened when I'd first come to the troupe, I would have already been packing my things to leave, to get as far away from Vasilia as possible. But now . . . now I wasn't sure what I wanted.

Oh, I wasn't planning to spill my guts and tell Serilda who I really was, much less let her use me in her palace games, but I wasn't going to slink away quietly into the night either. Paloma was my friend, my true friend, and I didn't want to leave her behind, any more than I had wanted to leave Isobel and Alvis behind at Seven Spire.

Cho, Aisha, Theroux, even Serilda. I cared about them all. And Sullivan . . . well, I felt more for Sullivan than I should have, something that went far beyond just fighting and fucking.

And if what Serilda and Cho had said was true, then the entire troupe was in danger. I couldn't just ignore that threat and walk away. Vasilia had already taken too much from me. She wasn't going to take anything else. I wanted to stay and help, in whatever small way I could. Besides, I'd promised myself that I would protect the people I cared about, instead of abandoning them to die.

I couldn't live with myself if I did anything less.

"Well, if I had known that a little bit of gold could shock you into silence, I would have tossed you a couple of crowns long ago," Serilda drawled, breaking the silence.

I couldn't tell her my thoughts, so I shook my head, as though I was still stunned by the figure. "I can't believe you're giving me this much money."

"Well, the winner usually only gets ten thousand, but you negotiated for triple that, remember?" Serilda arched an eyebrow. "Besides, you earned every single crown."

"What do you mean?"

She picked up the bottle and poured more sangria into her glass. "The odds against you were terrible. Emilie was a fifty-to-one favorite to win. Your thirty thousand crowns is only a small part of the even bigger fortune that I made when you defeated her."

"You actually bet on me to win? Why would you do that?"

"Let's just say that I could see beyond the odds." She smirked and took another sip of sangria.

See beyond the odds? What did that mean? My gaze focused on the black swan on the white pennant on the wall behind her. Anger surged through me. I was tired of Serilda Swanson and all her damn riddles. I reached into my pocket, drew out one of the black feathers from my costume, and tossed it down onto her desk.

"Why did you really bet on me?" I growled. "And why did you dress me up as a black swan?"

"Come with me."

She topped off her glass with more sangria, then opened one of the glass doors in the back wall and stepped outside. More anger surged through me that she hadn't answered my questions, but my curiosity won out, and I followed her.

Serilda ambled along a path that ran beside the stream that flowed through the gardens. I had wondered where the stream led to, and tonight, I got my answer. We walked over a stone bridge, and I realized that the stream fed into a large pond in the very back of the gardens.

Two streetlamps stood at the end of the bridge, their glows

stretching out across the pond and making the water gleam as brightly as all those gold crowns that I had won. Tall brown cattails ringed the area like soldiers standing guard, while blue and white water lilies bobbed up and down on the pond, twirling this way and that, as if they were dancing on top of the rippling current, just like the two creatures in the center of the water.

Black swans.

Midnight-black feathers; long, curved necks; sharp blue beaks; bright blue eyes. The two swans were exquisite, the epitome of beauty and grace, as they slowly drifted back and forth. For the first time, I understood why Serilda had chosen the creature as her own personal crest.

Serilda leaned against the whitewashed wooden fence that separated the pond from the rest of the gardens. I took up a position a few feet away. We stared at the swans, watching the creatures snatch bugs and bits of plants off the surface of the water.

"Have you ever seen a black swan before?" Serilda asked.

"My mother took me to a menagerie once. They had a pair of black swans. We got there at feeding time, and she let me toss flowers into the water for them to eat."

I had almost forgotten about that long-ago outing. My mother and I had spent the whole day at the menagerie, walking around; feeding the gargoyles, strixes, and caladriuses; and eating cornucopia and other treats ourselves. For a moment, the faint echoes of our happy laughter filled my ears, but the wind whistling over the pond quickly drowned out the sounds.

"When I was at Seven Spire, I would often go down to the river, to this hidden cove with water lilies and cattails growing up out of the rocks. The water was much calmer there, and

I would sit on the shore and watch the black swans." A wistful note crept into Serilda's voice.

I knew the exact spot she was talking about. It was a good place to hide from palace plots and politics, although I had never seen any black swans there. "It sounds lovely."

"It *was* lovely." Her face darkened. "Until someone killed the swans."

"Why would someone kill the swans?"

"Because she could," Serilda spat out the words.

A vague memory rose up in my mind, from the first time I had been to the cove. It hadn't been lovely then. The cattails and water lilies had been scorched to ash, and the smell of death had filled the air, so strong that I had only stayed for a few minutes. I remembered another scent from that day, one that I would recognize anywhere—the stench of Vasilia's lightning.

Vasilia had killed the swans. That had to be who Serilda was talking about. Even as a child, Vasilia would have had the power to do that, and slaughtering innocent creatures wouldn't have fazed her at all. But of course, I couldn't tell Serilda any of that, so I went with a simple commiseration instead.

"I'm sorry." And I truly was. I knew what it was like to lose something you loved to Vasilia.

Serilda shrugged as though it didn't bother her, although I could see how much it did. She didn't speak again for the better part of a minute. "Black swans are quite ugly when they first hatch. Everything about them is a dull, mottled gray, from their eyes to their beaks to their feathers."

"So?"

"So, as the swans grow, their eyes and beaks brighten, and their feathers darken until they look like these." She gestured at the two graceful creatures floating around the pond. "Just like you were ugly when you first got here. Well, not ugly in a physical sense. *Unskilled* would be a better word. But tonight, in the arena, you transformed yourself into something else, something greater than you had been before. Just like the swans change as they grow."

I snorted. "That's the most ridiculous thing I've ever heard."

"Why is it ridiculous? I saw your potential that very first day when you faced Sullivan in the training ring."

"Because I used a sword instead of a shield?" I snorted again. "Paloma told me about your little test. It doesn't mean anything. The sword was lighter than the shield. That's why I used it."

"And tonight you used both weapons," Serilda countered. "If that's not progress, then I don't know what is."

"A woman is dead. I would hardly call that *progress*."

"Sure it is," she replied. "Especially since you're not the one who's dead."

I couldn't argue with that.

Serilda took another sip of her sangria, a speculative look in her eyes. "I've trained a lot of people over the years. Palace guards and gladiators alike. You could be one of the best. You're quicker than Paloma, more determined than Cho, more ruthless than Lucas. One day, you might even be better than me, Evie."

It was the first time that she had called me anything other than *girl*, but I still laughed. "You've drunk too much sangria."

"Oh, I haven't drunk *nearly* enough. I'm not maudlin and rambling about the good ole days yet, but I will be soon enough." She drained the rest of the sangria, then toasted me with the empty glass.

"And what gives me so much *potential*?"

She didn't even have to think about it. "Your rage."

"Rage? I don't have any rage."

As soon as I said the words, I could smell the smoky lie of them in the air. I did have rage. I had *always* had rage, ever since my parents had been murdered, and everything that had happened to me since then had only fed it—growing up at the palace, being the royal stand-in, Vasilia's cruelty, losing Isobel, Cordelia, and everyone else in the massacre.

Serilda laughed. "Oh, you have plenty of rage. I don't know what happened to you, or who fucked you over, but they did a royal job of it. You've been oozing rage since the moment you got here."

I grimaced. If only she knew how true the *royal* part was.

"Some people pretty it up, call it drive or determination or ambition. But I like to call it what it is—rage." She shrugged. "It's not a bad thing. You actually have the best kind of rage."

I couldn't help but ask the inevitable question. "And what kind is that?"

"Most rage is hot, reckless, stupid." She tilted her head to the side, studying me. "But yours is cold, controlled, calculated. You think everything through before you say a word, take a step, make a move. Just like you did tonight in the arena when you dropped your sword. You had a plan, and you knew that the next time you picked up that sword you were going to kill Emilie with it. Cold rage is always the best rage."

"And what kind of rage do you have?"

"Right now? The sloppy drunk kind." Serilda toasted me with her empty glass again. Her cheeks were flushed, and her eyes were bright, but I didn't believe that she was drunk. Not for one second.

I shook my head. "You're wrong about me. I'm not a gladiator, I'm not a warrior, and I am certainly not a black swan."

"What are you then?" Her voice was soft but challenging.

My gaze moved past her, and I focused on the palace in the distance. Lights blazed on every level of Seven Spire. Before the massacre, I would have thought that the golden glows softened the rocky walls and made the palace seem warm and inviting. Tonight, they reminded me of the eyes of some monster, lurking in the dark and waiting to leap out of the shadows and gobble up everything and everyone in its path. I shivered and looked at Serilda again.

"I don't know what I am," I muttered. "Other than tired of this conversation. I'm going to bed. You should do the same."

I stared at the black swans again, but the creatures were still gliding across the pond, nibbling on tender shoots of water lilies and cattails. I envied their simple life of serenity. I sighed and turned to leave.

"Cold rage, Evie," Serilda called out behind me. "That's what saved your life in the arena tonight, and that's what will save it again someday. Mark my words. So you might as well embrace it!"

Her voice rang with a truth that I couldn't deny. Not tonight. Not after killing Emilie. But I didn't want to listen to any more of her riddles, so I ducked my head, crossed my arms over my chest, and hurried away.

Serilda's laughter chased me out of the gardens.

PART THREE

THE QUEEN'S CORONATION

CHAPTER TWENTY-ONE

The next morning, I went to the dining hall like usual, even though I didn't know what might greet me. After all, Emilie had been with the troupe a long time, and I had killed her.

The second that I stepped into the kitchen, everyone stopped what they were doing and turned toward me. Theroux, the other cook masters, the servers. Everyone stared at me.

And then they all started clapping.

"Congratulations!"

"We knew that you could do it!"

"Way to go, Evie!"

Everyone smiled, clapped, and called out greetings. I tried to smile, although I could feel my face twisting into a disgusted grimace. I dropped my head and hurried over to my prep station.

Two hours later, I was passing out raspberry-crème danishes when Serilda strolled into the dining hall, followed by Cho and Sullivan. All conversation stopped, and everyone focused on the troupe boss.

"First of all, I want to thank you all for putting on not

one great show but two of them last night. Vasilia was pleased with your performances." Her lips puckered, as though saying Vasilia's name left a bad taste in her mouth. "And, of course, I want to congratulate our Black Swan for giving the crowd such a thrilling match."

She started clapping. Everyone looked at me and joined in. Once again, I tried to smile, although my face twisted into another grimace.

Serilda could see how uncomfortable the attention was making me, but she was rubbing my face in it anyway. Smug, arrogant bitch. No matter what she thought, I wasn't a black swan, and I certainly wasn't going to become *her* black swan.

Finally, the applause died down, and everyone looked at her again.

"I have one final announcement, which I think you will all enjoy," Serilda said. "We're going on tour."

Excited whispers rippled through the crowd, along with more applause and even a few whistles. Apparently, going on tour was a much bigger deal than I'd realized.

"I want to capitalize on the success of last night's black-ring match and show everyone that the Black Swan is the best troupe not only in Bellona, but in all the kingdoms," Serilda said. "We leave as soon as possible. Cho and Sullivan have your assignments. So eat up, my lovelies. You're going to need your strength."

My job was to help Theroux and the others pack up pots, pans, and food for the trip. But packing wasn't more important than training, because Theroux eventually shooed me out of the kitchen.

So I went to the barracks, changed into my fighting leathers, and headed over to the training ring with Paloma. I stopped at one of the gates and stared at the other gladiators already gathered inside, stretching, warming up, and sharpening their weapons.

"Why did you stop?" Paloma asked. "You know that Sullivan hates it when anyone is late."

"Because I killed Emilie. She wasn't some random person, or some gladiator from a rival troupe. Like it or not, she was one of us. She ate and slept and fought alongside everyone else, and for a whole lot longer than I have."

Paloma laid her hand on my shoulder. "Don't worry. Everything will be fine. Everyone will honor the code."

"Code? What code?"

She gave me a serious look. "That the dead are the dead, and we don't harbor grudges against those who killed them in the arena. Fighting others, hurting them, sometimes even killing them, is a gladiator's life. It's *your* life now, Evie. And whether you like it or not, you're actually pretty good at it. So you might as well embrace it."

Before I could protest that I didn't want to be good at killing people, she opened the gate and pushed me through it. Paloma headed over to the weapons racks, and I followed her. I glanced around, waiting for someone to scream at me for killing Emilie, or perhaps even brandish their sword and attack me, but the exact opposite happened. Everyone smiled and nodded, and a few folks even stepped back out of my way so that I could walk past them.

The other gladiators actually *respected* me now.

Before, they had simply tolerated me, but now that I had killed Emilie, they saw me as an equal. With one thrust of my sword in the arena, I had graduated from newb to full-fledged gladiator. I wasn't sure how I felt about that, but Paloma was right. This was my life now, so I went over to the weapons racks, where I found another surprise. Emilie's name had been erased from the blackboard that denoted the gladiator rankings, and mine had been scrawled in its place, right under Paloma's name. I grimaced.

One of the gates creaked open, and Sullivan strode into the ring, carrying a black leather scabbard.

I hadn't imagined that you would be so handsome. Or so very polite. Then again, I suppose bastard princes have to mind their manners more than most, don't they? Vasilia's snide voice echoed in my mind.

I had encountered more than one bastard royal at Seven Spire, and all the clues that Sullivan was one of them had been right in front of me—the luxurious furnishings in his home, the fine cut of his coat, and especially the strong, confident way he carried himself. Lucas Sullivan and I had far more in common than I'd imagined with our royal upbringings. Still, I wondered how an Andvarian bastard prince had ended up with a Bellonan gladiator troupe.

He marched over to Paloma and me. He nodded at Paloma, who nodded back, grabbed a sword from the rack, and joined the other gladiators.

Then Sullivan turned to me, wariness flickering in his gaze. I knew that look. Bastard royals were often used quite ruthlessly in palace games. He probably trusted people even less than I did.

"Hello, Sully." I drawled his name the same way that I had a hundred times before.

He blinked in surprise. He had expected me to mockingly call him *princeling* again, but I would never do that. Not when I knew how much that word hurt him.

Sullivan dropped his gaze from mine and shifted on his feet. "I didn't get a chance to tell you before now, but I thought you did quite well in the arena last night."

I arched an eyebrow. "I killed Emilie, and all I get from you is *quite well*? How disappointing. Aren't you going to clap and tell me how amazing I am like everyone else has?"

"Well, I wouldn't want you to get any more arrogant than you already are."

"Ah, I'm afraid it's far too late for that."

I grinned, and he actually grinned back at me. For some reason, seeing that small lift of his lips eased some of the disgust, worry, and tension inside my own chest.

But Sullivan's grin faded all too fast, and he held out the scabbard in his hand. "Here. Serilda wants you to start training with this. It's lighter than the other swords."

I took the scabbard from him. It was nothing fancy, and the surface was plain, except for the swan crest that was stamped into the black leather.

I grimaced. "Why does Serilda want me to train with this?"

"You would have to ask her."

I looked over at the manor house. Serilda was on the second-floor balcony, relaxing in her chair. She smiled and toasted me with her glass, like she had by the pond last night.

"I am not a bloody swan," I muttered.

Sullivan frowned. "What did you say?"

Serilda mockingly saluted me with her glass a second time.

"Nothing," I muttered again, turning away from her. "Nothing at all."

The next few days rushed by, and a week after the black-ring match, the Black Swan troupe left Svalin.

A few people stayed behind to keep an eye on the compound, but everyone else piled into enormous wagons with wooden walls and flat roofs topped with pointed spires that were hauled by the troupe's older, tamer gargoyles. Serilda, Cho, and Sullivan rode in a lavish, cushioned carriage pulled by a team of Floresian horses, while Paloma and I were stuffed in a wagon with several other gladiators. Paloma wedged a pillow between her head and the wall and went to sleep, but I stared out the window at the scenery.

We left the Black Swan compound before dawn, so the city was dark, except for the lights that burned in the bakeries and butcher shops. Those folks were already hard at work kneading the day's breads, pastries, and croissants, as well as slicing up cuts of meat.

Besides the occasional city guard, the only other people out this early were the miners. They all wore heavy blue coveralls and black work boots, with tin lunchboxes swinging from their hands and fluorestone headlamps resting like crowns on top of their hard, ridged helmets.

I smiled as we rolled down the streets next to them. My father, Jarl, had been one of them, although he had been fortunate enough to eventually buy and establish his own mine near Winterwind, my mother's estate. Some of my favorite memories were of spending time in the cool, dark mines with him, moving from one shaft to another, staring at the interesting rock formations, and chiseling bits of tearstone out of the walls.

The troupe's wagons followed the miners to the rail stations at the edge of the city. From here, the miners would climb into carts that would take them up to the top of the Spire Mountains that surrounded the city. Then the miners would take another series of carts down into the shafts where they would dig fluore-stones and more out of the bellies of the mountains.

The wagons stopped in front of one of the rail stations to let the miners go by, but they weren't the only people here. Dozens of guards dressed in fuchsia tunics and gold breastplates roamed through the crowd. All the guards were holding swords, and a few were also clutching long black whips.

I frowned. The miners knew their business better than anyone, and guards had never been posted at the rail stations before. At least, not so many. And none with whips.

One of the guards raised his whip and slammed it down on the ground at the feet of a miner who was barely shuffling along. The miner flinched and lurched away.

"Let's go!" the guard shouted. "Move it! Those rocks aren't going to dig themselves out of the mountains!"

He cracked the whip against the ground again, and the miner hurried to climb into a metal cart. All the miners ducked their heads, as if they were afraid that the guard was going to bring his whip down across their backs next.

This had to be Vasilia's doing, since the guards were wearing her colors. Mining was one of the city's—and kingdom's—main industries. It had always been hard, dirty, dangerous work, but now it seemed as though Vasilia wanted it to be a form of slavery as well.

I had known that Vasilia would take control of everything in the capital and beyond, but seeing the miners hammered home just how much her cruelty would affect everyone in Bellona in one way or another. Serilda was right about one thing—any Blair would be a better ruler than Vasilia.

Even me.

I grimaced and shoved that thought away. I was staying with the troupe. I was protecting my friends. I was doing my part. But for the first time, I wondered if it was *enough*.

My heart squeezed tight, but I couldn't help the miners. After a few more minutes, and several more cracks of the guard's whip, the wagons rolled on.

We left the city behind and headed into the countryside, with its rocky ridges, forested hills, and clear streams. This was the first time that I had been out of Svalin since I had come to the capital fifteen years ago, and I stared out the window, drinking up the beautiful scenery.

Still, the farther we got from the city, the more worried I became. Serilda set a brutal pace, and we rode from sunup until well after sundown each day, with only a few short breaks for lunch and dinner. We were far away from the capital now, but I could see the worry in Serilda's face whenever we stopped for a quick bite to eat, and I could hear it in the sharp voice she used with the guards who stood watch at night. She thought that Vasilia was going to come after the troupe, come after her.

Two weeks after we left Svalin, we reached the mountains where the borders of Bellona, Andvari, and Unger met. Everyone grew tense and quiet, including me. Most of the troupe members were Bellonans, and we were wondering how we would be received in Andvari, given the impending war between the two kingdoms. Plus, the Ungers were notorious about patrolling and protecting their borders. One wrong turn, one wrong step into Unger, and the entire troupe could be detained—or worse.

We had a quick breakfast of hot oatmeal with honey and almonds, then climbed back into the wagons to travel the final few miles from Bellona to Andvari.

And that's when the snow started.

At first, it was only a few flurries, which was no real surprise. Even though it was spring now, we were high up in the mountains, and snow wasn't unusual at this elevation. Everyone pulled out their coats, gloves, scarves, and hats, and the wagons rolled on.

By midmorning, the flurries had turned into steady showers that covered the ground.

By lunchtime, the showers had turned into a blizzard, and the wind howled like a pack of greywolves nipping at the wagon wheels.

By midafternoon, the snow was so deep that not even the gargoyles could trudge through it anymore, and we were forced to stop and make camp. The wagons were maneuvered into a circle, which helped to block some of the snow and wind, although both still whistled in through the gaps. Several of the stronger gladiators dug down through the snow to create stone fire pits, which Sullivan and the other magiers lit with their power. Everyone huddled around the pits, drinking hot chocolate and mochana, but there was little conversation, and people's faces were tense and grim. Everyone realized that we would die from the cold if the snow didn't stop soon.

I stood at the gap between two of the wagons, peering into the blizzard. Even though the cold seared my lungs, I drew in a breath, letting the air roll in over my tongue and tasting all the scents in it. This was no natural storm, no mountain squall, no freak spring blizzard.

Every flake of snow dripped with the stench of magic.

Serilda had been right to flee Bellona, but she had still run straight into Vasilia's trap. Vasilia didn't need to send an army of assassins to kill us. All she had needed was a weather magier to create a storm and strand us on the mountain. Now we were stuck, like flies caught in a spider's icy web, and the magier was using each blast of snow and gust of wind to slowly freeze us to death. Worst of all, when our bodies were found, our deaths would be considered tragic accidents, and Vasilia would once again get away with mass murder.

Unless I figured out some way to stop the storm.

"What are you doing?" Paloma grumbled, stomping her feet. "Come back to the fire."

I kept breathing in, tasting the magic in the air, and trying to pinpoint where it was coming from. The magier had to be close by in order to control the blizzard and make sure that the storm stayed centered on our location. Maybe it was the snow blotting out everything else, all the other colors, textures, and shapes, but I could actually *see* the magier's power, like a seam of pale purple ore running through the tunnel of white in front of me.

I had never been able to see magic like this before. Then again, I had never been caught in a magier's storm before either. I squinted into the snow and wind, wondering if my eyes were playing tricks on me, but there it was, that seam of pale purple magic, rippling through the air before disappearing into the blizzard. If I could see the magic, then maybe I could track it back to its source. If I found the magier, then maybe I could force him to stop the storm—one way or another.

I didn't particularly like killing people, but as Paloma had pointed out, I seemed to be good at it. And if killing the magier meant saving myself and the rest of the troupe, well, what was one more death on my conscience at this point? Protecting my friends was the reason that I'd stayed with the troupe, instead of taking my prize money and disappearing, and I hadn't come all this way to abandon them now.

Besides, if the magier killed me, then I wouldn't have to deal with my growing guilt about breaking my promise to Cordelia. About the fact that I was hiding and running away with the troupe instead of staying in Bellona and fighting Vasilia.

"Let's go, Evie," Paloma grumbled again. "Before my toes freeze any more than they already have."

I moved away from the gap. "I need to talk to Serilda."

Paloma sighed, but she fell in step behind me. We trudged past the people huddled around the fire pits and over to a large tent that had been set up inside the wagon circle. I lifted the heavy canvas flap so that Paloma could slip inside. I followed her and let the flap drop into place behind me.

A fire crackled in the pit in the corner, making this area marginally warmer than the space inside the wagon circle. Sullivan, Cho, and Serilda were gathered around a table that was covered with maps. Sullivan and Serilda were bundled up like Paloma and I were, but Cho was wearing only a short red jacket. The dragon morph's inner fire was most likely keeping him warm. He was probably the only one of us who would survive the cold.

"You have to let me go out there," Sullivan growled, pacing back and forth. "I have to find the bastard who's controlling the storm and kill him before we all freeze to death."

"We've already wandered off the road to Andvari," Serilda replied. "We have no idea where we are, much less where the magier is."

"And you can't kill him if you can't find him," Cho added.

Sullivan gave them both a frustrated look and kept pacing.

"What if I can find him?" I said. "What if I can track the magier?"

The three of them looked at me. So did Paloma, who was stamping her feet to try to warm them up.

"And how can you do that?" Sullivan growled again. "You can barely see your hand in front of your face out there."

"I don't need to see him to track him." I tapped my nose. "All I have to do is follow the scent of his magic."

The four of them looked at me, doubt filling their faces. Another gust of wind howled against the tent, and the icy air cut through the heavy canvas like it wasn't even there. This time, everyone shivered, including Cho.

"Sully's right," I said. "Someone has to try to find the magier, and I have the best chance of doing that."

Sullivan stepped forward. "If you can track him, I can kill him."

I nodded at him, then looked at Serilda. Her eyes narrowed, and her gaze flicked back and forth between Sullivan and me. Once again, I got the impression that she was seeing far more than just the two of us standing here.

"All right," she said. "You two track down and kill the magier. Paloma, Cho, and I will stay here with the troupe and keep watch, in case the storm is a distraction for some other attack."

We split up. I left the tent, trudged back through the snow to the wagon where my things were, and put on every single piece of clothing that I had. By the time I finished, I felt as fat as one of the marshmallows that Isobel had always whipped up for hot chocolate, if not nearly as warm. Instead of wearing my belt on my leggings like usual, I buckled it on top of the blue jacket that I had stolen from Sullivan. I hooked my new, lighter sword to the belt, then pulled the poisoned white feather out of my black bag of treasures and slid it into my jacket pocket. Sullivan would most likely kill the magier, but I wanted to be prepared for anything.

I pulled a blue toboggan down low on my forehead, stuffed my hands into some matching gloves, and left the wagon. Sullivan was waiting for me by one of the gaps. He too was bundled up in a black toboggan and gloves, and he had also buckled his belt and sword on top of his gray coat. More snow and wind blasted through the gap, making us both grimace and step closer together. For a moment, I felt the warmth of Sullivan's tall, strong body next to mine, but the wind howled around us again, stealing it away, along with my breath.

"Are you sure you can do this?" Sullivan asked.

I drew in a breath. The stench of the magier's power was as strong as ever. "I can find the bastard."

A crooked smile curved his lips, and he gestured with his hand. "Then lead the way, highness."

I nodded back at him, and together, we plunged into the storm.

Back at the wagons, I had thought that I couldn't possibly get any colder than I already was.

I was wrong.

The wind slapped me in the face over and over again, along with the stinging flakes of snow. With every step I took, the three feet of snow already on the ground threatened to soak through my three pairs of leggings, along with my boots and my five pairs of socks. I felt like I was grinding my face into a bowl full of icy needles and slogging through cold, gritty sand at the same time, but I ducked my head and trudged on.

Sullivan walked next to me, his hand curled around his sword. I didn't know if he was being vigilant, or if his hand was simply so cold that he couldn't remove it from the weapon. Either way, he looked as miserable as I felt.

We were both so busy plowing through the snow that we didn't speak, but I didn't mind the silence. This was by far the most companionable thing we had ever done together.

Serilda was right. We quickly became lost in the snow. We hadn't gone more than a dozen feet from the wagons before they disappeared altogether. Even though I knew that the wagons were behind us, I didn't know if I could have found my way back to them through the storm. But there was no going back now. Only forward, until Sullivan and I either froze to death or found and killed the magier.

Every few feet, I stopped and drew in a breath, tasting the air. I turned around in a circle, searching for where the stench of magic was the strongest. Then I moved in that direction until I lost the scent and had to stop and find it again. Sullivan watched me with open curiosity, but he didn't say anything, and he didn't mock me, not even once. Perhaps he knew that my nose and my mutt magic were the only chance we had to survive.

I also kept looking for the magier's power. Despite the snow, I could still see that pale purple vein of magic shimmering in the air. Maybe it was my imagination—or desperation— but the longer we walked, and the deeper into the storm we moved, the brighter the magic became until it almost seemed like an arrow telling me exactly where to go.

I didn't know how far or long we walked. All I was aware of

was the snow stinging my eyes, the wind chilling my cheeks, and the stench of magic filling my nose—

And just like that, we stepped out of the storm.

One moment, Sullivan and I were trudging through a blustery blizzard. The next, we were standing in a clearing in the middle of the forest. Both of us staggered to a stop and looked around, blinking in surprise.

Oh, snow still covered the ground, but only three inches, instead of the three feet that we had been slogging through, and the wind was a faint breeze, instead of a howling gale. It certainly wasn't warm and sunny, but I didn't feel like I was trapped in a snow globe that someone was violently shaking anymore either.

I glanced behind me. A few feet away, the storm raged on, like a swirling wall of white that had been erected in the middle of the forest.

"You did it," Sullivan whispered. "You actually led us out of there."

He let out a loud *whoop*, picked me up, and spun me around in a circle. I laughed with delight, and he spun me around twice more before setting me down. The motions made me dizzy, and I swayed toward him, grabbing the front of his coat. Sullivan wrapped his arm around my waist, steadying me.

And then he smiled at me.

It was the first wide, true, genuine smile that he'd ever given me, and it was even more dazzling than the sun peeking through the clouds overhead. Suddenly, I didn't feel quite so cold anymore, and I found myself smiling back at him. At least, I thought I smiled back. I couldn't really feel my face at the moment.

Our breaths steamed in the air, mixing and mingling together, even as we held on to each other. Sullivan's gaze dropped to my lips, and hunger filled his face, the same hunger that I felt. Images of all the deliciously wicked things we could do together flashed through my mind. Oh, no, I wasn't nearly as cold anymore.

In that moment, I made another promise to myself—I would have Sullivan. I would have him every which way I wanted him and however he wanted me. But later, when we both weren't half frozen and the rest of the troupe wasn't still in danger.

I playfully tapped his chest and stepped away from him. "Did you ever doubt me, Sully?"

"Not for one second, highness. Not for one bloody second." He smiled at me a moment longer, then yanked off his gloves, stuffed them in his coat pocket, and pulled his sword out of its scabbard. "Now let's find the bastard and end this."

I yanked off my gloves and pulled my sword out as well, and we walked on.

Without the snow blotting out everything else, I couldn't see that purple vein of magic in the air, but I could still smell the magier's power. Every few feet, I stopped, tasted the air, and oriented myself as to where the magic was coming from, just like I had inside the storm. The process went much faster this time, and Sullivan and I quickly left the clearing behind and stepped into the forest, moving from one tree to the next and searching for the magier.

I finished tasting the air again and was about to step forward when Sullivan lunged over, grabbed my arm, and yanked me back.

"What are you doing?" I hissed.

"Trap," he whispered.

He pointed at the ground, and I spotted a metal bear trap

half hidden in the snow. The razor-sharp teeth glinted in the sunlight filtering down through the trees. I grimaced. Those teeth would have broken my ankle for sure.

"He's close," Sullivan whispered. "Stay behind me, and step where I step."

He took the lead, creeping through the woods and scanning everything, including the ground, but we didn't come across any more traps. Eventually, Sullivan stopped and peered around a tree. I sidled up next to him and did the same.

A clearing stretched out for about fifty feet before the pines took over on the far side. A canvas tent had been erected in the open space, along with a stone fire pit. No one was inside the tent, and no flames flickered in the pit. The magier wasn't here, although his footprints dotted the snow in the clearing.

"Where is he?" I whispered.

Sullivan shook his head. "I don't know. Probably somewhere closer to the storm, feeding his magic into it. I'm going to double back and see if I can pick up his trail. You stay here in case he returns."

I nodded, and Sullivan moved off into the forest. I looked around again, but I didn't see the magier, so I stepped out from behind the tree and went into his camp, keeping an eye out for more traps buried in the snow. But the ground was clear, and I slipped under one of the flaps and went into his tent.

A sleeping bag, a knapsack full of food, some other odds and ends. The magier had traveled light in order to catch up with the troupe, given the blistering pace that Serilda had set, but nothing in his things gave me any clue to his identity. I set his knapsack back down where I had found it and started to leave the tent when I noticed a book sticking out from underneath his sleeping bag. I crouched down and pulled it out.

It was a red ledger.

I opened the book, already knowing what I would find—a list of names, written in a neat, familiar hand. *Serilda Swanson, Cho Yamato, Lucas Sullivan.* I flipped through the pages. *Paloma, Theroux, Aisha.* I had wondered what Felton had been writing in his ledger the night that he, Vasilia, and Nox had visited the arena. It was another list of all the people Vasilia wanted dead.

Including me.

Oh, Felton hadn't recognized me any more than Vasilia had, but he had made a small star at the bottom of one of the pages next to a final name, or rather title—*the Black Swan gladiator.*

"Felton," I growled. "You and your damn checklists. You bastard."

A branch cracked in the distance. I froze, wondering if I had only imagined the sound, but a second later, another branch cracked.

Someone was coming this way.

I tossed the ledger on top of the sleeping bag, grabbed my sword from the ground, and crept up to the tent flaps. My gaze darted from one tree to the next, but a moment later, Sullivan walked into the clearing, still clutching his sword.

I let out a relieved breath and stepped out of the tent where he could see me. Some of the tension in his face eased, although he shook his head. He hadn't found the magier. Sullivan opened his mouth to say something, and that's when I saw a shadow darting through the trees, heading straight for him.

"Look out!" I screamed.

But my warning came too late.

A magier dressed in a long midnight-purple coat stepped out of the trees. Bits of bright purple magic crackled on his fingertips, like snowflakes dancing on the wind, and he reared his hand back and threw his power at Sullivan. As the flakes arced through the air, they transformed into sharp, jagged needles of ice. Sullivan lurched out of the way. The ice needles punched into the tree where he had been standing, like darts sticking out of a board.

Sullivan spun around, raised his hand, and threw his lightning at the magier, but the other man ducked behind a tree, letting Sullivan's power scorch it instead of him. Then the magier leaned around the trunk and let loose with another wave of his icy needles, making Sullivan scramble behind another tree for cover.

The two men exchanged blast after blast of magic, neither one able to wound the other, given all the trees in between them. I was still standing by the tent, but the magier was focusing his deadly magic on Sullivan, and he wasn't paying any attention to me. I tightened my grip on my sword, sprinted away from the tent, and crossed the clearing.

"No!" Sullivan shouted over the continued blasts of magic. "Don't!"

I didn't know if he was talking to the magier or me, but it didn't matter. This bastard had tried to kill everyone in the troupe. He wasn't getting away with that.

I darted through the trees, heading toward the magier and hoping that I could stab him in the back before he realized that I was there. He threw another blast of power at Sullivan, who cursed and fell to the ground. I couldn't tell if Sullivan had been hit or if he had just slipped in the snow, but anger scorched through me, and I picked up my pace.

The magier must have heard the crunch of my boots in the

snow because he whirled around, snapped up his hand, and sent a wave of icy needles shooting out at me. I threw myself down and rolled to the side. Needles *thunk-thunk-thunk*ed into the ground all around me, sending up sprays of snow, along with the dirt and dead leaves underneath.

None of the needles hit me, but I rolled into a tree. My left shoulder smacked into the trunk, making me growl with pain. But all these weeks training with Sullivan, Paloma, and the gladiators had taught me how to absorb a hard blow, and I scrambled back up onto my feet and kept going.

The magier blinked, surprised that I was still running toward him. He snapped up his hand to blast me with his magic again, but I plowed into him, knocking him off-balance and sending us both tumbling down to the ground.

I got back up onto my knees, but I had lost my sword, and I didn't see where it had landed. The magier snarled, scrambled up onto his knees as well, and lifted his hand, like he was going to blast me with his magic and drive his icy needles straight into my face. Even with my immunity, I doubted I would survive that, and I certainly didn't want to find out. So I reached for the only other weapon I had—the poisoned feather that Sullivan had given me.

I yanked the feather out of my pocket and lashed out with it. The needle on the end slashed across the magier's palm, surprising him, and his magic dissolved into a shower of purple snowflakes. The magier hissed, but he curled his hand into a fist and punched me in the face. He must have had a bit of mutt strength as well, because the blow hurt far more than rolling into that tree trunk had. Pain exploded in my left cheek, my head snapped back, and my legs slid out from under me. In an instant, I was flat on my back in the snow.

The magier climbed to his feet, leaned down, and plucked the feather off the ground, twirling it around in his hand. "A feather?" He laughed. "What were you going to do? Tickle me to death?"

I was too busy sitting up and trying to ignore the pounding ache in my face to answer. The magier laughed again and flicked the feather away. It landed on the snow next to my hand.

My head was still spinning, but I could see the smear of blood on the needle. Had I not sliced him deep enough with it? Why wasn't the poison working? Why wasn't he dead yet?

"Evie!" Sullivan yelled in the distance. "Evie!"

But he was too far away, and he couldn't help me.

"Time to die," the magier hissed.

He raised his hand, and snowflakes swirled around his fingertips again. The magier gave me an evil smile, and I reached for my immunity, hoping that it would save me from his icy needles. The magier's smile widened, and he drew back his hand to blast me with his magic.

And then he froze—he just *froze*.

He stood there, locked in place, the muscles in his neck, shoulders, and arms bunching and flexing, as though he was straining to move. A horrible, acrid stench filled the air, and the icy flakes swirling around his fingertips blackened and dropped to the ground, smoldering like bits of hot ash before melting into the snow. The magier looked at me, and I realized that his eyes were completely black, as though he was burning up from the inside out. He let out a strangled cry, and a thin trickle of black blood dribbled out of his mouth. Then he collapsed.

The magier landed in the snow next to me. I grimaced as a few cold pellets sprayed against my face, but he didn't move.

My breath escaped in a relieved rush. Sullivan's poison had worked, and the magier was dead.

A shout rose up in the distance, boots crunched in the snow, and Sullivan sprinted around a tree, his sword in one hand and his blue lightning crackling in his other hand. He hurried over and dropped to his knees beside me.

"Evie! Are you okay? Did he hurt you?"

"I'm fine. Just a little banged up." I gestured at the white feather that was lying in between the dead magier and me. "What kind of poison was on that?"

His lips pressed into a thin line. "Does it matter?"

"No, I suppose it doesn't. I'm just glad that I managed to stab him and not myself."

"Me too," Sullivan murmured. "Me too."

He stared at me, his blue gaze steady on mine, and reached out with his hand. At first, I wondered what he was doing, but then his fingers touched my cheek where the magier had punched me. Despite the fact that we had been tromping through a blizzard, his hand was warm, although the feel of his skin against mine still made me shiver.

Sullivan paused, as though he was feeling the same things that I was, then gently pressed all around the wound. His fingers lingered on my cheek a moment before he dropped his hand and sat back on his heels.

"No broken bones," he rasped. "Just a nasty bruise. You should put some snow on it to help with the pain and swelling."

I let out a bitter laugh. "Right now, I never want to see snow again, not one more flake."

A crooked grin lifted his lips. "Me neither."

I smiled back, but the motion made my face ache again, and I grimaced.

"The storm should have stopped the second you killed the magier," Sullivan said. "Let's get back to the wagons, so we can get warm and tell the others what happened."

I nodded, and he grabbed my arm and helped me to my feet.

CHAPTER TWENTY-TWO

We went back to the magier's tent. I grabbed the red ledger with the troupe members' names and showed it to Sullivan. He recognized it as an assassination list. His face darkened with anger, and he took the book from me and slid it into one of his coat pockets.

We searched through the rest of the magier's things, but there was nothing else of interest, so we left his camp. I thought we might have trouble figuring out where the wagons were, but Sullivan had come across the magier's tracks during his earlier search, and we followed them back to the edge of the storm. Without the magier to power it, the blizzard had disappeared, although more than three feet of snow still covered the ground.

Up ahead, smoke rose over the tops of the trees from the fire pits that had been set up inside the wagon circle. I pointed out the smoke to Sullivan, and we headed in that direction.

We were almost back to the wagons when I noticed the silence.

Snow still covered everything, so it had been quiet the

whole time that we'd been walking, but given how close we were to the wagons, noises should have filled the air. Boots stomping through the snow, shovels scratching into the ice, snatches of conversation. But I didn't hear any of those things. No boots, no shovels, no voices.

And most troubling of all, I smelled magic in the air again.

"Stop," I said.

Sullivan was a few steps ahead, since it was his turn to break the path, but he stopped and glanced over his shoulder at me. "What?"

I didn't see anything other than snow and trees, but someone was out here. My nose twitched. I could *smell* them.

"Something's wrong. We need to get back to the wagons."

We both drew our swords and quickened our pace. A few minutes later, we stepped out of the trees. The wagons stood in the center of a clearing, still arranged in a large circle. I could smell and see the smoke and the flames from the fires that were burning in the stone pits, but I didn't spot anyone moving through the gaps in between the wagons. Not that unusual, given how cold it still was, but the smell of magic was much stronger here than it had been in the trees.

I drew in a deep breath, tasting the air and trying to place the scent. I had smelled this kind of magic before, and the wet fur aroma reminded me of . . .

Lady Xenia.

"Morphs," I whispered to Sullivan. "There are morphs here—"

One second, we were alone. The next, we were surrounded.

More than three dozen men and women appeared. Most of them stepped out from between the gaps in the wagons, while a few came out of the trees behind us. They were all shapes and sizes, but they all had three things in common. One, they were carrying spiked maces, battle axes, and other large, heavy weapons. Two, they were wearing hip-length black jackets with two rows of red buttons running down the front in the traditional Ungerian style. And three, every single one of them had a morph mark on their neck.

And not just any mark—they were ogres.

My gaze moved from one mark to the next. The ogre faces peered at me, their liquid eyes blinking with curiosity, examining Sullivan and me. A few of the ogres smiled, then licked their jagged teeth, telling me exactly what they were thinking. I shuddered.

Sullivan lowered his sword and slid the weapon back into its scabbard. I did the same. There was no use fighting against this many morphs. They would tear us to pieces in seconds.

"Ungers," Sullivan muttered. "The storm must have forced us into their territory."

The Ungers were extremely protective of their borders. People who tried to sneak into their kingdom without the proper papers or authorization were often jailed—or worse.

One of the Ungers stepped forward. He was tall, even for an ogre morph, topping out at about six and a half feet. His black jacket strained to cover his broad shoulders, and his legs looked as thick as tree trunks. He had a strong jaw, although his nose had a lump in it, as though it had been broken long ago. His short hair was a dull copper against his bronze skin, and suspicion filled his hazel eyes.

"Bring them," he called out in Ungerian. "We'll put them with the others."

The other men and women stepped up and brandished

their weapons at us, and Sullivan and I had no choice but to step through one of the gaps and into the wagon circle.

Well, now I knew where everyone was. They had been herded to the back of the circle in front of Serilda's tent. Everyone looked tense and worried, and a few folks were sniffling and fighting back tears, but they all seemed to be okay.

Except for Serilda, Cho, and Paloma.

The three of them had been separated from the rest of the troupe and were kneeling in the snow off to one side with guards clustered around them. They must have fought back against the Ungers. Serilda's left arm hung limp and useless by her side, as though it had been broken, Cho's face was a mess of bruises, and Paloma's hands were covered with blood, although I couldn't tell if it was hers or someone else's.

The Ungers must have thought that Sullivan and I were dangerous too, because they herded us over and forced us to kneel in the snow beside Serilda, Cho, and Paloma.

"What happened?" Sullivan whispered.

"They came from out of nowhere," Serilda muttered. "After the storm stopped, we started digging the wagons out of the snow. One second, we were alone. The next, they were inside the wagon circle. Cho, Paloma, and I tried to drive them back, but you can see how well that worked out. We're lucky they haven't killed us all yet."

She fell silent, and I listened to our captors. They were speaking Ungerian, but I could understand them perfectly, thanks to all those years of language lessons at Seven Spire.

A short, burly man with black hair, dark brown eyes, and onyx skin was talking to the tall, redheaded man, who seemed to be the leader.

"It's possible that they just became lost in the storm, Halvar," the short man said, stroking his long, bushy beard.

"No, Bjarni," Halvar, the leader, replied. "They are spies for the Bellonan queen. Otherwise, they would have all been here, taking shelter from the storm. But instead, those two were off in the forest." He stabbed his finger at Sullivan and me. "So what were they doing, if not spying? Besides, she told us to be careful. So careful we shall be."

She? Who was she? And why were the Ungers so worried about us being spies? What were they hiding?

"And she would not want us to be hasty either," Bjarni replied. "We have enough problems already. Do you really want to add to them by killing all these people? Think of how long it will take us just to bury their bodies."

Halvar sighed, and the two men engaged in a long conversation about what to do. Finally, Halvar won, and it was agreed that everyone in the troupe had trespassed, so everyone would be killed as punishment.

Serilda must have spoken at least a little Ungerian, because her face hardened. She held her right hand out to her side, slowly got to her feet, and stepped forward. The Ungers tensed and brandished their weapons, but she stood straight and tall.

"If you're going to kill someone, then kill me," she called out. "I am the leader of this gladiator troupe, I am the one who led us on this route, and I am the one who got us lost in the storm. This is my fault. Everyone else is innocent."

Halvar studied her. For a moment, I thought he might agree, but then, he shook his head. "Kill her," he said in the common tongue so that everyone could understand him. "Kill them all."

The Ungers raised their weapons and moved forward. Everyone in the troupe pressed in tighter together, yelling and screaming and crying. My stomach twisted. The magier hadn't managed to murder us with the storm, but we were still going to die.

I should have been worried, panicked, terrified. But instead, I found myself thinking about those long hours and weeks that I had spent learning that Ungerian dance. All that time wasted on a silly tradition, and now here I was, about to die at the hands of the Ungers anyway—

My eyes widened, and a crazy idea popped into my mind.

"Wait!" I called out in Ungerian. "Wait!"

Halvar stopped and looked at me, surprised that I was speaking his language. So did everyone else. But it was the only thing that might save us now, along with another one of my many useless skills.

"Evie!" Paloma hissed. "What are you doing?"

Instead of answering, I scrambled to my feet and darted forward, so that I was standing next to Serilda.

"I demand to perform the Tanzen Freund!" I called out, still speaking their language.

Shocked murmurs rippled through the Ungers, and they looked at me with surprise and interest. Well, that was better than killing us.

Halvar strode forward and stabbed his finger at me. Anger glinted in his hazel eyes, as well as in those of the ogre on his neck. "What do you know of our dance?" he asked, switching to the common tongue. "How dare you even speak of it!"

He probably expected me to wilt in the face of his fury, but I'd gotten rather good at standing up for myself these past few months, and I remained calm and confident.

"Oh, I know plenty about it. For example, I know that once the offer to dance is given, it cannot be rescinded, and the dancer and all those who are with her are granted safe passage until the dance is finished." I paused. "Unless you want to dishonor your own tradition?"

Bjarni snickered. Halvar glared at him, but the other man shrugged.

"Perhaps she does know the dance. She has certainly twirled you into a corner, my friend." Bjarni let out another snicker.

But Halvar wasn't to be so easily twirled. He stabbed his finger at me again. "Well, then, if we are going on tradition, then you must perform the dance *perfectly*. Otherwise, it will be seen as an insult, and your life will be forfeit. One false move, one hesitant step, and you will be killed on the spot."

"*My* life is forfeit, but the lives of my friends are *not*," I snapped right back at him. "According to tradition, as long as I perform the Tanzen Freund and accept the consequences of failing, my friends will not be harmed by you and yours."

Halvar's lips pressed together. He didn't want to agree to my terms, even though they were tradition. I stepped closer and stabbed my finger at him this time.

"My friends will *not* be harmed by you and yours," I said in a loud, strong voice. "You will provide them the full extent of your hospitality, as you would any honored guests. That means food, clothing, warmth, and shelter for as long as they require it. Are we agreed? Or will you dishonor yourself and your people?"

Halvar looked at the other morphs, who were still regarding me with curiosity. Bjarni seemed highly amused, a grin stretching across his face.

"Fine," Halvar snarled. "If you want to perform the dance

so badly, then you will get your wish." He smiled, showing me his teeth, as did the ogre on his neck. "But when you fail, I will tear you to pieces with my bare hands for daring to insult me and my people this way."

I smiled back at him. "Then we are agreed."

Halvar's eyes narrowed, as if he was disappointed that I wasn't quivering with fear, but he nodded. "Agreed."

He stared at me a moment longer, then waved his hand at the other morphs. "Bring them."

The Ungers helped dig the troupe wagons out of the snow. Once everything and everyone was loaded up inside the wagons again, the Ungers retrieved their own horses from where they had hidden them deeper in the forest.

And then they took us to their castle.

It was carved out of a mountain, the same way that Seven Spire was, although it was much smaller than the Bellonan palace. Large, round windows were set into the dark gray granite walls, offering sweeping views of the surrounding forest, while tall, round turrets topped with black slate roofs soared up into the air. I glanced up at the turrets, expecting to see crested flags flapping in the wind, but the pinnacles were empty, as if whoever lived here didn't want to announce their presence to the outside world. Curious.

The castle was less than three miles away from our camp, and if we had continued on our path, we would have passed right by it. No wonder the Ungers had thought that we were spies. We had practically marched up to their front door.

Under the watchful eyes of Halvar, Bjarni, and the rest of

our escorts, the wagons crossed the stone drawbridge that led to the castle and stopped in a large courtyard. More Ungers appeared, all of them morphs as well, to help the troupe workers take care of the horses and gargoyles. Once that was done, everyone grabbed their supplies from the wagons. Halvar grunted and jerked his hand, and we followed him into the castle, still surrounded by our escorts.

We walked past room after room filled with mahogany tables and chairs, stained-glass lamps, and other fine furnishings. Tapestries depicting forest and mountain scenes covered the walls, while thick rugs stretched across the floors, softening the hard stone underfoot. Everything was simple, but well-made. It was far less luxurious than Seven Spire, but it was warm and dry, which was all I cared about after being out in the cold and snow.

Still, the longer we walked, the more I noticed the ogres.

Ogre faces and figures glared at us from every furnishing in every corner of the castle. They were carved into the table-tops, pieced together in the stained-glass lamps, threaded into the tapestries, and even chiseled into the walls, just like the gladiators in the columns at Seven Spire. I grimaced as I walked across a rug that featured a snarling ogre face that was more teeth than anything else. It seemed as though whoever lived here wanted everyone to know exactly how powerful and dangerous they were.

I expected Halvar to insist on my performing the dance immediately, but instead, he led us to a large dining hall. Halvar grunted again, then pointed at the tables, telling us to sit. Serilda took the seat at the head of the table. I wound up sitting next to her, with Paloma beside me. Sullivan was across from me, with Cho next to him. The rest of the troupe sat down as well.

More Ungers appeared with trays full of food and drinks, which they deposited on the tables before stepping away. They didn't go far, though. The Ungers lined the walls, their hands clasped behind them, watching us.

Halvar scowled at me, then everyone else. "Well?" he snapped, throwing up his hands. "What are you waiting for? Eat! Drink!"

Serilda, Paloma, Sullivan, and Cho looked at me, the same silent question on all their faces, wondering if I could smell any poison on the food. I drew in a breath, but I didn't sense any scents that shouldn't be here. I nodded at them, then did the same thing to Halvar.

"You honor us with your hospitality," I said in a dry tone.

An angry flush stained his cheeks, but he nodded back at me, then strode out of the dining hall. Bjarni remained behind, standing along the wall, an amused look on his face again. Well, at least I was entertaining someone.

The meal was simple—beef, potatoes, and other vegetables in a seasoned stew—but it was warm, hearty, and filling, and served with crusty bread slathered with honey butter. We washed everything down with tall mugs of spiced apple cider.

For several minutes, the dining hall was quiet, except for the scrapes of forks and spoons on dishes and bowls as everyone dug into their meals. Eventually, the food and drinks warmed everyone enough for them to start whispering. People stared at the Ungers, then at me. I grimaced, but I couldn't stop the speculative stares and whispers, so I concentrated on my food.

After all, this was most likely my last meal.

Several minutes later, I pushed my empty dishes aside. So did Serilda, Paloma, Sullivan, and Cho. They all looked at me, more questions in their eyes.

"How do you know how to speak Ungerian?" Paloma asked.

I could have lied. I probably *should* have lied. But it had been a long day, and I was tired. Even more than that, I was tired of lying, of always watching my words, of always worrying that I was going to do or say something that would give away my true identity. Besides, what was the point of lying now? I would be dead soon enough.

"I know lots of languages."

"And do you really know this dance that you've demanded to perform?" Cho asked.

I shrugged. "More or less."

"But the Ungers said that if you don't perform it perfectly, every single step, then they will execute you on the spot." Worry rippled through Sullivan's voice.

"Yes, they will. But on the bright side, they can't lay a finger on any of you now," I said. "Don't you dare let them renege on that. You remind them of their bloody tradition and honor, and you hold them to their word."

Serilda stared at me. "So you've traded your life for all of ours. Why?"

"Well, it was either that or watch everyone get slaughtered. Believe me, I've seen enough innocent people die already." My lips twisted into a bitter smile. "Besides, I wanted to finally do something useful with all the useless skills that I've learned."

She frowned, wondering what I meant. So did the others, but I didn't explain my cryptic words.

Finally, the meal ended. Halvar strode back into the dining hall and crooked his finger at me.

Showtime.

I pushed back from the table and followed him. Serilda, Paloma, Sullivan, and Cho followed me, with everyone else from the troupe trailing along behind them. The Ungers were at the back of the pack, still watching everyone.

Halvar led us to an open-air courtyard on the back side of the castle. By this point, the sun had set behind the mountains, and night had fallen over the land like a midnight blanket. The air was quite cold, although thankfully no more snowflakes fell from the sky.

A second-story balcony set with glass doors wrapped around the courtyard, while a series of columns and archways at the opposite end divided the area from the lawn in the distance. And just like in the rest of the castle, images of ogres adorned everything, from the glass in the doors to the stone rails in the balcony to the columns in the distance.

The balcony, columns, and archways were studded with small, diamond-shaped fluorestones that bathed the court-yard in soft white light. The steady glow of the fluorestones gave life to the ogre figures, making them seem as if they were watching and waiting to attack us. Still, I would have thought it a fierce, lovely scene, if not for the fact that I most likely wouldn't be leaving here alive.

To my surprise, chairs lined one side of the courtyard, and a group of Ungerian musicians were softly tuning their instruments in the corner. Lady Xenia certainly would have approved of that. She had always had live musicians perform at her finishing school, even when the students were just prac-ticing their dance steps.

Halvar grunted again and stabbed his finger at the chairs, and the troupe members went over and took their seats. Above them, on the second-floor balcony, several glass doors opened, and more Ungers streamed outside and sat down in the chairs on that level.

When everyone was seated, a door in the center of the balcony opened, and a tall figure stepped outside. A long black coat obscured the figure's body, while a black hat and a thick veil covered its head, hiding its features. I couldn't tell if it was a man or a woman. The figure stopped a moment, studying me, then sat down in a plush chair. Whoever the figure was, it had the best seat in the courtyard, and the other Ungers nodded their heads respectfully to it.

"Who's that?" I asked.

"Your judge," Halvar growled.

Of course.

"You have five minutes to prepare yourself," he growled again.

He strode across the courtyard and began speaking to the musicians. That left me alone with Serilda, Paloma, Sullivan, and Cho.

"Maybe Halvar will change his mind," I said.

"About what?" Cho asked.

"Maybe he'll cut off my head instead of ripping me to pieces with his teeth and talons."

The others looked at me, shock filling their faces. They might be gladiators and used to seeing people fight, bleed, and die, but my nonchalance about my own impending demise surprised them. I shrugged. I wasn't going to sugarcoat things. Not here, now, at the end.

"It's not too late. We can still try to fight our way out of here." Paloma eyed the other ogre morphs, and her fingers flexed, as if she was thinking about her own inner teeth and talons and how she could use them to rip into the Ungers.

I shook my head. "No, this was my decision. I knew the risks, and I'll accept the consequences. Besides, according to tradition, if I don't perform the dance, everyone's life is forfeit. Better for me to die than all of you."

Paloma stared at me, concern filling her eyes. Then her face hardened, as if she'd made an important decision. She turned so that she was standing directly in front of me, drew in a breath, and slowly let it out.

And then she morphed.

Paloma was already tall, but in an instant, she shot up several inches, until she was well over six feet. The muscles in her arms, chest, and legs expanded, along with the rest of her body, and her fingernails lengthened, darkened, and sharpened into long black talons. Her lips drew back in a grimace, revealing the sharp, jagged teeth in her mouth. Her amber eyes gleamed as brightly as candles, and her blond braids glinted and rippled with the same golden light.

Paloma grimaced again, as if she was afraid that I was going to call her a monster the way her father had, but she held her ground, lifted her chin, and looked at me. My heart squeezed tight. She really did trust me, and she really was my friend—the first true one that I had had since my parents had died.

And now I had to say goodbye to her.

I stepped forward, put my hands on her massive arms, and gave them a gentle squeeze, although her hard muscles didn't move. I would have hugged her, but I couldn't have gotten my arms all the way around her now.

"Thank you for showing me this. You are so strong and fierce and brave and beautiful. And don't you dare let anyone else tell you otherwise."

Paloma's grimace turned up into a smile. She stared at me a moment longer, then dropped her head and stepped back. An instant later, her teeth, talons, and muscles vanished, and she was her regular human self again. Then she stared at me, an expectant look on her face.

My turn.

Serilda, Cho, and Sullivan glanced back and forth between Paloma and me, wondering what was going on. They had all helped me in their own way, and they deserved to hear the truth too.

I nodded at Paloma, then grabbed the black velvet bag from its hiding place on my belt loop. I opened the drawstrings and poured the contents into my hand. Then I held my palm out where the others could see my treasures. The opal memory stone, one of the black feathers from my gladiator costume, the silver bracelet with its tearstone crown. Serilda, Cho, and Sullivan all frowned, not understanding the importance of the items—yet.

I handed the bag to Paloma, who took it and slipped it into her pocket. I didn't have anything for Cho, so I simply bowed low to him in the Ryusaman style. He returned the gesture. Then I faced Sullivan and Serilda.

I held the memory stone out to Sullivan. Before the black-ring match, I had told Paloma to give the stone to Serilda, but I hadn't known about Sullivan's royal Andvarian blood back then. He was the right person to give it to now.

His frown deepened, but he took the stone, his fingers lingering against my skin. I drew in a breath, tasting his cold, clean, vanilla scent.

"What's this?" he asked. "Why do you have a memory stone? What's on it?"

"Proof that the Andvarians are innocent and that Vasilia was behind the Seven Spire massacre."

He sucked in a surprised breath. So did Paloma and Cho. Serilda was also surprised, but her shock quickly vanished, and her eyes narrowed in thought.

"Bastard princes are still princes," I said in a soft voice. "Sometimes, they are the best princes. Use it wisely, Sully."

So many emotions flared in his eyes. Surprise, gratitude, and something much, much deeper. Something that made my heart ache with longing for what might have been. Something that was never going to be, since I would most likely be executed in the next few minutes.

Sullivan must have seen those same emotions reflected in my own eyes, but he couldn't do anything about them any more than I could. His fingers curled around the stone, and he pressed his fist to his heart and bowed low to me in the Andvarian style. I gave him the perfect Bellonan curtsy in return. A small sad smile curved the corners of his lips. Yeah. Mine too.

Finally, I turned to Serilda and held out the feather to her. "I'm sorry to disappoint you, but I was never a black swan."

She took the feather from me and twirled it back and forth between her fingers. After several seconds, she raised her gaze to mine. "Who are you? Who are you *really*?"

I knew what she was asking, what they were all asking, but I didn't answer. I wanted to hold on to this moment for a few seconds longer. So I looked at the silver bracelet. The seven tearstone shards that made up the crown glittered like tiny swords in the soft, dreamy light. I slipped the bracelet onto my wrist, then pushed my sleeve up so that it was clearly visible. I might as well wear it, since this would most likely be the last chance I ever had to enjoy it.

My fingers traced over the crown, along with a few of the

thorns. Then I dropped my hand to my side, lifted my head, and faced my friends again.

I looked at each one of them in turn. Trusting Paloma. Curious Cho. Cynical Sullivan. Suspicious Serilda. I drew in a deep breath and slowly let it out.

"My name is Everleigh Saffira Winter Blair, and I am a Winter queen." My lips twisted into a grim smile. "Whatever that bloody means."

Paloma frowned with confusion, while Cho gave me a speculative look. Sullivan's face hardened. In an instant, it felt as though he had put up a glass wall between us, with him on one side and me on the other.

But it was Serilda who had the most interesting reaction. Her blue eyes grew dark and distant, even as she peered at me more closely than she ever had before. Her searching gaze swept over my features, from my short black hair to my gray-blue eyes to my cheeks, nose, and chin. I got the impression that she was comparing me as I was now to whatever dim memories she might have of me as a girl running around Seven Spire.

Her gaze swept lower and focused on the bracelet glinting on my wrist. Recognition dawned in her eyes. She knew that Alvis had made the bracelet, just as he had made the black-swan pendant that ringed her throat.

That was the moment when she finally believed me.

She shuddered out a breath, and I could have sworn that tears gleamed in her eyes, although I had no idea why she would be so emotional.

Serilda opened her mouth, but she didn't get the chance to speak since Halvar chose that moment to walk back over to us.

"Your time is up," he growled.

I looked at my friends again. I thought about asking them to wish me luck, but I decided not to. I would need far more than luck to get through this.

I nodded at my friends, then strode out into the courtyard to meet my fate.

CHAPTER TWENTY-THREE

I stopped in the center of the courtyard. Halvar stepped up next to me and gestured at the musicians.

"Once they start playing, you cannot stop the Tanzen Freund, and you cannot start over," he said. "You have to keep going until you make it through all twelve sections. Stopping for any reason will mean your immediate death. Do you understand?"

"I understand. Although the dance has thirteen sections, not twelve." I glanced over at the musicians. "Please don't forget the last section. I would really hate for Halvar to kill me just because you all got tired of playing."

A few of them laughed at my joke, as did many of the Ungers sitting on the balcony, but Halvar glared at me.

I smiled in the face of his anger, then sat down in the courtyard and took off my boots and socks, all five pairs. Paloma came over and took them from me, and I stood up again.

I had always wondered why the dance was performed barefoot, and as soon as my feet touched the ground, I learned the answer—because the flagstones were coated with magic.

I had been so focused on my friends that I hadn't noticed it before, but the courtyard reeked of magic. My nose twitched. And not just any magic. Every single stone was covered with invisible, icy needles that were already stabbing into my bare feet. In a way, the sensation was even worse than trudging through the magier's storm, and my feet felt frozen and throbbing at the same time.

It was another fucking *test,* as if the dance itself wasn't difficult enough.

Halvar noticed my discomfort. "Any time you're ready to begin." He arched an eyebrow. "Unless you want to save yourself the embarrassment and forfeit your life now?"

I forced myself to smile as though nothing was wrong. "Just waiting for you to get out of my way. Unless you want me to twirl you around the courtyard a few times first?"

Bjarni and some of the other Ungers snickered, but Halvar's eyes glittered with anger. He gave me a short, mocking bow, then whirled around and stalked over to the musicians.

That left me standing alone. Everyone stared at me. Halvar, Bjarni, and the other Ungers. The mysterious figure in black on the balcony. Paloma, Cho, Sullivan, Serilda, and everyone else in the gladiator troupe. If I had done nothing else with my life, I had at least saved them from death.

Now I had to save myself.

I closed my eyes, thinking back to all those lessons, all those long hours spent with Lady Xenia barking out the moves and pounding her cane on the floor, beating out the rhythm of the dance. I hadn't practiced the Tanzen Freund since my last lesson with Xenia all those weeks ago, but I could hear the music playing in my mind. I drew in a breath, and I almost thought that I could smell her peony perfume wafting over me.

I concentrated on the scent and the memories that it brought along with it.

I could do this. I had to do this, or I was dead. Perhaps it was petty, but I had been through too much, I had *survived* too much these past few months, to die in some strange courtyard this far from home. I was going to perform the dance perfectly, every single step, and not just because my life depended on it. No, I was going to perform the dance for *me*. Because I had put the time, energy, and effort into learning it, just as I had all those other useless skills, and because I never did anything less than my best.

That was what being Lady Everleigh Saffira Winter Blair really meant to me.

With that determination surging through me, I opened my eyes and lifted my hands into the first position. I nodded at the musicians, telling them that I was ready. They picked up their violins, flutes, and other instruments, and the opening strains of music floated through the courtyard.

And then I danced.

The first section of the dance was very much like a Bellonan waltz, slow and elegant, with lots of twirls and elaborate hand flourishes. If I had been dancing on a regular ballroom floor, I would have enjoyed it immensely, but the icy needles of magic that coated the flagstones stabbed into my feet with every step, and I had to grit my teeth against the pain. Not only that, but the stones were chipped and uneven in places, and the sharp edges sliced into my feet, drawing out drop after drop of blood. I gritted my teeth and kept dancing.

As I spun around, my gaze roamed over the crowd. Paloma, Cho, and the troupe members stared at me with curious faces, having never seen the dance before. Halvar, Bjarni, and the Ungers studied me with furrowed brows, following and analyzing every single step of my feet and sweep of my hands through the air. Sullivan and Serilda both stared at me with sharp, narrowed eyes, and I could almost see the thoughts whirling around in their minds, much the same way that I whirled around the courtyard.

Slowly, the music changed, becoming lighter and faster as it moved into the second section, and I shut out everything else and focused on the dance. The steps became more intricate and complicated, the arm flourishes grander, the twirls longer and quicker. Sweat trickled down the back of my neck, and my breath steamed in the frosty air. And my feet. Oh, my poor, poor feet. I felt like I was dancing on a bed of cold nails, and I could see my steps tracing out the dance patterns from where my cut feet had smeared blood all over the flagstones.

Still, despite all that pain, discomfort, and blood, I was *enjoying* this.

Dancing had always been one of those things that I was naturally good at, even better than Vasilia. And it was the one thing that she had never tried to compete with me at, had never beaten me at. Of course that was largely due to the fact that she had always been surrounded by a flock of admirers during any royal ball. But it was still the one thing that she had never used to humiliate me.

For the first time—for the very first time—I didn't have to worry about Vasilia seeing me or someone whispering in her ear that I was actually better at something than she was. For the first time, I was completely free to dance the way that I had always wanted to—without fear. Even if I made a mistake, even if I forgot a step, even if Halvar lunged forward and ripped me to pieces, I was going to enjoy every single second of the dance up until that moment.

Once I made that decision, once I fully embraced the dance, my breathing became easier, my steps quickened, and my feet even quit hurting. I didn't know if my immunity had kicked in and nullified the magic that coated the flagstones, or if my feet were so cold now that I simply couldn't feel the pain pulsing through them anymore. It didn't matter. I still had eleven more sections of the dance to go, and I was going to enjoy every single one of them.

So I stomped my feet and laughed, moving into the next part of the dance. "Faster!" I called out to the musicians. "Faster! You're falling behind!"

The notes stuttered, as though the musicians were surprised by my request, but they accommodated me, and the music ramped up to a fast, lively level. As I whirled around and around, loud, enthusiastic clapping replaced the dull slap of my feet on the stones. The Ungers were actually clapping along to the music and the dance. Bjarni was smiling wide, and even Halvar was dutifully clapping along with everyone else.

One by one, I performed all the sections of the dance. Eventually, the music wound down, and my movements became shorter and slower until the notes faded away altogether. I held the last position, my eyes closed and my face tilted up to the sky. Then I dropped my head, opened my eyes, and looked at Halvar. Disbelief filled his face, along with grudging respect.

But there was one more part to the dance, the most difficult thing of all. So I bowed my head to Halvar and took the final position. I dropped to my knees, sat back on them, and placed my forehead on the stones, even though they were slick with my own blood. Then I held my arms out wide to my sides, leaving myself completely vulnerable.

Nothing happened for several seconds, but then footsteps scraped on the stone. I couldn't see what was happening, but that was the point. This was a matter of trust, and there could be no real friendship without trust. Maybe that was the reason why I had finally told Paloma and the others who I was. Because I wanted real friends, after all these long years of having none.

Something cold and sharp touched the back of my neck, and I gritted my teeth to keep from flinching. Halvar was standing over me, holding a sword up against my skin. Given my position on the ground, he could easily thrust the blade through my neck and kill me. No doubt he was tempted to, given how I had challenged him at every turn. But I had twirled him into a corner, like Bjarni had said, and now tradition demanded that he see the dance through to the end or sully his own honor.

So I held my position and waited.

A minute passed, then two, then three, and still Halvar kept his sword pressed up against my neck. No one moved or spoke, and the tense, heavy silence stretched on and on. I used the time to get my breath back and gather my strength for the final act of the Tanzen Freund.

Someone—Bjarni, I think—pointedly cleared his throat, telling Halvar to get on with it. Halvar sighed, then removed the sword from my neck, bent down, and slapped the hilt into my outstretched hand.

"Try not to take my head off with it," he muttered.

Then he stood up and stepped back exactly three feet. I let out a breath and curled my fingers around the hilt of the sword. It was a large, heavy weapon, far too large and heavy for me, but I had to wield it—correctly—or I was dead.

I could still hear the music of the dance playing in my mind, so I imagined matching my movements to the quick, steady beat, just as I had done with the other steps. I drew in a breath, sucking air deep down into my lungs and visualizing what I had to do next. Then, still listening to that steady beat, I surged to my feet, whipped up the sword, whirled all the way around, and sliced out with the blade.

Halvar was standing straight and tall, with his arms by his sides, although his hands were clenched into tight fists. The sword zoomed straight toward his neck, and everyone in the courtyard gasped in surprise, even the Ungers.

This was the moment of truth.

At the very last second, I stopped the blow, so that the blade was merely resting against his skin, instead of cutting through it. My arm trembled from the strain of wielding such a heavy sword, but I held the position for thirteen beats—seconds—as tradition dictated. Then I slowly lowered the sword. I grabbed the weapon by the blade, even though it cut into my palm, and held it out to him hilt first.

Halvar stared at me, disbelief in his eyes, but he had no choice but to take the sword. He bowed to me, then turned and looked up at the second-floor balcony where the black-shrouded figure was still sitting. Ah, yes. I had forgotten about my judge.

The figure tilted its head to the side, studying me again, then rose to its feet. All the other Ungers stood as well.

"The dance has been completed to my satisfaction," the figure called out in a loud voice. "This woman is now our friend. Until the mountains crumble to ash."

"Until the mountains crumble to ash." All the Ungers repeated the phrase, then bowed their heads to me.

I frowned, staring up at the figure. Perhaps it was my imagination, but I could have sworn that I knew that voice.

The figure turned and vanished through one of the balcony doors. I started to limp over to where my friends were standing at the edge of the courtyard, but Halvar held out his arm, stopping me. Everyone fell silent again.

A minute later, a series of *tap-tap-tap*s rang out, growing closer and louder. I frowned again. I could have sworn that I knew that sound too. The steady *tap-tap-tap*s continued, and the black-shrouded figure appeared in one of the archways and headed this way.

The figure stopped in front of me, and I realized that it was holding a cane. And not just any cane—one topped with a silver ogre head. My eyes widened in shock.

The figure reached up and pulled the black hat and veil off its head, revealing coppery red hair, amber eyes, and a face that I had never thought that I would see again.

"Xenia," I whispered.

Lady Xenia smiled at me, as did the ogre on her neck.

I smiled back at her. In fact, I couldn't *stop* smiling, the expression so wide and happy that it made my cheeks ache. But smiling wasn't enough, and I started laughing. I wasn't quite sure why. Perhaps it was the sheer, utter happiness filling my heart.

Xenia was alive.

Halvar frowned, not sure why I was laughing. So did everyone else, but I didn't care. It felt so good to laugh right now.

It took me the better part of a minute, but I finally managed to stop my crazy chuckles, although tears started streaming down my face instead. I didn't care. For once, they were tears of joy instead of sorrow.

Xenia bowed low to me and straightened back up. I executed the perfect Bellonan curtsy in return, even though my feet were dripping blood and had swollen to twice their normal size. Small white stars winked on and off in my eyes, but I ignored them, along with the pain and exhaustion steadily rising up in my body.

Xenia tried to give me a stern look, but her lips twitched up into another smile. "That was the best rendition of the Tanzen Freund that I have ever seen. Every step, every movement was perfect."

I smiled back at her. "That's because I had a most excellent teacher."

The words were the final straw. Those white stars in my eyes grew bigger and bigger, and darker and darker. The pain and exhaustion rose up, even stronger than before, and the blackness dragged me under.

I was being tested.

I sat in a chair, watching a magier arrange objects on a table. Seeds, potted flower bulbs, chunks of stone, candles. All those items and dozens more covered the wood.

Today, I would be tested to determine what kind of magic I had, just as every member of the royal family, every Blair, was when they were twelve years old. I could have told the magier not to bother, that I already knew exactly what powers I had— my enhanced sense of smell and my immunity.

And that was the problem.

Everyone already knew about my enhanced sense of smell,

but my mother had always warned me never to tell anyone about my immunity. She had said that other people knowing about it would make me a target in more ways than I could possibly imagine. I hadn't really understood what she'd meant, but I had always kept my power a secret, like she had told me. But how was I going to hide it during the testing?

"Don't worry, Everleigh," a soothing voice murmured. "Just do your best."

I looked at Vasilia, who was sitting next to me. I had been at Seven Spire for a few weeks now, and the two of us had been inseparable ever since that first day. We did everything together, from eating our meals to learning our lessons to playing with the other children. I even slept in a room down the hall from hers. Vasilia was my best friend, and I was so glad that she was here.

"I don't see why I have to be tested," I said for the tenth time in as many minutes. "Everyone already knows that I don't have any magic, other than my sense of smell."

"You have to have something more useful than your silly nose." Vasilia's voice was strangely flat, and she tapped her fingers against her chair arm, as though she was annoyed.

I frowned, wondering at her odd mood. Vasilia had been fidgety and impatient all morning. Perhaps she was nervous for me. I reached out and squeezed her hand, trying to reassure her as much as myself. She hesitated, then squeezed back, although her smile didn't warm her pretty face the way that it normally did.

The magier finished arranging the objects and gestured for me to approach. Nervous butterflies quivered in my stomach, but I let out a breath, got to my feet, and walked over to begin the testing.

For the next hour, I picked up one object after another to see if I had any magic related to it. A plant master's ability to make *seeds grow and bulbs bloom. A stone master's power to carve and command rocks. A magier's fire to light candles.*

One by one, I picked up the objects and concentrated, and one by one, I set them all down again after nothing happened. No new skills, no fire, nothing on my part. The only thing that I had any reaction to was a perfume bottle. At first scent, the bottle seemed to be filled with a pleasant aroma. I drew in another breath, crinkled my nose, and put the bottle down. I could smell the rot lurking underneath the deceptively sweet scent.

"An enhanced sense of smell, as expected," the magier murmured. "Nothing else so far."

Over in her chair, Vasilia sighed, rolled her eyes, and started tapping her fingers again. She seemed more annoyed and impatient than before. What was wrong with her?

The magier made me pick up the rest of the objects to make sure that I didn't have any other powers. Everything was fine until I reached the item at the very end—a long, slender tearstone sword.

Unlike the other objects, which were dull, ordinary things, the sword was full of magic. My nose twitched. I could smell the power radiating off it. The magier nodded at me, and I had no choice but to pick up the sword, even though I knew how much it was going to hurt.

As soon as my fingers closed over the sword, sharp, invisible jolts of lightning sizzled against my skin. In an instant, my hand felt like it was on fire from the stinging power, and my immunity rose up, wanting to snuff out the magic. I started to unleash my power, but then I realized that the magier was watching me far more closely than before, as if this object was more important than all the others combined. Even Vasilia had quit fidgeting and was leaning forward.

This wasn't a test to see if I had magic—it was a test to see if I could destroy it.

"*Do you feel anything?*" *the magier asked.* "*Any magic? Any tingling? Any sensation of any sort?*"

I kept my face blank and shook my head, as though I didn't feel the magic shocking my fingers over and over again. "*I'm sorry. It just feels like a sword to me. Nothing more.*"

The magier sighed. "*Put it down then.*"

Even though I wanted to drop it like a hot rock, I slowly laid the sword on the table. I looked at Vasilia, expecting her to be smiling now that the first part of the testing was finished, but she got to her feet, turned away, and left the room without a backward glance.

"*Vasilia?*" *I called out.* "*Where are you going?*"

She didn't answer. My stomach twisted with worry, but I pushed it aside. Vasilia might be my best friend, but she was also the crown princess. She had probably been called away on some royal business.

The magier made me pick up all the objects again, double-checking to make sure that I didn't have any other powers. When the testing was finished, I hurried to Vasilia's playroom. The doors were closed, although I could hear faint giggles inside. Vasilia must already be in there, along with some of our other friends. I smiled and pulled on one of the knobs.

The doors were locked.

I yanked on first one door, then the other, but they didn't budge. Strange. So I raised my hand and knocked. "*Vasilia? Are you in there? It's Everleigh.*"

More giggles sounded, louder than before, although they seemed to have a sharp edge to them. I knocked again, and several seconds later, the door finally opened. Vasilia was in the playroom, wearing her favorite pink dress and diamond tiara. Behind her, three girls were sitting around the table having a tea party with tiny cakes and steaming cups of hot chocolate.

I started to step inside, but Vasilia put her arm on the door, blocking me from entering.

"What do you think you're doing?" she snapped.

"Joining you and the others for cakes and chocolate like always."

Vasilia shook her head. "You're not welcome here. Not anymore."

"Of course I'm welcome here. I'm your friend."

She let out a small, mocking laugh. "Oh, Everleigh. You have no idea what's going on, do you? I always knew that you were nothing more than a silly little country bumpkin."

"What do you mean? What's going on?"

"I can't believe that I wasted my time sitting through your testing." A sneer crept into Vasilia's voice. "Although that wasn't nearly as tedious as all the time that I've wasted listening to you cry about your dead parents. You're such a weak, whiny, pathetic thing."

I reared back in shock. She had never spoken to me like this before. Why was she saying all these cruel things?

"Putting up with your sniveling might have been worth it, if you had had even a lick of magic. But you don't." Vasilia sneered at me again. "You don't have any magic, which makes you completely useless."

Every word she said was like a dagger slicing off another piece of my heart, and I struggled to push away my pain and surprise and focus on her words.

"But—but you're my friend. You're my best friend." I

couldn't keep the tremor out of my voice. "You shouldn't care if I have magic or not."

Vasilia let out another laugh, this one louder and even more mocking. "I am not your friend. I was never your friend. I was just playing along to see if you could be of any use to me." She lifted her chin. "I will be queen one day, sooner than anyone thinks, and I need the right people around me. Strong people, strong allies like the girls in this room."

She jerked her thumb over her shoulder, and I looked at the girls sitting around the table. One was a senator's daughter, the second had wealthy guilder parents, and the third was training to become a powerful stone master.

I opened my mouth to protest that I was strong, and that in my own way, I had just as much magic as Vasilia did with her lightning. I longed to tell her about my immunity. In that moment, I wanted to reveal my power to her more than anything. She would take me back, she would be my friend again, if only she knew about my immunity. I was sure of it.

But something held me back. Perhaps it was my mother's voice whispering a warning in my mind. Or how closely the magier had watched me when I had picked up that tearstone sword during the testing. Or the way that Vasilia was staring at me now like I was a stain on the floor, something far, far beneath her notice. Maybe it was all of them together. Whatever the reason, I choked back my words.

"Face it, Everleigh. You're just a little lost orphan girl with no parents, no money, and no magic. And now that I know how weak and useless you really are, I don't have to waste any more time pretending to care about you." Vasilia's gray-blue eyes were as cold and hard as the tearstone columns. "Don't come back here, and don't ever bother me again."

She slammed the door in my face. A moment later, I heard the click of the lock sliding home, followed by another round of giggles from the other girls. The sounds rammed into my heart, one after another, shattering it into a hundred pieces. Hot tears gathered in my eyes and streaked down my face, but they were nothing compared to the sharp shards that were twisting and twisting in my chest, cutting me to shreds from the inside out . . .

My eyes fluttered opened. I was lying in bed, clutching my chest, as if I could somehow ease the pain of Vasilia's long-ago betrayal. But I had never been able to do that, and this time was no different. So I dropped my hand and stared up at the fresco on the ceiling, which featured ogres running through a forest . . .

Wait. Why were there ogres on the ceiling?

For a moment, I didn't remember where I was, but then it all came rushing back. Killing the weather magier. Being captured by the Ungers. Performing the Tanzen Freund. Realizing that Xenia was here.

I sat up and looked around. I was lying on a large four-poster bed covered with soft sheets and thick blankets that stood in the back of the room. A nightstand, an armoire, and a vanity table with a mirror hugged the walls around the bed, while a round table flanked by several chairs stood in front of a fireplace that took up most of another wall. An open door to my left led into a bathroom with a white porcelain tub mounted on silver ogre heads. Sunlight streamed in through the white lace curtains on the windows, telling me that it was around noon.

My nose twitched, and I glanced down at my body. Someone had cleaned me up, and I was now wearing blue silk pajamas, instead of all the layers of clothes that I'd had on in the courtyard. I wiggled my arms and legs. Someone, probably Aisha, had healed me as well, although I still felt tired and sore. I peeled back the covers to find that my feet were heavily bandaged. I flexed my toes inside the white bandages. My feet felt as sore as the rest of me, but at least they were still attached to my body.

Someone cleared her throat. My head snapped to the right. I hadn't noticed her before, but Lady Xenia was sitting in one of the chairs by the fireplace, reading a book.

She smiled at me. "Hello, Everleigh."

CHAPTER TWENTY-FOUR

A m I dead?" I asked.

Xenia's face crinkled with confusion. "Why would you say that?"

"Because you keep smiling at me. You never smiled at me before. Not once in all the weeks that we worked together."

Her eyes narrowed. "That is a problem that is easily fixed."

I grinned. "Ah, there's the Xenia that I know. Stern and demanding."

She snorted. "And there's the Everleigh that I know. Cheeky to a fault." She pointed to a blue silk robe lying at the foot of the bed. "Put that on, and we'll have a drink."

I got up, shrugged into the robe, and slid my bandaged feet into a pair of soft, padded slippers beside the bed. Then I plodded over and sat down in the chair across from Xenia.

She had traded in her long black coat for a dark green tunic topped by a short, matching jacket, along with black leggings and boots. Her silver cane with its ogre head was leaning next to her chair. She picked up a crystal decanter, also shaped like an ogre, and poured a healthy amount of amber liquid into a glass. Apple brandy, from the smell. She passed the glass to me, then poured herself a drink before setting the decanter aside.

"To us." Xenia lifted her glass. "The survivors."

I grimaced, but I clinked my glass against hers, leaned back in my seat, and took a sip. The brandy was as cold as ice in my mouth, with a sweet taste, like a bloodcrisp apple. I swallowed, and the brandy heated up as it slid down my throat before forming a warm pool in my stomach.

Xenia and I sipped our brandy in companionable silence. It was several minutes before she spoke again.

"I've always preferred a good, strong brandy to anything else. Especially champagne."

"You didn't drink any champagne at the luncheon," I said. "That's why you were able to shift when none of the other morphs could. That's why you were able to fight back."

She nodded and took another sip of her brandy.

"What about Gemma, the Andvarian girl? What happened after you disappeared with her?"

"Maeven hurt me pretty badly with her lightning, but I managed to carry the girl inside the palace." Another smile flickered across Xenia's face. "You made quite an impression on Gemma. She kept screaming that we had to go back and help you."

"But you couldn't come back."

Xenia shook her head. "No. The guards chased after us, so we had to run. Gemma started yelling that we had to go to the master's workshop, and I realized that she was talking about Alvis, and that you had told her to find him."

My breath caught in my throat, and my fingers clenched

around my glass. I had lost Isobel, and I had thought that Alvis was dead too. "And did you?"

She nodded again. "Alvis was in his workshop. As soon as he realized what was happening, he used his magic to collapse part of the ceiling and block the door. We could hear the guards outside, but they couldn't get through his barricade."

"But how did you get out of the workshop if Alvis had barricaded you inside?"

Xenia shrugged. "He pressed in on a stone in the wall and opened up a secret passageway."

I blinked. In all the years that I had worked for him, I had never suspected that there was a secret passageway in his workshop. Then again, it was just like Alvis to keep something like that to himself.

"The passageway led into some of the old mining tunnels that still run under Seven Spire," Xenia continued. "Alvis knew all about the tunnels. He said that we could use them to escape, and he was right. We trudged through the tunnels from the palace, all the way under the Summanus River, and came out in an abandoned mine on the outskirts of the city."

Those must be the same tunnels that Serilda and Cho had been talking about after the queen's vigil. The ones that they had said were blocked and that they couldn't use to rescue Captain Auster.

"All of the turncoat guards were still at Seven Spire, so it was relatively easy for us to escape from Svalin. We ran into some trouble after that, but we eventually made it to safety." Xenia gestured out at the room with her glass. "I've been here ever since. Castle Asmund has been in my family for generations, although few people know that it belongs to me. Halvar, my nephew, takes care of it during the months that I'm in Bellona."

"And Alvis and Gemma?" I asked, my fingers clenching around my glass again.

"Safe in Andvari. They're being protected by the king."

I sighed with relief. Alvis and Gemma had escaped Vasilia's clutches. I longed to see the metalstone master and the girl, but it was enough to know that they were alive and well.

Xenia leaned back in her chair and studied me. "But it seems that my adventure pales in comparison to yours. I didn't know what to think when Halvar returned to the castle yesterday claiming that some woman had demanded to perform the Tanzen Freund in order to save her gladiator troupe. At first, I thought that it was some trick and that Vasilia's minions had found me. But then you appeared in the courtyard."

I snorted. "I wouldn't call it an adventure."

"Then what would you call it?"

"Survival."

A sharp knock sounded, the door burst open, and Serilda stalked inside, followed by Cho, Paloma, and Sullivan, who closed and locked the door behind him. The four of them walked over to the table where Xenia and I were sitting.

My friends had all been healed and cleaned up, and they showed no ill effects from the magier's storm or anything else. Cho and Paloma both smiled, telling me that they were glad to see me. Serilda and Sullivan did not. Peppery anger radiated off both of them, especially Serilda.

"Well, isn't this cozy?" Serilda drawled. "Although I would think that it would be too early in the day for brandy, Xenia."

"It's never too early for brandy, Serilda. Especially when I have such distinguished guests." Xenia mockingly toasted the other woman with her glass.

I glanced back and forth between them. "You two know each other?"

"Oh, yes," Serilda drawled again. "I know all the Ungerian spies in Bellona. Still reporting to your cousin, the queen?"

Xenia shrugged. "Only when I have something of interest to report."

Serilda stepped forward, her hand dropping to the sword belted to her waist. "If you've told anyone about us, if anyone knows that we're here—"

"You'll do what?"

Serilda gave her a thin smile. "I'll carve that ogre out of your neck—before I slit your throat."

Xenia's amber eyes glowed with a dangerous light, and she put her glass down and surged to her feet. I set my own glass down, scrambled up, and stepped in between them.

"Enough." I held my hands out. "That's enough. We are all friends here. Not enemies."

Serilda and Xenia kept glaring at each other, but Serilda didn't pull her sword, and Xenia didn't morph.

"Why don't we all sit down, have a drink, and talk?" I suggested.

"Yes," Sullivan said in a cold voice. "Let's talk. We can start with you telling us who you really are, *highness,* and especially how you got your hands on this."

He slapped the opal memory stone onto the table, hard enough to make the brandy slosh around in its decanter. Sullivan stepped back and crossed his arms over his chest. I had expected him to be angry, but not quite this angry. And the way he snarled out *highness* made it seem as though I had somehow hurt him, although I had no idea how I could have done that.

"What Lucas is trying to say is that we would like an explanation, Everleigh," Cho said in a calm, reasonable voice.

"Evie," I muttered. "My name is Evie."

Cho glanced at Serilda, and the two of them exchanged a look that I couldn't decipher. "Very well . . . Evie."

Paloma touched my arm. "Tell us what happened. Please."

I flashed her a grateful smile, reached up, and squeezed her hand. She nodded back at me, and I faced the others again.

"Cho's right," I said. "I owe you all an explanation. So sit down, and I'll show you exactly what happened."

Everyone sat down at the table. Xenia offered the others a glass of brandy, although Cho was the only one who accepted. Serilda glared at him, but Cho grinned back at her. Apparently, he loved spirits as much as he did desserts.

Once we were all settled, I gestured at the memory stone and looked at Sullivan. "Did you watch it?"

"No," he growled. "I wanted to see what you had to say for yourself first."

I still had no idea why he was so angry, but everyone was waiting, so I angled the memory stone toward a space on the wall that was free of tapestries. I drew in a breath and let it out, bracing myself. Then I tapped on the memory stone three times and sat back in my chair.

The opal started glowing with a pure white light, and the blue, red, green, and purple flecks in the surface glimmered as well. One by one, those flecks of color rose up out of the stone and hovered there like stars suspended in midair. Then they shot across the room and attached themselves to the wall. The colors grew larger, brighter, and sharper, and finally coalesced into one solid image, as though we were watching a moving painting.

My face was the first thing that appeared.

I was staring at the stone, making sure that it was recording. Then I stepped to the side, and the royal lawn appeared with its tables and clusters of people. I grimaced, knowing that it was only going to get worse.

And it did.

The memory stone had recorded everything from the time that I had turned it on, to Vasilia arriving at the luncheon, to her stabbing Prince Frederich, to her admitting to poisoning everyone and ordering the turncoat guards to attack. After that, the sounds, screams, and shrieks of the battle rang out. The very last image was of my hand closing over the stone.

I leaned forward and tapped on the stone three more times, preserving the memories until the next time that someone wanted to view them. No one said a word for the better part of two minutes.

Serilda turned to Xenia. "I'll have that drink now."

Xenia poured everyone a glass of brandy, and we all sat there, sipping our drinks.

"What happened after you put the memory stone in your bag?" Cho asked, breaking the silence.

I gulped down the last of my brandy, then told them the rest of it. Helping Gemma and Xenia escape, fighting my way over to Cordelia, Vasilia stabbing the queen and blasting me over the wall. Waking up in the river, trudging back to the city, seeing the first gladiator show, sneaking into Sullivan's house.

When I finished, everyone fell silent again. Xenia, Paloma, and Cho gave me sympathetic looks. So did Sullivan, who seemed far less upset with me than before, although fresh pain filled his eyes at what had happened to the Andvarians. But Serilda glared at me, the peppery scent of her anger stronger than ever.

"Who are Maeven and Nox?" Paloma asked. "Who do they really work for?"

"Nox is a nephew to the Mortan king," Xenia said. "As for Maeven, even my spies haven't been able to find out who she really is, but if I had to guess, I would say that she's a bastard royal, a sister to the king."

Serilda nodded, agreeing with her.

"Why is that important?" I asked.

"For years, there have been rumors that the Mortan royal family uses their bastard offspring to do their dirty work as spies, assassins, that sort of thing," Xenia said. "That way, if any of them are ever caught, the royal family can deny having any involvement with their bastard relatives' crimes. From what I've seen, Maeven fits that mold."

Once again, everyone fell silent, but Xenia looked at me, her lips puckered in thought.

"There's one thing that I still don't understand," she said. "Vasilia's lightning is quite powerful. How did you survive a direct blast of it?"

"Yes, highness," Sullivan murmured. "Do tell."

I sighed. I had told them the rest of my secrets. What was one more? Besides, Paloma already knew, and the others would figure it out soon enough. "I'm immune to magic."

Everyone except Paloma stared at me with a blank expression. I sighed again, got to my feet, and went over to a fluorestone lamp sitting on the nightstand. I turned on the lamp. When the fluorestone flared to life, I wrapped my hand around the stand and let loose with my power. An instant later, the bright glow flickered, then vanished altogether.

Xenia and Cho sucked in surprised breaths, while a thoughtful look crept over Sullivan's face. Serilda kept staring at me with angry, narrowed eyes.

"So that's how you managed to save Paloma from the wormroot," Sullivan said. "You used your immunity to neutralize the poison."

"Something like that."

"That's also how she took away Emilie's speed in the blackring match," Paloma added.

"You throttled Emilie's speed so you could kill her." Cho looked at me as if he had never seen me before, as did the dragon on his neck. "That's impressively ruthless."

My mouth twisted. "That's what growing up in a pit of vipers will do to you."

Serilda drained the rest of her brandy, then got to her feet. She stared at the empty glass in her hand, then turned and threw it against the wall. The crystal shattered, and everyone jerked in surprise, except for Cho, who sighed, as if he knew what was coming next.

Serilda stabbed her finger at me. "You stupid, reckless, foolish girl!" she snarled. "I should wring your bloody neck."

Anger surged through me that she was dismissively calling me *girl* yet again, and I shot to my own feet. "For what? For surviving?"

Serilda stabbed her finger at the memory stone on the table. "For keeping that to yourself all this time." Then she stabbed her finger at me again. "And especially for not telling me who you were."

I opened my mouth to snap back at her, but she cut me off.

"Do you know what would have happened if you had been killed in the arena? Or if the magier had murdered you in the woods? Or if the Ungers had executed you? Bellona would have been lost. *Everything* would have been lost." Serilda's blue eyes burned with rage, her hands curled into fists, and her entire body shook with emotion. "I could *see* it. I could see how horrible, how *hopeless,* it would be for everyone."

Her obvious distress made me bite back my snarky retort. "What do you mean you could see it?"

"Don't you know? Serilda is a bit of a time magier," Xenia murmured. "She gets visions of the future. Her visions were quite useful to Cordelia. At least, until the queen stopped listening to them."

Serilda's jaw clenched, but she didn't deny it.

My mind spun around. Serilda, a time magier? But then I thought of how her silent scrutiny had always seemed more intense than anyone else's, as though she was peering into my thoughts. And I remembered something that she had said to Cho the night of the queen's vigil.

I told Cordelia that this would happen. I told her. Over and over again. For years. But she didn't listen to me.

"You knew that the massacre was going to happen," I whispered. "You saw it with your magic."

"No," Serilda muttered. "I don't see the future. Not really. I see possibilities, things that might happen. But magic or not, I always saw Vasilia for *exactly* what she was, ever since she was a little girl, and I always knew that she was going to be the cause of Cordelia's death. As soon as Maeven and Nox showed up at Seven Spire, I knew that that day was fast approaching, and I warned Cordelia yet again. And this time, she finally listened to me."

But the truth is that killing you would be a mercy to all the people of Bellona and beyond. My only regret is that I waited too long to do it.

This time, Cordelia's voice whispered in my mind. She had said that to Vasilia during the massacre. I had wondered who the queen had hired to kill her own daughter, and now I knew.

"You," I whispered again. "*You* were the one that Cordelia was talking about. You were going to kill Vasilia." My gaze cut from Serilda to Cho and back again. "That's why you came back to Bellona after all these years. That's why you built the Black Swan compound. So you could keep an eye on things at Seven Spire. Cordelia gave you the property as a down payment for assassinating Vasilia."

"Cordelia didn't give me a damn thing. I bought that property fair and square. I've been preparing for Vasilia's betrayal for a long, long time." Serilda's mouth twisted, as if she was thinking back over all those preparations, whatever they had been. Then she shook her head and focused on me again. "But yes, a few months before the massacre, Cordelia reached out to me, and Cho and I started making plans to assassinate Vasilia."

"And Vasilia somehow found out about it."

Serilda and Cho both nodded.

So many things suddenly made sense, including why Vasilia had come to the arena the night of the black-ring match and why she had sent that weather magier to kill Serilda, Cho, and everyone else in the troupe. Vasilia had wanted to eliminate her would-be assassins before they could do their job.

"Do you have any idea how long and hard Cho and I searched for news, for a hint, for the faintest whisper that someone had survived? And you were right under my nose the whole fucking time. I don't know whether to admire your cleverness or strangle you for it." Serilda let out another bitter laugh. "I could see everything but *you*, thanks to your damn immunity."

"Why didn't you come to us like Cordelia told you to?" Cho asked. "We would have protected you."

"Everyone I had ever known had just been slaughtered," I said. "All I knew about Serilda was that she was a disgraced guard. I didn't know if I could trust her. I didn't know if I could trust anyone."

Cho nodded, accepting my explanation, then looked at Serilda and raised his eyebrows, telling her to do the same. She huffed, but she let out a breath, and some of the anger and tension drained out of her body.

"What did Cordelia say to you?" she asked in a low voice. "At the end?"

"She said to tell you that she was sorry. About everything."

A ghost of a smile flickered across Serilda's face, and her hand crept up to the sunburst scar at the corner of her right eye. And I realized that Cordelia must have given her that scar when Serilda had warned the queen about Vasilia all those years ago. Cordelia had had many rings fashioned with her rising-sun crest, and she was the only person who could have ever hit Serilda and lived to tell the tale.

Serilda dropped her hand from her scar and shook her head again, as if clearing away the troubling thoughts of her past with the dead queen. "Well, Cordelia was right about one thing. We must begin your training immediately."

"Training for what?"

"For the royal challenge," she answered. "For when you fight Vasilia for the right to be queen."

My heart dropped, and my stomach clenched. I had known that she would want something like this, but I had still hoped to avoid it. "No. That was never my ambition. I have no interest in being queen. That's not why I told you who I was."

"So what is your ambition?" Sullivan asked in a soft voice. "What is your heart's desire, highness?"

I forced myself to keep my face blank as I looked at him. "To leave Seven Spire for good. To restore my family's estate in the mountains. To finally be *free*. From all the palace politics and infighting and backstabbing. From being the royal stand-in, the royal puppet. And most of all, from Vasilia and her cruelty."

Sympathy flickered in Sullivan's gaze. "I can understand that."

"What did Vasilia do to you?" Paloma asked.

"She pretended to be my friend, but as soon as she thought that I was of no use, she dropped me." Somehow, I managed to keep the hurt out of my voice. "That was when I finally understood what being a royal, what being a Blair, really means."

"And what is that?" Serilda asked.

"That I'm just a tool that other people want to use. Nothing more, nothing less." I stared at her. "Just like you want to use me now."

She shook her head. "I don't want to use you, Everleigh—"

"My name is *Evie*," I snarled. "Not Everleigh. I will *never* be Everleigh again."

I wasn't just talking about the names. Evie was strong and confident with a friend who truly cared about her. Everleigh had been and had none of those things.

"All right, Evie," Serilda said. "Let's calm down and talk about this—"

I stabbed my finger at her. "Don't you *dare* play that cajoling game with me. I've been playing it for the last fifteen years, and I'm much, much better at it than you are. Besides, I heard you talking to Cho the night of the candlelight vigil. What was it you said? Oh, yes. That you wanted to find a Blair, any Blair. You didn't care who."

Serilda's lips pressed together, while Cho winced.

"Of course you want to use me. You think that I can help you get back everything that you lost when you left Seven Spire." I crossed my arms over my chest. "Let me guess. You've already picked out your title. Personal advisor to the queen or something like that, right?"

Serilda stepped forward, her hands clenching into fists and anger sparking in her eyes again. "I don't care about bloody titles. I care about Bellona. And you can save people— *your people*—from being led into a pointless war by a treacherous bitch who only cares about herself."

Her words punched me in the gut, but I still tried to deny them.

"Why? Because I'm some chosen one? Some special snowflake with a unique power that no one has ever seen before? Because I can take on Vasilia and the evil Mortan empire and win?" I let out a soft, bitter laugh. "You're dreaming if you think I can do any of that. I was seventeenth in line for the throne. No one ever chose me for anything, except to be a target for their games."

"I don't think that you can do it." Serilda's voice was soft and serious. "I *know* that you can do all that and more."

"Why?"

"Because you're a Winter queen."

I threw my hands up in exasperation. "I don't even know what that *means*. So what if I'm a Winter queen? It's just some old fairy-tale rhyme."

Serilda and Cho exchanged a glance, although I couldn't decipher its meaning.

"It's so much more than just an old fairy-tale rhyme," Serilda said. "And you know exactly what it means because you've been acting like a Winter queen this whole time, since the moment the massacre started."

"What do you mean?"

This time, Serilda was the one who threw up her hands. "I mean that you've been helping people this whole time. First, during the massacre, when you saved Gemma. Then, at the Black Swan, when you used your immunity to heal Paloma. When you volunteered to go after the weather magier who was trying to kill us. And then when you agreed to trade your life for the entire troupe's and perform the Tanzen Freund. You've been helping people all along. And *that* is what a Winter queen really does, Evie."

I didn't know how to respond to that.

Cho cleared his throat and got to his feet. "What Serilda is trying to say is that now you have a chance to help everyone. All the people in Bellona and Andvari who are caught up in Vasilia's plot. All the innocent people who are going to war for no reason. All the innocent men and women who are going to die if you don't do something about it."

His words made me think of the miners I had seen when we'd left Svalin. Of the guards cracking whips and forcing the workers into the carts. Those were just some of the people

Vasilia had already hurt, and her war with Andvari would devastate the citizens of both kingdoms and beyond.

Unless I stopped her.

Over the last few months, I had learned how to stand up for myself. Even more than that, I had *enjoyed* it. I had enjoyed carving out my place in the troupe, becoming a gladiator, and showing everyone that I was a force to be reckoned with. And now I had a chance to stand up for all of Bellona, for everyone that Vasilia could potentially hurt, the way that she had hurt me for so many years.

You have to protect Bellona. Promise me you'll do that. Cordelia's voice whispered in my mind.

When I had made that promise, I had just been trying to comfort my dying queen. I hadn't thought that I would get off the royal lawn alive, much less survive this long. But here I was now, months later, and I finally had a chance to honor that promise, along with the one that I had made to myself to never be weak and helpless and useless again.

Perhaps I hadn't escaped Seven Spire and all the hard lessons I'd learned there. Perhaps I could *never* escape being a Blair and doing my royal duty to my kingdom, to my people. Or perhaps I just wanted a chance to finally get my revenge on Vasilia for all the heartless things she'd done to me. But I couldn't sit by and let her plunge two kingdoms into war just because she wanted more power.

Not even if it cost me my own life.

I sighed, giving in to the inevitable. "Even if I did battle Vasilia in a royal challenge, she almost killed me with her magic during the massacre. She could easily do that again, or run me through with her sword. Vasilia is a highly skilled warrior, and she's always been better at fighting than me. I never won a single bout against her, not even when we were kids."

"I wouldn't say that," Sullivan said. "You saved yourself from her magic when she blasted you off that cliff. You won when it really mattered."

"Just like you won against Emilie in the arena," Paloma chimed in.

"And against the turncoat guards during the massacre," Xenia finished.

I looked at them all in turn. Steady Cho. Hopeful Paloma. Sly Xenia. Strong Sullivan. Determined Serilda. They really thought that I could do this. That I could actually challenge Vasilia for the throne—and win. Their confidence warmed my heart, if not my cynical mind.

"All right," I muttered, and looked at Serilda again. "All right. I'll be your royal stand-in. One last time. But don't blame me if it ends in disaster, and we all wind up dead."

A smile spread across her face, and she dropped into a perfect Bellonan curtsy. I wasn't sure whether she was mocking me or not.

"Oh, stop that. I'm not queen yet."

Serilda rose, her smile sharpening. "But you will be, if I have anything to do with it."

She marched over to the armoire, threw it open, and grabbed some of the clothes inside. Then she turned around, came over, and slapped the clothes up against my chest.

"Get dressed and meet me in the courtyard. Your training starts now."

CHAPTER TWENTY-FIVE

Serilda, Cho, Sullivan, and Xenia headed out of the bedroom, leaving me alone with Paloma. I got dressed, and
she led me to the courtyard.

By this point, it was midafternoon, and people moved
through the castle, going about their chores. Everyone was far
more relaxed than they had been last night. Apparently, the
Ungers took that vow of friendship very seriously. Several Ungers were working side by side with Theroux and the kitchen
staff to prepare the evening meal, while others were playing
darts and games with the gladiators in the common rooms.

Paloma and I stepped out into the same courtyard where
I had performed the dance. The chairs were gone, and it was a
courtyard again, except for one thing—the musicians were set
up in the corner with their instruments.

Xenia was talking to the musicians, with Serilda standing
next to her. Paloma and I walked over to Cho and Sullivan, who
were leaning against the wall next to a table covered with weapons. The two men stopped their conversation and straightened

at our approach. Paloma shifted on her feet and chewed on her lip, as if she was debating whether she should bow to me or something silly like that.

"Don't do that," I snapped in an angry voice. "Don't you *dare* do that. Any of you."

"Do what?" Paloma asked.

"Treat me any differently than you would have before." My hands curled into fists. "I don't want to be different."

"But you are different." A low, sad note rippled through Sullivan's voice. "You are very different now, highness."

"No, I'm not. I'm still the same Evie, and I'm still your friend. I'll *always* be your friend."

Paloma and Cho nodded, accepting my words. Relief filled me. I had worked too hard and had come too far to lose them now. Especially since they were the first real, genuine friends that I had ever had.

And Sullivan, well, I didn't know what Sullivan was to me. He didn't nod, and I could almost feel him pulling away and stepping back behind that same invisible wall he had put up when I had told everyone who I really was.

"Will you still make me pies?" Cho asked in a hopeful voice. "Every once in a while?"

I let out a relieved laugh. "Yes, I will still make you pies."

That broke the tension, and Paloma and Cho peppered me with questions about the massacre, Vasilia, Seven Spire, and everything else. Sullivan listened, but he didn't say anything.

A door opened, and Halvar and Bjarni walked over and bowed to me. I glanced at the others, but Sullivan shook his head, answering my silent question. Xenia and Serilda hadn't told them about me yet. Good. The fewer people who knew that I was a Blair, the better.

"You're looking quite well today, Evie," Bjarni said. "How are your feet feeling?"

"Much better. Thank you for asking."

Halvar wasn't as polite, but he wasn't quite as hostile as before either. "How did you learn the Tanzen Freund?"

I gestured at Xenia. "Your aunt beat it into me with that bloody cane of hers."

Halvar's eyes narrowed, making me wonder if I'd said the wrong thing, but then he threw back his head and laughed. "Oh, she does love that cane, doesn't she? You wouldn't believe all the times she poked me with it whenever I would misbehave as a boy . . ."

And just like that, Halvar and I were fast friends.

Halvar regaled us with tales of Xenia and her cane until the lady herself came over to our group, along with Serilda.

"My ears are burning from all your lovely stories," Xenia said in a dry tone.

Halvar cleared his throat. "I was just showing Evie and her friends a bit of hospitality."

"Well, you can go show the kitchen staff some hospitality by helping them prepare dinner," Xenia ordered. "You too, Bjarni."

Bjarni had been snickering at his friend's chastisement, but his laughter cut off. The two men smiled at us again, then went inside the castle. Xenia followed them, leaving me in the courtyard with Paloma, Cho, Sullivan, Serilda, and the musicians.

"Now that they're gone, we have work to do." Serilda gestured at the musicians. "If you will all be so kind."

The musicians nodded at her, smiled at me, and started tuning their instruments.

"What's going on?" I asked. "Why are they here?"

"The music is going to help with your training, just like it helped you perform the dance."

"Someone told me that dancing is not fighting." I looked at Sullivan, who shrugged.

"The principles are the same. Step and counterstep. Strike and counterstrike. You're just battling for your life instead of moving to music," Serilda said. "Besides, if Xenia can teach you to dance, then I can teach you to fight."

Surprise rippled through me. "You? *You're* going to teach me? Not Sully?"

"Lucas can't teach you what I have in mind."

"And what is that?"

Instead of answering, Serilda turned toward the table. I thought she might grab one of the swords or spears, but she ignored them and went over to a black cloth bundle lying on the corner. She took hold of the bundle and unrolled the cloth so that it was lying flat on the table.

Three items gleamed a dull silver against the black fabric— a sword, a dagger, and a shield.

It was the same set of weapons that I had noticed hanging on the wall in Serilda's library. Now that I was seeing them up close, I realized that small shards of midnight-blue tearstone had been set into the hilts of the sword and the dagger, as well as into the center of the shield. They all formed the same, familiar design.

A crown.

My gaze dropped to my wrist. The exact same crown that the tearstone shards formed on my bracelet.

I tapped my finger on the crown crest in the sword's hilt. "Alvis made these, didn't he? This shard design, this crown design, is his signature." I shook my head. "I didn't even know that he could make weapons."

"Yes, Alvis made these," Serilda said. "He used to make all sorts of weapons. He gave these to me a long time ago for safe-keeping."

I waited, expecting her to say more, but she fell silent, so I tapped my finger on the crown crest again. "Icy crowns made of frosted shards. Do these weapons have something to do with that old fairy-tale rhyme?"

Serilda and Cho exchanged an inscrutable look, then Serilda cleared her throat.

"Alvis always told me that he liked the look of that crown crest."

Once again, I waited, and once again, she didn't offer any more information. So I picked up the sword, the dagger, and the shield all in turn.

They weighed much less than the weapons that the gladi-ators usually trained with, and even less than the sword that Serilda had given me before we had left the Black Swan com-pound. The sword, the dagger, and the shield felt as light as, well, feathers in my hands. I drew in a breath. And they all smelled cold and hard, just like my bracelet did. Surprise filled me.

"These are made of tearstone."

Serilda nodded. "Yes, they are."

Tearstone might be used in jewelry and found in columns like the ones at Seven Spire, but tearstone weapons were rare. The stone could be temperamental to work with, especially when you were trying to shape it into a sword, and it had a ten-dency to shatter, unless the master who was crafting it knew exactly what he was doing. I had thought that my bracelet was exquisite, but this set of weapons easily outstripped anything that I had ever seen from Alvis. But even more than that, I could smell how strong they were. And given that tearstone could both absorb and deflect magic, Alvis could have sold the weapons for an immense fortune.

"Those tearstone shards are blue, so they will deflect a fair amount of magic," Serilda said, echoing my thoughts. "The weapons should help bolster your own immunity when you face Vasilia."

I arched an eyebrow. "So you think Vasilia will kill me with her lightning after all?"

"I didn't say that."

"You didn't have to."

Serilda rolled her eyes, but she gestured at the sword, and I picked it up again.

"Tearstone is also surprisingly lightweight," she continued. "You don't have the upper-body strength to use a traditional sword and shield like the other gladiators do. Those weapons are far too heavy, and all they do is slow you down. This sword will help maximize your speed. So will the dagger and the shield. You showed everyone how well you can move during the Tanzen Freund. Your speed, movement, and fluidity are weapons too. All we need to do is combine them with that sword in your hand."

"Now it almost sounds like you think that I have a chance to defeat Vasilia," I drawled.

"You're far more powerful than you know," Serilda murmured.

I got the sense that she was talking about more than my meager fighting skills, but I didn't ask her to explain. She wouldn't tell me anyway, just like she hadn't told me everything she knew about what it really meant to be a Winter queen.

"And once I get through training you, you will be more than a match for Vasilia and anyone else who dares to challenge you. All you have to do is trust me. Can you do that, Evie?"

Serilda held out her hand, a serious expression on her face. Cordelia had told me to get Serilda to train me. But now that the moment was here, I wasn't sure that I was ready for any of this. But there was no backing out now, so I nodded, blew out a breath, and put my hand in hers.

Quick as thought, Serilda spun her body into mine and flipped me over her shoulder. My sword flew out of my hand, and once again, I ended up flat on my back on the ground, trying to keep my eyes from spinning around and breathing through the pain pulsing through my body.

Serilda leaned over me. "First lesson—never trust anyone."

I groaned. It was going to be a long day.

It wasn't just a long day. It was one long bloody day after another.

From sunup until well past sundown, all I did was train. I crawled out of bed, ignored my many aches and pains, and stumbled down to the courtyard. Serilda was always there, always waiting, always ready, willing, and eager to attack me.

And she wasn't alone.

The musicians were always in the courtyard too, their instruments at the ready. Cho, Paloma, and Sullivan joined us as well, although not nearly as early. Sometimes, Halvar and Bjarni would train with us too. Xenia preferred to watch from her cushioned chair on the second-floor balcony, her silver cane tapping out a steady beat.

Serilda took an entirely different approach to training me than Captain Auster and Sullivan had. She treated each fighting sequence like a dance, complete with music, and made me learn all the steps first. When to attack, when to retreat, how to whirl out of the way and then move back in for my own strike.

Once I had mastered that part of each "dance," she went on to the hand movements, or weapons portions. How to hold my sword, dagger, and shield, and how to block, parry, and attack with them. When she was satisfied that I sort of knew what I was doing, she made me put the steps together with the weapons, until I had learned the complete "dance."

To my great surprise, her methods actually worked.

Perhaps it was the fact that I had always loved dancing and music, but I had far more success training with Serilda than I'd ever had with anyone else. Even when I wasn't training, I could still hear the music playing in my mind, and I often twirled down the hallways, moving through the fighting sequences. In a way, I supposed they were like sections of a dance. Only these dances ended with blood, pain, and death, instead of bows, smiles, and claps.

Serilda was also right about the sword, dagger, and shield. The tearstone weapons were so lightweight that they felt more like extensions of my hands, rather than something separate, just like a morph's talons or a magier's lightning were a part of who and what they were.

Every day was different. Sometimes, all I did was work with the sword. Sometimes, only the dagger, or only the shield. Sometimes, all three together. Sometimes, no weapons at all, except for my fists and my wits.

My sparring partners were also different. Cho, Paloma, and Sullivan were always there, but I battled them in different groups, from one-on-one to all three at once. Sometimes, Halvar and Bjarni joined in as well, trying to cleave me in two with their maces. All the while, Serilda circled me, barking out orders to keep my hips square, my sword up, and my eyes on my enemy.

While I trained, the rest of the troupe integrated themselves quite nicely into Castle Asmund. Everyone from the acrobats to the gladiators to the bone masters practiced their routines, skills, and magic, keeping themselves sharp, and fascinating the Ungers with dazzling displays of acrobatics, fighting, healing, and more.

One morning about three weeks into my training, I stepped into the courtyard to find it deserted, except for Serilda. But instead of sitting on the table, sipping mochana like usual, she was standing in the middle of the courtyard, holding her own personal sword and shield.

I eyed the weapons. They gleamed a dull silver and were made of tearstone, just like mine, and they bore Serilda's swan crest—jet shards with a blue tearstone eye and beak. I wondered when Alvis had made the weapons for her—and why—but I didn't ask. She wouldn't tell me anyway.

Serilda gestured for me to face her. I sighed and did as she commanded. This was going to hurt.

"Today, you are going to fight until you can't fight anymore," she said.

"And then what?"

"And then we'll see how much progress you've really made."

I opened my mouth to ask what she meant, but she raised her sword and attacked. I snapped up my own sword and shield, and the fight was on.

And I lost spectacularly.

I had never fought Serilda before, but I quickly realized why she was the leader of the Black Swan troupe—because she was the best fighter. Cho, Paloma, and Sullivan were all skilled warriors, but they couldn't compare to Serilda, who was faster, smarter, and far more ruthless. We were barely three moves into the fight before she disarmed me, flipped me over her shoulder, and pressed her sword up against my throat.

"You're dead," she snapped. "Now get up."

I shook off the blow, got back onto my feet, and grabbed my sword and shield. And once again, she attacked and killed me in only a few moves.

"Again!" she snapped. "Again! Again!"

I rapidly came to despise that word. It was painfully apparent that I couldn't beat her—that I was *never* going to beat her—but every time she killed me, I got back up and braced myself for another attack.

After the twelfth—thirteenth?—time that Serilda flipped me over her shoulder and onto my back, she glared down at me, disgust stamped all over her features. "You're thinking too much. You need to react, defend, attack. You need to just fucking *move* like you did during the Tanzen Freund. You're too worried about everything else."

"Like you knocking me on my ass again?" I grumbled.

She huffed, then ordered me to get up so that she could knock me right back down again.

This went on for *hours*.

People came and went in the courtyard, but no one interrupted Serilda or kept her from beating me. We didn't even stop to eat. Every time we sparred, Serilda attacked me with the same level of strength, speed, and determination. No wonder she had been Cordelia's personal guard. The woman was bloody *relentless*.

Finally, around midnight, Serilda let me go back to my room, although not before ordering me to return to the courtyard bright and early in the morning. I was far too tired to argue, so I stumbled inside the castle. I was a sweaty, bruised mess, and every single part of my body ached, from my head down to my toes. Even my hair hurt.

No one was around to see my misery. Everyone else had already gone to bed, even the Ungers, who loved to drink ale and cider, sit by the fire, and play games late into the night. I rounded the corner and spotted the door to my room at the far end of the hallway. A hundred more feet, and I could crawl into bed and not move a single aching muscle until morning—

A shadow detached itself from the wall to my left. I blinked, thinking that I was so tired that I was hallucinating. Then I saw a flash of silver, and I realized that it wasn't a hallucination. Some assassin was in the castle, rushing toward me.

For a moment, I stood there, frozen in place. Then all those lessons that Serilda had been beating into me took hold, and my feet moved of their own accord, propelling me out of the way. I rushed back so quickly that I banged into a painting hanging on the wall behind me.

But the assassin didn't stop, not for one second, and she raised her sword for another strike. I pivoted to the side just in time to keep her blade from skewering me.

The assassin had committed all her strength and speed to the blow, and her sword sliced through the canvas and got stuck in the frame. She grunted, but she pulled the weapon out of the wood and whirled around to face me again. She was so fast that I barely had time to yank my own sword out of my scabbard and lift it up to block her next blow.

Clang!

Our swords crashed together in a thunderous roar, and the assassin bore down with her weapon, trying to use her strength to wrest my sword out of my hand. I gritted my teeth, tightened my grip, and threw her off. Then, before the assassin could come at me again, I whipped up my own sword and attacked.

Back and forth we fought through the hallway, each one of us lashing out with our weapons and doing our best to kill the other. Perhaps it was my worry or exhaustion or both, but sometime during the battle, I realized that I could actually *hear* the music from all the training sessions playing in my mind. I grabbed hold of the phantom music and let it sweep me away, moving to the beats just as I had during the Tanzen Freund. Only this time, I wasn't dancing. I was going through all the steps, all the strikes and counterstrikes, that Serilda had drilled into me.

And for the first time, the music, the dancing, the fighting all came together, and it actually *worked*.

I managed to keep the assassin from killing me, although I couldn't wound her in return. The longer we fought, the more I found myself humming along to the music in my mind. I blocked out everything else except for the music, the feel of my sword in my hand, and the steps that I needed to perform in order to survive.

The assassin was clothed in black from head to toe, including the knit mask that covered her face and head. All I could really see was the glitter of her eyes and the flash of her sword in the shadows. Vasilia must have found out that I was still alive and had sent this assassin after me.

Cold rage surged through me, and I grabbed hold of the emotion, using it to drown out the exhaustion that threatened to topple me with every step. This assassin was not going to kill me. Vasilia was *not* going to kill me. Not like this.

The assassin came at me again, and I stepped up to meet her attack, lashing out hard with my sword. And I did something that I hadn't been able to do so far—I disarmed her.

I knocked away her sword, which skittered down the hallway. I whipped up my blade and pressed my advantage, but the assassin spun away, reached up, and ripped off her mask, revealing her blond hair and the sunburst scar at the corner of her eye.

Serilda—I had been fighting Serilda this whole time.

"A test?" I screeched. "It was all a bloody *test*?"

She gave me a smug smile. "Of course it was a test. One that you passed."

I wanted to attack her again, but I was too tired. "You couldn't do this earlier? When I wasn't covered with blood and bruises and about to pass out from exhaustion?"

"I've been trying to do it all day, but you've been thinking too much. So I decided to force you to stop thinking and just react." She shrugged. "To force you to let go and tap into all of that delicious cold rage deep inside you. Still think it's not there?"

My lips pressed together. She was right about the rage. It was the only thing that had let me beat her, and it still hummed through my veins, beating in perfect time with my heart.

"I hate you right now," I muttered.

"You might hate me, but I've taught you how to fight," Serilda said, even more smug than before. "Now the real work can begin."

chapter twenty-six

I didn't think that it was possible, but after that night, Serilda trained me even harder.

And I actually started to get better—I actually started to get *good*.

As much as I hated to admit it, Serilda's sneak attack unlocked something in my mind, something that was holding me back, and I started putting the steps, movements, and training together into a cohesive fighting style. Oh, I still wasn't as good as Cho, Paloma, or Sullivan, but I managed to hold my own against them, and I even won some of our sparring bouts.

Even Serilda couldn't kill me inside the first minute anymore. Sometimes, it took her three minutes, or five, or longer. Sometimes, I even managed to disarm her, although she always got the better of me before I could move in for the final strike.

But training wasn't the only thing we did. We also planned how we could take down Vasilia, Felton, Nox, and Maeven.

One morning, about six weeks after we had come to Castle Asmund, Serilda, Cho, Paloma, Sullivan, and Xenia were gathered around the table in my bedroom poring over maps of Seven Spire and the surrounding city.

I stood by the window, holding back the white lace curtain and staring down at one of the courtyards. The acrobats were tumbling across the flagstones, while the wire walkers were practicing their flips on the cables they had strung up. The gladiators were also there, going through their drills and formations.

"It doesn't matter how well Evie is progressing in her training if we can't get her close enough to actually issue the royal challenge to Vasilia," Xenia said.

"I know that," Serilda snapped. "But my sources say that Vasilia is holed up inside Seven Spire, preparing for the coronation, so we have to find some way to sneak Evie inside the palace."

Xenia sniffed. "Your spies are inferior. Mine are reporting that Vasilia has been seen out and about in the city several times."

"Yes, my spies have reported that too. They have also reported that Vasilia never sets foot outside the palace without a heavy guard. So even if we could find out when she was leaving the palace, we still wouldn't be able to get close to her without engaging her guards. Which, of course, would give Nox and Felton plenty of time to get Vasilia to safety, and then we would lose our chance to issue the challenge altogether."

Xenia sniffed again, conceding the other woman's point, but just barely.

Serilda rolled her eyes and went back to her maps. Xenia's fingers curled around the top of her cane, as though she was thinking about braining the other woman with it. I didn't know their history, but it had quickly become apparent that they knew each other well and that everything was a competition between them and their soldier-versus-spy mentalities. Serilda wanted to cut straight through any problem she encountered, while Xenia preferred to knock the legs out from under her enemies first before she went in for the kill.

"I agree with Serilda," Cho said. "Sneaking into the palace is still our best bet."

Paloma and Sullivan joined in the conversation too, but I kept quiet.

I knew how we could get close enough for me to challenge Vasilia. I had known the answer for weeks now, ever since we had started dreaming up this crazy plan, although I hadn't said anything. I stared at the acrobats, wire walkers, and gladiators again.

I hadn't wanted anyone to sacrifice their lives for me.

But Vasilia's coronation was only about a month away now, and we were running out of time. Once she was formally crowned queen, she would declare war on Andvari, and there would be no stopping her.

So, with a heavy heart, I dropped the curtain and faced the others. "The coronation. That's how we get into the palace, and that's how we get close to Vasilia."

Paloma frowned. "But all sorts of nobles, senators, and guilders are supposed to attend. There will be more guards than ever. We can't sneak past all of them."

I shook my head. "We won't have to sneak past any of them. Vasilia will invite us."

"And why would she do that?" Sullivan asked.

"Because she will be absolutely delighted to have the Black Swan troupe perform at her coronation."

Silence fell over the room as the others absorbed my words.

"Think about it," I said. "Vasilia wants Serilda and Cho dead for working with Cordelia. She's already tried to kill them once. And not just them, but the whole troupe, anyone who could possibly be a threat."

"So?" Xenia asked.

"So she'll try again. Her weather magier never reported back, so she knows that he failed, and that Serilda is still alive. So let's give her exactly what she wants—the entire troupe at her coronation. Vasilia will think that we're walking right into her trap. She'll never suspect that we have a trap of our own planned."

"And how do you know that she won't slaughter us the second that we walk into the palace?" Sullivan asked.

I gave him a grim smile. "Because I know my dear cousin better than anyone. She'll want the troupe to perform before she orders her guards to kill us. Vasilia likes to play with her food before she eats it."

Silence fell over the room again as everyone thought about my plan.

"It could work," Xenia said. "Vasilia has invited several troupes to the coronation, but none as prestigious or well-known as the Black Swan."

Serilda snorted. "Evie's right. Vasilia will leap at the chance to have us perform before she tries to kill all of us."

"Yes," I said in a low voice. "That's the problem. *All* of you."

Sullivan's eyes narrowed. "You're worried about everyone."

"Yes. Vasilia won't settle for anything less. She'll want the entire troupe there so she can murder us all at once." Worry twisted my stomach. "Even if I challenge her, even if I kill her, we don't know what might happen afterward. There could be casualties."

I didn't mention what would happen if I didn't win—that we would all be summarily executed, starting with me.

"We owe you our lives," Cho pointed out. "We wouldn't even be having this conversation if it wasn't for you. We would have died in that storm if you hadn't tracked down the magier."

"Or the Ungers would have killed us," Serilda added, throwing a nasty look at Xenia.

I rubbed my aching head. "But that doesn't give me the right to ask the rest of the troupe to do this. To potentially die for me. They didn't ask to be part of this. *None* of you asked to be part of this."

"And you didn't ask to be part of the massacre," Xenia said. "We all make the best choices that we can; we all do the best that we can."

"Besides," Serilda said, a dark note in her voice. "If we don't do this, if you don't do this, thousands more will die. I've seen it with my magic, such as it is."

"I know all that, but it still doesn't make it right, or ease my guilt."

"We're your friends, Evie. That means that your problems are our problems too." Paloma shrugged, and a wry grin curved her lips. "Your problems just happen to involve the fate of kingdoms."

I snorted, but I flashed her a grateful smile.

The others gathered around the maps and continued their plotting. I returned to the window, pushed the curtain back, and peered at the courtyard again. Everything was the same as before. Acrobats tumbling, wire walkers balancing, gladiators drilling. Yes, everything was the same, right down to the guilt and dread twisting my stomach.

Using the Black Swan troupe was the only chance I had of getting close enough to challenge Vasilia, but I couldn't help but wonder how many people I was leading to their deaths.

That night at dinner, Serilda told everyone that we were packing up and returning to Bellona in a few days. She had barely sat back down before Xenia got to her feet and announced that the Ungers would be hosting a ball to give us a proper send-off. Naturally, everyone was more excited about the party than the packing, and Xenia shot Serilda a triumphant smile. Always a competition between those two.

The next few days passed by quickly, and the night of the party arrived. Xenia had opened up the castle's grand ballroom, and Paloma and I stood by the entrance.

The ballroom was a large area with a second-floor balcony that wrapped around it, but instead of common flagstones, the floor here was made of pale gray marble that gleamed like a sheet of glass. Even the ogre faces set into the stone were as smooth and shiny as mirrors. The gray marble continued up the walls before giving way to a lovely forested fresco that stretched across the ceiling a hundred feet overhead. Several chandeliers, their crystals shaped like ogre heads, dangled down from the ceiling, bathing the ballroom in soft light.

Several tables had been set up against one wall, each one boasting an impressive spread of food and drinks. My gaze locked onto one of the dessert tables, which featured everything from tiny chocolate petits fours to strawberry tarts to towers made of apple strudels that were held together with thick ribbons of vanilla icing. I wished that Isobel was here. She would have loved seeing the desserts that the Ungerian cook masters had created.

Paloma and I were among the last to arrive, and everyone was already talking, laughing, drinking, and eating. The musicians who had performed during my training sessions were sitting on a raised dais in the corner, playing waltzes, reels, and other tunes, although no one was dancing yet.

I scanned the crowd. Cho was at a dessert table, tasting and debating the merits of the various delicacies with Bjarni. Serilda and Xenia were standing near the musicians, sipping brandy and probably trying to outdo each other with their biting comments. Theroux, Aisha, and the other troupe members were mixing and mingling with the Ungers, and everyone looked relaxed and happy.

Paloma nudged me with her elbow. "Lucas is in the corner."

I tensed. "I wasn't looking for him."

"Of course you weren't."

My gaze zoomed in that direction. Sullivan was sipping brandy and talking with the Ungers. He was wearing his gray coat over a black shirt, leggings, and boots. His dark brown hair gleamed under the lights, and his eyes crinkled as he smiled at something his companions said.

We were leaving at dawn. From there, it would be a long, hard trip back to Bellona, and then a final bit of training and planning before Vasilia's coronation. Tonight was the last free night that I would have for the foreseeable future. It might be the last free night that I would *ever* have, and I wanted to make the most of it.

With him.

I had never been in love. I had never *let* myself be in love. I knew that Vasilia would eventually destroy anything she realized I cared about, so I took great pains not to care about anything at all. Not people, not animals, not even a favorite dress or book or piece of jewelry. Isobel and Alvis had been the two exceptions, and I had only let myself care about them because I knew that Vasilia wouldn't bother with two servants. They were even more below her notice than I was.

But I had wanted to know what all the women giggled about, so when I was twenty, I had very discreetly and carefully seduced a visiting noble. I had done weeks of research, taken all the appropriate herbs, and studied the man's every word and action for days after he had arrived at Seven Spire. Finally, when I felt confident that he had no ulterior motive other than whiling away an evening, I had slept with him.

He hadn't been Prince Charming, and he certainly hadn't set my heart—or any other part of me—aflutter, but he had been nice and skilled enough. Truth be told, I had been rather disappointed with the whole process. A year later, I had tried again with a different visiting noble to the same mediocre results, and I hadn't been tempted to do it again since then.

Until Sullivan.

I didn't love Sullivan, but I wasn't immune to him either. Far from it. Physically, he was tall, strong, and handsome, as were many men in the troupe, but something about his hair, eyes, features, and scent intrigued me in a way that no one else ever had before. And he touched and challenged my emotions just like he challenged me in the training ring. Sullivan made me feel all sorts of things—anger, annoyance, care, concern, desire.

And now I was finally going to do something about my brewing feelings.

Ever since the massacre, I had been fighting. To stay alive. To find some way to stop Vasilia. To figure out who I was and what I was supposed to do.

Tomorrow, I would return to Bellona for perhaps the final fight of my life. But tonight, I didn't want to fight. No, tonight, I wanted to lose myself in this current that continually sparked and snapped between Sullivan and me. I wanted something that was mine and mine alone, and not done out of necessity or duty.

I wanted *him*.

Sullivan must have sensed my stare because he looked in my direction. Our gazes locked and held across the ballroom. This was my moment. I drew in a breath and headed toward him—

Halvar stepped in front of me, blocking my path. He smiled and held out his hand. "Hello, Evie. May I have this dance?"

I looked past him, but Sullivan had vanished. I glanced around the ballroom, but I didn't see him anywhere.

Halvar frowned. "Is something wrong?"

"Of course not. I would be honored to dance with you."

I forced myself to smile and put my hand in Halvar's. He grinned and led me onto the dance floor.

My earlier performance of the Tanzen Freund had had a far more profound effect than I'd realized, because every single Unger wanted to dance with me. Men, women, even the children. I whirled from one partner to the next, from one section of the ballroom to the opposite side and back again, from waltz to reel to quickstep. Whenever I got a chance, I looked for Sullivan, but I didn't see him anywhere.

Finally, after about two solid hours of dancing, I managed to escape from the ballroom. I was a bit overheated from the last quickstep, so I slipped out one of the doors and wound up in the training courtyard. Spring had come and gone while we had been at the castle, and summer was taking hold, but the air was still a bit chilly here in the mountains. After the noise, heat, and commotion of the ballroom, I welcomed the cool quiet, and I walked through the courtyard and stepped out onto the grass beyond.

The lawn here wasn't nearly as large as the one at Seven Spire, and I quickly reached the stone wall that cordoned off the grass from the steep drop below. Castle Asmund overlooked the surrounding mountains, and the sticky scent of the pines and other evergreen trees filled the air. A sliver of the moon hung in the midnight sky, gilding the rocks and trees in a silver frost.

I didn't know how long I stood there before I heard footsteps echoing through the courtyard and then swishing through the grass behind me. I drew in a breath, and Sullivan's scent filled my lungs.

He stepped up beside me and stared down at the steep drop. "If you're thinking of jumping, I wouldn't advise it," he said in a light, humorous tone. "That's far too long a drop until you hit the bottom for you not to regret what you've done."

I barked out a laugh. "I was thinking just the opposite. That I should go ahead and jump. That I should stop this madness and put myself out of my misery."

Sullivan stared down at the drop again. "What went through your mind? When Vasilia blasted you off the side of the palace, and you started to fall?"

"Well, my life didn't flash before my eyes, if that's what you're asking."

"So what did you think about?"

"How angry I was," I said in a soft voice. "That Vasilia had gotten the best of me yet again. That she had killed everyone. My cousins were never particularly kind, but they didn't deserve to be slaughtered. But most of all, I wished that I had done something else, something *more,* something to fight back against Vasilia and all the horrible things she did that day and all the others at the palace. I wished that I had found a way to stop her."

"And now you have," he said. "Do you regret it? Coming to the Black Swan? Becoming a gladiator?"

I shook my head. "No. Even though I have worked harder than I have ever worked, even though I've been in danger and almost killed more times than I can count, these last few months have been the happiest of my life since before my parents died. For the first time in years, I could be myself and not have to weigh my words and actions and how someone might use them against me. I could just be me, *Evie,* and no one else. I was finally free."

Sullivan raised his eyebrows. "And now?"

I blew out a breath. "And now I feel like a gargoyle being forced back into its cage. And that's not even the worst part."

"And what would that be?"

"Knowing that you, Paloma, Serilda, Cho, and everyone else are going to risk your lives, just on the mere hope that I can kill Vasilia."

"It's more than a mere hope."

This time, I raised my eyebrows at him.

"Serilda Swanson is one of the finest warriors that I have ever seen."

"So?"

Sullivan shrugged. "So I've watched you go toe to toe with her all day, every day for weeks."

I shook my head again. "But she still beats me. She still kills me every time."

"But she has to *work* for it. And she has to work *hard* for it. How long do you think that it's been since Serilda has gone up against anyone that she couldn't beat within a matter of minutes? She's not letting you win. She has too much pride for that. But you're challenging her. Someday, you're going to be even better than she is, and she knows it. That's why she is pushing you so hard now, and that's why she is going to keep pushing you every day until you kill Vasilia."

I smiled. "You make it sound like a certainty."

"It *is* a certainty. You will do it, Evie. You will face Vasilia and win. I believe in you."

Conviction blazed in his eyes, making them glitter like blue stars, while the silvery moonlight gilded the handsome planes of his face. He really did think that I could defeat Vasilia. It was the first time anyone had ever thought that I was better than her, and it touched something deep inside me—too many things deep inside me.

I drew in a breath, letting his scent sink deep into my lungs. The cold, clean vanilla aroma sent a shiver through me, and a hot spark flared to life in my stomach. I didn't want to talk about the future and all the death that it might hold. No, tonight, I didn't want to do any more talking at all.

His hand was resting on top of the wall, and I reached out and laid my fingers on top of his. Sullivan jerked, as though my hand burned him, but he didn't pull away. Understanding filled his face, along with a touch of amusement.

"I thought you hated me, highness."

"I did. At first."

He arched an eyebrow. "And now?"

"I'm starting to see some of your finer qualities. You can be quite pleasant, Sully. When you're not blasting me with magic or knocking me flat on my back in the training ring." I smiled, stepped closer, and tilted my head up so that I was looking directly into his face. "Although there are certain instances where I wouldn't mind being flat on my back with you looming over me."

His eyes narrowed, and hunger flickered across his face. I wet my lips and moved closer to him . . . and closer . . . and closer still . . .

The warmth of his body mingled with mine, and I drew in another breath, tasting his delicious aroma. More heat spiraled through my body, and I could see the same desire shimmering in his eyes, making them glow brighter than the moon above. I reached out with my other hand to cup his face and draw his lips down to mine—

Sullivan pulled away.

One moment, our breaths were kissing each other's cheeks, our lips were only an inch apart, and we were as close together as two people could be without actually being in each other's arms. The next, he had stepped back, and the night air swirled in between us, in the space where his body had been. It felt like a cold slap across my face.

"I've just made a monstrous fool out of myself, haven't I?" I couldn't keep the bitterness out of my voice.

"No," he replied in a low, husky tone. "Not a fool at all."

"Then what's wrong?"

Sullivan's lips pressed into a tight, thin line, as though he didn't want to answer. But after several seconds, he cleared his throat. "You will be queen of Bellona soon."

"You think—*hope*—that I will be queen."

He shook his head. "No, I *know* that you will be queen."

"So? What does that have to do with tonight?"

A muscle ticked in his jaw. "Because I wouldn't be satisfied with just one night with you, highness. I would *never* be satisfied with that."

Hope flooded my chest. "It wouldn't have to be one night—"

His bitter laugh drowned out my words. "Of course it would. Because you will be queen. Do you have any idea what that means?"

I stiffened. "I lived at the palace for fifteen years. I know exactly what it is to be queen."

"And I know exactly what it's like to be a bastard prince," he growled.

Understanding rushed in, drowning my hope. Sullivan gave me a grim smile. He could tell that I was thinking about all the implications of my becoming queen—implications that I had never fully considered until now.

"As soon as you are on the throne, your allies and enemies alike will expect you to marry," he said in a soft voice. "And to marry well—someone with money, power, magic, connections. Someone who can help you secure the Blair line and Bellona's future."

I had been so focused on my training that I hadn't thought much about what would happen if I actually defeated Vasilia, but he was right. Sooner rather than later, I would be expected to marry, and marry well.

A cold light filled Sullivan's eyes. "My father is the king of Andvari. My mother has been his mistress since before I was born. I spent my childhood at the royal palace, and I grew up with the rest of the king's children—his legitimate children."

I thought back to the massacre. "So Prince Frederich was your half brother, and Gemma is your niece."

He nodded. "Yes. I had the same tutors and learned the

same skills and went to the same balls as Frederich and my other royal relatives, but I was never really one of them. I was never their *equal*."

I grimaced. I knew exactly what that was like.

"So I made a promise that I would never let myself be treated that way again, that I would never let myself be seen as *less* than anyone else just because of the circumstances of my birth." He smiled, but the expression was even colder than his eyes were. "We both know that bastard princes don't get to consort with queens."

I wanted to tell him that he was wrong. That his being a bastard and my being queen wouldn't matter. But I couldn't say the words because I knew what a lie they would be.

Sullivan stepped forward and raised his hand. For a moment, I thought he had changed his mind, that he was going to pull me close and kiss me anyway, despite his harsh words. But his fingertips stopped an inch away from my cheek, as though I was a marble statue in a museum that he didn't dare touch, not even for the briefest moment.

"You will be a wonderful queen. Kind, caring, compassionate. Strong, cunning, and ruthless when you need to be. But I can't break my promise to myself. I *won't*. Not even for you, highness." The last word came out as a low whisper, but somehow, it shattered my heart more than if he had been shouting curses at me.

Sullivan's fingers hovered in the air next to my cheek. Then he dropped his hand to his side, gave me a sad smile, and walked away.

chapter twenty-seven

The next morning, we gathered in the main courtyard to say goodbye to the Ungers. But we weren't saying goodbye to all of them. I was standing with Serilda when Xenia, Halvar, and Bjarni announced that they were returning to Bellona with us.

"Aunt Xenia told us what you're planning. We would be honored to assist you. One of us is worth twenty soldiers," Halvar said, a proud note rippling through his voice.

Bjarni nodded. "You'll need our help when you challenge Vasilia."

Serilda crossed her arms over her chest and glared at Xenia. "Going back to Bellona to spy on us?"

"I told you before. I'm only a spy when I have something interesting to report." Xenia eyed me. "And I think that this royal challenge will be very interesting."

"I don't think that *interesting* is the right word for it," I muttered. "Suicidal, perhaps."

Xenia smiled. "We'll see."

She strode across the courtyard to make sure that her bags

were properly loaded onto her carriage. Halvar and Bjarni followed her, while Serilda went over to speak to Cho and Paloma. That left me standing alone next to the doors, watching as everyone prepared to leave.

Footsteps sounded inside the castle, growing closer and louder. My breath caught in my throat. I would know his footsteps anywhere.

A moment later, Sullivan appeared in the doorway.

He was wearing his gray coat and had a gray leather knapsack slung over his shoulder. Stubble darkened his jaw, his brown hair was mussed, and his eyes were tired, as though he'd had a long, sleepless night.

He wasn't the only one. After he had walked away, I had gone back to my room and spent the rest of the night lying in bed, glaring up at the ogres in the fresco on the ceiling and alternating between being angry and sad that he had rejected me. I understood his reasons, but they didn't lessen my own pain and disappointment, and they certainly didn't banish the complicated feelings that I had developed for him. Perhaps the truly sad part was that his bloody honor made me like him even more.

Sullivan stopped when he saw me. I made sure to keep my face perfectly blank and not let any of my true feelings show. His jaw clenched, as though he were having trouble pushing down his own emotions. He nodded at me and walked on.

I tracked him through the courtyard as he called out greetings to everyone. He didn't look at me again, but I could smell the peppery anger and minty regret radiating off him.

I sighed. It was going to be a long trip back to Bellona.

A long trip? More like interminable. Not only were things between Sullivan and me extremely awkward, but Serilda and Xenia sniped at each other the whole way back to Svalin. Still, we made good time, and we reached the Black Swan compound two weeks later.

But our work was just beginning.

As soon as we returned, Serilda wrote to Vasilia, congratulating her on her upcoming coronation and offering the troupe's services to add to the celebration. Vasilia replied to the letter the next day, saying that she would be honored to have the troupe perform.

And so Vasilia set her trap for us, and we set ours for her. Only time would tell which one of us would be victorious.

Sullivan was right in one of his dire predictions. Serilda trained me even harder than before, working with me from sunup until well past sundown every day. The other gladiators wondered what was going on, and Cho told them that I was to perform a special drill for Vasilia, since I had won the black-ring match. I didn't know if the other gladiators believed him, but they all gave me sympathetic looks, grateful that I was the one working so hard instead of them.

The days passed by quickly, until it was the night before the coronation. I finished my final round of training with Serilda, took a shower, and collapsed into bed. My eyes slid shut, and I started to dream, to remember . . .

I didn't know how long I stood in front of the playroom door that Vasilia had slammed in my face, listening to her laugh at me through the heavy wood. Tears leaked out of my eyes, but I couldn't move. I couldn't scream. All I could do was stand there and cry.

Eventually, one of the servants came and led me to my room. Only, it wasn't the large, spacious bedroom filled with toys and pretty clothes down the hall from Vasilia's chambers. No, this room was on one of the upper levels, tucked in a dark, deserted corner, and full of hand-me-down clothes and worn-out furniture, with nary a toy in sight.

And that was only the beginning of my miserable fall from grace.

The day after my testing, Captain Auster came to my room and told me that I was being apprenticed to Alvis, the royal jeweler. Auster led me to Alvis's basement workshop. The metalstone master took one look at me, then went right back to his work.

The only one who was remotely kind to me was Isobel, one of the cook masters. She felt sorry for me, the girl no one wanted, and she plied me with sweet treats, trying to make me feel better. Plus, Vasilia and the other children had servants to fetch them food and drinks, so they never visited the kitchen. At least while I was in the kitchen, I didn't have to listen to their laughter.

My heartbreak didn't ease, not really, but as the days passed, another emotion rose up to join it—rage. This cold, cold rage that beat in my chest whenever I looked at the crown princess, whenever I saw her smile or heard her smug laughter.

Vasilia didn't want to be my friend? Fine. I would show her exactly what she was missing. I was still a royal, still a Blair, and still attending the same lessons, parties, and training sessions as her. If I couldn't be Vasilia's friend, then I would be better than her—at everything.

So I studied my lessons and memorized the party dances and trained with the guards and did everything that I could to best her.

And for a while, it worked.

I excelled at my lessons, especially the languages and the dances. My only frustration was that I could never quite get the hang of fighting, but two out of three wasn't bad.

Vasilia realized what I was doing. She knew that she had crushed my heart, and at first, it amused her to see me trying so hard to get back at her, to show her that I was just as good, just as special, as she was. But she slowly grew bored of it, and she turned on me again.

Oh, Vasilia didn't lift a finger to hurt me. She didn't have to. The other children did it for her.

They stole my homework and ripped my papers to shreds. Tripped me during the dances. Punched, kicked, and sliced me with their swords during the training sessions. Through it all, Vasilia stood by and watched with a satisfied smile. The other kids had already realized that pleasing Vasilia could be beneficial to them and their parents right now, as well as in the future.

Even Bellonan children are very good at playing the long game.

Still, all the cruel pranks, tricks, and beatings only fueled my rage and made me that much more determined, and I kept right on going.

One day, I showed up at Alvis's workshop with a black eye from when the other kids had roughed me up during training. Alvis watched me while I grabbed a rag and wiped the dirt off my face. Isobel had given me a bag of ice, and I held it up to my eye, hissing at the fresh sting of pain that the cold brought along with it.

"There's no future in fighting," Alvis said. "Not right now, anyway. The other brats are going to keep right on beating you until they beat the spirit right out of you."

Startled, I lowered the bag from my eye. Up until this point, he had communicated in annoyed grunts. This was the first time that he had ever actually spoken to me.

"I have to keep fighting," I mumbled through a mouthful of loose teeth. "I can't give in. I can't let her win."

Alvis shook his head. "Sometimes, it's not so much about winning as it is about surviving. Quit trying to beat her, and Vasilia will forget about you. You'll be much happier and far less bloody. Trust me."

It took me a few more weeks and several more beatings, but I eventually took his advice. Oh, I still did my schoolwork, memorized the dances, and trained with the other kids, but I didn't raise my hand in class anymore, and I didn't volunteer to demonstrate anything. As much as I hated it, I always made sure that I never challenged or outshined Vasilia in any way.

Alvis was right. After she was satisfied that I had learned my place, Vasilia ignored me. No, it was worse than that. It was like she forgot that I even existed, despite the fact that I saw her every day. Which, of course, broke my heart all over again and filled me with even more rage. I wasn't even good at being her bloody nemesis.

But there was nothing that I could do to wound her in any way, so I gave up trying to hurt her and started counting down the days until I could finally leave Vasilia and Seven Spire behind forever . . .

A loud snore startled me awake. For a moment, I thought I was back in my room at the palace, sleeping in my old bed. Then the snore came again, and I realized that I was in the barracks. My entire body was tense, and my hands were fisted into the sheets, as though I was still fighting all those long-ago battles with Vasilia and the other children. I drew in several deep breaths and forced myself to relax.

The snores were coming from Paloma, who was fast asleep in her cot, along with the other female gladiators. Everyone was resting up for the big day tomorrow. But I couldn't sleep, not with all those horrible memories swimming around in my mind, so I got up, threw on a robe, and slipped out of the barracks.

I wandered around the compound, but everyone else had already gone to bed, except for a few guards manning the front gate. A light burned in Sullivan's house, but I didn't dare knock on his door. I had no desire to be rejected again. Lights burned in the manor house as well, but I didn't want to see Serilda, Cho, or anyone else, so I slipped into the gardens.

I ended up at the pond with the black swans.

The two swans were gliding through the water, just as they had been when Serilda had brought me here after the black-ring match. Tonight, instead of eating bugs and plants, they were swimming side by side, nuzzling each other with their beaks.

I watched the swans for a while, enjoying their displays of affection, then looked up at the palace.

Seven Spire loomed over the city, with lights burning on every level. No doubt everyone was still hard at work pulling together the final details for the coronation. If everything went according to her plan, Vasilia would be crowned queen by midnight tomorrow, and everyone in the Black Swan troupe would be dead.

When I had first come to the compound, the thought of

facing Vasilia again would have filled me with dread. I had been the useless royal for so long that I had actually started to think of myself that way.

But I wasn't useless—not anymore.

I thought about all the memories that I'd had of Vasilia since the massacre. How deceptively kind she had been to me those first few weeks. How she had slammed that door in my face once she thought that I didn't have any magic. How she had stood by with an amused smile and watched while the other children tortured me.

I couldn't take Alvis's advice. Not now. I couldn't give in to Vasilia again. Not even for one second, or she would kill me. And not just me, but Paloma, Serilda, Cho, Xenia, Sullivan, and everyone else I had cared about. She had already murdered our family. I wasn't going to let her kill my friends too.

Perhaps I should have been thinking about Bellona and all the innocent people who would die if Vasilia declared war on Andvari. Perhaps I should have been thinking about my duty to protect them. Perhaps I should have been contemplating Cordelia's last words about how I needed to do what was best for our kingdom.

But I wasn't thinking about any of that. Not really. No, I was thinking about my own heartbreak.

Serilda had been right when she had said that I was full of cold rage. Vasilia was the source of a lot of that rage, and if I was brutally honest with myself, I didn't want to kill her because of the massacre or the potential war with Andvari or to save Bellona.

I wanted to kill her for *me*.

For how she had so casually broken my heart. For all the cruel things she had done to me since then. For all the countless times she had tortured, dismissed, and ignored me. I wanted to kill Vasilia for all that and more—so much more.

And tomorrow, I would finally get my chance.

I stared up at the palace for a moment longer, then dropped my gaze and walked back to the barracks to get what sleep I could for the night.

CHAPTER TWENTY-EIGHT

The next morning, I stood in one of the barracks bathrooms, staring at my reflection in the mirror.

I was wearing black fighting leathers and sandals, along with my tearstone sword, which was sheathed in its scabbard and hooked to my belt. And once again, I had been made up to look like a black swan, just like I had during the black-ring match. Only instead of paint, an actual mask covered my face today.

The mask was made of black cloth and secured to my head with a thin black band. Several rows of tiny silver crystals fanned out across the mask, arranged in feathery patterns. Blue crystals gleamed at the corners of my eyes, also arranged in feathery patterns, to further play up the swan theme. More silver and blue crystals had been glued to my black hair, which had been slicked back into three knots, all of which were bristling with black feathers. To complete the fierce look, blood-red gloss coated my lips, and silver glitter shimmered on my arms, hands, and legs.

Serilda had insisted on my wearing the mask. She didn't want someone recognizing me before we got close enough for me to issue the royal challenge to Vasilia. Her reasoning made sense, but staring at the mask and my distorted reflection made my stomach clench with worry.

I still didn't think that I was a black swan. But I could certainly end up as a dead one—and so could everyone else in the troupe.

So many things could go wrong today, and my death wouldn't be the worst of it. If I didn't kill her, Vasilia would make everyone in the troupe suffer in horrible ways that I didn't want to imagine but couldn't stop thinking about. So many people could die. So many people could be slaughtered because of me.

The irony of the situation didn't escape me either. Six months ago, Vasilia had been doing the exact same thing that I was—plotting to kill the queen. To get rid of all the Blairs and anyone else who could stand in her way. To take over Bellona for her own ill ends.

Perhaps I was more like my murderous cousin than I wanted to admit.

A sick weariness filled me, and I leaned down and braced my hands on the sink, letting the feel of the cool porcelain steady me. I could do this. I *had* to do this. Not just for myself and my friends, but for all the innocent people Vasilia was planning to hurt.

Paloma stepped into the bathroom. She too was dressed in black fighting leathers, with her spiked mace dangling from her black leather belt. Her blond hair was pulled back into an elaborate braid, and gold, feathery streaks shimmered on her face, bringing out her amber eyes.

"It's time," she said.

I nodded, reached out, and picked up the memory stone that was sitting on the sink. The opal felt as heavy as a lead weight, but I slipped it into my kilt pocket. My silver bracelet with its tearstone shards glinted on my right wrist. I hadn't taken it off since I had performed the Tanzen Freund. I traced my fingers over the crown of shards, then dropped my hand and faced Paloma.

"Promise me something."

"What?"

"That if Vasilia kills me, you will get the others out of the palace. That you will get them and yourself to safety. Don't do something stupid like try to avenge me. Okay?"

Paloma glared at me. So did the ogre face on her neck. "Don't be stupid. Of course I will avenge you, no matter what. That is the gladiator way; that is *our* way."

I groaned. "You're not making this any easier."

"That's because it's not going to be easy," Paloma said in that matter-of-fact tone that I both admired and hated. "It's going to be one of the hardest things you'll ever do. But you *can* do it, Evie. So buck up, and let's go kill your bitch of a cousin before she ruins any more lives."

Despite the seriousness of the situation, I couldn't help but laugh. "Well, when you put it that way, you almost make it sound like it's going to be fun."

I smiled at Paloma, then hooked my arm through hers. Together, we went to meet the others.

The wagons were waiting outside the arena. Everyone loaded up their supplies and climbed on board, and away we went.

We weren't the only ones heading to the palace, and the streets were packed with wagons, people, horses, and gargoyles. Only invited guests and performers would be allowed into Seven Spire to witness the coronation, but it was tradition for the people to line the streets directly across the river from the palace, as well as the bridges leading to the palace itself. Once the queen was crowned, she would walk to the edge of the royal lawn and wave to the people below, letting them know that Bellona was in good hands for as long as she reigned. The crowd would cheer, and the celebrations would last all night.

I was riding in a wagon with Paloma, Halvar, Bjarni, and Sullivan. The three ogre morphs were sharpening their weapons again, even though they were already as sharp as could be. Sullivan had his eyes closed and his hands stuffed in his coat pockets.

Me? I couldn't sit still. I kept touching the black-swan mask on my face, my sword belted to my waist, and the memory stone in my pocket, checking them over and over again, even though nothing had changed since the last time I had checked them a minute ago. I reached for my sword again, but a hand closed over mine, stopping me.

"Relax," Sullivan said. "Just relax. Everything is going to be fine."

"Do you really believe that?"

"Yes. And more importantly, I believe in you."

This was the most he had spoken to me since that night in Unger. Oh, I had seen him every day since then, but he had nodded and gone on about his business as though our conversation at Castle Asmund had never happened.

Sullivan stared at me. I expected him to remove his hand, now that he had done his best to reassure me, but he slowly threaded his fingers through mine. Heat spiked through me at his touch, and I curled my fingers into his. We didn't speak after that, but we held hands as we rode through the city.

Finally, the wagon rattled across one of the bridges that led from the city over the river to Seven Spire. The wagon stopped in the main plaza in front of the palace, and I peered out the window.

Serilda and Cho had already gotten out of their wagon and were speaking to the guards manning the gates. They had a lengthy conversation, and Serilda showed the guards the necessary papers that proved that she, Cho, and the troupe had been invited to perform.

Vasilia might want the Black Swan troupe here so she could murder us, but the guards still inspected every wagon, including ours.

Paloma, Halvar, and Bjarni tensed and gripped their weapons a little tighter, while Sullivan curled his free hand into a tight fist, ready to unleash his lightning. The guards stared curiously at my black-swan mask, but they didn't order me to take it off. A minute later, they moved on to the next wagon, and ten minutes after that, we were rolling through the gates. I let out a quiet sigh of relief.

We were in—but the danger was just beginning.

The guards directed us to a courtyard that was used for food and other deliveries. Even though it was just after eleven o'clock in the morning and the coronation wasn't going to take place until this evening, the area was already a madhouse, with servants carrying food, flowers, tables, and chairs into and out of the palace, across the courtyard, and even back through the gates. Dozens of conversations filled the air, along with the high whinnies of the horses and the low grumbles of the gargoyles.

I got out of the wagon with the others, and we all gathered up the costumes, props, and other supplies for our show.

Serilda was wearing her white tunic with the black-swan embroidery, while Cho looked dashing in his red ringmaster's coat. The gladiators were sporting black fighting leathers, given the special occasion, and the acrobats, wire walkers, and other performers had already donned their costumes as well.

The guards gave me curious looks, wondering why I was wearing a mask, since our show wouldn't start for several hours yet. Then Xenia climbed out of her wagon, and she became the center of attention.

Xenia was also wearing a mask to hide her identity, and hers was far more gruesome than mine. Her mask was made of thick, stiff paper that had been painted to look like an ogre's face, complete with sharp, bloody teeth. The ogre mask matched the morph mark on her neck, and more than one guard shuddered and looked away from her.

We carried our supplies into the palace. The second that I stepped inside, the faint scent of musty paper and crushed rocks—Seven Spire's unique aroma—filled my nose. I drew in a deep breath, and a thousand memories flickered through my mind.

I just hoped today would be filled with more good than bad.

Eventually, we wound up in a library on the first floor. Normally, this area was used for teas, recitals, and other gatherings, although today, it had been turned into a storage and staging area, and all sorts of performers crowded into the room.

The Scarlet Knights, the Blue Thorns, the Coral Vipers. I recognized the names, colors, costumes, and crests from when those gladiators had come to the Black Swan arena to battle Paloma and the others. Although today, the mood between the various troupes and performers was one of friendly rivalry, rather than the more serious and lucrative business of the arena fights.

Some of the acrobats practiced their flips, while others peered into the mirrors on the walls and applied their makeup. Magiers tossed balls of fire, ice, and more through the air at a dizzying pace, while wire walkers practiced their moves on the cables they had strung up at knee-high level between the bookcases. Conversations trilled through the air, and the powdery scents of makeup tickled my nose, along with dozens of different perfumes and colognes.

"Ah, Serilda, there you are." A familiar, snide voice cut through the chaos.

I looked over my shoulder. Felton was striding toward Serilda, his high-heeled boots snapping against the floor, his black hair and mustache waxed to a high gloss, and his red ledger dangling from his fingers.

I couldn't move away from Serilda without drawing attention to myself, so I ducked my head and pawed through a box of feather boas, as though I was looking for a certain one.

Felton stopped right beside me. He glanced at me for the briefest moment before turning to Serilda. "I was starting to wonder if you were going to show up."

"Really?" she murmured. "Why is that?"

Despite the fact that he was several inches shorter, Felton still somehow managed to look down his nose at her. "Because you're late. Queen Vasilia abhors tardiness of any sort, but especially today."

His chiding, superior tone made me grind my teeth. Down in the box, my hands fisted around the feather boas, and I was tempted to yank one out, wrap it around his neck, and squeeze the life right out of him. But I couldn't do that, since a few guards were stationed around the room, keeping an eye on everyone. If I attacked him now, I would never get close enough to issue the royal challenge to Vasilia. As much as I wanted to kill Felton, I forced myself to settle for strangling the feather boas, instead of him.

"My apologies," Serilda murmured.

Felton eyed her, wondering if she was being sincere, but he must have been satisfied that he had put her in her place, because he looked at the performers. "It seems like you're going to put on quite a show."

"Oh, we're going to give Vasilia and everyone else something that they'll never, ever forget."

Felton's eyes narrowed with suspicion, but Serilda gave him a bland smile in return.

After a few more seconds, he opened his red ledger. "I wanted to double-check the list of performers . . ."

Felton told Serilda that the Black Swan troupe would be the last to appear, right before Vasilia was crowned queen. Of course she would make us go last. No doubt after our performance, she would have us all herded out to the center of the lawn and executed.

Felton flipped over to a list of names. He glanced around and started making little check marks next to the names of the more prominent troupe members, including Cho and Sullivan.

My hands strangled the feather boas a little tighter. The bastard was making sure that everyone was here, just like he had before the massacre—

Felton turned to me. "And I take it that you're the gladiator who won that black-ring match that Queen Vasilia attended a few months ago?"

My mouth opened, but I couldn't risk speaking for fear that he might recognize my voice. If he realized who I was, Felton would bellow for the guards, and our mission would end right here and now.

Serilda stepped in between Felton and me. "Yes, she is the Black Swan. Why do you ask?"

He shrugged. "Queen Vasilia requested that you present only your best gladiators today."

My hands wrapped even tighter around the feather boas. Vasilia just wanted to make sure that I was slaughtered along with everyone else.

"Oh, this gladiator will do a special performance just for the queen's enjoyment," Serilda drawled.

Felton must have picked up on the double meaning in her words because he gave her another sharp look. My breath caught in my throat. If he suspected what we were really up to, none of us would leave this room alive. Felton's lips puckered, but he had no reason to argue, since Serilda was agreeing to his demands.

"Excellent." He made another little check mark in his ledger. "I'll leave you to prepare for the show. Until then."

Serilda dipped her head to him. "Until then."

Felton snapped his ledger shut, spun around on his bootheel, and left the library. I let out a quiet sigh of relief. We weren't caught.

Not yet.

We spent the next few hours in the staging room, making the final preparations for the show. The minutes flew by all too fast, and before I knew it, we were being summoned to the royal lawn as the final performance.

Under the watchful eye of several guards, we left the library and walked through the hallways. I had traveled this same route a thousand times before, and everything was eerily familiar and yet sickeningly different.

The last time I had been in the palace, Cordelia's red and gold colors and rising-sun crest had dominated. Now the hallways were adorned in Vasilia's garish fuchsia-and-gold palette and sword-and-laurels symbol, from the banners that hung down from the ceilings to the ribbons that wrapped around the columns to the yellow carpets underfoot, which were printed with a fuchsia paisley pattern that looked like bloodstains.

The guards led us to the final staging area, a large room that was just off the royal lawn. The troupe members milled around, warming up and making a few final adjustments to their costumes and props. My friends all gathered around me—Serilda, Cho, Xenia, Halvar, Bjarni, Paloma, and Sullivan.

"Does everyone know what they're supposed to do?" Serilda asked in a soft voice.

We all nodded. We had gone over the plan so many times that I could have recited it in my sleep.

Led by Cho as the ringmaster, the troupe members would perform their regular routines, while Serilda, Xenia, Halvar, Bjarni, Paloma, and Sullivan slipped into the crowd and discreetly took up positions around the lawn. Once the show ended, Halvar and Bjarni would make sure that the troupe made it over to the palace doors, and if things went badly, they would get people to safety. Serilda had also told Theroux, Aisha, and a few of her most trusted gladiators that we might run into trouble and to be on high alert, although she hadn't given them any details.

Once the troupe was out of the line of fire, I would step forward as the Black Swan gladiator. Everything would be up to me then, including whether we all lived or died.

I looked from one face to another, but none of my friends showed the faintest flicker of fear. Well, I couldn't really tell what Xenia was feeling, given the mask on her face, but the ogre on her neck winked at me.

So many emotions filled me, like a magier's lightning jolting through me over and over again, but the one that was stronger than all the others was my worry. Vasilia had beaten me so many times before. Could I really defeat her now, when it counted most? I didn't know.

Serilda must have sensed my concern, because she laid a hand on my shoulder. Her blue gaze locked with mine. "You're ready. You can do this, Evie. I know you can."

I shook my head. "But I've only been training for a few months. Vasilia has been planning for this her entire life."

"Planning is not winning," Serilda said in a soft voice. "Remember that."

She squeezed my shoulder, then stepped back. I looked at the others again, and they all nodded back at me. There was so much that I wanted to say to them, but the words were stuck in my throat, so I did the only other thing that I could to tell them how much they meant to me.

I made an elaborate flourish with my hand, then dropped down, executing the perfect Bellonan curtsy.

I held the curtsy far longer than was necessary, far longer than protocol dictated, before rising. One by one, the others bowed back to me. Serilda, Cho, Xenia, Halvar, Bjarni, Paloma, and Sullivan.

Tears pricked my eyes, but I cleared my throat and finally managed to say a few words. "To the end?"

"To the end," they all murmured in unison.

A knock sounded on the door, and a muffled voice said that it was time to take our places for the performances.

It was time—to finish this.

CHAPTER TWENTY-NINE

We left the staging room, walked down a hallway, and stepped out onto the royal lawn.

The area in front of the doors was open, just as it had been during the massacre. Several long buffet tables had been set up against the palace wall, and people filled plates with all sorts of delicacies, including bite-size chocolates that had been molded to look like tiny crowns. Beyond the tables, people milled together in groups, sharing the latest gossip. Servants moved through the throngs there, handing out more food and drinks.

My gaze swept over the crowd. Senators, guilders, noble lords and ladies. Vasilia had invited everyone who was anyone in Bellona to her coronation. Everyone was dressed in their finest formal suits and ball gowns and adorned with their most impressive jewels. The scents of beauty glamours and other magic radiated off their rings, necklaces, and bracelets, and I had to twitch my nose to hold back a sneeze at the strong aromas.

Next, I studied the guards. A couple of them were stationed at either end of the buffet tables, with a few more roaming through the crowd, but there weren't nearly as many as I had expected. Then again, why would Vasilia bother with dozens of guards? She thought that she had already won, that there was no one left to challenge her, and that the ceremony was a mere formality. And so did the guards, judging from their bored expressions. Some of them were even eating and drinking, instead of being alert to potential danger. The lack of guards gave me a tiny spark of hope. Maybe we could actually pull this off.

Finally, I focused on the centerpiece of the evening—the arena.

Gray wooden bleachers circled much of the lawn, creating an arena on the grass. The bleachers towered high into the air, each section topped with a fuchsia flag bearing Vasilia's gold sword-and-laurels crest. The sun had set while we had been waiting inside the palace, and the moon and stars were gleaming in the sky. A gray-blue twilight bathed the makeshift arena in a soft haze, but the summer air was still warm, despite the faint breeze.

Felton was standing at the wide gap between the bleachers that served as the arena entrance. He held up a hand, telling us to stop, since another troupe was still performing. He glanced at Serilda and Cho, making sure that they were about to walk into Vasilia's trap. Then he turned his gaze back to the other performers on the lawn.

And that's when the rest of my friends moved.

One by one, Xenia, Halvar, Bjarni, Paloma, and Sullivan slipped away and vanished into the crowd. I held my breath, wondering if Felton might notice them and wonder where they were going, especially Xenia, who was rather conspicuous in her ogre mask, but he was focused on what was happening on the lawn. So far, so good.

A few minutes later, the troupe on the lawn finished their performance to loud, hearty cheers. The performers waved to the crowd and hurried off the grass.

Our turn.

The Black Swan troupe was announced, and Serilda strutted out to the delight of the crowd. She smiled and waved until everyone quieted down, then turned and bowed to someone that I couldn't see, although I knew that it had to be Vasilia.

"We are honored to be here to usher in a new queen for Bellona," Serilda said in a loud voice. "One who will lead our kingdom to even greater prosperity."

The crowd buzzed, puzzled by her proclamation, since everyone knew that war with Andvari was coming, but Serilda smiled through the murmurs.

"But for now, we offer up this humble performance. Enjoy the show!"

The crowd roared, and Serilda waved to different sections of the arena. The familiar calliope music started, and Cho and the performers ran out onto the lawn. Serilda hurried over to where I was standing. Felton eyed her a moment, then turned his attention back to Cho and the others.

Serilda touched my shoulder, and I nodded, telling her that I was okay. She nodded back at me, then slipped into the crowd to take up her position.

The acrobats started their tumbling passes, the wire walkers climbed up to the platforms that had been erected around the lawn, and the gladiators gathered in their formations. Hearing the music and seeing the routines helped me to relax.

As long as I kept thinking of this as just another show, I was fine. Dwelling on the knowledge that mine was the most important part was what filled me with worry.

The Black Swan troupe gave a grand performance, pulling out all the stops. The acrobats tumbled faster and farther, the wire walkers did more flips and dips, and the gladiators slashed their swords and crashed their shields together harder and more violently. The show ran far longer than normal, although it seemed to fly by. All too soon, the acrobats stopped tumbling, the wire walkers climbed down, and the gladiators lowered their weapons.

The performers saluted the crowd a final time, then ran off the lawn. A low, roaring drumbeat filled the arena, and a spotlight fell on Cho, who was standing in the center of the grass.

"And now our main event," Cho called out, his voice booming like thunder. "The winner of our recent black-ring match. The Black Swan!"

The crowd roared, just as they had done in the arena when I had killed Emilie. I just hoped that they would still be cheering for me when this was all said and done. I drew in a deep breath, then slowly let it out. Then I pulled my sword out of its scabbard and focused on the feel of the cold tearstone in my hand, letting it steady me.

Showtime.

I strode out to the middle of the lawn where Cho was standing. He touched my shoulder, like Serilda had, then left the arena, leaving me to face the crowd alone.

The people in the bleachers yelled and cheered and clapped

and screamed at the top of their lungs. But they weren't screaming for me. Not really. No, they were cheering for the blood sport that I represented. But these were my people and this was our way, so I lifted my chin, squared my shoulders, and bowed to first one section of bleachers, then another.

I worked my way around the arena until I came to the final section, which was situated up against the wall, right where Cordelia had died and I had taken my forced swan dive. Instead of bleachers, a gray stone dais took up that section of the arena.

That's where Vasilia was.

She was sitting on the queen's throne, an enormous chair made of jagged pieces of tearstone that had been dug out of Seven Spire and fitted together centuries ago. Normally, the throne stayed in the grand ballroom, which also served as the throne room, but tonight, it had been placed in the center of the dais. The chunks of tearstone gleamed with a soft, muted light, their color shifting from lightest starry gray to darkest midnight-blue and back again. The shifting colors and gleams of light represented the Summer and Winter lines of the Blair royal family, as well as the everlasting strength of the Bellonan people.

I had never paid much attention to the throne before, but my gaze locked onto the top of the chair, and for the first time, I realized that the seven jagged pieces of midnight-blue tearstone were arranged there in a very deliberate way to create a familiar pattern.

A crown of shards.

"Frosted crowns made of icy shards." I whispered the fairy-tale rhyme, even though no one could hear me above the continued roar of the crowd.

I stared at the crest a moment longer, then focused on my cousin.

Vasilia was wearing black boots and leggings, along with a fuchsia tunic embroidered with her gold sword-and-laurels crest. A sword and a dagger were belted to her waist, and a small gold crown studded with pink-diamond laurel flowers rested on her head. It was the same crown she had worn to the black-ring match. I was surprised that she wasn't already wearing the queen's crown, but she was probably saving that moment for the official coronation.

I had been expecting her to wear something far more formal, but the casual outfit made sense. Vasilia wouldn't want to dirty up a ball gown on the off chance that she had to chase down and kill the troupe members when she ordered the guards to massacre us. Perhaps she was even planning to battle Serilda and Cho herself, just as she had killed her mother and sister.

Despite her casual clothes and modest crown, Vasilia looked stunningly beautiful. Her hair hung in loose waves around her shoulders, each strand gleaming as though it was made of polished gold, and her gray-blue eyes were bright and luminous. Murderous power agreed with her. But even more than that, she seemed genuinely *happy*, and the wide smile that stretched across her face only added to her beauty. She should be happy, ecstatic even. She was on the verge of getting everything she'd ever wanted.

And she wasn't alone.

Nox was lounging in a smaller, cushioned chair next to her, looking as handsome as ever with his golden hair and tailored tunic. He must have been a bit bored, since he signaled a serving girl to climb up onto the dais and refill his wineglass. Nox looked the girl up and down before winking at her. The girl tittered and rushed off the dais, but Nox followed her movements, a hungry expression on his face.

Vasilia didn't seem to notice his wandering eye, but Maeven did. She was sitting on his other side, and she narrowed her eyes at him in a clear warning. Nox shrugged and sipped his wine. He wasn't concerned if Vasilia caught him ogling anyone.

Maeven's lips pressed together, but she turned her attention back to the arena. She was dressed in a glittering gown that was the same midnight-purple as the amethyst choker that ringed her neck. Her blond hair was sleeked back into its usual bun, and she looked far more regal and queenly than Vasilia did, despite the fact that the younger woman was the one wearing the crown. Then again, if Xenia was right, Maeven was a royal too, albeit a bastard like Sullivan was.

One more person was on the dais, but he wasn't sitting in relaxed, luxe comfort. This man was standing stiff and tall in a metal cage that was lined with hundreds of thin, needlelike spikes. He couldn't move, not even an inch, and he couldn't relax, not even for a second, or the spikes would dig into his skin. It was a cruel, prolonged torture. Bruises covered his face, and a dirty, blood-crusted red tunic hung in tatters from his thin frame, as though he had been wearing the garment since the last time I had seen him here all those months ago.

Captain Auster.

I shouldn't have been surprised that he was still alive. Of course Vasilia would wait until tonight to execute him. She would want to make a spectacle of him too.

Maeven stared at me, and her lips puckered, as though she was wondering why I was so interested in Auster. I couldn't afford for her to recognize me, so as much as it pained me, I dropped into a low bow in front of Vasilia.

I held the bow as long as was necessary, and not a moment longer, just as Serilda had done, then straightened back up. Vasilia fluttered her hand, graciously telling me to proceed.

I waited for the music to start, feeling vulnerable and exposed, since I wasn't carrying my shield or wearing my dagger on my belt. Only a sword was required for this routine, and Serilda had thought that it would look suspicious if I took any other weapons into the arena. So I tightened my grip on my sword, hoping that it would be enough, hoping that *I* would be enough.

The music blared to life, and I snapped up my sword and moved through the gladiator drills that Sullivan and Serilda had spent so many long hours teaching me. The things that had seemed so impossibly hard just a few months ago were as easy as breathing now, and I executed every single position with perfect, beautiful, fluid precision.

My gaze cut from one section of the arena to the next, searching for my friends. Cho was standing next to Felton, while Sullivan and Paloma had stationed themselves behind a group of guards. Halvar and Bjarni were standing in front of the troupe members, whom they had shepherded back to the palace doors. Serilda and Xenia had discreetly taken up positions behind the guards on either side of the royal dais. Everything was going according to plan. Now the rest was up to me.

I finished the drills, the last strains of the music faded away, and another hearty round of applause rang out. I bowed to each section of bleachers, then faced the dais again. Everything was the same as before. Vasilia smiling, Nox guzzling

wine, Maeven frowning at me, Auster standing at forced attention inside his cage.

Now or never.

I pulled the memory stone out of my pocket. I could feel and
smell the magic flowing through the opal, and I kept a careful hold on my own immunity, lest I accidentally snuff out the
memory stone and the shocking truth that it contained.

The applause finally died down, but I stayed in the middle
of the arena.

"I have a special treat for everyone," I called out. "Something you will all want to see, especially the woman who would
be our queen."

I held the memory stone up where everyone could see it.
Then I angled the opal out toward the empty lawn and tapped
on the stone three times.

The opal started glowing with a pure white light, as did the
blue, red, green, and purple flecks in the surface. The flecks
quickly attached themselves to the smooth lawn and coalesced
into one solid image—my face.

From there, the massacre played out as it had in real life.
Screams and shouts filled the air, but they weren't from the
crowd this time. Now the cries of everyone who had died that
day rang out instead. Eventually, my hand closed over the
stone, and the images vanished. I tapped on the stone again
three times to deactivate its magic, then tossed it over to Cho
for safekeeping.

A stunned silence fell over the crowd, and everyone stared
at Vasilia, who was just as shocked. Even Nox and Maeven
seemed startled. The only one who was remotely happy was
Captain Auster, who was beaming inside his cage.

Vasilia shot up off the throne. Anger and embarrassment

mottled her cheeks, and a bit of white lightning crackled on her fingertips, telling me how pissed she was.

"What is the meaning of this?" she hissed.

"To tell everyone the truth," I called out. "To show them what really happened during the royal massacre."

Vasilia opened her mouth, but I cut her off before she could deny all the evil things she'd done.

"Captain Auster and the Andvarians didn't assassinate Queen Cordelia and the other Blairs. It was Vasilia and Nox and Maeven and Felton." I stabbed my finger at each one of them in turn. "And if you crown Vasilia queen tonight, then she will lead you into a false war against a kingdom and a people who have done nothing wrong. She will lead you to ruin. And for what? Nothing but her own greed and ambition."

Everyone looked from me to Vasilia and back again, and uneasy murmurs rippled through the crowd. Vasilia realized that she was losing control of the situation, even more so than she already had, and she stalked forward to the edge of the dais, even more lightning crackling on her fingers.

"What trickery is this?" she demanded. "And who are *you* to say what happened? All you have is a pretty rock. Everyone knows that magic can be manipulated, designed to show whatever we want."

"I know what happened because I was there."

Vasilia sucked in a breath, and more uneasy murmurs sounded. Her gaze locked onto me, and I could tell that she was thinking back to that day, trying to figure out who I was and how I could have possibly survived. I waited for recognition to dawn in her eyes, but it never came. Even now Vasilia still didn't see me. Well, she would realize her mistake soon enough.

I drew the black swan mask up over my face and head and tossed it onto the grass. I looked at the crowd, turning this way and that, and letting them stare at me. Most of the people in the bleachers frowned, not recognizing me any more than Vasilia had, but one voice rose up.

"That's Lady Everleigh Blair!" a man called out.

I hid my grin. That was Cho, doing his part and using his booming voice to full effect.

I looked at Vasilia again. She stared at me for several seconds, blinking and blinking, as if she couldn't believe that I was still alive, as if she were desperately hoping that her eyes were playing tricks on her. But they weren't, and her face quickly hardened into a tight mask of barely restrained rage, and more lightning flashed on her fingertips. She wanted to raise her hands and blast me into oblivion with it, just as she had tried to all those months ago.

"My name is Lady Everleigh Saffira Winter Blair," I called out. "And I hereby issue a royal challenge to you, Vasilia Victoria Summer Blair. A challenge to determine who will be queen of Bellona. I challenge you to a fight to the death."

CHAPTER THIRTY

Shocked gasps rippled through the crowd, but I tuned them out and focused on Vasilia.

I had spent the last fifteen years watching her, and I could tell the exact instant when she realized how thoroughly I had fucked up her big moment. Her eyes burned, more anger stained her cheeks, and lightning crackled all around her clenched fists. I smiled in the face of her rage. Now the bitch knew exactly how I had felt all these long years here.

By this point, everyone in the arena was on their feet, including Nox and Maeven on the dais.

"Guards!" Maeven called out. "Kill that woman! Kill the imposter!"

I snapped up my sword, bracing for a fight.

But it never came.

Serilda and Xenia stepped up and rammed their swords into the backs of the guards that Maeven had ordered to attack me. Paloma and Sullivan did the same to the guards who threatened me from the other side of the arena. Halvar and Bjarni took out the guards closest to the troupe members, while Cho held a dagger to Felton's throat.

Still more guards advanced on the troupe members, but Theroux, Aisha, and the gladiators raised their swords, daggers, spears, and shields and stepped up to meet them. The gladiators easily cut down the guards who dared to attack them, then moved into a tight circle, shielding the acrobats, wire walkers, and other troupe members, and protecting their own, like Serilda had asked them to.

I had once thought that I could never hurt Vasilia, not even if I'd had an army at my disposal. I hadn't realized back then that I didn't need an army.

All I needed was a gladiator troupe.

Our plan worked perfectly. In less than three minutes, my friends and the gladiators had dispatched more than three dozen guards, something that made the others hesitate.

"What are you waiting for?" Maeven yelled in frustration. "Kill her! Now!"

The guards looked from the gladiators to me and back again, but they didn't move to attack anyone else. They had seen how easily their compatriots had been killed, and they didn't want to be next.

"Fine," Maeven hissed. "I'll do it myself."

A ball of purple lightning popped into her hand, but Xenia stepped in front of the dais and ripped the ogre mask off her face.

"It's Lady Xenia!" Once again, Cho's voice rang out, causing more shocked whispers to ripple through the crowd.

Maeven's eyes widened with surprise. My coming back from the dead was disturbing enough, but she hadn't expected Xenia to be here too.

Xenia smiled, showing the magier the sharp jagged teeth that were suddenly protruding from her mouth. Xenia hadn't fully morphed, but she could easily do that and attack Maeven before the magier managed to throw her lightning at me.

"You'll have to go through me to get to her," Xenia hissed. "And I still owe you for last time."

Maeven's eyes narrowed with fury, but she lowered her hand to her side, although that purple lightning kept crackling on her fingertips, waiting to be used.

Since Maeven was standing down, at least for now, Vasilia turned her attention back to me.

"How did you survive?" she demanded.

"You mean after you blasted me off the side of the palace with your lightning?"

More gasps and whispers surged through the crowd, along with some low, angry mutters. The people weren't liking these ugly revelations about their new queen.

I shrugged. "Your lightning threw me clear of the rocks and tossed me out into the middle of the river. The current carried me downstream, but I managed to get to shore. You really should have sent Nox and his men to check and make sure that I had drowned."

Vasilia glared at Nox, who shrugged. She glared at him a moment longer, then turned back to me.

"So you survived. So you're here. So what?" she sneered. "Do you really think that you and your friends are going to kill me? I'll burn you all to a crisp, every last one of you, and anyone else who gets in my way."

Even more lightning crackled around her fists, and uneasy murmurs surged through the crowd.

"My friends aren't going to kill you—*I* am."

Vasilia sneered at me again. "And how are you going to do that, Everleigh? You don't even have any real magic."

"Seems like your hearing isn't as nearly sharp as your tongue is," I mocked her. "Didn't you hear me before? I issued a royal challenge to you."

"So what?"

"So you either fight me here and now, or you forfeit the throne."

"That's ridiculous!" Vasilia hissed. "*I* am the queen, and no one is going to take the throne away from *me*. Especially not *you*."

I shrugged again. "It's not ridiculous. It's the *law*. You should have paid more attention in history class."

Vasilia opened her mouth to insult me again, but I turned away from her and held my arms out to my sides, taking my case to the crowd.

"Bellona was founded by a gladiator," I called out. "And we still love our gladiators and their blood sport to this day. So let's settle this like two gladiators would—in a fight to the death. What do you say? Don't you want to see which one of us is truly strong enough to be your queen?"

I hadn't planned the speech, but it was far more effective than I'd expected. Everyone yelled, screamed, and whistled so loud that the bleachers shook from the thunderous roar. The commotion went on and on until I lowered my hands to my sides and faced Vasilia again. Harsh whispers rang out, telling people to quiet down, and a heavy, expectant silence dropped over the arena again.

"The people have spoken," I said. "Once again, I challenge you to a black-ring match. Right here, right now."

Vasilia stared at me for several seconds. Then she started laughing.

Her laughter rang out across the lawn, and the light peals echoed in my ears the same way they had countless times before. I ground my teeth, but Vasilia saw the anger, frustration, and old memories in my eyes, which only made her laugh even louder. Several people in the crowd snickered as well.

Finally, she quit laughing. "You're actually serious, aren't you?" A smile stretched across her face. "*You* really want to fight *me* in a black-ring match for the right to be queen? You should just go ahead and cut your own throat. It would be far more merciful than what I'll do to you."

Maeven and Nox both sidled closer to her, and Maeven opened her mouth, probably to advise Vasilia to reject my offer and once again order the guards to murder me. But Vasilia snapped up her hand, cutting off the other woman.

"If Everleigh wants to challenge me, then I accept," she called out. "My dear cousin is right about one thing. We'll see who is strong enough to be queen."

The crowd roared in response.

Vasilia smirked at me, then turned and started speaking to Maeven and Nox. My cousin obviously thought that she could beat me, but I wouldn't put it past her to try to cheat. She was probably telling Maeven and Nox to kill me if they got the chance, despite the fact that Serilda and Xenia were still watching them.

I held my position in the middle of the lawn, my sword still in my hand. One by one, I looked at my friends around the arena. Halvar, Bjarni, Theroux, Aisha, and the gladiators protecting the troupe members. Paloma and Sullivan watching the guards. Cho restraining Felton. Serilda and Xenia still close to the dais, keeping an eye on Maeven and Nox. They all nodded, once again showing their confidence in me.

Now it was time for me to truly earn that trust.

I thought Vasilia might drag out the process, but less than two minutes later, she stepped off the dais, strode out onto the lawn, and stopped in front of me, much to the delight of the cheering crowd. She drew her sword and twirled it around in her hand. I did the same thing with my weapon, matching her move for move.

Vasilia sneered at me again. "Looks like someone has been training with Serilda. Do you really think that a couple of months with that flimsy little sword is going to let you beat me?"

I shook my head. "I haven't been training for just a few months. I've been battling you my entire life, ever since we were kids."

Vasilia laughed again. "It's not much of a battle when you always lose, Everleigh."

"You might be right about that. But even if I lose today, I've still won."

"How so?"

"I exposed you for what you really are—a coldhearted bitch who doesn't care about anything but her own ambition. The people aren't going to adore you. Not anymore. Not when they know that you're planning to plunge them into war against an innocent kingdom. Even if you kill me, you'll never win with them. I've ruined your name, your reputation. I've ruined *you*. Do you really think that any of these people are going to believe a word you say? Do you really think that any of them are going to cheer for you ever again?"

Vasilia looked at the people gathered in the bleachers and

all around the lawn. The senators, the guilders, the noble lords and ladies. The palace servants. The remaining guards. Before, they had stared at her with a combination of admiration and envy. Now, disgust and derision filled their faces.

Vasilia frowned, as if it had never occurred to her that people would treat her any differently after they learned the truth. But the more she glanced around, the more she realized that she had utterly, completely lost them.

"Let's go, Evie!" Paloma yelled, breaking the silence. "Kick her royal ass!"

Once that first cheer rang out, more and more sounded, each one louder than the last. Vasilia looked confused and even a little lost. For the first time in her life, the crown princess wasn't everyone's favorite. I was—and it *infuriated* her.

Anger mottled her cheeks, and her lips drew back into a snarl. Her eyes narrowed to slits, and her fingers clenched even tighter around the hilt of her sword. I had been watching Vasilia for a long, long time, and I knew exactly what was coming next.

With a loud scream, Vasilia snapped up her sword and charged at me.

Vasilia raised her sword high and brought it down, trying to kill me with that first blow.

And she almost succeeded.

I had made her far angrier than I'd expected, and she put all her strength into that initial strike. But I brought my own sword up, and I managed to block her blow. We stood there in the middle of the lawn, muscles straining, seesawing back and forth. Our swords scraped and screeched together in a low, sinister chorus as each one of us tried to get the advantage.

"You know what, cousin? I'm glad that you're still alive," Vasilia snarled. "I'm going to enjoy killing you in front of your friends and adoring fans."

"Funny. I was going to say the same thing about you," I hissed back.

Vasilia snarled again and threw me back, and we started circling around and around, each of us studying the other. I blocked out everything else. The crowd's screams. My friends' tense faces. Maeven and Nox still standing on the dais, along with Captain Auster in his spiked cage. I blocked it all out and focused on Vasilia.

For the first time in a long, long time, I went on the offensive, attacking Vasilia and trying to cut through her defense. She blocked every one of my blows and then launched her own counterattacks, slashing her sword at me over and over again. I parried her blows as easily as she had thwarted mine, and our duel, our dance, continued.

The longer the fight raged on, the more Vasilia slowly started to wear down. She was a fine warrior who had spent years perfecting her skills, but she hadn't spent all day, every day, training like I had for the last several weeks. Serilda hadn't just been teaching me to fight—she had also been building up my strength and endurance for this moment.

Vasilia was usually able to end a fight in a few quick moves, and she didn't know what to do when I kept matching her blow for blow. Finally, her defenses slipped, and I took advantage. I stepped forward and knocked her sword out of her hand, sending it flying across the lawn like an oversize arrow. Vasilia watched the sword sail away, her eyes widening in surprise.

And I saw something else in her gaze, something that I had never seen before.

Fear.

But she recovered quickly. I slashed my sword through the air, trying to end the fight, but she threw herself forward and rolled across the lawn as nimbly one of the troupe acrobats, although she lost her gold crown in the process. I still managed to slice my blade across her arm, causing her to let out a surprised shriek, but she kept going.

Vasilia scooped her sword from the grass and came up into a low crouch. She glanced down at the blood running down her left bicep and dripping onto the lawn. She blanched a little, but the crowd had an entirely different reaction.

They cheered even louder.

Fear sparked in her eyes again, a little stronger and brighter than before, but she growled and went on the offensive.

Vasilia surged to her feet and banged her sword into mine over and over again, trying to break through my defenses. And she finally did. The edge of her blade bit into my left forearm, making me hiss with pain. Blood slid down my arm and dripped onto the lawn, just like hers was still doing. Once again, the crowd roared in response. They might have turned against Vasilia, but they still wanted to see a bloody good match, in every sense of the words.

"Do you hear that?" Vasilia yelled over the raucous cheers. "They want me to kill you. They're *begging* me to kill you. You haven't won anything, Everleigh. Not one damn thing!"

I didn't waste precious breath responding to her taunt. Instead, I whirled around, brought my sword up, and attacked her again.

The wound on my arm kept dripping blood, but I ignored

the stinging pain and kept fighting. Vasilia ignored her injury as well, and we battled on. Our swords crashed together over and over again, although the cheers, yells, screams, and whistles drowned out the harsh clangs.

But the longer the fight dragged on, the more certain I was that I was going to win.

For the first time since I'd come to the palace all those years ago, Vasilia actually looked a bit disheveled. Blood, grass, and dirt covered her fine clothes, exertion stained her cheeks a bright red, and sweat dripped down the sides of her face and soaked into her now-limp blond hair. She kept gulping down breath after breath, as though she couldn't get enough air into her lungs, and perhaps worst of all, she'd lost her pretty crown, which was now lying somewhere in the grass.

I was a dirty, bloody, sweaty mess, just like she was, but my breathing was still smooth and even, thanks to my training with Serilda and the others. So I pressed my advantage, going through the steps that I knew so well now. That phantom music had been playing in my mind the whole time that we had been fighting, but the beat, the tempo, quickened, and I upped my pace, my attacks, to match it. I knew that the music, the moves, were building to the grand finale of the piece—Vasilia's death.

Vasilia kept gulping down breath after breath, but she couldn't keep up with the brutal pace that I set, and she was barely managing to block my attacks. Less than two minutes later, I knocked her sword out of her hand for the second time.

Gasps surged through the crowd, and Vasilia and I both stopped, just for a moment, to watch the sword. This time, the weapon sailed even farther across the lawn than it had before, too far away for Vasilia to grab it before I cut her down from behind. She knew it too, and she snarled and backed away. My resolve hardened, and I surged forward, determined to finally end this—

And that's when Vasilia unleashed her magic.

Lightning flashed on her fingertips, and she reared her hand back and then snapped it forward, tossing a white bolt of magic at me. I barely had time to throw myself down to the ground and roll out of the way. Even though I avoided the blast, I could still feel and smell the sharp sizzle of it streaking through the air.

The bolt zinged across the arena, and people screamed as it hit one of the poles planted in the lawn, shearing the wood in two and causing the flag on the top to topple to the ground. This flag featured Vasilia's fuchsia colors and sword-and-laurels crest, and the fabric smoked from where her magic had scorched it.

I came up into a low crouch, my sword still clutched in my hand.

Vasilia sneered at me, even as more lightning crackled in her palm. The glow of her power matched the murderous rage gleaming in her eyes. "I don't need a weapon to kill you, Everleigh. I can just do it with my magic."

She reared back and tossed another bolt of lightning at me. Once again, I rolled out of the way, avoiding it. This time, the bolt hit the base of one of the bleachers, making the wood smolder. The people sitting in that section screamed in surprise and started leaping out of their seats and off the sides of the benches, trying to get to safety.

Vasilia threw back her head and laughed. She wanted to kill me so badly that she didn't care if her lightning fried the crowd as well. I hadn't wanted the troupe members to get hurt, but I hadn't realized that everyone else would be in danger too. There was only one way to end the fight now.

I had to let her hit me with her lightning.

I didn't know if I could survive it a second time, given how angry she was. Those last two blasts had been much stronger than what she had used on me during the massacre. But I couldn't let Vasilia hurt anyone else, especially not the people I was supposed to protect. So I got back up onto my feet and moved so that I was standing in front of her. Still holding on to my sword, I held my arms out wide, just as I had done when I had first addressed the crowd. Everyone immediately quieted down, although I could still hear the stamp of footsteps as people continued to leave the smoldering bleacher.

"Go ahead. Hit me with your magic. Blast me into oblivion if you think you can."

Vasilia let out a loud, mocking laugh. "Do you really think that you can survive my lightning? You might have gotten lucky once, but you've grown quite arrogant if you think that you can walk away from it a second time."

"You want to kill someone, then kill me," I called out. "Leave everyone else alone. They don't have anything to do with you and me. They never have."

Vasilia glanced around at the crowd, which had gone utterly, eerily still and silent. Her mouth twisted with disgust. "They're all a bunch of fools. Cheering for you. Thinking that *you* can beat *me*. Thinking that *they* can stand against *me*. I'll kill you, and then I'll show them exactly who their queen is."

Everyone heard her threats. A few folks gasped, but people remained in their seats. They were too afraid to move right now for fear of drawing her attention and wrath.

I raised my arms even higher. "I'm not going to stop you. Go ahead, cousin. I dare you."

If there was one thing that Vasilia could never, ever refuse, it was a dare. Even when we were kids, it was the one way that I always knew that I could still get under her skin. Vasilia sneered at me a final time, then reared back and threw her lightning at me.

I stood there and let the bolt hit me square in the chest.

For a moment, my vision went completely white, as though I were standing in the middle of Vasilia's lightning, watching it flicker all around me. Then her magic hit me, and I started screaming.

And I couldn't stop.

Vasilia had hit me with her lightning before, when she had knocked me over the wall and into the river, but that had just been a small, brief sting of her power. But this—this was an all-out, full-frontal assault by a powerful magier.

That first bolt knocked me down to the ground. Once again, I was lying flat on my back with my opponent looming over me, and once again, there was nothing that I could do to block the attack that I knew was coming next.

Vasilia stepped forward and hit me with another bolt of lightning. And then another, and then another, until I felt like I was in the center of a storm cloud. The lightning zipped up my arms, across my chest, and down my legs, before rushing back in the opposite direction. My fingers spasmed, my toes curled, and my entire body jerked and flailed. I opened my mouth to scream again, and the lightning sizzled down my throat and burned my lungs.

Through the blasts, I could see Vasilia towering over me, smiling wide. I had been wrong before. She hadn't been happy merely sitting on the throne. Not really, not completely. No, this, killing me, this was what made her truly *happy*.

The sight of her smug face made my own cold rage rise up in response.

I had always pushed down the emotion, along with my immunity. It had been easier, safer, that way. But things were not easy right now, and they definitely weren't safe. And I didn't want them to be. Not anymore. For the first time, I wanted Vasilia—and everyone else—to see exactly how strong and powerful I was.

So I reached for the one thing that could save me—my immunity.

I ignored the burning pain pulsing through my body and focused on my own strength, my own power. I reached deep down inside myself, bringing all that cold rage up to the surface, along with my immunity. I imagined wrapping that power around my fists, like it was an icy, unbreakable shield covering both my hands. Then, when I had a good grip on my magic, I used that power in my fists to start pounding away at the lightning, punching it apart piece by piece, even though my hands weren't actually moving.

I punched away the lightning zinging through my lungs, and my breathing became easier. I hammered at the bolts blasting my arms and legs, and my body quit flailing. I drove through the stinging tendrils wrapping around my head, and my vision cleared.

Oh, the lightning was still sparking, snapping, and crackling all around me, but it wasn't actually *touching* me anymore, thanks to my immunity. Now came the hard part.

Finally finishing this.

I looked past the lightning at Vasilia, who was still looming over me, pouring all her magic and energy into killing me. I let the hate filling her eyes fuel my rage.

Still holding on to my immunity, I rolled over onto my knees. My sword had slipped from my fingers when I had hit the ground, and I crawled over to it and wrapped my hand around the hilt. Serilda was right. The tearstone deflected some of Vasilia's magic, and the feel of the sword in my hand bolstered my own immunity and further steadied me, as did Alvis's bracelet, which was still on my wrist. Using the weapon as a crutch, I stabbed the blade into the ground and pushed myself to my feet.

I was dimly aware of the crowd gasping in surprise, but I tuned out the noise. With every move I made, Vasilia's lightning threatened to break through the cold, protective shield of my power, and it was all that I could do to push back against her magic.

Slowly, very, very slowly, I turned around and faced her again. Vasilia snarled and blasted me with even more of her lightning, but I ground my teeth, dug my boots into the grass, and remained upright.

Then, when I felt steady enough, I started walking toward her.

One step, then two, then three. My boots dragged through the grass, along with the dirt underneath, but I managed to put one foot in front of the other, even though she was still blasting me with magic the whole time. Paloma was right. It was the most difficult thing I had ever done, and with every step, I was aware of Vasilia's lightning crashing into my body, trying to break through the icy shield of my immunity and fry me alive.

But I didn't let it.

I didn't give in to her as I had so many times before, and I didn't let my magic waver, not even for an instant. This time, I kept right on fighting the way that I had wanted to for so long.

I shuffled closer to Vasilia. She blinked in surprise, and more fear flashed in her gaze, even as the lightning streamed out of her fingers. She snarled and hit me with another blast, forcing me to stop. But my immunity snuffed out her power, and I walked on.

Vasilia backed up, still throwing lightning at me, but I followed her, every single step. Finally, she let out a loud, frustrated scream, drew both her hands back, and hit me with every single shred of magic that she had left. But my immunity snuffed out this blast like it had all the others, and I kept creeping toward her.

Desperate, Vasilia tried to call up another bolt of lightning, but only a few weak sparks crackled on her fingertips. She was out of strength, out of magic. She sucked in a shocked breath, but she slowly lowered her hands to her sides.

"Why—why aren't you dead?" she whispered.

"Do you remember the day of my testing? When the magier said that I didn't have any magic? When you told me that I was useless and slammed your playroom door in my face?"

Confusion filled her features. "What does that have to do with anything?"

I moved even closer to her, lowering my voice so that only she could hear it. "Because the magier was wrong, and so were you. I'm immune to magic. I always have been."

Her eyes narrowed. "It doesn't matter. You're still useless, Everleigh. Your precious immunity won't save you from this."

She reached for the dagger belted to her waist, her last line of defense, her last resort. Her desperate action might have worked against anyone else, but I had studied my cousin's treachery for a long, long time, so I was expecting the trick, and I didn't give her the chance to hurt me again.

I snapped up my sword and buried it in her heart.

Vasilia screamed then, screamed with all the life and rage that she had left. I looked into her eyes and twisted the blade in deeper.

"Do you remember what you told Captain Auster after the massacre?" I asked. "Because I've thought about it a lot over these past few months."

Vasilia stared back at me, pain and tears filling her gray-blue eyes—eyes that were so much like mine.

"Traitors always pay for their sins," I hissed.

I twisted the blade in deeper still. Vasilia gasped, and an agonized cry escaped her lips, along with a thin trickle of blood. She looked at me a moment longer, then toppled over onto the lawn with my sword still buried in her heart.

The queen was dead.

Again.

CHAPTER THIRTY-ONE

I stared at Vasilia a moment longer, then reached down and yanked my sword out of her chest.

A few people in the crowd gasped, and a tense, heavy silence fell over the lawn again. I held my sword up high where everyone could see it, as well as Vasilia's blood sliding down the blade and dripping onto me. Then I twirled the weapon around in my hand and lowered it to my side.

I looked at the bleachers, my gaze moving from one section to the next. Every single person was on their feet and staring at me, a mixture of horror, fear, and admiration filling their faces. The queen's coronation had not gone how they had anticipated. Not at all.

"I might not be the queen that you expected, that you wanted," I said. "But I'm the one you've got. If anyone else wants to challenge me for the throne, speak up."

No one said a word, and that tense, heavy silence stretched on and on. But it was finally broken by a most surprising source.

Maeven.

She stepped to the front of the dais and started clapping. Nox looked at her like she was mad. So did everyone else.

"Bravo." She tilted her head to me. "Truly. Well done, Queen Everleigh."

I couldn't tell whether she was mocking me or not. "Why are you congratulating me? Your puppet queen is dead. There will be no war with Andvari now."

"We'll see about that. This is far from over. Besides, there are other ways to get what we want."

"And what do you want?"

She gave me a thin smile. "What we've always wanted—everything."

Her words sent a chill through me. Out of the corner of my eye, I could see Serilda and Xenia creeping closer to the dais, ready to attack Maeven and Nox.

Maeven spotted them too, and purple lightning sparked to life on her fingertips, far more powerful than what Vasilia had thrown at me. Serilda and Xenia stopped and looked at me. I shook my head. I didn't know what Maeven was up to, but I didn't want them to get hurt.

"You're not the first Winter queen that I've battled," Maeven said. "But you *will* be the last. And when you are dead, Bellona will belong to Morta, as will the rest of the continent. Until we meet again, Queen Everleigh."

Maeven clapped her hands together. Lightning erupted, along with thick clouds of dark purple smoke that obscured the entire dais. People screamed in fear and confusion. I raised my hand against the bright glare and rushed forward, even though I couldn't see where I was going.

Several seconds later, the glare faded, and the smoke wisped away. The dais was empty, except for Captain Auster, who was still trapped in his spiked cage.

Maeven was gone, and so was Nox.

My head snapped back and forth, but I didn't see them anywhere. Serilda and Xenia circled all around the dais and then rushed across the lawn, but a few minutes later, they returned and shook their heads, telling me that Maeven and Nox had escaped.

Rage surged through me, and I wanted nothing more than to pound my sword into the dirt. But the crowd had finally calmed down, and everyone was staring at me again. I stood in front of the dais, shifting on my feet, not sure what I was supposed to do now. I had been so focused on killing Vasilia that I hadn't thought about what would happen after that.

But Sullivan had.

The magier crossed the lawn, his long gray coat swirling around his body. He stopped in front of me, then went down on one knee. Sullivan tilted his head up, his blue eyes warm in his face, and held his hand out to me.

"Your people are waiting for their new queen to take her rightful seat. Please, let me do the honor of escorting you." His mouth curved up into a small grin. "Highness."

I nodded and took his hand in mine. Sullivan rose to his feet and escorted me over to the dais. I thought he would walk all the way up there with me, but he stopped at the bottom of the steps. He bowed low to me in the Andvarian style, with his fist pressed to his heart, then straightened up. I grinned back at him. Then, before I could think too much about what I was doing, I climbed up the steps and strode out to the middle of the dais.

I stared at the throne, my gaze focused on those seven shards that made up the crown at the top of the chair.

You have to live, Cordelia's voice whispered in my mind. *You have to survive, no matter what you have to do, no matter who you have to cheat and hurt and kill, no matter what the cost is to your heart and soul. Do you hear me, Everleigh? You have to live. You have to protect Bellona. Promise me you'll do that.*

"I promise," I whispered, and hoped that she could hear me, wherever she was.

I stared at the crown a moment longer, then turned and faced the crowd again. Everyone was still quiet and on their feet. All those faces staring back at me was a bit overwhelming, so I focused on my friends.

Halvar and Bjarni, grinning wide and standing in front of Theroux, Aisha, and the other Black Swan troupe members, who had looks of awe and confusion on their faces. Paloma, also smiling, even as she hefted her spiked mace a little higher on her shoulder. Cho, beaming at me, his dagger still up against Felton's throat. Xenia, who had released Captain Auster from his spiked cage and was helping him stand upright. Sullivan standing at the end of the dais, his gaze steady on mine.

And finally Serilda, also standing at the end of the dais, a satisfied look on her face and the gleam of tears in her eyes. I wondered what she was seeing right now, what possibilities, good and bad, were flashing before her. Part of me didn't want to know.

I wouldn't have made it this far, I wouldn't be here tonight, without all of them. Serilda had been right when she said that my rage made me strong, but so did my friends. I wasn't going to forget that—ever.

"Evie!" Paloma called out, and stabbed her spiked mace into the air. "Queen Evie! Long live the queen!"

The rest of the crowd quickly took up her *Evie! Evie! Evie!* chant, and soon, my ears were ringing with the noise. It was something that I had never thought I would hear, that I had never wanted to hear, but I was the only one left, and I would do my duty, just as the rest of the Blairs, just as the rest of my family, had done.

To the end.

I raised my bloody sword high, then swept it down in a flourish and executed the perfect Bellonan curtsy. That really made the crowd roar.

I held the curtsy far longer than necessary, showing them the same respect they were showing me. Then I straightened up, turned around, and sat down on the throne, with my sword lying across my lap.

The people kept yelling, cheering, clapping, and whistling, the sounds louder and stronger than ever before. In the center of the arena, Vasilia's body lay crumpled on the ground, her bloody hand stretched out toward her golden crown, which was resting on the grass beside her. I stared at her a moment longer, then focused on the crowd again.

Everyone was still cheering, but some people were just going through the motions of celebrating, and I could already see the calculation creeping into the faces of certain noble lords and ladies as they thought about how my killing Vasilia and taking the throne would impact them.

Maeven was right. This was far from over. It was just beginning. Maeven, Nox, Felton, and Morta weren't my only enemies. There would be many more, both abroad and here at home.

Tonight, I would enjoy this moment and everything that I

had won. I would squeeze every last drop of pleasure and happiness from it that I could and tuck them away in my heart to always remember. Then, tomorrow, I would get started on the hard, dirty work of securing my throne, weeding the turncoats out of Seven Spire, and repairing relations with Andvari.

I was a Bellonan, and I was just as good at playing the long game as everyone else. And through it all, I would keep one thing in mind, the most important thing that Vasilia had ever taught me, and perhaps the one thing that would keep me alive through all the coming trials and tribulations.

Someone *always* wanted to kill the queen.

Read on for a sneak peek at the

next thrilling installment in

Jennifer Estep's

Crown of Shards series!

PROTECT THE PRINCE

Coming in 2019

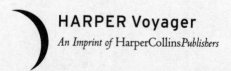

HARPER Voyager
An Imprint of HarperCollins*Publishers*

chapter one

Pretty, pretty princes,
All in a row.
Who will they marry?
Where will they go?

This girl, that girl,
Maid, lady, queen.
Who snares the princes' hearts
Remains to be seen.

—ANDVARIAN COURT SONG

The day of the first assassination attempt started out like any other.

With me girding myself for battle.

I perched stiffly in a chair in front of a vanity table that took up the corner of the room. The long, rectangular table was made of the blackest ebony and adorned with all sorts of drawers and cubbyholes, along with crystal knobs that glinted at me like mocking eyes.

The morning sun slipped in past the white lace curtains and highlighted the tabletop, which featured carvings of gladiators clutching swords, shields, and daggers. I looked down at the figures, which were embossed with bits of metal, along with tiny jewels. They too seemed to stare at and mock me, as if they knew that I shouldn't be here.

I leaned forward and traced my fingers over the carvings, wincing as the metal tips of the weapons and the sharp facets of the jeweled eyes dug into my skin. I wondered how many other women had sat here and done this same thing. Dozens, if not more. I also wondered if they'd all been as uncomfortable as I was.

Probably not.

After all, this table and all the other fine furnishings in these chambers had been their birthright, passed down from mother to daughter through the generations. The women who'd come before me hadn't stumbled into this position by accident like I had.

Someone delicately cleared her throat, and I leaned back into my previous stiff perch. Fingers fluttered all around me, adjusting my sleeves, smoothing down my hair, and even slicking berry balm onto my lips. A minute later, the fingers retreated, and I raised my gaze to the domed mirror that rose up from the table like gladiator arenas did from the Svalin city landscape.

More figures were carved into the band of wood that encased the mirror. Gargoyles with sapphire eyes and curved, silver horns that were pointed at the strixes, hawklike birds with onyx feathers that glinted with a metallic, amethyst sheen. The creatures looked like they were about to leap out of the wood, take flight, and tear into each other, just like the gladiators on the table did. A single pearl-white caladrius with tearstone eyes adorned the very top of the mirror, as though the tiny, owlish bird was peering down at all the other creatures below, including me.

Someone cleared her throat again. I sighed and finally focused on my reflection.

Black hair, gray-blue eyes, pale, tight face. I looked the same as always, except for one notable thing.

The crown on my head.

My gaze locked onto the silver band, which was thin and surprisingly plain, except for the small midnight-blue pieces of tearstone that jutted up from the center. The seven tearstone shards fitted together to form a crown, as if the silver band itself wasn't enough indication of who and what I was now.

But it wasn't the only crown that I was wearing.

I reached over with my left hand and touched the bracelet that circled my right wrist. It was made of curls of silver that had been twisted together to resemble sharp thorns, all of which wrapped around and protected the elegant crown in the middle of the design. The crown embedded in the bracelet was also made of seven tearstone shards, but it contained one thing that the actual crown on top of my head did not.

Magic.

Like other jewels, tearstone could absorb, store, and reflect back magic, but it also had the unique property of offering protection from magic—deflecting it like a gladiator's shield would stop a sword in an arena fight. Each midnight-blue shard in my bracelet was filled with a cold, hard power that was similar to my own magical immunity. The cool touch of the jewelry comforted me, as did the magic flowing through it.

I was going to need all the help that I could get today.

Someone cleared her throat for a third time, and I dropped my hand from my bracelet and focused on my reflection again.

I slowly tilted my head to the side, and the silver crown

swayed dangerously to the right. I straightened up and tilted my head to the other side, and it swayed in that direction.

"I still feel like this stupid thing is going to fall off at any second," I muttered.

"It will *not* fall off, my queen," a low, soothing voice murmured. "We've put plenty of pins in your hair to make sure that doesn't happen."

A woman stepped up beside me. She was on the short side, and the top of her head wasn't all that much higher than mine, even though I was sitting down. She was about my age—twenty-seven or so—and quite lovely, with blue eyes, rosy skin, and dark honey-blond hair that was pulled back into a pretty fishtail braid that trailed down over her shoulder. She had a thick, strong body, but her fingers were long and lean and freckled with small white scars from all the pins and needles that had accidentally poked into her skin over the years.

Lady Calanthe had been Queen Cordelia's personal thread master for the last few months of the queen's life. And now she was mine. As were her two teenage sisters, Camille and Cerana, who were hovering behind her.

"Are you pleased with your appearance, my queen?" Calanthe asked.

I studied my blue tunic in the mirror. A crown of shards had been stitched in silver thread over my heart, while still more silver thread scrolled across my neckline and then down my sleeves, as though I had wrapped myself in thorns. Black leggings and boots completed my outfit.

"Of course," I said. "Your work is exquisite, as always."

Calanthe nodded, accepting the compliment, and pride gleamed in her eyes. She reached up and adjusted the long bell sleeves of her blue gown, even though they were already perfectly draped in place. They too were trimmed with silver thread, in keeping with the colors of the Winter line of the Blair royal family.

My colors now.

"I still wish that you had let me make you something more formal," Calanthe murmured. "I could have easily done it with my magic, despite the limited time."

She was a master, which meant that her magic let her work with a specific object or element to create amazing things. In Calanthe's case, she had complete control over thread, fabrics, and the like. My nose twitched. My own magic let me smell her power on my tunic, a faint, vinegary odor that was the same as the dyes that she used to give her garments their bold, glorious colors.

Calanthe had tried to get me to don a ball gown for today's event, but I'd refused. I wasn't the queen everyone had expected, and I certainly wasn't the one they wanted, so draping myself in layers of silk and cascades of jewels seemed silly and pointless. Besides, you couldn't fight in ball gowns. Although in that regard, it didn't really matter what I wore, since every day at Seven Spire palace was a battle for me.

"Forget the clothes," another voice chimed in. "I still can't believe that people sent you all this stuff."

I turned around in my chair and looked over at a tall woman with braided blond hair and beautiful bronze skin who was lounging on a velvet settee. She was wearing a forest-green tunic that brought out her golden amber eyes, along with black leggings and boots. A large mace was propped up next to her on the settee, with the spikes slowly sinking into the cushions.

Paloma waved her hand at the low table in front of her. "C'mon. How much stuff does one queen need?"

Every available inch of the table was covered with baskets, bowls, and platters brimming with everything from fresh produce to smelly cheeses to bottles of champagne. The other tables scattered throughout the room boasted similar items, as did the writing desk, the nightstand beside the four-poster bed, and the top of the armoire that took up one wall. Not to mention the cloaks, gowns, and other garments that were piled up in the corners, or the paintings, statues, and other knickknacks that were propped up against the walls. I'd gotten so many welcome gifts over the past several weeks that I'd resorted to perching them on the windowsills, just so that I would be able to walk through the room.

Paloma grabbed a white card out of a basket on the table. "Who is Lady Diante, and why did she send you a basket full of pears?"

"Lady Diante is a wealthy noble who owns fruit orchards in one of the southern districts," I said. "And it's a Bellonan tradition to send the new queen a gift wishing her a long and prosperous reign."

Paloma snorted. "Funny tradition, sending a gift to someone you're plotting against."

Calanthe's lips puckered, and her two sisters let out audible gasps. Calanthe was a Bellonan courtier who was traditional and polite to a fault. She didn't much care for Paloma's bluntness about Diante's lack of fealty, but she didn't say anything. She might be a talented master, but Paloma was a much stronger morph.

Calanthe stared at the morph mark on Paloma's neck. All morphs had some sort of tattoo-like mark on their bodies that indicated what monster or creature they could shift into. Paloma's mark was a fearsome ogre face with amber eyes, a lock of blond hair, and plenty of sharp teeth.

The ogre must have sensed Calanthe's disapproving gaze, because its blinking liquid amber eyes shifted in her direction. The ogre stared at her a moment, then opened its mouth wide in a silent laugh. Calanthe's lips puckered even more, and she let out an indignant sniff, which only made the ogre laugh again.

"Well, then, perhaps you should taste test the pears," I sniped. "Just to make sure that Lady Diante isn't trying to poison me with fresh fruit."

"I think that's an excellent idea," Paloma drawled. "Especially since I know that mutt nose of yours would never be able to stand having a basket of poisoned fruit in here."

Calanthe winced, and her two sisters gasped again at Paloma so casually calling me a *mutt,* since it was a derogatory term for those who had little to no magic. But I didn't mind. I had been called far worse things. Besides, Paloma was my best friend, and I found her honesty refreshing, especially after so many years of people smiling to my face, then spewing poison behind my back the second they got the chance.

I gave Paloma a sour look, but she plucked a pear from the basket and sank her teeth into it. She grinned at me, as did the ogre face on her neck.

"See?" she mumbled. "No poison at all."

I rolled my eyes, but I couldn't help but grin back at her.

"Well, eat fast," I said, getting to my feet. "Because now that I'm properly attired, it's time for our first battle of the day."

❧

I thanked Calanthe and her sisters for their services. The thread master curtsied to me, gave Paloma another disapproving sniff, then left. While Paloma polished off that first pear and ate another one, I cinched a black leather belt around my waist, then hooked a sword and a dagger to it.

A queen shouldn't have to carry weapons, at least not inside her own palace, but then again, I was no ordinary queen.

And these were far from ordinary weapons.

The sword and the dagger both gleamed a dull silver, and both of their hilts featured seven midnight-blue shards that formed my crown crest. But what made the weapons special was that they were made entirely of tearstone. The sword and the dagger were far lighter than normal blades, and they would also absorb and deflect magic, just like the tearstone shards in my bracelet would.

A matching silver shield was propped up beside my bed, but I decided not to strap it to my arm. Carrying a sword and a dagger was noteworthy enough, but taking the shield as well would make me seem weak, something that I could ill afford, given my tenuous grasp on the throne.

I traced my fingers over the crown crest in the sword's hilt. Despite their dark blue hue, the tearstone shards glittered brightly. Part of me hated the crown of shards and everything it stood for. But in a strange way, the symbol comforted me as well. Other Blairs, other Winter queens, had survived life at Seven Spire. Perhaps I could too.

Time to find out.

Paloma finished her second pear. Then she got to her feet, grabbed her spiked mace, and hoisted it up onto her shoulder. The weapon made her look even more intimidating. "You ready for this?"

I blew out a breath. "I suppose I have to be, don't I?"

She shrugged. "It's not too late. We could still sneak out of here, run off, and join a gladiator troupe."

I snorted. "Please. I wouldn't get across the river before Serilda and Auster hunted me down and dragged me back."

Paloma shrugged again, but she didn't dispute my words. Then she grinned at me, as did the ogre on her neck. "Well, then, you should give Serilda, Auster, and everyone else what they've been waiting for."

I snorted again. "The only thing they've been waiting for is to see who makes the first move against me. But you're right. I might as well get on with it."

I touched my sword and dagger again, letting the feel of the weapons comfort me, then walked over and stopped in front of the double doors. Just like on the vanity table, gladiators and other figures were carved into the wood. I stared at them a moment, then let out a long, tense breath, schooled my face into a blank, pleasant mask, and threw open the doors.

As soon as I stepped out into the hallway, the two guards posted by the doors snapped to attention. They were both wearing the standard uniform of a plain silver breastplate over a short-sleeve blue tunic with black leggings and boots, and each one had a sword buckled to their black belt.

I smiled at the guards. "Alonzo, Calios, you're both looking well this morning."

The guards bowed their heads, but that was their only response. Several months ago, back when I'd just been Lady Everleigh, the guards would have talked, laughed, and joked with me. Now they just stared at me with wariness in their eyes, wondering if I would do or say something to hurt them. I tried not to grimace at their watchful, distrustful silence.

I forced myself to smile at them again, then set off down the hallway. Paloma fell in step beside me, her spiked mace still propped up on her shoulder. In addition to being my best friend, Paloma was also my personal guard, and the former gladiator took great pride in casually threatening anyone who came near me.

The queen's chambers were located on the third floor, and we quickly wound our way down several flights of steps until we reached the first level.

Seven Spire palace was the heart of Svalin, the capital city of Bellona, and just about everything in the wide hallways and spacious common areas was a tribute to the kingdom's gladiator history and tradition, from the tapestries that covered the dark gray walls, to the statues tucked away in various nooks, to the wooden display cases bristling with swords, spears, daggers, and shields that famous queens and warriors had used long ago.

But the most obvious signs of Bellona's past were the columns that adorned practically every hallway and room. Before it was a palace, Seven Spire had been a mine, and the columns were the supports for the old tunnels where my Blair ancestors had dug fluorestone and more out of the mountain. Over the years, the columns had been transformed into works of art, and now they were covered with gladiators, weapons, gargoyles, strixes, and caladriuses, just like the furnishings in the queen's chambers.

But what made the columns truly impressive was that they were all made of tearstone, which could change color, going from a light, bright, starry gray to a dark, deep midnight-blue, and back again, depending on the sunlight and other factors. I had always thought that the tearstone's shifting hues brought the gladiators and creatures to life, making it seem as though they were circling around the columns and constantly battling each other.

I stared at the column closest to me a moment longer, then forced myself to focus on the people inside the palace. After all, they were the ones who could truly hurt me.

Even though it was early on a Monday morning, people filled the hallways. Servants carrying trays of food and drinks. Palace stewards heading to their posts to oversee their workers. Guards stationed here and there, making sure that everything proceeded in an orderly fashion.

Everyone went about their business as usual—until they saw me.

Then eyes widened, mouths gaped open, and heads bobbed. Some people even dropped down into low, formal bows and curtsies, only rising to their feet after I had moved past them. I gritted my teeth and returned the acknowledgments with polite smiles and nods of my own, but the bowing and scraping were nothing compared to the whispers.

"Why isn't she wearing a gown?"

"Doesn't she know how important today is?"

"She won't last another month."

The whispers started the second that I moved past someone, and the hushed comments chased me from one hallway to the next, like a tidal wave that was rising up and about to crash down on top of me. If only. Drowning would be a far more merciful death than what I'd gotten myself into here.

From the rumors I'd heard, the servants and guards had started a pool, placing bets on how long my tenuous reign would last. I was wondering that myself. I'd been queen for only about two months, and I was already thoroughly sick of all the politics, infighting, and backstabbing that were the palace's equivalent of the gladiator fights that were so popular in Bellona.

Even Paloma with her spiked mace and the glaring ogre face on her neck couldn't quiet the chatter. I gritted my teeth again and hurried on, trying to ignore the whispers. Easier said than done.

Paloma and I rounded a corner and stepped into a long hallway, which was empty, except for the usual guards stationed in the corners. My gaze moved past them and focused on the enormous double doors that stretched from the floor all the way up to the ceiling at the far end. The doors were standing wide open, and I could see people moving around in the area beyond.

The throne room.

My stomach dropped, and my heart squeezed tight, but I forced myself to keep walking forward, one slow step at a time. There was no turning back, and there was no running away. Not from this.

A lean, muscled, forty-something man wearing a red jacket over a white shirt and black leggings and boots was standing by the windows off to one side of the doors. The sunlight streaming inside made his black hair seem as glossy as ink against his golden skin, and it also highlighted the morph mark on his neck—a dragon's face made of ruby-red scales.

The man was giving his full and undivided attention to a silver platter filled with bite-size cakes that was perched on the windowsill. He selected a cake, popped it into his mouth, and sighed with happiness.

He must have noticed Paloma and me out of the corner of his eye because he glanced in our direction. He quickly popped another cake into his mouth while we walked over to him.

"Ah, there you are, Evie," he said. "I was just enjoying some treats before the main event."

In addition to being a former queen's guard and ringmaster, Cho Yamato also had a serious sweet tooth, as did the dragon on his neck, since its black eyes were still locked onto the tray of cakes.

"I'm glad to see that Theroux is making himself at home as the new kitchen steward," I said. "And doing his best to ply you with desserts. Or did you steal those from some poor, unsuspecting servant?"

Cho grinned at my teasing. "I stole them, of course. Theroux's desserts aren't as good as what you could make, but some sugar is better than no sugar, right?" He didn't wait for an answer before he downed another tiny kiwi cake.

Joking around with Cho loosened some of the tension in my chest. I might not like being queen, but at least I had friends like him and Paloma to help me with the dangerous undertaking.

He finished his cake, then eyed me. "Are you ready for this?" he asked in a more serious voice.

"As ready as I'll ever be."

He gave me a sympathetic look, as did the dragon face on his neck. "Well, then, let's start the show."

Cho dusted the cake crumbs off his fingers and smoothed down his red jacket. Then he strode over so that he was standing in the center of the open space between the doors.

"Announcing Her Royal Highness, Queen Everleigh Saffira Winter Blair!" Cho used his ringmaster's voice to full effect, and the words boomed out like thunder, drowning out all the conversations in the throne room.

He stepped to the side, and everyone fell silent and turned

to peer at me. I gritted my teeth yet again, fixed my bland smile on my face as firmly as I could, and stepped inside.

The throne room was easily the largest area in Seven Spire. The first floor was an empty, cavernous space, except for the massive tearstone columns that jutted up to support the ceiling high, high above. Shorter, thinner columns also rose up to support the second-floor balcony that wrapped around three sides of the room.

More gladiators, weapons, and creatures were carved into the columns, and the ceiling was one enormous battle scene made of gleaming stone, glass, metal, and jewels. In the center of the ceiling, Bryn Bellona Winter Blair, my ancestor, had her sword raised high, about to bring it down on top of the Mortan king, whom she had defeated in combat so long ago to create her kingdom.

My kingdom now.

As much as I would have liked to just stare at the ceiling and pretend like the rest of the world didn't exist, I forced myself to focus on what was in front of me.

A long, wide blue carpet with silver scrollwork running along the edges led from the doors all the way across the room before stopping at the bottom of the raised stone dais at the far end. As if the carpet and the dais weren't intimidating enough, Bellonan lords, ladies, senators, guilders, and other wealthy, influential citizens lined both sides of the carpet, all of them staring at me.

It was a brutal gauntlet if ever there was one.

Still holding on to my benign smile, I squared my shoulders, lifted my chin, and strode forward, as though this had been my birthright all along, and not something that I had blundered into by accident after the rest of the Blair royal family had been assassinated.

People stepped up to both sides of the carpet, nodding, smiling, and calling out inane pleasantries. I returned the words and gestures in kind, keeping my face fixed in its benign mask and not letting any of my worry or apprehension show. I might not know how to be queen, but I excelled at keeping my true feelings bottled up inside where no one could see them.

Back behind the line of well-wishers, Paloma walked along, keeping pace with me. Her suspicious gaze scanned over everyone, and she still had her mace hoisted up onto her shoulder. She was taking her duties as my personal guard seriously, even though I'd repeatedly told her that I wasn't in any physical danger from the nobles.

They would all be quite happy to eviscerate me with their cruel words and sly schemes instead.

Finally, I left the crowd behind and reached the steps that led up to the dais. Three people were standing off to the side.

One of them was a forty-something woman and obviously a warrior, given the sword and dagger that were holstered to her black leather belt. Her short blond hair was slicked back from her face, revealing the sunburst-shaped scar at the corner of one of her blue eyes. She was wearing black leggings and boots, along with a white tunic that featured a swan swimming on a pond, surrounded by flowers and vines, all of it done in black thread.

Serilda Swanson, the leader of the Black Swan gladiator troupe, and one of my senior advisors, tilted her head at me, then executed the perfect Bellonan curtsy. I clenched my teeth a little tighter to hide a grimace. I would never get used to people curtsying to me, especially not someone as strong, lethal, and legendary as Serilda.

The second person was also a woman, although she was older, somewhere in her sixties, with short red hair, golden amber eyes, and bronze skin. She was wearing a forest-green tunic, black leggings, and boots and was leaning on a cane that featured a silver ogre head. It matched the morph mark on her neck.

Lady Xenia, an Ungerian noble, also tilted her head at me, although she didn't drop down into a curtsy.

The third person was a fifty-something stern-looking man with short gray hair, dark bronze skin, brown eyes, and a lumpy, crooked nose that had obviously been broken many, many times. Like the other guards, he was wearing a short-sleeve blue tunic, along with black leggings and boots. My gaze locked onto his silver breastplate, which featured a feathered texture and my crown of shards emblazoned over his heart. Despite the fact that he had been sporting the breastplate for weeks now, I would never get used to seeing him wearing my crest instead of Queen Cordelia's rising sun.

Auster, the captain of the queen's guards and all the others in the palace. My captain now.

Captain Auster's fingers flexed over the hilt of the sword strapped to his belt, and he gave me a traditional Bellonan bow, holding it far longer than necessary, as if each extra second showed his devotion—and his determination not to let me be assassinated like Queen Cordelia had been.

Auster finally straightened up. I gave him a genuine smile, and his stern features softened a bit, if not his readiness to pull his sword free and defend me with his dying breath.

Even though they weren't standing anywhere close to the

been du~

The throne ~ Auster all stepped even farther

starry gray to m~ path to the throne.

umns did. The chan~ he perched on top of the dais.

Winter lines of the Blair ~eces of tearstone that had

strength of the Bellonan peo~ together centuries ago.

I had seen the throne many,~ ight, shifting from

that it was mine, I found it far more ~ just like the col-

since the top featured the same crown of ~ Summer and

my tunic, bracelet, sword, and dagger. I had n~ everlasting

tention to that symbol before the royal massacre,~ now

was everywhere I went. Sometimes, I thought that I wou~

been far happier if I had never seen it at all. I certainly wo~

have been much safer.

Summer queens are fine and fair, with pretty ribbons and flowers in their hair. Winter queens are cold and hard, with frosted crowns made of icy shards.

The words to the old Bellonan fairy tale echoed in my mind, as though all the queens who had come before me were somehow whispering them to me over and over again. I listened to the echoes a moment longer, then exhaled, slowly climbed up the dais steps, turned around, and sat down on the throne.

That was the signal everyone had been waiting for, and all the lords, ladies, senators, guilders, and others strode forward, stopping a few feet away from the dais. They quickly split into their usual cliques and began gossiping among themselves, while servants circulated through the crowd, handing

More nobles milled out kiwi cakes, fres... ing, and watching me, kling blackberry... as far less important than I looked up... or.

around up t... when I noticed a man sitting by although t... the balcony. He was wearing a long the ones... nic, leggings, and boots. His dark brown I... the lights, while a bit of stubble darkened him... His handsome features were as blank as mine ...ouldn't tell what he was thinking, although his blue ...ed into mine with fierce intensity.

...y nostrils flared. Even though he was as far away from me ...possible, I could still pick out his scent—cold, clean vanilla with just a hint of spice—above all the other ones in the room. I drew in another breath, letting his scent sink deep down into my lungs and trying to ignore the hot spark of desire that it ignited inside me.

Lucas Sullivan was the magier enforcer of the Black Swan troupe, a bastard prince of Andvari, and my . . . Well, I didn't know what Sully was to me. Much more than a friend, but not a lover, despite my pointed advances on that front. But I cared about him far more than I wanted to think about, especially right now, when I was facing yet another battle inside my own palace.

So I dropped my gaze from his and looked back out over the nobles again. Even though I had been queen for several weeks now, ever since I had killed Vasilia, the crown princess and my treacherous cousin, this was my first formal court session. Everyone had come here to discuss business and other matters with me, and it was important that things went well. I doubted they would, though. The nobles weren't going to like some of the things I had to say.

While the nobles chattered and downed their food and drinks, I discreetly drew in a breath, letting the air roll in over my tongue, and tasting all the scents in it. The people's floral perfumes and spicy colognes. The fruity tang of the sangria. The pungent aroma of the blue cheeses that the servants were slicing on the buffet tables along the walls.

I opened my mouth to start the session, when one final scent assaulted my senses—jalapeño rage so strong that it made my nose burn with its sudden, sharp intensity.

Most people might scoff at my mutt magic, but my enhanced sense of smell was quite useful in one regard—it let me sense people's emotions, and very often their intentions. Garlic guilt, ashy shame, minty regret. I could tell what someone was feeling, and often what they were plotting, just by tasting the scents that swirled in the air around them.

I'd had years to hone my mutt magic, so I knew that jalapeño rage meant only one thing.

Someone here wanted to kill me.

ABOUT THE AUTHOR

Andre Teague

Jennifer Estep is a *New York Times, USA Today,* and internationally bestselling author who prowls the streets of her imagination in search of her next fantasy idea.

In addition to the **Crown of Shards** series, Jennifer is also the author of the **Elemental Assassin, Mythos Academy, Black Blade,** and **Bigtime** series.

For more information on Jennifer and her books, visit her website at www.jenniferestep.com or follow her online on Facebook, Goodreads, and Twitter—@Jennifer_Estep. You can also sign up for her newsletter at www.jenniferestep.com/contact -jennifer/newsletter.